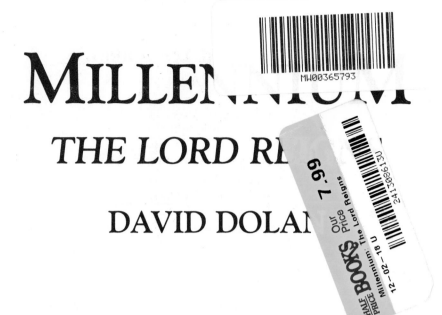

MILLENNIUM

THE LORD REIGNS

DAVID DOLAN

"THE LORD REIGNS, LET THE PEOPLE TREMBLE. HE IS ENTHRONED ABOVE THE CHERUBIM, LET THE EARTH SHAKE! THE LORD IS GREAT IN ZION, AND HE IS EXALTED ABOVE ALL THE PEOPLES. LET THEM PRAISE THY GREAT AND AWESOME NAME. HOLY IS HE."

PSALM 99:1-3

To Jill

MILLENNIUM: THE LORD REIGNS

DAVID DOLAN

HOUSE OF DAVID PUBLISHERS
2536 Rimrock Ave Ste. 400-383
Grand Junction, CO 81505

ISBN: 978-1-936417-45-2

Apart from the biblical characters named in this novel, all of the other characters are fictional, although based somewhat on real people the author knows in Jerusalem. The names of several living or deceased celebrities are mentioned only to give the work more of a sense of reality. Apart from biblical quotes, the words attributed to Yeshua the Messiah are fictional. The use of the name "Android" comes from the author's first novel, originally published in 1995, and has absolutely no connection to the subsequent cellphone technology known by that name.

Cover photo taken by David Dolan off the Mediterranean coast of Tel Aviv Israel. Cover design by Robert Benson and Damien Mayfield.

ADDITIONAL COPIES of this novel, plus David Dolan's companion first novel, **THE END OF DAYS** and his other books may be purchased at special discounts via his web site, **www.ddolan.com** Bulk orders at special prices are available from Your Israel Connection, by phoning toll free in North America 888-639-8530 or by email: **orders.millennium@gmail.com**

AUTHOR'S THANKS: I suspect few men would get much right without the help of some good women. I want to thank four in particular-Pam Smith (a true wordsmith) living in green Wales, Lis Stubbs in beautiful Washington State, Barbara Joy Neiman in the "show me" state of Missouri—for faithfully praying for this novel and for critiquing the text and helping to edit it—and Patsi Day for helping to get it published.

DAVID DOLAN is an American author and journalist who has lived and worked in Israel since 1980. He reported from early 1988 through the year 2000 for the New York-based CBS radio network. Before that, he worked for CBN television and radio news out of Jerusalem, the Chicago-based Moody radio network, and has also appeared on many television and radio programs around the world. Dolan currently reports weekdays for *Eye on the Middle East*, heard on hundreds of radio stations around America and on the Friends of Israel web site, and is a regular guest on the Prophecy Today radio program broadcast on Saturdays around the USA. He has written the monthly Israel News Review for CFI-UK since April 1986, also posted on his website: **www.ddolan.com**. David Dolan is a popular international public speaker, addressing audiences in over twenty countries in North America, Europe, Africa, Eastern Asia, and in Australia and New Zealand. To schedule David Dolan to speak anywhere in North America, write to **alohashalom@gmail.com**. For other places around the world or comments about this novel, contact: **millennium.thelordreigns@gmail.com**.

OTHER BOOKS BY DAVID DOLAN

- · HOLY WAR FOR THE PROMISED LAND (Thomas Nelson, 1991)
- · ISRAEL: THE STRUGGLE TO SURVIVE (Hodder & Stoughton, 1992)
- · THE END OF DAYS (Baker/Revell, 1997)
- · ISRAEL AT THE CROSSROADS (Baker/Revell, 1998)
- · ISRAEL IN CRISIS: WHAT LIES AHEAD? (Fleming H. Revell, 2001)
- · HOLY WAR FOR THE PROMISED LAND (Revised update, Broadman and Holman, 2003)
- · THE END OF DAYS (21st Century Press, 2005)

TO ORDER COPIES OF THESE BOOKS, VISIT **www.ddolan.com**

David Dolan's books have also been published in Germany, Brazil, Holland, Finland, Norway, and Denmark.

Author's Foreword

As I write this foreword, the solemn Jewish fast day held on the Ninth of the Hebrew month of Av is just ending. As every year, many Jews here in Jerusalem went to the nearby Old City's Western Wall to mourn the destruction of the First and Second Temples, said to have taken place on this date along with several other calamities that befell the Jewish people over the centuries. Although Israel's contested capital city was thankfully relatively quiet during the fast this year, many other parts of the world were shaking as stock markets fell sharply and violent lawlessness gripped many UK cities. North of Israel, Syria was in turmoil while famine spread in the drought-plagued Horn of Africa to the south.

This novel is about the time when all that comes to an end, replaced by the tranquil reign of Immanuel, Hebrew for *God with us*, ruling the world from His exalted throne here in Jerusalem. It was written almost entirely in the Holy City, vividly picturing that upcoming peaceful era which I and many others believe is drawing very near. This book places many of the characters from my tribulation novel *THE END OF DAYS* (which you might want to read first, although I do reintroduce them all to my readers) into the Lord's magnificent Millennial Kingdom. Although it is obviously a work of fiction, it is based, like my previous novel, on many prophetic biblical scriptures that speak of the Lord's glorious reign over a restored earth. In these turbulent days of worldwide upheaval, I trust it will act as an island of comfort and joy as readers contemplate the wonderful era that lies ahead for those who faithfully put their trust in Israel's Sovereign Lord.

Still, this novel contains significant drama in its pages as well. The prophet Isaiah and John the Apostle were among several biblical writers who indicated that some sin-prone people will survive into a literal millennial age. John foretold that the Lord Yeshua-Jesus in English-will rule the nations "with a rod of iron" (Rev. 19:15), signaling that fallen human beings will still be present during His prophesied thousand-year reign. That forms the basis of the conflicts I describe in this novel, culminating in one final satanic attempt to overturn the Lord's righteous rule, as foretold in Revelation 20:7-9.

I realize there are other views of the prophesied millennium. Some teach such an era is not literally going to occur at all, or that it coincides with the increasingly "peaceful" church age (a position that became harder to maintain during the last, blood-soaked century featuring two world wars). I take the various prophecies about it quite literally, especially John's writings in Revelation, as reflected in this novel. Even if you disagree, I hope you will be blessed by reading this book.

The name of the youth gangs in the novel, *Androids*, comes from my earlier book with no connection to the subsequent mobile phone technology known by that name. The words attributed to the Lord Yeshua and other biblical characters are obviously my own creation. Still, my text is based on what they actually said and did during their recorded lifetimes. I don't claim that the scenarios I lay out are prophetically factual, only that they are based on scriptural patterns and teachings. For example, who is actually in the Lord's ruling band and exactly what they do remains to be seen. Thankfully, we have been graciously given enough prophetic oracles to construct a fairly accurate model of the *MILLENNIUM*, the majestic time when *THE LORD REIGNS!*

David Dolan
JERUSALEM

CRASHING DOWN

Gina stared in silence, her moist olive-colored eyes transfixed on the unimaginable scene unfolding before her. Tears rolled down like pebbles into her baby's blue cotton bib. The trembling mother held him tenderly over her left shoulder, burying his pale face in her long auburn hair. Even though he was only eight months old, Gina did not want the baby to view this horrific scene. Her world was literally coming to an end.

Standing alone with her beloved infant son on her fourth floor New Jersey balcony, a distant memory sadly serenaded the young woman. Slowly it rose to the surface like a deep sea diver trying to avoid the bends. And then it came back to her in full. She had indeed experienced this nightmare before, and it happened at this very same spot. Enfolding Gina on his left hip, her sobbing father, Giuseppe Marino, had gripped his seven year old daughter a bit too tightly as the second tower came crashing down, shielding her eyes with his sinuous right hand.

Gina gasped as the burning 1,776 foot high *One World Trade Center* began to collapse, its windows previously shattered in the massive earthquake that ripped through the planet's crust several hours before. Popularly known as the *Freedom Tower*, the construction of America's tallest skyscraper had helped refill the black hole which the destroyed twin towers had burrowed in Gina's childhood psyche. As if in some deranged sci fi flick, the tower's celebrated replacement was now crashing to the ground as well.

Fires raged all over lower Manhattan. The unprecedented world-wide epileptic shaking had brought dozens of buildings down and left most others severely damaged. Flaming asteroids had subsequently struck many skyscrapers and Central Park as well, adding to the hellish conflagrations. A nine-inch gap had opened up on the western side of Gina's own five floor apartment building in Newark, splitting the red brick façade in two. Portions of taupe stucco ceiling had tumbled down in her modest living room. Toppled lamps and fallen pictures were scattered everywhere. Shattered dishes littered the kitchen floor.

Decked out in her favorite designer jeans and a light summer top, Gina had been eating canned corn while watching the World News Network's mid afternoon international report when the terrible trembling began. Her baby was snoring softly in his nearby mahogany crib—a "good luck" wedding gift from her older sister Teresa whose two precocious children were by then already into their teen years.

Like billions of viewers tuned in all over the globe, Gina was astounded when the two elderly Jews who had tormented the earth suddenly bolted up from their prone positions. They had lain dead for seventy-two hours outside of the main Jaffa Gate entrance into Jerusalem's ancient walled Old City. Just three days before, she'd witnessed the Emperor Andre's exhilarating triumph over the men he called 'the Antichrist and False Prophet,' slaying the two 'imposters' who had distressed people everywhere with their frequent pronouncements of impending judgment and doom. The zestful European-born monarch had then stridently commanded that their limp bodies be left to rot on the curb just outside the stone gate, providing a vivid testimony of what would happen to all on earth who resisted his glorious international rule.

With dozens of television cameras still focused on the putrefying bodies, the dead men had stirred without warning, prompting networks everywhere to switch live to the scene. The elderly bearded Jews had opened their eyes, slowly raised up their arms, and then sprung to their feet before rising supernaturally into the sky. As they did so, a thunderous voice called out from the heavens. Gina gasped, instantly recalling the words of her older sister Teresa who had warned of this very scenario several years before—as if she was some prophetess or soothsayer instead of a boring Connecticut housewife who spent too much time reading her Bible and volunteering at church.

Seconds later, the gigantic earthquake began to rattle the greater New York City area. It was apparent from the frantic WNN reporter that the ferocious seismic activity was pummeling Jerusalem, seven thousand miles away, as well. In reality, the violent shaking was rocking the entire planet. Tectonic plates crashed into each other like bumper cars at a theme park. The earth's molten core had heated up to an unthinkable temperature. Hundreds of volcanoes erupted on every continent and on myriad islands, spewing tons of billowing smoke and ash into the atmosphere. The air blanketing the decimated earth had already become severely polluted some three years before when the Emperor launched his European Union nuclear missiles at Russia and China at the beginning of his worldwide reign, which was closely followed by another horrifying nuclear warhead exchange, this time between the United States and China.

Gina stood weeping on her balcony as she watched New York City burn to the ground like Rome of old. Numerous buildings in her own city of Newark were also engulfed in rapacious flames. The usual roar of commercial jets taking off from Liberty International Airport six blocks away had ceased, replaced by the dreadful din of crackling fires and the piercing shouts and screams of frightened people scurrying about on the streets.

Then out of the corner of her teary right eye, Gina caught the first glimpse of the 64 foot high tidal wave striking the shoreline in nearby Bayonne. The tsunami took just one minute to reach her neighborhood, although thankfully it was only half as tall when it struck. Blood red and brimming with decaying sea creatures, the rancid wall of Atlantic Ocean water swept away a family of five hiding in an abandoned first floor apartment in her building. At least it also doused some of the coastal fires.

Gina knew she needed to quickly exit her crumbling building if she had any chance of keeping herself and her precious baby alive.

Determining that nowhere would be safe in the teeming metropolitan area, she decided to head up to her late sister's suburban home in Westport Connecticut. She moved like a spinning atomic particle as she gathered up a few personal items and her remaining tins of tuna fish, chicken and canned milk. Thankfully, she had left the family Ford on the fifth floor of the nearby neighborhood parking garage, so it was spared damage by the frightful tidal wave, which was rapidly descending into Newark's netherworld sewer system.

The young widow wept while stuffing some adult and baby clothes into her polyester suitcase, recalling with mixed emotions her childhood years in the three bedroom, one bathroom apartment. Her father Giuseppe and mother Catrina, hard working immigrants from Italy, had bought the place soon after their marriage in Brooklyn. The doting parents had showered the two sisters with generous gifts every Christmas and on their annual birthdays, adoring their cute daughters above all else.

Gina inherited the comfortable flat from her parents two and a half years before when they moved just a few miles away to a new gated community in the city of Elizabeth. Giuseppe said at the time that with Andre's new economic reforms bringing glimpses of global prosperity, he was ready for an upscale transition. He would miss the panoramic view from his sunrise-facing balcony, but even that was not the same in the sorrowful wake of 9/11. He'd certainly not miss the constant airport noise and mushrooming crime rate in his old neighborhood.

After turning the key to lock the familiar apartment door for the last time, Gina pulled her black suitcase down two flights of stairs while clutching her son over her right bosom. As she descended, the frightened widow fought back fresh tears. The young mother was leaving home without the love of her life, who'd been murdered in an ambush six months before.

When she joyously announced her engagement to George Kirintelos, who was a fellow student at the Newark branch of Rutgers University, her parents had expressed minor irritation that she intended to marry a non-Italian. But they blessed the nuptial anyway. "At least he's not a Protestant," said Catrina at the time with appropriate seriousness, adding with a sly smile and a wink that "he *is* very handsome." She also liked the fact that the beefy young man whose family came from Greece overtly appreciated her spicy cooking.

At Gina's suggestion, George had gone to the local pharmacy to pick up some medicine for their coughing baby boy, who was apparently not handling the polluted air blanketing his nascent world very well. Although the shelves were nearly bereft of products, the concerned father had rapidly located some kids' cold medicine and began to head for the cash register. He bore the necessary government-issued mark to buy and sell. Then George identified the portentous sound of rushing footsteps behind him. Two young thugs belonging to an Android street gang—who prided themselves in their often brutal enforcement of the Emperor's commands—sped up behind him.

"I think you can tell this is not a stick of gum I'm holding against your lower back, man!" the taller one spat out while the other plunged his stout teenage hand into George's right-side back pocket, where the outline of his leather wallet was evident.

Proudly possessing a black belt in karate, the muscular body-builder instantly devised a plan. He'd drop like a sack of lead to his knees, then swing his substantial right arm around and hit the robber's legs before wrestling the gun from the taller guy's hand. The bullet tore through his spine before he could hit the filthy tiled floor.

Back at the badly damaged apartment building, Gina frantically knocked on a second floor apartment door like a machinegun discharging bullets. When it opened, she cried out "You've got to come with me!" without even saying hello.

Rosa was like a grandmother to Gina. Pleasantly plump and cheerful most of the time, she had often babysat the girls when their parents went dancing at the local *Napoli* nightclub, or sauntered out to dinner with friends. Widowed for decades and childless, Rosa had eagerly 'adopted' the two sisters; knitting them adorable little sweaters and baking them sweet goodies.

"Oh honey, I *can't* go with you. Look, it's all falling apart." Rosa pushed her thick glasses up on her prominent nose while turning to point at the ominous gap in her living room wall, which revealed just a sliver of the chaos raging outside.

The older woman slowly turned back toward the door while brushing a strand of gray hair from her sweaty forehead. "Where are you going anyway, Gina? Where *is* there to go?"

George Jr. let out a sharp cry. "Hush little bambino, it'll be alright," cooed Rosa, not actually believing a syllable she was uttering.

"I'm heading up to Teresa's home in Westport. I think we'll be fairly safe there." Then Gina pleaded, "I *really* need your help Rosa, I'm all alone!"

"Oh, lovely Gina, lovely Gina, I must to die in my own bed. Anyway I don't think you'll make it that far honey; I don't think you *can* make it that far. Please just stay here with me. I will take care of you like always before."

Gina was tempted to accept Rosa's heartfelt offer when the outer wall let out a loud groan as two inches were added to its burgeoning breach. "I want to stay Rosa, I really do. But I need to think of my baby." She stretched out her free arm and hugged her dear friend for the last time as mixed emotions flooded her torn soul. "It's time to go. Goodbye sweet Rosa," she uttered gently amid swelling tears.

With teardrops mirrored back, the squat lady stood on her tiptoes and gave Gina a moist kiss on her pink left cheek. "Goodbye my darling child. May God go with you." Then she pecked the baby on his rotund little forehead.

With that, Gina turned tail and, unlike Lot's wife, she did not look back.

When she got to her undamaged car, Gina tried once again to reach Chad on her cellphone. She was thrilled when he apparently answered.

"Hello, this is 'The Stud' Chad Scarcelli. I'm not able...you know the routine. Leave me your fine words and I'll try to get back to ya, a-s-a-p."

Beep. "Hi Chad, this is your Aunt Gina. I just wanted to check on the condition of your family house. I was thinking...."

"Hey Gina, how are you? I'm surprised you got through!"

"Oh Chad! Thank God you answered. I'm not very well. I'm also surprised we connected. I don't think many phone towers are still standing, and there is no electricity down here in Newark. Things are falling to pieces! You must be aware of that?"

"Well, I'm located in the underground Android command center here in Westport, so not seeing everything you are I guess. You probably got me on one of our backup generator-driven phone lines and reinforced cell towers. Andre's government had lots of those built in New York City and the surrounding areas."

"Chad, I wanted to check on your parents' house. Do you know if it's still standing, and do you think I'd be safe there? My apartment building is about to crash down, and I suspect the entire area is going to be destroyed. I still have a copy of their house key."

"From the reports we're getting Gina, I don't think you'd be able to make it here. Many bridges are out, the road pavements are cracked, and they say there're dead bodies everywhere. What about Grandpa and Grandma's place in Elizabeth? That's a heck of a lot closer."

"True Chad, but it's also located in the metro area, and I don't think it'll be safe anywhere around here. So I'll try to get up there, and let you know if I succeed."

"Okay, Aunt Gina. Give my little cousin Georgie a big hug from me, and drive as safely as possible. Hopefully talk to you soon!"

Gina had driven less than two blocks before realizing she could not possibly travel all the way to Connecticut. Slimy fish were scattered amid mud-covered bodies which littered the fractured sidewalks. Rubble was strewn over the walkways and the adjacent buckled streets. With power lines down everywhere, the only light came from fires consuming area buildings. Thick smoke choked off the sky. Realizing she could not go on, Gina gingerly eased her silver Taurus around and headed for her nearby parents' home.

In a way, the fleeing mother was relieved that she could not make it to Westport with her now-wailing baby boy. Gina deeply disliked her seventeen-year-old nephew, suspecting he had been behind her sister's ugly demise. Born out of wedlock when Teresa was in her junior year in high school, Chad had been an embarrassment to her Roman

13

Catholic parents from the get-go. Although glad her beau was at least of Italian descent, they had pointedly not attended Teresa's modest wedding to Leo Scarcelli, who graduated from high school in Connecticut some four months before Chad was born. The couple had met at a Catholic summer camp in the Catskill Mountains. However despite their hurt, the premature grandparents had eventually warmed to the lad; handsome and intelligent as he was.

Whatever her faults and mistakes, Teresa Scarcelli certainly didn't deserve to die, not to mention Leo and their 13 year old daughter Angelica. Gina thought her older sister was often well over the top with her fundamentalist religious beliefs, adopted soon after Andre was crowned 'Emperor of the World' during a beautiful cere-mony in Rome. Sure, she and George had resisted her sister's pleas to refuse Andre's implant in their right hands. After all, the world ruler's new economic system made good sense, as the Emperor himself had pointed out, cutting the need to carry cash and reducing the chances of identity theft. But what had Teresa's rigid stand gotten her, along with Leo and Angelica? Cruel beheadings! Where was the good in such an atrocious outcome?

In fact, Chad had played a starring role in that dark disaster film.

"What's it to you if I want to drink beer and smoke pot with my buds in my own bedroom! Would you prefer we sit here on the living room couch?" he bellowed with a sardonic smirk on his lightly-bearded face.

"You are not yet 16 years old young man, and you think you're going to call the shots around here?" barked Leo as he turned the color of a ripe tomato. "It's not going to happen! And I don't want to tell you again, son, to stop hanging out with that screwball Android gang! Pronto!!"

"I can do *anything I want*...I'm an Android!" boasted Chad as he hoisted his substantial frame from the plush sofa. He slowly approached his father's indigo velvet easy chair and then belted out a command.

"Lift up your right hand, old man!!"

Not nearly as fit as his steroid-taking son, Leo glanced nervously at his wife Teresa standing rigidly next to him wearing a plain yellow apron over her tan slacks and blouse. "I, uh, why should I do that?"

"You don't have Emperor Andre's required mark, do you dad? And neither do you mom!"

Pressing wet hands against her apron, Teresa answered with a rising pitch in her voice. "You already know we don't, Chad. You know we do not believe in his claims to be some…some divine god. We will not worship that beast!"

"And we have convinced your sister Angelica to follow our example, thank God," added Leo.

"You and your constant 'god' talk! I'll do whatever the hell I want to in this house, and outside as well, and you can't possibly stop me!!" Chad's wavy brown hair was spiked with dyed blond highlights. A woven band of smiling red devils wielding pitchforks was tattooed around his toned left bicep. He folded his muscular arms across his substantial chest, drunk with triumph over his cowering parents.

"And hell is *exactly* what you will get," sighed his mother, more in sorrow than anger.

It took only two hours to make all the arrangements. By mid-evening, Chad was sprawled across his king size bed playing with two soft teenage girls. A nearly empty vodka bottle and three ice-filled glasses sat on the table next to the bed.

Widely admired, if not envied, for her slim demure figure and stylish clothing, the twenty-something widow had never felt this alone. She drove her Ford Taurus past the unmanned open front gate and up the winding side street that led to her deceased parents' familiar town-house. The walled community usually resembled a carefully coiffured golf course. Today it looked like a category-five hurricane had blown through it.

Gina avoided a dead dog and some fallen tree branches cluttering the still wet road, and soon arrived at Giuseppe and Catrina's driveway. Despite the dirty water mark on the beige townhouse's front wall, along with debris scattered all over the soaked green lawn, and broken panes in the large picture window to the left of the front door, Gina quickly surmised that her parents' abandoned home was still basically intact. She pulled out her silver key, opened the carved wood-paneled door, and switched on her flashlight.

Flood damage was immediately evident in the living room, along with many fallen items. The ceiling and walls displayed several substantial cracks, but were still holding up.

Gina rushed into the kitchen to see if there was any stored food in the pantry. The canned goods she had left in the house after her parents' mysterious disappearance were still there! She was always hoping that dad and mom would somehow show up again. Maybe they had been kidnapped like so many people were these days, especially older folks with money. Or maybe they were "raptured" like Teresa expected them to be after she "led them to the Lord," as she put it, a couple years before? The immigrant couple's stubborn elder daughter had also persuaded them to refrain from receiving Andre's implantation, so maybe they were arrested and beheaded like Teresa, Leo and their innocent granddaughter? The grieving Gina just didn't know, so she'd left some canned food in the house, hoping they might return to it one day.

Gina lit the brass oil lamp that her graying father had attached to the kitchen wall in her presence after he purchased the new home. With adequate light now bathing the room, she grabbed the empty plastic bottle out of her large cloth diaper bag before heading for the stove. The exhausted mother was happy to discover that the gas was still working. Giuseppe's installation of reserve tanks in the two-car garage had apparently paid off. He had stated at the time that he wanted a backup for the time when things would "fall apart at the end of the Antichrist's 42 month reign," whether he'd be around to experience that or not. Maybe he was thinking of his youngest daughter Gina?

The shaken widow hummed a familiar tune while emptying a can of milk into her son's nippled plastic bottle. Despite how she felt inside, Gina wanted to act as calm and normal as possible, realizing her fragile offspring was already scared half to death, as she was herself. The trembling mother turned on the cold water tap and then shook her head before heading back to the pantry to fetch some bottled water. After placing the milk in the warming liquid on the stove, she put the can opener back in its designated drawer near the sink.

As she closed the drawer, a potent aftershock began to rattle . through her parents' weakened townhouse. Gina fell backwards onto the marble kitchen floor, almost hitting the baby-chair that her father had bought soon after she became pregnant. George Jr. threw his tiny arms into the dusty air as he let out a bloodcurdling scream.

As the room swayed back and forth like a drunken hobo, the terrified woman ping-ponged her eyes as if they were lightning bolts striking a forest, desperately searching for somewhere safe to place her screaming baby. For his sake alone, Gina managed to get back onto her feet and grabbed little Georgie and his Spiderman blanket with one hand as she flung open the oven door with the other. She shoved her little son inside as if he were a leg of lamb before slamming the door shut, deliberately oblivious to his frantic wailing.

Just then, a chunk of concrete fell from the ceiling, striking Gina's left shoulder and pinning her to the floor. Blood poured from her savage wound. Within six minutes, Gina Kirintelos was dead.

"Where will I go now?"

Maria Alvarez sat on the gritty bench two hours before dawn, her legs crossed tightly in front of her. She wept as she gazed at the ruins of her crumbled south Newark apartment building. The shy woman was only twenty-one, but her life appeared to be over. Her family was dead. She had no food or possessions at all, only the dirty clothes she was wearing.

Then Maria remembered the townhouse where she had cooked and cleaned for Giuseppe and Catrina Marino. She still had a key. Successfully talking herself up off the bench, the former maid located the key in her purse and began the two mile trek to their home.

The young woman with a pleasant smile and thick raven hair was relieved to discover that no one was guarding the compound's open metal gate. It had been a while since she labored in the community and she feared they might not let her in under the circumstances. The woman whose parents hailed from Puerto Rico marched with renewed strength up to the townhouse and turned the key in the lock.

Flickering light streamed in from the kitchen, just enough to reveal some of the damage in the living room. Someone must be here!

She paused and listened. Yes, there was a muffled sound...of a crying baby!

Maria rushed to the kitchen door and quickly discovered that part of the far corner ceiling and wall had caved in. Then she spotted Gina's limp body. The new mother was lying face up in a pool of blood near the kitchen table, obviously dead. Mumbling something about Jesus in Spanish, Maria rushed to her side. She bent over Gina's severely injured body and started to cry. She could not stay in that position for more than a few seconds. The baby demanded her immediate attention. She traced his piercing screams to the oven, opening it in a flash. With all the gentleness she could muster under such traumatic conditions, Maria cradled the sobbing infant in her arms. "Hush little Georgie, I'm here for you now."

But what could she really do? The house might collapse in the next aftershock. There was food in the pantry, but not much, and only a couple of plastic bottles filled with water. The sink faucet offered only stale air. How could she care for this needy baby?

Gently weeping while cradling the infant boy, who was now sucking on the bottle she had uncovered under some rubble near the flaming front stove burner, Maria realized what she must do. She'd half noticed that the stone Baptist church building three blocks away was still basically undamaged when she rushed past it toward the gated community. She was aware that the church operated an orphanage next door.

Maria talked kindly to George Jr. as she rummaged through his diaper bag. She was glad to find his birth certificate inside, along with Gina's driver's license. Holding the orphan over her shoulder, Maria avoided the debris as she picked her way over to his mother's flaccid corpse. She wiped the salty water from her weary face. "I'll make sure your little lamb is taken care of, Gina. Go now and rest in peace."

After quickly changing the baby's diaper and wrapping him in his wool blanket, Maria tossed some canned milk into the rust-colored cloth bag. She then heaved the infant over her right shoulder and headed for the door. The agitated former maid strode more carefully than before, not wanting to slip on the slimy pavement while carrying her whimpering bundle.

Minutes later, Maria caught sight in her peripheral vision of a male racing across the street right toward her. He thrust his arm out to grab the diaper bag, intending to rip it out of her clenched fingers. The former maid made a swift 45 degree turn and kicked him in a most sensitive spot, casting the cursing young man to the debris-strewn sidewalk.

Markedly picking up her pace, Maria spotted the large white cross rising above the corner tower of the old Baptist church. A pizza parlor and a dry cleaning outlet burned with alacrity across the street, shedding dancing light upon the stone facade. Most of the stained glass windows were shattered, but otherwise the hoary edifice was still standing. The same was true for the adjacent orphanage.

Maria slowly walked up the three muddy steps and placed the cloth bag near the orphanage's large front door. She gingerly lowered the now quiet baby onto some soft diapers at the bottom of the bag, making sure that his birth certificate was easily visible next to him.

The thin woman's dark brown eyes moistened once again. "Be well, little one. Grow and be strong!"

Maria pounded on the metal door and then disappeared like a ghost into the noxious night.

"FOR A CHILD WILL BE BORN TO US, A SON WILL BE GIVEN TO US; AND THE GOVERN-MENT WILL REST ON HIS SHOULDERS; AND HIS NAME WILL BE CALLED WONDERFUL COUNSELOR, MIGHTY GOD, ETERNAL FATHER, PRINCE OF PEACE. THERE WILL BE NO END TO THE INCREASE OF HIS GOVERNMENT OR OF PEACE, ON THE THRONE OF DAVID AND OVER HIS KINGDOM, TO ESTABLISH IT AND TO UPHOLD IT WITH JUSTICE AND RIGHT-EOUSNESS, FROM THEN ON AND FOREVERMORE. THE ZEAL OF THE LORD OF HOSTS WILL ACCOMPLISH THIS."

ISAIAH 9:6-7

ONE

THE LORD REIGNS

Hallelujah! For the Lord our God the Almighty reigns! Let us rejoice, and be glad, and give the glory unto Him!

Untold millions of rich melodious voices rang out with the joyous proclamation. Israel's Crucified Messiah, the Risen Lord, had returned to Jerusalem three days before in unparalleled splendor. Countless redeemed saints and holy angels had accompanied the Lamb of God as He rode from the center of the universe to the Mount of Olives on His majestic white stallion. The faithful and true King of Kings was wearing a gleaming white robe dipped in blood. A silk woven breast-plate made of fine gold-colored thread was draped over His powerful chest. Multiple crowns were regally perched upon His radiant head.

The Word of God and His companions had begun their celestial journey several months before when the last trumpet spoken of in the biblical book of Revelation sounded at the beginning of Rosh Ha Shana, the Jewish New Year holiday known in the Bible as the annual Feast of Trumpets. Now it was the third day of Hanukkah, the winter-time festival of cleansing and dedication, and the Conquering King was seated in the Holy of Holies on a deep blue throne made of precious lapis lazuli stone. Thousands of redeemed saints, or Holy Ones—*Kadoshim* in Hebrew, which would become the official language of the Sovereign Lord's worldwide realm—danced the circular *hora* before Him. All were rejoicing as never before. The Lion of the Tribe of Judah, with glistening hair and penetrating eyes of flaming fire and feet glowing like burnished bronze, had returned to rule and reign forever! *Glory to the Lamb!!*

Among those chosen to actually dance inside the Jerusalem Temple before the Lord of Lords was a small band of Kadoshim who had ministered in the Holy City during the dark days of the Antichrist's worldwide rule at the end of the previous age. They had labored alongside Yochanan and Natan-el, the two anointed witnesses spoken of in chapter eleven of the New Testament book of Revelation.

Ascending as elderly men into the night sky from just outside of the walled Old City's Jaffa Gate, the pair now enjoyed the youthful spiritual bodies which all of the redeemed possessed. Appearing to be around thirty years old, Yochanan and Natan-el spun around with the same high spirited energy displayed by Benny and Tali, who had served with them as children just months before but now also inhabited eternal bodies featuring the outward and inward characteristics of young adults. Even though they had been rejoicing non-stop for three days and nights, no one felt the slightest bit tired, or hungry, or thirsty. Those things were traits of their former human lives. Those needs no longer featured in their days.

Jonathan and Sarah Goldman were holding hands and dancing vigorously with Yochanan—also known as the Apostle John, the Lord's most beloved disciple during the days of His ministry in ancient Israel. In the passing era, the American-born Israeli couple had parented Benny and his older sister Tali. The four had lived together in a comfortable two-floor townhouse in southeast Jerusalem.

Eli Ben David, Jonathan's closest friend during his short human life in Israel, joyously thrust out his legs next to the swirling couple, followed by Benny and Tali. As children, they had eagerly adopted Eli as a surrogate father (or was it the other way around?) after Jonathan was killed in a Syrian chemical warhead attack on the Golan Heights just before the Antichrist, the European-born Emperor Andre, suddenly sprang onto the international stage.

Yoseph Steinberg from New York, who had founded and led the small Beit Yisrael Messianic congregation in Jerusalem which the brethren had been members of, tightly gripped Yochanan's left hand.

Smiling next to Yoseph was Cindy, his devoted wife in the previous era. Natan-el, whose name in English was Nathaniel, came next, clasping hands and swinging around with several other former members of the tight-knit congregation who had ministered everyday with the two witnesses in the expansive stone plaza next to the Western Wall.

The uncountable millions of Kadoshim who could not fit into the spiritually cleansed Temple danced and sang in triumph on the plaza outside, or rejoiced while floating in the air all around the sacred structure. The Temple's white marble walls had become transparent to their eyes the moment the Bright Morning Star dismounted from His celestial steed and strode into the magnificent building three days before. The Conquering King had quickly slain Andre, the Man of Sin, who was pompously seated naked on a golden throne inside the Holy of Holies. The Emperor's pretentious false prophet during the dreadful three and a half year tribulation period, Urbane Basillo from Italy (who was typically always found standing in Andre's shadow) was also instantly killed.

With eyes possessing telescopic vision and ears that could detect a feather dropping miles away if so desired, every single Holy One could clearly see the Lord of Life seated upon His luminous royal throne. Above Him stretched a brilliant shimmering rainbow. Millions of angels hovered in the upper atmosphere over Jerusalem, savoring every second of the sacred celebration taking place below them. Heavenly choirs and orchestras joined in the hallowed festivities. The Good Shepherd had returned to earth to rule over His redeemed friends, never to depart from them again.

Dozens of thundering trumpets instantaneously sounded as the Wonderful Counselor sprang to His feet. The shofars signaled that King Yeshua was preparing to speak. The joyous dancing ceased as all prostrated themselves before the Son of God.

"My precious children, whom I have longed to gather under My wings! Today you are with Me in My glorious kingdom, forever!!

The Kadoshim lifted their heads and joined their voices together in a Spirit-led utterance of heartfelt praise: *Worthy are You, our Lord and God, to receive glory and honor and power! For You created all things, and because of Your will they are, and were created!*

In a rich baritone voice resembling the sound of pure rushing water, Israel's hallowed Messiah began to deliver His message. "I have yearned for this day since before the dawn of creation! I have pined for the time when I would be united with you in everlasting joy! You will each spend some time sitting individually next to Me on My glorious throne in the tranquil years that lie ahead. My banner over every single one of you is love!"

King David's Greater Son tilted His crowned head and glanced in Yochanan's direction, displaying a beautiful smile that radiated deep affection.

"We will continue our wedding feast celebrations here in the Temple, and on the ground and in the skies above, until the end of Hanukkah in five days."

The Kadoshim reflected the Lord's warm smile back to Him. However their faces turned more somber as the Judge of All the Earth uttered His next words.

"At the end of the feast, you will each appear individually before My judgment seat to give an account of your earthly lives, as our brother Shaul foretold in the his letter to the Kadoshim in Rome." Yeshua turned his penetrating gaze toward the Apostle Paul, who had been dancing with youthful feet in another circle next to Yochanan and his brethren.

"Do not fear my dear friends. You will all live forever! My reward is with Me to render to each one according to what you have done." The Great High Priest stepped further away from His throne. "Many of you will serve as priests before Me, never leaving the presence of My throne. You will be as pillars in my Holy Temple. Some will rule with Me during My thousand year reign over the restored earth. Others will have various roles to play here in Jerusalem, the City of the Great King and our new world capital, or out in the new national provinces that we will establish."

The Sovereign Lord's glowing expression turned more serious as He continued. "Only some thirty million human beings remain alive after the Antichrist's brutal reign. Nearly two-thirds of them are children who did not receive his death-dealing mark. I was forced to perform My strange work of judgment upon Andre's satanic empire, sending all who had worshipped that beast and received his mark to their eternal home away from My presence."

Having missed the recent horrific tribulation period to which the Sovereign Lord was referring since he was already in heaven with his beloved Savior when it began, Jonathan glanced at Sarah and his two transformed children, who had successfully endured that evil time with the help of their Heavenly Father and earthly friends.

"In the devil's iniquitous grip, the world was decimated. The Creator of the Universe, standing before you at the beautiful dawn of this new day, will quickly restore the earth to its original blissful state, with your help and participation. The fresh holy water flowing out from underneath this Temple Mount right now will also help bring swift healing to the nations. Many of you will soon carry the therapeutic leaves and fruit from the Trees of Life—already swiftly growing next to the sacred waters—to the millions of hungry, hurting human souls around the globe. You will act as My ambassadors of life!"

The Kadoshim bowed their heads at the humbling prospect of being used as the Lord's channels of healing and love to their devastated world.

"Billions of people all over the earth sadly rejected My authority and the words of warning issued daily by our brothers Yochanan and Natan-el." The Word of Life again glanced in the direction of His two intimate friends. "The rebels are now consigned to the fiery flames of hell, and will remain in that justified condition forever. Their followers will remain dead until the prophesied second resurrection will take place at the end of My magnificent thousand-year reign." Sarah squeezed Jonathan's hand, thinking in sorrow of her rebellious younger sister Donna from California who had constantly mocked Israel's Glorious Messiah while living with her and the children in the Goldman family Jerusalem home during the last days of the previous era.

"Regular ingestion of the leaves and fruit from the Trees of Life, which will only grow here in the Promised Land and in the nearby restored Garden of Eden, will bring health and longevity to the human race. It will take ten years for a person to age as much as humans did in just one year in the passing era. Therefore, as in the days before Noah, people will live many hundreds of years. Clean air, pure water, abundant food, the lack of warfare and the elimination of most diseases will add further years to human life spans."

The Prince of Peace paused and looked down briefly toward His gleaming feet. "However I must warn you, despite the fact that I am now physically present with humanity on earth as their resplendent King of Kings, some will yet rebel against Me. At the command of My Father, the human race retains free will to either worship the Alpha and Omega from their hearts, or to turn away and face the consequences of their serious error." Eli's bright eyes met Jonathan's; faint frowns on each of their youthful faces.

"Some of you will be ruling over human populations either locally or regionally with a rod of iron. In doing so, you will help shepherd millions to eternal salvation, like many of you did in the previous era. When you stand before My judgment seat after this joyous Hanukkah festival is over, I will give you your personal assignments if you are not notified of them before then. Some of you who will govern with Me will be free to choose your own helpers. I will also hand you a white stone with your new name on it: a name that no one else will know but you and Me alone." The Kadoshim were smiling broadly once again.

"My rewards are with Me to render to each one according to what you have done."

The Passover Lamb gazed tenderly at the redeemed servants standing in awe before Him. Then He slowly raised His countenance to gaze at the millions listening closely from above the sacred Temple. His stunning brown eyes had turned misty. "I have loved you with an everlasting love! Therefore I have called you My friends!"

The King of the Universe, the eternal Holy One of Israel, raised His strong right arm and blew a gentle kiss to the Kadoshim assembled before Him. Their hearts melted inside them.

The Bridegroom then continued His discourse with His purified Bride. "King David, My esteemed servant and faithful friend, will now be called the Prince of Israel, as foretold long ago by another faithful friend, the Prophet Ezekiel." The Author of Life turned His eyes toward the ancient seer that uttered those words long ago, who had been dancing in the same circle with Shaul. "Prince David will now share a few words with you."

Wearing a small silver tiara and an embroidered white silk robe with a regal purple sash around his trim waist, the now youthful monarch with a cropped crimson beard slowly stepped up to his Greater Son's right side. He reverently bowed low before the Beginning and the End, and then began to speak.

"King Yeshua, we all love You so much!!" Loud shouts of affirmation erupted in the sacred Temple and beyond it, lasting several minutes. When the ecstatic voices finally died down, Prince David continued. "We worship You Lord with all that is within us! We remember the blood that You shed, the personal price that You paid, to redeem us!"

Yochanan looked again at the dark red scars still visible on his beloved Savior's hands and feet. They would remain there forever. Like all of the saved ones present before the Master's throne, he now had tears of sorrow mixed with joy dribbling down from the corners of his wise brown eyes.

Prince David raised his arms into the air in a sign of triumphant victory as he quoted his own prophetic words recorded in Psalm 110. "You are now stretching forth Your strong scepter from Zion and will rule in the midst of Your enemies! We, your people, will volunteer freely in this day of your power!" He then turned his engaging gaze toward the Kadoshim gathered before him. "In holy array, from the womb of the dawn, Your youth are to You as the dew!"

King Yeshua's sparkling eyes became even mistier as He smiled at his worshipful forebear. The sweet psalmist of Israel then addressed his fellow holy ones. "We are so privileged to serve our Savior and King with all of our hearts and minds and strength!" he proclaimed, to resounding shouts of *amen!* David thought of his queen, Batsheva, as he turned again to face the Bread of Life. "None of us is worthy to stand before Your anointed eternal throne. It is by grace alone that we are here on this wonderful day." Another round of affirming amens burst forth from the redeemed ones as Prince David turned back to face them.

"Most of you will be living under my governance here in our Lord's special land, which will also be known as *Mahane-Adonai*, the Camp of the Lord. The Holy City of Jerusalem will be greatly expanded. Its western border will run along the bottom of the foothills of Judea and Samaria adjacent to the coastal Plain of Sharon. The northern boundary will be at the base of Mount Gilboa, where it meets the Jezreel Valley. The eastern border will stretch down into the Jordan Valley, still the lowest spot on earth. It will become lush and verdant by means of the living water pouring out from freshly sprouting springs all over the land, and also from the healing waters flowing down from the Temple Mount into the nearby Dead Sea, which will be restored back to life. In the south, the new municipal boundary will run beyond the Hebron hills, where they meet up with the Wilderness of Zin in the northern portion of the Negev Desert."

Prince David paused to look around at his sanctified audience, listening with rapt attention to his every utterance. "By the Word of the Lord, homes will materialize at the end of this festival in every section of the territory I just mentioned. Located on the slopes of the hills, many will have majestic views as the Lord's beloved land comes back to abundant life. Springs of water will rise up all over the hills, in the valleys, along the coast and in the southern desert, producing many refreshing streams and small lakes. Parks to stroll and play in will be everywhere. The dry and thirsty Promised Land will be reborn!"

Having grown up near the beach in Santa Monica California, and then spent most of her married life in waterless Jerusalem, Sarah thrilled at the fertile picture in her heart that David's vivid words inspired.

"However the homes will not be totally private dwellings." The handsome young prince paused and smiled. "I realize that particular fact might not excite all of you. My earthly son, Solomon, can testify what it's like to live with more than one partner!" Standing about thirty feet back from the throne, Solomon bowed with mock reverence and then smiled back at his precious earthly father.

"You will each dwell with other Kadoshim who'll be assigned to share your living space. Mostly they will be those you knew well while living as human beings in the passing era." Many Holy Ones glanced at intimate friends and former family members gathered around them.

"To prepare room for the homes, some of you will be directed to go out in teams from tomorrow to begin removing the debris left behind from the Man of Sin's final military assault upon our sacred city and land. Buildings lie in ruins everywhere, and most must be removed. You will do that by means of the powerful Word of the Lord." Benny, who had loved Superman films when he was a human boy, poked his elbow in his earthly father Jonathan's ribs and winked, thrilled at the prospect of such a supernatural assignment.

Israel's new regal governor turned solemn as he carried on. "Every afternoon, beginning at the end of this joyous festival of rededication, Yeshua our Eternal King will appear in the Holy Temple on His exalted throne at exactly 5:00 PM local time. After the shattered international communication system is restored—and some of you will begin work on that immediately after the Hanukkah celebrations end—people everywhere on earth will be able to view the wonderful worship as it takes place. It will be early morning in the western half of North America, mid morning in the east, early afternoon in South America, mid to late afternoon in Europe, Africa and our region, early evening in western Asia, and late evening in the Far East and Australia." The listening Kadoshim, who had come from every region on earth, were elated over the news that people everywhere would have the opportunity to witness the sacred worship they had just experienced.

"For around two hours every day, we redeemed ones will gather here to worship our wonderful Savior and Lord. On the weekly Shabbat, the King of the Ages will spend all day on His royal throne. Of course, He's already told us that many will serve Him day and night as priests here in His Temple, which will be further transformed very soon. I think you all realize by now that with our new spiritual bodies, we can make the transition from the farthest corners of earth in the twinkling of an eye." Delighted over the prospect of worshiping the worthy Righteous One every day, the sanctified children of God smiled broadly at one another as they relished with deep appreciation and thanksgiving the magnificent gifts which their gracious Heavenly Father was bestowing upon them.

"Finally my hallowed brethren, I'm extremely honored to announce to you that we'll hold a holy formal coronation of our majestic King of Kings here in Jerusalem in just over forty days time, soon after the severed worldwide communications network is repaired. Of course, Yeshua already is our King but this will be a ceremonial proclamation of his Millennial Kingship for all to see. We want every human being alive on earth, especially the children, to watch that awesome ceremony. So prepare your hearts for that splendid day as you praise and worship our unmatchable King of Glory!!"

The Kadoshim cheered as Prince David turned once again to face his beloved Savior and Lord. As they warmly embraced, the myriad celebrants began to dance the hora once again, praising Israel's Conquering Messiah and rejoicing in their eternal salvation.

TWO

RIVER OF LIFE

"Cry aloud and shout for joy, oh inhabitants of Zion! For great in your midst is the Holy One of Israel!!"

It was day number four of the eight-day Hanukkah festival, and the mighty Son of God was still seated upon His glistening throne with jubilant Kadoshim celebrating all around Him. His glistening splendor filled the Holy Temple with glory. In front of the throne, four large white wax candles, two feet in diameter and seven feet tall, were positioned in a golden eight-branched *Hanukkiah* that was flickering with brilliant light, marking the first four days of the annual Jewish festival.

However David the Prince was not dancing this wonderful winter morning. Acting on King Yeshua's behalf, he was moving about the swirling Kadoshim, pulling or motioning some aside to give them his instructions for the day. Eli Ben David was one of those he spoke with.

Prince David uttered an exuberant greeting to Eli, who had been one of the 144,000 sealed Jewish males that ministered with signs and wonders during the Antichrist's atrocious reign. "Good morning, Child of the Eternal Father!"

"Good day, my Prince!" Eli volleyed back with a wide smile, displaying his pearly teeth between a dark brown mustache and meticulously cropped beard. The Jerusalem-born Israeli was the product of a Sephardic father and an Ashkenazi mother in his previous life, and he still retained the russet skin color of his father Baruch, born in Basra Iraq, and the bright blue eyes that he inherited from his mother

Rivka, whose parents moved to the Holy Land from Germany soon after Adolph Hitler rose to power.

Although Eli had only met Israel's illustrious new Prince two days before amid the ongoing celebrations of the Sovereign Lord's return to earth, he'd felt an immediate kinship with him. After all, they were both handsome young Jews who'd spent much of their human lives in Jerusalem, although their earthly roles hadn't been at all similar. Another difference was that Eli had never been married.

"I have an assignment for you, my brother," Prince David stated after giving Eli a brief embrace. "Our Master wants you to head up one of the teams that will go out today and tomorrow in order to cleanse the city in preparation for the new housing and other buildings that will soon appear."

Eli bowed his strong upper body until it was parallel with his trim waist. "I'm most honored to be asked to serve, Prince David."

"Thank you, my son," replied Israel's renowned new provincial governor. "Can you quickly assemble a team of seven or eight brethren to go out with you? You'll be working not far from here, in the southeastern portion of the city."

"Certainly, your grace," Eli replied with surety, quickly realizing that Prince David was referring to the section of Jerusalem where his friend Jonathan Goldman and his family had lived. He strongly suspected that Big Benny, at least, would be eager to jump on board, and probably his parents and their other close friends as well.

"Good Eli, we knew we could count on you. Now all you have to do when you get there is spread out a bit and give the command in the Name of the Lord for the rubble and anything else in front of you to be removed, and it will be instantly dissolved."

"*Cool!*" squealed Benny, who had noticed the nearby conversation and employed his newly-keen hearing to listen in. Eli turned slightly toward his young friend and feigned a frown before cracking a smile, still marveling at the reality that the stocky young man had been a mere eight-year-old lad until his recent transformation.

Eli grinned at the equally amused Prince. "I think I've located our first recruit!" The royal governor slapped him affectionately on the back and wished him "Godspeed!" as he skipped away to search for his next divine appointment.

It took just a few seconds for Eli to enlist his friends Jonathan and Sarah Goldman, plus their daughter, Tali, who'd been an eleven-year-old girl until the Root of Jesse returned to Jerusalem, but now was nearly six feet tall. Jonathan then volunteered to go speak with two other Kadoshim who had kindly assisted his fatherless family after his untimely death on the Golan Heights. Eli nodded his grateful permission.

Before the unprecedented Great Tribulation began, Craig Eagleman was a language student at Hebrew University on Mount Scopus, located northeast of the Temple Mount. The Gentile American guitarist also served as a worship leader at their Beit Yisrael Messianic congregation in Jerusalem, and later ministered with Yochanan and Natan-el at the Western Wall and other parts of the Holy City and the world.

"Shalom Craig, how goes the dancing?"

"Hey, Jonathan! I'm enjoying myself immensely! I can't even begin to express the joy in my heart, being in the presence of the Lord with all of you." Craig stopped speaking, slightly bent his knees and dramatically grabbed hold of his robe-covered thighs as a sly smile stretched over his face. "And although I look like I must weigh at least 220 pounds—all hard muscle of course—this new body is actually lighter than air!"

Jonathan laughed along with his longtime friend, still blond and blue eyed as ever. "Listen brother, we can use your hulky help today. Eli's heading a team that'll go out and dissolve the rubble in parts of southeast Jerusalem by means of the Word of the Lord. The rest of my family are also signed up to help, especially a very eager Benny. I was thinking maybe you and Ken Preston could join us."

Craig pointed at Jonathan's transformed children who had resumed dancing with their loving earthly mother in a nearby hora circle. "I still find it hard to believe that the big guy over there is actually your son Benny, dancing with a very tall Tali and Sarah. I mean, I look almost the same as before the Lord returned, since I was about the age I seem to be now in this new body. And you look pretty much like you did when you went off to fight against Lebanon and Syria. But Benny and Tali were just *youngsters* until Yeshua came back, and now look at them!"

"Yah, it's all a bit odd for me too, Craig, as you can imagine. And don't forget, you were with my kids sheltering in the desert until fairly recently, but I last saw them before I was called up for the war almost five years ago. Benny was only four and a half then, and Tali just six, although her seventh birthday was coming up the week after I headed north with Eli and the rest of our army unit. I'm so proud of them both, and, of course, of their brave mother."

Jonathan paused as his eyes followed his happy transformed family dancing the hora. Then he turned back to Craig. "I've been hearing some stories of what you all did while ministering with Yochanan and Natan-el near the Western Wall. You really risked your lives for your faith. Plus Benny told me how you and Eli and some of the other guys took such good care of my family after I was killed in that surprise Syrian gas attack." A tear touched his left eye as he paused again and put his arm around Craig's broad shoulders. "How can I ever thank you?"

"Aw, it was nothing you wouldn't have done if the conditions were reversed. And by the way Jonathan, we were all so proud that you died while bravely defending your country after that unprovoked Hizbullah rocket attack sparked off the war. I mean, you were only a reserve soldier already well into your thirties, but you joined up with your unit in the middle of the night without prior notice or question. Eli told us all about it. He really loved you Jonathan, as we all did, and of course still do."

Jonathan squeezed his arm more tightly around Craig's shoulders. "The feeling's mutual, brother."

The American guitarist continued speaking about Jonathan's closest friend. "Despite witnessing your death, and then being taken captive by the Syrians, Eli started helping out your family the minute he got back to Jerusalem after the prisoner exchange. And that was in the midst of deep sorrow after losing his best buddy." Craig's sky-blue eyes met Jonathan's dark amber eyes square on. "I don't think Sarah would've made it without Eli's help."

"She's told me a little bit about that, Craig, but I still haven't spoken to Eli himself; to thank him properly I mean. Too much dancing going on I guess! Maybe I'll get a chance to do that today. Hey, I heard from Sarah that you met my parents at my funeral here in Jerusalem, and then saw them again when you all went with the two witnesses to minister in Chicago. She said you were actually at their home in Skokie when Andre's security forces arrested them for not having his implantation under the skin on their right hands. She told me they would've all been arrested if it hadn't been for you and Eli. I'm so grateful guy, but tell me, what exactly did you do?"

Craig now placed his own burly arm around Jonathan's shoulders. "We were sitting around talking and eating your mom's tasty pizza when your dad got a phone call from someone in his synagogue. The caller warned him that Andre's United World thugs were arresting Jews in the area who didn't have his mark implanted on their right hand or underneath the skin on their forehead. When the doorbell rang, we all rushed down to the basement where your dad said we could hide in his large unused coal bin. Sarah stuffed Benny and Tali inside, and then she and Eli and I got in—a tight fit but we made it. Your parents had meantime gone back upstairs to answer the door, knowing they couldn't possibly escape, but hoping at least we'd be safe. When the soldiers came down the stairs, Eli and I pushed down hard on the inside metal door handle, which had a matching handle outside. We heard them say it must be rusted shut and so we escaped arrest."

Jonathan leaned over and kissed Craig on his neck. "Thank you my dear friend."

Craig blushed and pulled on his short beard before speaking. "Well Jonathan, again it was nothing you wouldn't have done for my family, if I'd had one that is! I really liked your parents, by the way. I'm sure Sarah told you she never heard what happened to them after that."

The robust American hesitated for a moment as he debated whether or not to ask Jonathan a question about a topic that had been on his mind for a couple days. He decided to go ahead. "Speaking of your family, can I ask you something that might be…a bit…sensitive?"

"Sure brother, anything at all."

"Isn't it somewhat…odd to have been married to Sarah when you last saw her, and now you are not, and she looks quite…different, even if not as much as your totally-morphed kids."

Jonathan paused again and gazed at his earthly family joyously dancing the hora. "Not as different as Tali and Benny for sure, but I get your point. Yes, it may take some time to become fully used to the transformations, Craig. I suppose we have at least a thousand years to adjust!

Craig chuckled as Jonathan continued. "But brother, we knew all along that the Lord had said there'd be no marriage for the redeemed once they received their eternal bodies, so it was not really a surprise. Still, it might take some time…anyway, back to today! Are you with us on the clean up crew?"

"Yes sir!" Craig answered as he gave an exaggerated army salute. "Do you want me to talk to anyone else about it?"

"That'd be great, friend. Sarah suggested Ken Preston might be a good candidate, but I don't really know him. I understand you led him to the Lord and then later you escaped to the desert with him and my family, led by Moshe Salam?"

That's correct, Jonathan. I'd be glad to recruit him."

"Thanks so much brother, let me know what he says."

Craig Eagleman had already spotted Ken Preston dancing in another circle on the other side of the Temple with his previous-era wife, Betty. Born and raised in North Carolina, she had been killed in a brutal rocket attack upon the two witnesses, launched by some young Orthodox Jewish hotheads who incorrectly thought the elderly prophets and their companions were bringing spiritual harm to their people.

"Hey Ken!" he shouted out in order to be heard above the melodious voices singing praises to the Rose of Sharon. Standing six foot four, Ken Preston turned around and rapidly exited the dancing ring, bringing Betty with him. They greeted Craig with warm hugs.

"It's so good to see you Craig!" said Ken as Betty nodded in agree-ment. "I noticed you over there yesterday and was planning to say hello, but you beat me to it!"

"I spotted you as well Craig, and I must say you look fantastic," said Betty with her characteristic southern drawl, adding "Like a foot-ball quarterback!"

"Well, you look great yourself Betty, about twenty years younger than when you were killed near the Western Wall." Craig stepped back to take a better look at Ken's former wife. "I must admit, I wouldn't have recognized you at all if you hadn't been dancing with Ken. Of course, you look a lot younger too, Ken, but your countenance is still basically the same. Betty, you are more stunning than ever!"

The couple smiled broadly and thanked Craig for the compli-ments. Then the worship leader spoke about the clean up assignment Prince David had given to Eli. Ken quickly affirmed that he'd be more than glad to join in, but he thought it best if Betty remained in the Temple.

Craig first met Ken when he was working in Jerusalem as a local cameraman and periodic reporter for the World News Network, based in America. The agnostic media man had covered the two witnesses for WNN in the Old City. He had strongly disliked the fact that his Evangelical Christian wife was often in the Western Wall plaza minis-tering with them and the other disciples, despite his frequent objec-tions. Soon after Betty was slain, Craig led a very shaken Ken in a prayer asking the Lord to forgive his sins and grant him eternal life.

While Craig Eagleman was chatting with Ken and Betty Preston, someone approached Benny Goldman from behind and thumped him on his shoulder. As if on a pogo stick, Benny jumped backwards out of the dancing circle to check out who this stranger was.

"Excuse me, are you Benny Goldman?" asked the handsome saint with hazel eyes and a four-day-old russet-colored beard.

"Yes I am brother, and who are you?"

"I'm the kid with thick glasses who helped you put Lego buildings and puzzles together, and watched Batman and Superman movies with you almost every day."

"Micah Kupinski! I can't believe it!!"

The two friends embraced harder than they should have, forgetting for a moment that they were now inhabiting muscular adult bodies. Micah, whose parents had immigrated to Israel from the city of Manchester in England, was Benny's best friend when they were neighbors in southeast Jerusalem. However they lost touch with each other after Benny moved with his mother and sister to live with the two witnesses and other brethren, including Eli and Craig, in a large house on the Mount of Olives. The childhood buddies had only seen each other briefly one time after that, when Micah's father reluctantly took his son to the Western Wall plaza to say hello to his ministering close friend.

"How did you recognize me Micah? You and I sure don't look *anything* like we did the last time we met!"

"Yah, we were both only five years old then…and that wasn't so long ago. Anyway, I guessed it must be you when I spotted your dad dancing next to you. He looks about the same as before, well, maybe a bit hunkier, but then we all look strong and healthy in these new bodies." He stopped speaking and pointed at one of the dancers. "Is that your sister Tali?"

"Sure is, can you believe it dude? She's all grown up too, in fact nearly as tall as me!" Benny smiled as he reached out and cupped his large left hand over Micah's right bicep, partially visible below the sleeve of his white robe. "I guess you've been working out!"

The two saints laughed with delight as they hugged each other again, this time more gently. Then Benny asked the question that had instantly come to mind when he realized he was talking with his childhood friend. "Micah, I remember that your dad warned me a couple times not to talk about Yeshua with you. Your parents didn't know the Lord at all, and didn't want to know him. I'm so thrilled you're here! But how and when did you give your life to Him?"

"Well, it was because of you and your dad."

"Me and my dad? But I only talked with you about the Lord for a few seconds in the Old City after you suddenly showed up and tapped me on the shoulder—kind of like today."

"That's true Benny, but you planted a seed that God watered. After hearing what you shared, and seeing Yochanan and Natan-el up close instead of just on TV, I became more and more curious about your faith. A few months later, I surrendered my life to the Lord, which obviously was the best thing I ever did!"

"Amen to that! But what did my dad have to do with it? He was long dead by then."

"That's also true Benny, but God works in mysterious ways, my dear friend. You told me I needed to read the New Testament, but I didn't know how to get hold of a copy. Then I thought maybe someone in your family had left a Bible in your house. So I went over there one afternoon when my mom was out buying some milk and rang the bell, and your Aunt Donna answered."

Benny interrupted Micah at the mention of his notorious aunt. "Was that Swedish United World soldier with her? You know, she kind of turned into a whore after we moved out. Mom said she actually employed some prostitutes there to service UW soldiers who occupied the city. They worked in all three bedrooms, including mine!"

"Ugh! No, she was alone, but I did notice a UW motorcycle jacket hanging on the back of one of your dining room chairs. Anyway I asked her if I could borrow a Bible, and she said I shouldn't waste my time on religion. Then after I told her I just needed to do some research for a school project, which I guess was kind of a white lie, she went up to your parent's bedroom and came back with your dad's leather Bible. She said 'Here is Jonathan's Bible. You can keep it since he won't be returning anytime soon,' which I thought was rather cruel. Still, I just thanked her and left. And Benny, I was so happy that night when I picked it up to read a bit in secret after my parents went to bed. A sweet picture of you with your family fell out! Your dad was wearing his army uniform, but you and Tali were in pajamas! I treasured that picture very much."

Benny brushed a tear from his left eye. "It was snapped on one of those old Polaroid cameras my dad had, the night he was called up with Uncle Eli for army duty—the last time I saw him until we were reunited in glory. He put the camera on automatic and placed it on a shelf. I guess he must have taken the photo with him to the Golan Heights."

"Speaking of Eli, later that week I discovered another picture of your dad standing with him, decked out in their army uniforms. Your dad was holding a rifle and they both looked very happy."

"Well Micah, I may have already told you, but it was a reserve combat unit they were part of. Dad was a marksman and Eli was the unit's medic. He tried to save my dad's life after Syrian soldiers fired a gas-tipped artillery shell that landed not far from him." Benny paused and wiped away another tear. "He held my dad's limp body in his arms."

Just then, a very alive Jonathan walked over to fetch his earthly son, with Eli just behind him. They were joined a moment later by Craig and Ken. "Its time to go out on our mission Benny," announced Jonathan, adding "I'll go get Sarah and Tali."

"Wait a second dad. I want you to say hi to Micah Kupinski. I'm sure you'll remember who he is."

"Of course I do! Hey big guy! My, have you grown up fast!" The six saints laughed heartily at Jonathan's cheeky remark.

Craig Eagleman suddenly stopped chuckling and gasped before proclaiming, "Jonathan!! I think it's your dad and mom!!"

Jonathan and Eli spun around in seconds and spotted a couple of Kadoshim galloping toward them. Like everyone else in the Holy Temple, they appeared to be about thirty years old. Craig had seen something specific on one of them that gave him an instant identity clue.

"Dad, is that you?" enquired Jonathan as tears of joy began to flood his eyes.

Abraham Goldman reached out and warmly embraced his earthly son, which answered Jonathan's question. By now, everyone in the small group was tearing up. It was clearly a day of sweet reunions.

Jonathan reached out and kissed his mother Rebecca, who then hugged him tightly. Soon Abe joined the bear hug, as did Benny— overwhelmed by having just been reunited with his best childhood friend, and now his beloved grandparents whom he'd last seen alive over two years before in Illinois.

After remaining in the affectionate hold for several more seconds, Jonathan reintroduced Craig and Eli to his parents, followed by Micah and Ken. After that, he asked Craig how he had recognized them since they were in their seventies the last time he saw them.

"It was *that*," said Craig as he pointed to Abe's forearm, where the tattooed concentration camp number was located.

"But we all have new bodies, dad" said Jonathan in astonishment. "Your own father Benjamin perished at Auschwitz. Why do you still bear that awful reminder of Hitler's hideous holocaust?"

"Because of Him," answered Abe as he pointed up to the Lord, seated in grandeur on His throne. The small group of Kadoshim turned to gaze at the King of Life; already looking their way and smiling.

Abe resumed speaking as he slowly turned his eyes away from his precious Savior. "You've probably heard, Jonathan, that we took in young Benny after Sarah and Tali decided to stay put in Israel when the American government evacuated many of its citizens during the early part of Andre's reign. We were so thrilled when Sarah and Tali showed up at our front door in Skokie two years later. They were with Eli and Craig, who were all in the Chicago area ministering with Yochanan and Natan-el. Benny had just turned seven, and he was, of course, ecstatic to see his mother again, along with his sister and friends. They hadn't notified us they were coming, for security reasons, so it was a total surprise for him." Benny smiled as he recalled the sweet reunion.

"Well Jonathan, the Emperor's goons showed up that same evening and arrested your mother and me after we hid our guests safely down in the basement. We hadn't taken Andre's identity mark, son, on Sarah's advice, so that was their excuse for nabbing us. We never made it back home. I don't think Sarah or the kids knew that we were...beheaded a couple days later for our faith."

Abe's last comment cut through Benny and Jonathan like a sharp blade slicing a taut rope. Then Benny spoke up. "I knew you were no longer answering the phone Grandpa, so I sort of guessed...."

Jonathan could not wait any longer. "Your faith?" he interrupted before realizing in a flash that his parents would not be standing before him in glorified bodies if they had not surrendered their lives to Yeshua.

"Yes son. We were incarcerated in a UW prison camp just north of Skokie." Abe directed his eyes once again toward his radiant Redeemer. "And then suddenly there He was, standing before us in our jail cell, shining brightly like He is today."

As Abe began to choke up over the vivid memory, Rebecca Goldman added to her husband's moving report. "We knew we weren't crazy Jonathan, or merely seeing a vision. Then the Lord spoke to your father. He asked him to reach out and touch the scar on His right hand, which Abe did. We were both speechless son, realizing it was the Jewish Messiah we'd heard about at your funeral; the One who Eli and Sarah had talked about just prior to our arrest. Benny also shared his faith with us many times as well."

The young saint reached out and grabbed hold of his grand-mother's hand, who was now lightly weeping while sharing the couple's special testimony.

"We knelt down before the Lord and asked Him to forgive our sins. He then touched us on our shoulders and said 'Today you will be with Me in paradise.' Then Abe said something amazing to Yeshua, Jonathan. He said, 'If you're bearing those scars for all eternity, then I want to bear the identity numbers the Germans gave me when I was just a boy, incarcerated in a Nazi concentration camp. I don't want to forget what they did to us.' The Lord answered Abe, saying 'It is done.' We were beheaded a few hours later, but now we are alive forever!"

The small band of saints again turned their gazes toward the Lamb of God, who promptly blew a tender kiss in their direction. There was not a dry eye among them.

Sarah Goldman showed up moments later, accompanied by Tali. They had not noticed Jonathan and the other saints gathered near the hora circle since they had ceased dancing when Benny left to speak to a stranger. Then mother and daughter headed for another group of dancers that included Sarah's longtime closest friend, Stacy Pearlman.

Sarah was about to ask Eli Ben David if Stacy could join their scheduled cleansing expedition when she spotted Abe's tattoo. Seeing her look of total astonishment, Jonathan said, "Sarah, say hello to my parents."

Sarah and Tali raced to the now youthful couple and threw their arms around them. "I am so *thrilled* you are here with us and the Lord!" exclaimed Sarah as Jonathan and Benny joined the embrace. "But how, I mean, when…I'm speechless!"

"I'll tell you all about it as we walk to our assignment," replied Jonathan. "We'd better be on our way. I can't wait to talk to you later today, mom and dad; I have so many questions to ask you. We must get going since we have some important work to do now, but I'll see you this evening for sure!"

"Oh, I almost forgot," Sarah uttered as Jonathan's last word came out. "Can Stacy Pearlman join us?" Eli nodded his head in affirmation.

"Hey mom and Tali, can you guess who this tall dude is?" asked Benny as he poked a thick finger in Micah's side.

"I haven't a clue," answered Sarah as she studied his robust face.

"Do you remember a little squirt with thick glasses and buck teeth who loved to build things with Lego blocks?" said a self-deprecating Micah with a placid smile pasted on his ruddy face.

"Micah Kupinski!" exclaimed Sarah and Tali in unison. More hugs were exchanged.

Then Micah turned to Eli. "Can I come along with you guys?" he enquired, not really knowing where they were going but wanting to spend more time with Benny and company. "Sure, big guy. Let's get going!" barked out Eli as if leading a unit of Israeli army warriors into battle.

Eli Ben David had already decided that the small band of Holy Ones would walk to their job site since he wanted to see the new river that ran down to the Dead Sea from underneath the Temple Mount. The biblical Mount Moriah, upon which the Temple Mount was located, had risen in height during the tectonic upheavals which shook the earth as the Lord was returning to Jerusalem, releasing pent up water underneath it. The Jerusalem Temple was now situated like a diamond on the tallest hill in the Holy City, some twenty feet above the nearby Mount of Olives.

The new river was called *Nahar Cha'im*, the River of Life. Its healing waters flowed briskly down into the Kidron Valley right below the Temple Mount, where the sacrificial Lamb of God had agonized over His pending crucifixion in the Garden of Gethsemane nearly 2,000 years before. From there it rushed south over the long dormant Ein Rogel spring at the bottom of the sloping valley. Ein Rogel had sprung back to life after being dry for many centuries. It was located at the corner of the ancient territorial boundary between the tribes of Judah and Benjamin.

Ein Rogel contributed more fresh water to the ever widening river, as did the Gihon spring south of the Temple Mount, which also gushed with renewed vigor. The cascading river—whose appearance had been prophesied by Ezekiel in the sixth century before the Lord was born in Bethlehem, and also spoken of by Yochanan in the book of Revelation—surged down a series of gorges until it reached the Dead Sea. The holy liquid miraculously purified the salty water. Therefore it would no longer be called the Dead Sea (or the Salt Sea as its name had been in Hebrew), but *Yam Cha'im*, the Sea of Life.

The abundant sacred water quickly filled up the depleted sea, which had shrunk considerably during the final centuries of the old era since its mineral rich water had been evaporating every day in the increasingly fierce desert heat. Adding significantly to the shrinkage, fresh water from the Jordan River to the north, which replenished the salty sea, had been mostly diverted for agricultural purposes from the 1950s onward.

The Yam Cha'im would soon become the source of another new river, called *Nahar Arava*, the name of the waterless valley that ran south from the Dead Sea to the Red Sea, where the Israeli resort city of Eilat was located. The new river flowed down a steep gorge created when the massive earthquake, which immediately followed the two witnesses' ascension in Jerusalem, reopened parts of the Great Rift that ran from central Africa up to Syria. Trees of Life were growing briskly all along the river's lush banks.

When the sacred water first reached the Red Sea, it instantly cleansed the ocean of all the blood, filth, destroyed ships, dead fish and pollution that followed in the wake of the Lord's final judgments upon

Andre's corrupt world empire. The salt also miraculously disappeared from the Red Sea and the adjacent Indian and Pacific Oceans, making their abundant potable waters excellent for both drinking and agricultural use. This would quickly help bring the devastated world back to life.

Four days earlier, another new river had also sprung up from underneath the Temple Mount. Called Nahar Yehuda, it cascaded down canyons and gorges in the western Judean hills, emptying into the Mediterranean Sea just south of Tel Aviv. In a similar fashion, the biblical sea and the adjacent Atlantic Ocean became instantly purified.

Eli Ben David explained a little bit more about the dissolution work ahead of them as he and his volunteer helpers set out for south-eastern Jerusalem. He warned that they would probably find many decaying bodies in the rubble. Eli explained that Prince David had come to him a second time with instructions about how to dispose of any corpses they might encounter. The bodies were to be dissolved along with the rubble. All who perished in the final wave of judgments had accepted the Antichrist's mark, he explained, and would not be honored with proper burials. Still, the work crews had to be careful to make sure that no living humans were trapped in the debris.

After Eli finished speaking, Jonathan slowed his pace a bit so he could converse with Sarah and Tali walking behind the rest of the group. He wanted to relate his parents' incredible salvation story. When he finished, Sarah again expressed her ecstatic amazement over the senior Goldman's testimony and the small role she had played in it. "You know Jonathan, I've heard so many stories of the Lord miraculously appearing to holocaust victims and survivors and leading them to His throne room. Which reminds me; after you were killed by the Syrians, I went to work as a volunteer at Hadassah Hospital in southwest Jerusalem. Frankly Jonathan, I needed to do something more positive with my time than just moping around grieving. Anyway, while there, I became very close to a Holocaust survivor named Yitzhak, with whom I often shared my faith. It was actually that friendship which prompted me to decide to stay put in Jerusalem when I sent

Benny off to stay with your parents in Skokie. I later led Yitzhak in a prayer of salvation, so I think he should be somewhere here among all the Kadoshim. I've been looking around for him, but haven't spotted him yet. Of course, he was a very old man when I last saw him, and I look a bit different now as well."

Tali Goldman radically changed the subject. "Dad, mom, don't you think that we might find Aunt Donna's body in our old home today? That's the last place you saw her mom, just before Benny went to America, and she was probably there when that gigantic earthquake struck right after Yochanan and Natan-el were called up to heaven. Plus I've heard Eli say there were many other earthquakes and meteors and those hideous stinging creatures after that. So she must be dead, correct?"

The great earthquake was actually unleashed when the Lamb of God opened up the sixth seal that Yochanan had written about in the book of Revelation. The demonic creatures were released to persecute Andre's followers as a result of the angelic blowing of the fifth shofar trumpet of judgment listed in the beloved Apostle's book.

"Indeed, Donna is probably deceased, honey," replied Sarah as a grimace crossed her face.

Jonathan picked up where his earthly wife left off. "I'm sure we'll see many bodies today, Tali, as Eli warned us. After all, it's only been a few days since the final judgments ended. So it's certainly possible that Donna's remains will be among them."

Sarah put her arm around Tali's shoulders. "Let's hope if she was still alive when the massive quake struck, someone was able to bury her afterwards; that is if it killed her, as may well have been the case. Your rebellious aunt certainly didn't know the Lord when I last saw her, Tali, and she didn't want to know Him, although at least she still hadn't received Andre's mark. Yochanan warned the world that everyone on earth who accepted his identity implant would perish, as I made sure she understood."

The small group paused for a few minutes to admire the new Nahar Cha'im river that was gushing down the ravine next to them. Then they examined one of the fast-growing Trees of Life which were sprouting up like weeds on the banks of the coursing waterway. Feeling refreshed, the demolition crew continued on their short journey to southeast Jerusalem. Eli had already announced that they would head to the Goldman house first. He thought it was best to put that emotional hurdle quickly behind them.

As they entered their former neighborhood, Sarah grabbed Jonathan's arm for comfort. Tali held her mother's other hand. Rubble was everywhere. Unlike their small private townhouse, most people in Jerusalem lived in apartment buildings. Almost all were destroyed. They spotted and smelled many rotting bodies lying under concrete slabs and fallen or burnt trees. Shards of glass littered the sidewalks and lawns. Many of the Jerusalem-stone buildings were still smoldering, having been partially or wholly incinerated during raging fires ignited by the various earthquakes, or by flaming chunks of cascading meteors.

When they turned the final corner onto the street where their family home was located, Tali began to whimper. The house had almost completely collapsed during the unprecedented shaking which gutted the planet. However as they drew closer to the rubble, they could also see that a small part of the back kitchen wall and a corner section of the ceiling above it were still standing. A column of gray smoke was wafting out of that area.

As they approached the house, it was now Sarah's turn to react. *"Donna!"*

THREE

Happy Birthday

Donna was wrapped in a dank wool blanket, sipping hot coffee while perched on a concrete block next to a small campfire. Its embers were glowing under the remaining corner ceiling of the Goldman's obliterated kitchen. Not having seen a single soul for days, she sat up straight when she noticed a group of white-robed people approaching the destroyed house out on the buckled street. Like a wounded gang member left stranded by its mates, she grabbed her long kitchen knife and prepared for the worst.

As the Kadoshim drew closer, Donna gasped with delight when she recognized her brother-in-law Jonathan and his close friends Eli and Craig, whom she had unsuccessfully tried to seduce more than one time. However she could not identify anyone else.

Looking pale and gaunt, the young woman slowly rose to her feet as a grimace of pain contorted her facial expression. "Jonathan, what a...total surprise! And Eli and Craig! You can't imagine how wonderful it is to see you all!"

"Hello Donna," said her former relative coolly, with just a hint of enmity in his voice.

"Shalom Donna," added Eli before adding, "We're really surprised and delighted to see you're alive."

After gently hugging the three saints, Donna noted how well they all looked. Then she gazed at the other six Kadoshim standing just behind them. "And who are the rest of these fine folk?" she enquired.

"Hey sis!" exclaimed Sarah as she gingerly took a couple steps forward over the debris. While Donna did not immediately recognize her by face, she quickly picked up on Sarah's distinctive voice, which was a bit lower in tone than before but more or less the same.

With soot littering her stringy hair, the American-Israeli immigrant—who obviously had not bathed in some time—hobbled over to her older sister and embraced her. "My, have you changed!" she proclaimed before moving on to squeeze Jonathan again around his waist.

Sarah spoke up. "Donna, this is Tali, and that's Benny and his best friend Micah, who you'll recall lived two doors down from here."

"Hello Aunt Donna," uttered Tali followed by Benny, as they moved toward their mother's grungy younger sister to give her a squeeze.

Donna examined them with intensity. "I can see some resemblance to the young Benny I knew, but hardly any to Tali. Is that really you dear?"

Tali wore an embarrassed smile. "Yes Aunt Donna, it's really me. We're all in our glorified bodies now, so a few changes have occurred, as you can see."

"Oh, so that explains all these white robes. Chic! You look like a group of monks or something!" she giggled, adding "But I do love those gold sashes." Tali glanced at her mother who swiftly picked up the ball.

"Donna, standing near Eli is my best friend Stacy Pearlman, who of course you know quite well, and next to her is Ken Preston, who worked as a reporter and cameraman for the World News Network."

"I thought that might be you, Stacy," replied Donna while tilting her head to examine the formerly plump New Yorker's face from a different angle. "My, you really do look quite...different as well. It's a nice look for you." Stacy's auburn hair was much shorter than before, but she still had rosy cheeks and ruby lips that went well with her emerald-colored eyes.

Sarah got right to the point. "Donna, I'm certainly very glad to see you, but quite amazed as well. How did you survive the final judgments?" Before her sister could answer, she issued a follow-up question; born more in hope than conviction. "Did you finally give your life to the Lord?"

"No sis, I didn't do that." Sarah's heart sank like a minnow that just swallowed a lead ball before she realized that Donna would be in a glorified body if that had indeed been the case. "But I *did* get married!" she announced as her burgundy eyebrows darted up on her bruised brow. "I know you must've noticed men's clothing lying around when you last came to check on me and your house." Sarah nodded curtly at the unpleasant reminder. "Well, they belonged to Lars Svenson, a Swedish United World officer who commanded this district. We fell in love Sarah, and he was living here with me. However after your last visit, I felt a bit guilty sleeping in your bed with him, so I asked him to marry me and he agreed. We were wed by the rabbi at that synagogue down the street, but only after Lars gave way to his demand that we raise any children we might have as Jews. I don't think Lars really meant it by the way, but he did love me, so he at least said the right words at the right time. So now I'm now Donna Svenson!"

"Oye!" yelped Eli automatically, before diverting his eyes.

"And where is this guy now?" asked Jonathan, more than annoyed to learn for the first time that his marriage bed had been used for an illicit tryst.

"Of course, he had Andre's economic implantation under the skin of his right hand, and he was often at his office or out on patrol. When the huge earthquake struck right after Sarah's two flame-throwing friends seemingly rose from the dead near Jaffa Gate, he was killed. The ceiling collapsed at his UW office, next to the promenade overlooking the city. I crept over to the area afterwards and spotted his body, which I could see from a distance was being placed into a truck by surviving UW soldiers. I miss Lars so much."

"And you did not take Andre's skin implantation?" quizzed Sarah before quickly deducing that this surely must have been the case.

"No, sis, don't you remember I told you I didn't want to disfigure my fair skin? And anyway, Lars said it would be okay because he was the local UW commander. He said to just stay near the house and I'd be fine; he'd have someone do all our shopping and such. He was really a love Sarah; six-foot-four, and so blond and sexy…kind of like you, Craig."

The former American worship leader did not appreciate the comparison.

Benny thought he'd better quickly change the subject. "But how did you find enough food to survive after the initial worldwide quake Aunt Donna, which happened over three months ago, followed by all those strong aftershocks and other stuff?" he enquired after noting again how emaciated his once very shapely aunt appeared.

"Actually the strongest quake of all was just last week. I've never felt anything like it before. The rest of the kitchen ceiling was still up there, and most of that wall was still standing, until it struck. Fortunately I was outside picking up some branches for my fire when everything started to shake, or I *would* be dead. Anyway Benny, soon after I got back from the area where the destroyed UW headquarters building is located, I went around the neighborhood and picked up tin cans of food and anything else edible I could find. Most people were dead and there were fires blazing everywhere. It was the scariest time of my life!"

Micah winced at her last comments. Donna noticed his expression, and turned to address him. "Micah, I'm sorry to tell you, but I found your dad's body under some roof tiles and other junk in his destroyed bedroom. I also uncovered some tins of tuna fish and beans and two six-packs of bottled water in the kitchen rubble, which I desperately needed. Just then two Arab teenagers made their way slowly past your house, driving one of those small delivery carts they use in the narrow Old City stone streets. They spotted me and pulled over, and then came rushing at me like animals and tried to steal the food I had in my hand. I grabbed this kitchen knife from a pile of rubble near me. The guys stopped cold when they saw it. Then I told them I'd give them each a bottle of water and some tuna fish, beans, and a carton of your mother's cigarettes if they'd help me remove your dad's body and take it with them on their cart, and either bury or burn it somewhere outside of town. I didn't want the…city dogs or the vultures to eat his remains in his own home. Hundreds of hungry dogs were roaming around in vicious packs, and the vultures were pecking at bodies everywhere. So they agreed to that offer, and away they went."

Copious tears were now flowing down Micah's cheeks, and for the first time since he received his new eternal body, they were not tears of joy. Benny put his arm around his dear friend as he gently laid his head down upon Micah's left shoulder.

"Thank you for doing that Donna. I really appreciate it. But what about my mother? Did you spot her body as well?"

Donna stepped over some ragged concrete to take Micah's hands in her own. "Oh honey, I'm so sorry, I guess I thought you knew. Soon after you disappeared, she came down with the Ebola plague and died just a couple days later. I accompanied your father and other neighbors to her funeral at the synagogue where I was married. The coffin was wrapped in a huge plastic bag because of the contagious disease."

Suddenly feeling like a human orphan, Micah said nothing as Jonathan, Sarah and Eli walked over to enfold him in their arms. "You may have lost your earthly family," said Jonathan tenderly after several seconds passed, "but you've gained a new one now. And that will last forever!"

While Donna was speaking to Micah, Tali wandered off to the area below where her second-floor bedroom had been located. She was searching for something special in the dusty debris. Oblivious to the solemnity that had descended over the small group; she suddenly burst into the destroyed kitchen and squealed with delight, "I found it! It was under the mattress of my bed! I had to dig a bit to rescue it."

"Oh Tali, I'm so thrilled for you!" exclaimed her earthly mother as she instantly recognized the object in her daughter's right hand. It was a silver menorah, about seven inches tall. Tali busied herself cleaning dust off the precious item as Donna revealed she'd hidden the Jewish artifact under Tali's mattress to prevent one of her 'guests' from stealing it.

"It's beautiful, sweetheart. Where did you get it?" asked Jonathan as he moved closer to examine the replica of the sacred seven-branched candelabrum which stood in the ancient Jewish Temple.

Sarah winked at Benny and Eli and then began to tell the sweet story. "Jonathan, everyone was so kind after the news about your death reached us. Stacy, I couldn't have made it without your constant help, and that goes for you Eli, and you Craig." Each of her friends smiled as they meekly absorbed the kind comment. "And Donna, you were a blessing as well, even if you did keep up a constant prattle against our faith. The kids also appreciated all of you very much." Tali and Benny nodded their affirmations.

Sarah shifted her head back toward Jonathan. "Nearly one year after the war ended honey, I realized it would've been your 35th birthday coming up on that April 4th. It was going to be the first one…without you. I steeled myself as best I could and placed a special rose-colored ribbon first thing that morning around your portrait, just over there above the sofa. But I hadn't reminded the children that your birthday was coming up. I thought I'd just mention it that day since I didn't want to add to their grief." Both of Jonathan's children lowered their heads and gazed at their littered kitchen floor as they vividly recalled those difficult days not so many years ago.

"Then Tali surprised me by walking into the living room carrying a package wrapped in blue and white paper. I asked her what it was and she answered 'It's a present for abba.' Then she added, 'God told me to buy it and give it to you to keep for him. One day, he's coming back to Jerusalem with Yeshua.' And there it is, and here you are!" Sarah took several steps forward and gave Jonathan a kiss on his right cheek.

Tali smiled misty-eyed at her father, alive forevermore, and then handed him his much delayed present. "Happy birthday, abba." Jonathan held the precious menorah next to his chest as he leaned over and gave his earthly daughter a kiss. Even Donna was tearing up by now.

Then Sarah continued. "Jonathan, there's still more to the story. Eli showed up a couple hours later with some food for the upcoming Passover meal and a lovely stem rose for me, which were hard to come by in those days. He admitted he'd recalled it was your birthday, and knew I certainly would've remembered as well, and he said he wanted to bring me a little bit of cheer. Then he noticed the ribbon around your portrait and the silver menorah that I'd placed next to it. He asked me where I'd gotten that, and when I explained it to him, he told me about...." Sarah could not go on at this point. She stopped to wipe her tears with a used dishcloth that Donna handed her.

Using the common Israeli nickname for Jonathan that he always employed with his closest friend, Eli took over. "Yonni, I told her that your daughter was a little prophetess. Do you remember you bought Tali a birthday gift when our army truck stopped on our way up to the Golan Heights, you know, at that gas station near Tiberius which sold souvenirs?"

"Sure I do brother. I bought Tali a silver menorah, almost like this one. You saw me do that." Jonathan paused a few seconds before adding, "But I never got to give it to her."

"Yonni, you told me the menorah was for Tali's birthday in early June, and then added, 'Seven branches for my seven-year-old little girl.' Well, when I picked up your body and held you against my chest just after you were...killed a few days later, I could feel the menorah inside your army jacket. I was so angry with myself later on that I didn't slip it into my pocket right then, because it wasn't with your personal items when they released us from the Syrian prisoner of war camp a few weeks later. But when I came to your home on your birthday almost one year later, there it was, or at least one almost identical to it. I was amazed at God's goodness, and so was Sarah." The two friends embraced as they and the other Kadoshim silently worshipped Immanuel, their Immortal King.

Hearing the wonderful story enhanced Micah's desire to get on with his burning project. "Eli, can I go and take a brief look at my family home before we begin our clean-up work?"

"Of course you can brother, and take Benny along if you like."

The two friends set off for the ruined Kupinski home two doors down as Jonathan and Sarah rummaged around the remains of their destroyed house, looking for any more items they might want to rescue before the rubble was dissolved.

As they strolled the short distance down the street, Micah quietly braced himself for the difficult scene he would soon encounter. He wore a frown after he noticed that all the walls were completely knocked down. Large piles of rubble were strewn everywhere. The apartment on the floor above had crashed down onto his first floor family home, entangling the contents in a harrowing mess.

Still, the young adult saint, who had lived in this place from the time of his birth until just one year before, wanted to uncover any remains he might find in his old bedroom. As he rummaged about, he informed Benny he was especially searching for Jonathan's Bible. "After I gave my life to the Lord, my father caught me one evening reading your dad's Bible. He ripped it out of my hand and hurled it against the wall. I'd never seen him so angry before. The very next day, he signed me up for one of those UW 're-education centers' where they worked to brainwash believers out of their faith."

"Oh Micah! My mom was sent to one of those as well, up near Ramallah, but she was miraculously set free by Yochanan."

"Yes, I heard that story later on. It's the exact same camp I was sent to, although to a separate section they called 'The Youth Division.' I was held for one month as they gave us these daily lectures and stuff, and then I was sent back home. My parents more or less left me alone after that until dad appeared at my door one night to tell me he'd set up an appointment for me to get Andre's mark in two days. When I protested, he said it was either that or I'd be sent straight back to the camp. So I sneaked out of my bedroom window that very night and never went back."

"Where did you go? I mean, you were only like seven years old."

"I'd heard while in the camp about a secret group of young believers living together on the flat roof of a south Jerusalem apartment building that had a storage shelter located on it. Someone had given me the address, so I made my way there, about a mile away. Later I escaped out of the city to the desert with a small group of saints led by a young guy from Tel Aviv named Danny Katzman. He was one of those sealed Jewish males who ministered all over Israel and the world in those days."

"Hey, I know Danny! He was one of Eli's roommates before we all moved up to the Mount of Olives. We escaped too, Micah; my mom, my sister, Craig and Ken Preston. We were led out to the desert by Eli's other sealed roommate, Moshe Salam. You know, Eli was one of the 144,000 sealed Jewish males as well."

"Yes, I know. Anyway I couldn't risk carrying a Bible through town, so I hid it underneath my drawer. So that's what I'm searching for now."

"Micah, our congregational leader, Yoseph Steinberg, went out secretly one night from our protected group home to visit some new believers he'd heard were hiding in south Jerusalem on an apartment building rooftop. It must have been your group. We only found out much later about it. Yoseph was shot and killed by UW troops on his way back to our Mount of Olives home."

"It was indeed him, Benny. I heard they'd murdered Yoseph later on as well. He shared so deeply with us that night; his teaching was very rich. We all learned so much. I was the youngest one there, but we were all pretty young, with the oldest maybe sixteen. We'll never forget his sacrifice, Benny. I want to meet him again and thank him. Will you introduce me?"

"Sure brother, you're now a member of our forever family!" Micah stopped rummaging for a second as the friends exchanged another embrace. Then he continued digging, with Benny probing as well.

"*Look!*" shouted Benny as he pointed with excitement to a pile of rubble on the other side of the destroyed bedroom. Micah then spotted a two-inch portion of brown leather protruding from under the cedarwood remains of what was apparently once his dresser. The mound also included a shattered mirror, broken lamps and other electrical items and large chunks of concrete from the caved-in ceiling. The friends rushed over toward the Bible as quickly as they could, pushing aside blocking junk with their feet and climbing over two heaps of debris too colossal to move.

Micah Kupinski easily lifted up the heavy concrete slab above the Bible as Benny pulled the precious book loose and dusted off the slightly-torn book cover, using the hem of his robe. Then Benny handed the Bible to his friend. Without a word, Micah immediately opened it and turned to the middle section where the two Polaroid pictures had been safely stashed away.

The holy ones smiled as they gazed at the slightly faded photos. "Yah, that's the one dad took of all of us the night he went off to war. Don't I look cute in those Superman pajamas?"

"Really super!" ricocheted Micah as a banana smile crossed his face. "But Tali looks even better in those Alice in Wonderland pajamas. Come on, let's get out of here! I want to give this to your dad right away." Before he exited the destroyed house of his youth for the last time, Micah found a soiled towel and wrapped the sacred Bible inside it. He wanted to surprise Jonathan. It worked.

"Hey dad, Micah's got a birthday present for you as well!" announced Benny loudly as the two saints carefully made their way past what was once the Goldman's front door.

"Guys, it's December, not April, and anyway my new birthday is the same as all of yours—the day we all got these new bodies from on high!"

Although Sarah laughed leisurely, she was intensely curious what this latest present might be. "Well, open it up!" she urged her former husband, adding with mock amazement, "My, it's wrapped so *beautifully* Micah!"

Amid chuckles all around, Jonathan ceremoniously unraveled the crusty green towel.

The surprised saint gasped in amazement as he held his prized Bible for the first time in almost half a decade. It had been a birthday present Sarah gave him soon after they surrendered their sinful lives to Israel's Holy Messiah.

"I'm, I'm speechless, Micah." Jonathan gave his newly adopted son another squeeze and then opened the sacred scriptures.

"Wow, what a day; and it's not even noon yet," uttered Craig as Jonathan reverently turned the pages.

"Dad, look inside the book of Micah," said Benny as he winked at his friend.

Jonathan rapidly did so, opening to chapter five where he discovered the pictures of himself with his family and his best friend Eli. After studying them for a moment, he read verse two from the open chapter out loud; a prophecy about Yeshua. *But as for you Bethlehem Ephratah, too little to be among the clans of Judah, from you One will go forth for Me to be ruler in Israel. His goings forth are from long ago, from the days of eternity.*

Sarah and Tali gathered around to study the photos. Both mother and daughter began to weep yet again as the memories of those last few moments with their husband and father in this very house flooded like a burst water pipe into their redeemed memory banks. Then Benny lightened the atmosphere by pointing out that Micah thought he looked 'super' in his superman pajamas; and Tali like a princess in hers.

The others sauntered over to examine the Polaroid pictures as Sarah explained that the family photo was taken while Jonathan was waiting for the army van to arrive the night he and Eli left for the Golan Heights. Then Eli revealed that the picture featuring him with his buddy was taken the morning they arrived at their outpost up on the strategic high ground claimed by both Israel and Syria.

"These are priceless as well, Micah. Thanks so much for this surprise gift. I'll treasure my 'born again Bible' and these photos forever, as I will your silver menorah, Tali."

"Okay crew, enough birthday presents for one day!" proclaimed Eli as he fired off a toothy smile toward his friends. We've got some important work to accomplish!"

FOUR

UNDER THE RUBBLE

Sarah rummaged through the rubble in her destroyed former home, looking for any piece of cloth that might be clean enough to help her minister some cleansing aid to her suffering sister. She had decided to stay behind with Donna as the other Kadoshim went off to work. Eli had readily agreed to the proposal, noting in a short private conversation with her that Donna looked to be about two steps away from death. The volunteers would return in a few hours and escort the two sisters back toward the Old City, dissolving the Goldman and Kupinski homes as their final act of the day.

Eli divided his eager band of redeemed ones into three groups. Craig would lead Stacy and Ken in one team, while Benny would head up the 'youth group' with Tali and Micah. Eli would work alone with his dear friend Jonathan. He wanted to talk privately with Yonni about an important proposal that he had in mind.

Jonathan yanked Eli aside seconds after he announced who would go off to labor with whom. "Do you think it's really wise to let the kids work completely on their own today? I'm afraid they might dissolve the whole universe, just for fun!"

Eli chuckled. "Jonathan, it's natural that you still think of them as children, but look at them! They're taller than me for sure, and probably stronger. I'm sure they'll do fine."

"I guess you're right. I've just noticed that they still seem a bit...childlike inside. I mean, they *were* only children until *very* recently."

"Suffer the little children to come unto Me, and do not hinder them." A smiling Eli was quoting the Lord, as Jonathan naturally realized.

"Okay brother, you win. But you can take responsibility if they end up 'accidentally' dissolving the Mediterranean Sea or something!"

The Youth Brigade did fine, as did the other two teams. Each was assigned a square mile area where they moved block by block, searching carefully for any living human beings or household animals trapped in the rubble. If they discovered any people or domestic pets still alive, they would remove them first, using their powerful heavenly bodies, or if necessary, supernatural methods. Then they would call out to alert the proper Kingdom authorities who'd appear to fetch them. If the coast was clear—as proved to be nearly always the case—the group leader would issue a solemn command in the Name of the Lord, and the debris and any dead bodies would instantly dissolve. In this manner, the Holy City of Jerusalem was made ready for the God-given housing and other buildings that were about to appear.

After successfully clearing several city blocks, Tali and Micah felt a tinge of emotion as they approached the ruins of the Yitzhak Rabin elementary school six blocks from their former homes. They'd both studied there not long before. Now they were preparing to send the destroyed building into oblivion.

Tali's experience at the public school had not been a good one overall. She was frequently taunted by several female classmates about her 'weird religious beliefs,' as one of the girls put it. On two occasions, she was more than verbally abused—she was physically attacked by three older boys who told her each time to shut up about Yeshua or get off the property. Sarah had pulled her distressed daughter out of the neighborhood school after Tali finished grade two, determined to teach her at home as she was already doing with Benny.

Micah Kupinski's experience at Yitzhak Rabin had been worlds apart. Although he was a bit geeky looking with his thick-rimmed glasses and prominent buck teeth, he was also a budding wizard in science and math. And even though he didn't get past the second grade himself, due to his nighttime escape from his family home,

Micah had gained some very positive notoriety by helping many of his young classmates with the rudimentary math problems they were puzzling over. His sudden disappearance was noted with sorrow by more than one classmate, as it was by his teacher, Mrs. Bernstein.

The three transformed young saints carefully checked over the ruins of the local elementary school. There was no sign of life. Everything was still. As they came to the last set of destroyed rooms on the south end of the property, where both Micah and Tali's last classes had convened, Benny put his finger to his mouth and signaled for silence.

Then he heard it again. Muffled sobs were escaping from under a thick concrete slab. Without hesitation, Benny turned his head toward the sky and called out in a loud voice for Eli and Craig to quickly bring their teams in order to help him. Possessing the same massively enhanced hearing that the former youngster enjoyed, the others detected his alarm call and instantly appeared.

Eli took command, directing his seven volunteers where to position themselves. The ex-army medic had done this before. With all eight Kadoshim surrounding the slab, Eli gave the command to "LIFT!" and all did so. The slab was removed in three seconds.

Tali gasped at the sight. Two young whimpering girls wearing torn cotton dresses were lying face up in the rubble. They appeared to be no more than six years old.

"Oh no, I can't believe it!" exclaimed Micah as he joined Jonathan and Craig clearing away small pieces of concrete from around the two girl's faces. "These are the twin daughters of my former teacher, Mrs. Bernstein!

"She was my teacher as well!" exclaimed Tali as she joined in the cleaning operation. "I last saw them when they were much younger, when Mrs. Bernstein's sister brought them to class for Show and Tell."

Employing his army medical training, Eli immediately checked to see if the girls had sustained any serious injuries. He quickly determined that the large slab of concrete had landed on nearby rubble piled up high on either side of the twins, creating a chamber that spared their young lives. Apart from some scratches, they appeared to be unhurt.

Micah asked Eli if he could pick up one of the girls. "Yes brother, but carefully," he answered, while preparing to slowly lift up the other twin.

"Hi Dalya, I haven't seen you in over a year. Are you okay sweetie?" A faint smile appeared as the girl's tears started to wane. "How did you know my name?" enquired Dalya in a barely audible voice as Micah suddenly remembered that he looked considerably different from when he had played with her the day his teacher brought the young twins to class to show them off to the students. "Well, I used to know your mother, Mrs. Bernstein. Like I just said, she was actually my teacher."

Eli wiped some dirt off of the left cheek of his still-weeping charge. "And what is this darling one's name?"

"That's Daniyella," answered Dalya as Micah nodded his head in affirmation.

"Hello Daniyella," cooed Eli softly as he slowly lifted her like a china doll into his robust arms. Then he asked, "Do either of you cuties have any areas of special pain to tell us about?"

They both signaled 'no' by moving their small heads from left to right several times in that synchronized manner seemingly reserved for identical twins.

"Good," stated Eli as he signaled with his eyes for Craig to make the emergency call.

The blond American galloped about fifty feet away and then shouted up into the sky. "*Emergency rescue services, we need you in East Talpiot right away!*"

Moments later, four servant-saints were pulling out stretchers and other equipment from what appeared to be an ambulance without wheels. It was a Kadoshim rescue squad put together by Prince David that very morning. Within seconds, they were able to supernaturally materialize anywhere they were needed in Israel. Similar teams would soon be established all over the globe.

"What were you girls doing here?" asked Micah as the rescue team trotted to the site.

"We were looking for our *ima*," answered Dalya, using the Hebrew word for mother.

"She didn't come home after the huge quake last week, and we thought maybe she was here," added Daniyella. "While we were looking for her, another strong shake happened and that wall came falling down on us. We thought we were going to die."

"Undoubtedly an aftershock," noted Ken.

"How long ago was that sweetheart?" asked Eli, knowing the rescue team descending on the scene would want to know as well."

"I think about five days ago," answered Dalya, prompting the team to work even faster. "But at least we had some water with us." She pointed to a plastic water carrier strapped around her neck. Her twin sister bore a matching carrier resting on her small chest. "Mine just ran out a little while ago."

"Mine too," echoed Daniyella.

Eli touched the two bottles and they were instantly filled with fresh water, which the twins eagerly gulped down. At the same moment, the small puddles of urine in the spots where the girls had been lying disappeared as their wet dresses turned dry. The eight volunteer workers then said their goodbyes as the Israeli twins were whisked into the medical van by the rescue team, moving like a whirlwind passing through a dusty field. In the blink of an eye, the van was gone.

"Benny, Tali, Micah, you guys did a super job," commended Eli as he turned and smiled at the three humble saints. "We're all really proud of you."

"It was Benny," interjected Micah, adding "He's the one who heard them crying and knew immediately what to do." The math and science wiz was obviously seriously proud of his new brother.

It suddenly dawned on Jonathan what the ruined building had been before it was destroyed. "Hey guys, maybe we should handle this one, okay?"

"Thanks abba, that's probably best," answered Tali.

Eli jumped in. "Benny, why don't you take your team down to the next block and we'll finish up here. Craig, you and your team can go back where you were. Thanks so much everyone!"

"Aye Aye, Captain!" said Craig as he deliberately fumbled an exaggerated salute, hoping to lighten the mood of the understandably shaken young saints.

"Do you realize what this building used to be?" asked Jonathan after the others had gone.

"No, but it sure was a large one," answered Eli.

"This was Tali's primary school. Mrs. Bernstein must have become her second grade teacher in the fall of the year when I went off with you to fight in the war with Syria and Lebanon."

"Of course, that's what Micah and Tali were referring to, and why the twins came looking for their missing mother here. It makes sense to me now. I also recall what you told me about the harassment she received here from some of her classmates. You shared that info while we were traveling up to the Golan Heights."

"That's right, Eli. So now you know why I thought it was best if we took over. Too many mixed memories for her here, and I suspect for Micah as well."

"Good call, brother. You're a scholar and a saint, well, at least a saint."

The two friends smiled just before Eli ordered the rubble dissolved in the Lord's powerful name.

As the two sanctified friends returned to their original work area several blocks away (they walked this time), Jonathan shared what had been on his heart since the moment Sarah first told him how fantastic Eli had been to her and his children in the wake of his death.

"Eli, I didn't want to get too sappy in front of the others earlier today, but I was about to tell you something important when Benny made that emergency call."

"What is it my eternal brother?"

"In the last few days, Sarah's clued me in on some of the marvelous, selfless things you did for her and the kids after I was killed. And I'm guessing from the story about the menorah that she and you shared today, I've not even heard the half of it yet. Brother, I can't begin to express my deep gratitude to you. It is times like that which test a man's true nature and worth, bud, and you came out smelling like a rose. I love you so much, and so does my family. I hope we can always serve the Lord together."

"Thanks, Yonni. I've never smelled like a rosebud before," joked Eli, a bit embarrassed by the heap of praise. "But my dear friend, it was pretty easy to do. Sarah is such a gem, and you both raised your children to be real champions in the Lord. And, I…kind of like you a little bit as well, and I really missed you. It was a great pleasure to help out anyway I could, friend. And speaking of always being together, I have something I've wanted to talk to you about all day."

"Shoot!"

"I was informed by Prince David early today, when we spoke for a second time just before we all exited the Temple, that I'll be assigned a governor's position somewhere on earth by King Yeshua."

"Congratulations Eli! You're more than worthy, brother."

"Well, I don't know about that. Only the Lord is truly worthy. Anyway, David said all the governors will need cabinet-style ministers and assistants, and he added that I should be thinking of some candidates. Yonni, I would be so very happy to have you on board. Would you join me wherever they send me?"

"For sure, Eli! Anything you and the Lord ask of me, I'll do. I am His servant, and would love to labor alongside of you."

Jonathan slapped his friend gently on his back and then gave him a sideways hug as they proceeded down the road toward their next dissolution.

Sarah said a short prayer over an empty plastic bucket that she uncovered in the ruins of her kitchen pantry. It was instantly filled to the brim with clean water. She then helped her sister Donna out of her reeking wool blanket, unbuttoned and took off her torn blouse, and then began giving her a much-needed sponge bath with a usable dish towel she found under the bucket.

"Thanks so much for staying behind, Sarah. I appreciate your help very much. It's been pretty rough for me here all alone. The heat alone over the past few months was unbearable!"

"That must've been the result of the fourth bowl of wrath being poured out upon the sun," noted Sarah. "Yochanan recorded in

Revelation 16 that the earth would be scorched with fierce heat when that occurred, just as the international armies were descending on Israel for the final battle of Armageddon."

"Well, whatever caused it, it was hotter than hell."

"I'm not so sure about that."

Donna quickly changed the subject. "Hey, where did you get that water? I only have one bottle left, and it's over there near my basket."

"Let's just say *Jehovah Jireh*, the Lord provides."

"Oh," uttered Donna, not really certain what she meant and reluctant to enquire. However she did ask Sarah the question that had ricocheted in her mind since it first dawned on her that she was looking at the face of her older sister, whom she hadn't seen in almost two years.

As the dirt and sweat came off her skinny body, Donna spoke up. "Sarah, what happened to you? Don't get me wrong, you look really healthy and strong, and your countenance is more stunning than ever. Your glowing eyes are simply gorgeous! But I think you look a little *too* strong, if you know what I mean. The same goes for Tali and Stacy. You all remind me of those steroid-taking Russian female athletes during the Soviet era; Big Bertha with a shot put!"

Sarah laughed as her sister went on. "You're definitely all taller, and...well...broader, and yet your breasts are clearly smaller than before. What happened to all of you?"

"It's not so easy to explain Donna, but I'll try. We're now in our glorified bodies, which I told you about when we were still living together as humans in this house. Do you remember that?"

Donna nodded as Sarah started scrubbing her left armpit. "You obviously must've realized that we'd been transformed, since Benny and Tali were just kids when you last saw them around three years ago."

"Yes, of course I did Sarah, plus Benny mentioned it this morning. Still, the other guys, except of course Micah, look more or less the same as before, apart from being more handsome than ever—and beefier too! That Craig is an absolute dreamboat!"

"Donna, don't start on him again! We're all Kadoshim now, which means 'Holy Ones' in Hebrew. He's not going to be seduced by

66

you." Sarah scrubbed silently for a moment and then continued. "Sis, do you recall I told you that Yeshua shared with His disciples many centuries ago that there would be no marriage among the saints living in His eternal kingdom?"

"Sure, I thought that was strange at the time. Then again, I really didn't, and still don't, understand a lot of what you all believe in. You and I were raised Jewish, although in a fairly non-observant home. So apart from those few classes we attended at the synagogue, I really don't know much about religion, and certainly not about yours!"

Sarah moved on to wipe off Donna's filthy back. "Well, that means Jonathan and I are no longer married. We're now just like the angels in heaven. You know Donna, the Bible never once speaks of any of them as female, always only as males, or at least with male names. And Genesis says that men are made in the likeness of God, and women in the image of man, although all are equally children of God. So we're just going back to the way things were before humans were created and placed in the Garden of Eden."

"Surely you don't believe in all those Jewish fables—Eve eating some forbidden fruit while totally stark naked, and then handing it to Adam, and then some snake slithers up and deceives them? It's like a fantasy novel to me."

"Actually I *do* believe in the biblical accounts of creation, although I'll admit some of it is still mysterious to me. I spoke sometimes to Yochanan about those sorts of things when we were all living in that large house on the Mount of Olives, and he explained a lot of things to me."

"So how is that old flame-thrower getting on...is he still, like, 2,000 years old?"

Sarah frowned. "I've asked you before not to call him that! Anyway, Yochanan is fine; and Natan-el as well. Like all of the redeemed, they're now in very strong heavenly bodies that appear to be around thirty years old, so they've been dancing up a storm with all us younger folks. You should see them fly!"

"What, did you guys open up a saloon or something?"

"Not quite," chuckled Sarah as she wiped down Donna's left calf below her filthy cream-colored shorts. "We've been celebrating in the

Temple before the Lord, dancing the hora and singing songs of praise and worship. It's been truly *wonderful*. And guess who showed up this morning? Jonathan's parents! They gave their lives to the Lord after we visited them in Skokie. Soon after we left, they were…beheaded for their faith, but now they're alive forevermore!"

"Wow, I don't even know how to reply to that information, but I'm glad for Jonathan's sake and the kids, that they're reunited with Abe and Rebecca.

Sarah began swabbing Donna's needy right arm pit. "Eli was asked to lead a work party to prepare the ground for new housing which will appear supernaturally this weekend. The others volunteered to help him. He said Prince David told him this morning that I'll be getting a new house in this exact location. Isn't that wonderful?"

"Prince David?"

"Yes, the King David of old. He's now Israel's new prince, and will serve as governor of the land under the administration King Yeshua's setting up to rule the earth. But let's get back to your original question, Donna. I still love Jonathan very much, and our kids as well. However, our relationship is…different now. We're all brethren in the Messiah, equally loving every single one of our fellow Kadoshim, and there are many millions of us I might add. Yet I'm certain I'll always have a soft spot for my previous era family. And somewhere in my heart, Tali and Benny will always be my babies, as is the case with most mothers even after their children grow up, I suspect."

Donna's soiled neck was Sarah's next cleansing project. "You used the term 'brethren' just now, but I would almost say 'brothers,' Sarah. I noticed from behind you and Tali and Stacy almost look like men. Don't get me wrong, I've always thought an athletic appearance is rather attractive on a young woman, but it's just…a real change from before, that's all."

"Well, we are *not* human men, Donna. But you see, we're not exactly human-style *women* anymore either. The Kadoshim do not bear babies, so those of us who were human women have no more need for wombs or suckling breasts. Plus we're definitely not trying to attract men. So we dress in white robes, as do all the Holy Ones. And frankly the best part is that we no longer have periods to deal with, or men harassing us all the time for sex."

"It all sounds a bit...boring," quipped Donna as her sister cleaned out her ears and wiped her brow with the wet towel.

"It might sound that way to you now sis, but if you could feel the sheer joy that we're experiencing every single moment, and taste the amazing new powers that we possess, you wouldn't think so—not to mention the fact that we'll never grow old, get all wrinkly, shrivel up and die!"

"Now you *are* making me jealous!" exclaimed Donna as Sarah began pulling out some of the twisted knots in her long dyed hair. "By the way sis, when did you become a blonde? I hate to inform you, but your Jewish roots are definitely showing through."

"Um, very clever," smirked Donna. "Sven asked me to join him as a blonde. He said I'd be safer that way, and I think it did help. Sarah, it was absolutely *awful* being here alone after he died. There were asteroids falling sometimes, and these massive hailstones came down last week when this humungous earthquake took place, the one that caused most of that wall to fall down. It was even stronger than the quake that occurred right after Yochanan and Natan-el rose up into the sky. And topping that for the last three months or so, these hideous creatures would sometimes come around and scare the heck out of me! They looked like giant locusts, and they were stinging people with their tails. They actually got me once in my left arm. I was in severe pain for three days. But whenever they came near after that, I hid in your solid oak cabinet, still intact in your bedroom. It was absolutely *horrible!*"

"Oh honey, I'm so sorry! How dreadful! You know, those creatures were actually written about by Yochanan in Revelation, I think chapter nine. He had a vision of them, revealing they'd be released to judge the people on earth who'd not been sealed by the Lord. Donna, he wrote these demonic creatures would be given freedom to act on earth for a period of five months, and yet they were released from the bottomless pit only three and a half months ago, right after Yochanan and Natan-el rose from the dead on the evening of Rosh Ha Shana. That must mean that the final period of wrathful judgment, as terrible as it was for you, was actually cut short by over one month. When Yeshua was sitting with Yochanan and the other disciples on the Mount of Olives just before His crucifixion, He foretold that the days of God's final wrath upon sinful humanity would be shortened for the sake of the remaining elect, or else no flesh at all would've been left alive on earth."

"Well then, thank God for that! I had Jonathan's shortwave radio and all those batteries you stored in your bedroom drawer, so I was able to follow the news until the BBC went silent about one month ago. That Russian-led attack nearly scared me to death, and then there were reports of around 200 million Muslim jihad warriors heading our way from the east, and Andre's UW forces massing in the north and west-it all frightened me so much! As if that wasn't enough, there was this blazing fire from the sky, intense lightning and all sorts of hideous things. One small flaming asteroid landed just a few blocks away! It really is amazing I'm still alive."

"It's the grace of God, no doubt, Donna, but Yochanan told me the entire eastern half of the city was taken over by mobs of marauding UW soldiers for a short time; and that they took captive most of the Jewish residents and imprisoned them outside the city. Actually that was also prophesied, in Zechariah chapter 14. How did you survive all that?"

"Well as you said, Sarah, they were mostly going after Jews, and I had my UW passport issued under my married name, Donna Svenson. I also had one belonging to Lars along with some of his military uniforms in the closet, so they basically left me alone."

Donna twisted her head so she could see Sarah's face as a tear glistened in her left eye. "Sarah, I lied to Micah earlier today. I simply couldn't tell him the truth. His father was killed in that initial massive quake like I said, but his mother, Chava, was actually still alive after it. It's true she caught Ebola a year before, but she somehow survived that. I heard her screaming one night about six weeks ago and rushed over to check on her. I hid in the bushes and could see what was happening through her crumbled bedroom wall.

There were about six UW soldiers brutally raping her like wild pigs. They killed her, Sarah. I later went and made a fire and threw her body on it. There was no one to help me bury her or take her corpse away. I didn't know what else to do."

"Oh, that's so tragic Donna, but I promise it will remain our secret. You did lie to Micah, but your motives were good. He obviously had enough to deal with after you told him about his father."

Finished with her cleaning project, Sarah pulled out a handful of healing leaves from her handbag. She picked them from the Tree of Life that the volunteer companions had examined earlier. The saint tossed them into the pot of weak coffee steaming on a metal oven rack over the fire. After the special leaves steeped for a few minutes, Sarah poured her malnourished sister a fresh cup. "This should help you feel much better," she stated without elaboration.

Two hours later, the eight satisfied Kadoshim workers returned to Sarah's home. Stacy suggested they call for the medical squad to take Donna up to the small Augusta Victoria Hospital that Eli had told her was treating human beings on the Mount of Olives. However, Donna protested. She wanted to see the new river that Sarah had told her about, and the other changes in the city. Secretly, she also desired to gaze at the millions of Kadoshim her sister said were happily dancing in worship around the sacred Temple.

"I'll carry you up there, Aunt Donna!" volunteered Benny eagerly. Sounding like a lumberjack who'd won an arm-wrestling contest, he added, "I'm pretty strong these days!"

"That should work fine," piped in Eli. "Well brethren, let's move out into the street and dissolve the ruins here like we just did to Micah's old home. Then let's get going, it's nearly 5:00 PM."

"Mom, you won't *believe* who we rescued today!" exclaimed Tali as she helped her mother pull Donna to her wobbly feet.

"We'll tell her all about that on the trip back to the Old City," instructed Eli, adding intriguingly, "I have a very important announcement to make on the way as well."

71

FIVE

MINISTERS OF LOVE

Benny hoisted his Aunt Donna up onto his large frame as if she was a sack of sweet onions. Already feeling much better after drinking her healing tea, the ersatz blonde passenger was looking forward to an unusual ride on her nephew's broad back through the nearly empty streets of Jerusalem. Micah walked next to his buddy. Sarah strolled behind him with Tali, Jonathan and Eli. Craig, Ken and Stacy brought up the rear.

Even though it was mid December, the fresh early evening air was warm. In fact, when the King of Kings returned to earth four days before, the planet's lower atmosphere and weather patterns were dramatically altered. Thick toxic smog and sulfuric ash instantly disappeared from the air as the Lord's celestial army neared Jerusalem. Ocean water levels stabilized after rising almost half a foot in just two months, swamping many islands and parts of Florida and other low-lying coastal areas around the globe, made worse by several massive tidal waves which roiled across the oceans. The deep cracks in the earth's tectonic plates were supernaturally glued back together.

Air temperatures had initially dropped several degrees in early autumn as a 'nuclear winter,' sparked off by the intense Israel-centered international warfare, blocked out most natural sunlight and totally obscured the moon and the stars. Then just over two months before Yeshua returned to earth with His heavenly hosts in tow, the sun had suddenly heated up to seven times its normal temperature, scorching the battered planet with unprecedented heat. That in turn warmed up the ocean waters and produced thick toxic fog all over the globe.

From now on, planet earth would mainly be watered by a late-evening mist rising from the temperate oceans and abundant lakes, as had been the case before the ancient biblical flood took place. By two or three each morning, the nightly mist condensed into clouds that dropped gentle rain all over the earth until just before dawn. Daytimes would be completely dry, although occasional clouds would float by, just for effect.

The Sovereign Lord had decreed that moderate weather would prevail everywhere on earth for the next thousand years. No more would hurricanes, tornados, droughts or floods ravish the earth. The variance in outdoor temperatures between the two poles and the equator—which had all shifted somewhat when the earth wobbled like a drunkard during the unprecedented earthquake that was unleashed just after the two witnesses rose from the dead—would be only about ten degrees. Summertime would be a bit warmer than winter in the two hemispheres, but not by much. For those missing snow and ice, it would soon reappear, along with glaciers, on the tops of many newly-created mountain peaks that sprang up around the world in the wake of the final gigantic earthquake, which was the strongest ever felt in human history, bringing down most of the existing mountain ranges already severely weakened by the previous seismic activity.

"Mom, I've just *got* to tell you what happened today!" blurted out Tali, bursting inside to share her unique story.

"Well honey, maybe Eli wants to deliver his announcement first?"

"No, that's fine Sarah. We have a couple miles walk ahead of us. My news can wait. You won't *believe* what Tali's obviously dying to tell you!"

Donna listened closely from her mobile high perch, arms flung around the sinuous neck of her now-strapping young nephew.

"Well mom, Benny, Micah and I were clearing away rubble in the area around my old elementary school, Yitzhak Rabin, where Micah also attended. Benny heard someone crying and called out for abba

73

and the others to come quickly, and all appeared in a flash. We joined together and lifted up this heavy slab of concrete wall like it was a cube of butter or something, and lying underneath were Mrs. Bernstein's twin girls!"

"My goodness honey! Were they hurt? They're such adorable little girls."

"They were fine," interjected Jonathan, "especially considering how long they'd been trapped. They told us they were in the air pocket for five days! It's really a miracle either girl's still alive, let alone both of them."

"I know all about that," added Donna as she lightly bounced up and down on Benny's back.

Tali continued. "The medical rescue crew came right away and whisked them off, mom. The twins had some water with them, so were able to survive that long. They told us they were out looking for their mother when the wall fell down. I suppose they're now orphans. I feel so sad for them, mom. I really liked Mrs. Bernstein."

"Me too," stated Micah from the front.

"Well, she was a lovely woman and a brilliant teacher," Sarah affirmed. "Dafna Bernstein was very sympathetic and helpful when you had those problems, Tali. I met with her several times, and the twins were there the last time I spoke with her after school. By the way, that's when I forgave you for the candy."

"For the candy?" asked a puzzled Jonathan, wondering how much more he'd learn about his missing years in the coming days.

"Jonathan, your kind parents sent Tali a nicely wrapped Mounds bar for her eighth birthday. Chocolate was hard to come by after the Syrian chemical attacks on us and the subsequent nuclear destruction of Damascus, so it really was a precious gift, and they knew she loves coconut. It was near the end of the school year, soon after Andre was crowned emperor in Rome. I knew what was inside the small package since Rebecca informed me over the phone. So I placed it in Tali's lunch box one morning just before her birthday and told her it was an early gift from your folks, and to unwrap it after she ate her sandwich."

Donna's stomach growled like a lion as Sarah continued her account. "When we sat down for dinner that evening, Tali told me the twins were brought to class that day by Dafna's younger sister, Gili. Tali said she was playing with them when the Lord told her to share the candy bar with the girls. So she gave it to them. I was frankly a bit cross with Tali. I mean, it was a very sweet birthday gift mailed to her from America by her grandparents; even if a token one. However when I later went to tell Dafna that I was pulling Tali out of school because of the harassment she was getting from some of the students, and saw the twins there, I realized why she couldn't resist sharing her candy bar with them. Besides, if the Lord had indeed spoken to her, who was I to contradict?"

Tali steeled herself as she prepared to reveal her gargantuan request. "Mom, dad, I don't think sharing my chocolate with the twins was just some meaningless gesture, nor the fact that Benny, Micah and I were the ones to find them alive today." Tali gulped before she went on. "Would you be upset if…I adopt the girls and take care of them; that is if their mother and aunt are truly deceased?"

"Oh sweetheart, that's such a *huge* commitment," replied Sarah, even as she realized more deeply than ever what a wonderful, compassionate daughter she and Jonathan had raised. "I think at the very least, you'd need more help. I have a sense from the Holy Spirit that I might be working in the medical field here in Jerusalem, so I'm not sure how much time I could contribute to help raise them. It's a *very* big job."

"And I'm not exactly Shirley Temple's mom with children," added Donna from the front. The 24-year-old Californian was fond of old movies produced before her time.

Eli interjected a thought. "I can at least check with Prince David to see if the twins are really orphans. King Yeshua will know for sure. And Sarah, they *are* quite adorable, and will need tender loving care from *someone* if their mother's gone, as seems likely. By the way, your offspring and Micah were marvelous today. They handled that situation like real pros. I was very impressed."

The three transformed 'kids' blushed as Donna gave Benny a warm pat on the head.

Sarah embraced her earthly daughter as she spoke. "Fine honey, we'll see what develops. But now I think it's time to hear Eli's big announcement. Speak, oh ye of great wisdom!" she proclaimed as she winked at her longtime friend.

"Sure thing, oh ye bearer of wise children!" replied Eli as if slamming a ball back in a friendly tennis match. Then his tone turned quite serious.

"Gang, let's stop for a second while I share with you. You can put your aunt down for a moment, Benny. I've got something to say that will affect every one of you to some extent, even you Donna. Turning in unison to face Eli, they formed a chorus of interested ears.

"Prince David informed me this morning that I will become governor of a province located not too far from here, but he didn't tell me exactly where." The small band of saints expressed their congratulations to him, including Jonathan who already possessed that information.

"Thanks everyone, I'm greatly humbled by such a high calling. Prince David also said I needed to think about candidates to serve with me as cabinet ministers and aids. I've been praying about it all day. I asked Jonathan a couple hours ago if he'd serve with me, and he immediately said yes." Eli walked closer to Jonathan and grasped his right hand. "Yonni, I want you to become my chief advisor and Foreign Minister."

Jonathan was moved by his close buddy's offer. "I'll be more than honored, Eli," he replied as he bowed his head before his highly esteemed friend.

The governor-designate then walked over to Ken Preston. He thumped him gently on the chest and asked, "Ken, will you serve as my Communications Minister?"

"Gladly," replied Ken with a glint in his eye.

"Great!" Eli then turned toward Craig and playfully pinched the end of his short blond beard. "Kind sir, will you become my Minister of Culture, Music and Sports?"

The Eagle-man was soaring. "Yes, Mr. Governor!" he enthusiastically replied as he gave Eli a hug.

Eli marched over to Micah Kupinski, who had just helped Donna disembark from Benny's back. "Micah, I remember well those intricate Lego buildings you used to put together, and your budding talent in science and math. Will you become my Minister of Construction, Housing and Science?"

Benny grinned at his childhood friend with joy gleaming from his eyes.

"Yes, Eli sir, with great pleasure."

"Very good big guy!" The governor—designate then reached out and affectionately grabbed hold of Benny's right arm. Eli paused for several seconds as gentle tears sprang forth from his deep brown eyes, prompting a similar response from Benny, Tali and her parents. "My sweet Benny—a passionate lover of fairness and truth! A man with no guile at all! Will you serve me as my new Justice Minister?"

"My son, the attorney general!" exclaimed Sarah in typical Jewish-momma fashion, her heart overflowing with Godly pride.

Everyone chuckled as Benny confirmed his millennial calling. "You know I will, Uncle Eli. I love you very much."

"Well, this calls for a party!" opined Donna with a smile as she was hoisted back up onto Benny's muscled back. "Did anyone bring some pretzels and cold beer?"

Eli Ben David continued speaking as the Goldmans and company trudged up a small hill. "Sarah, I wanted to ask you to serve as my Health Minister, but as you yourself confirmed, the Holy Spirit showed me He had some important medical work for you to do here in Jerusalem. And Stacy, I thought you'd make a great Minister of Education, since you were such a wonderful teacher of the children and adults at our Beit Yisrael congregation. But the Lord showed me you'll be working with Prince David."

"He showed you *what?*" gasped Stacy.

Sarah turned and gave her longtime best friend a warm embrace. "That's fantastic Stace! Godspeed with that!" Recalling that the aspiring actress had landed several small parts in Broadway stage shows before immigrating to Israel, she added with a wry smile, "You always did know how to hobnob with the glitterati."

A few minutes later, the small group of glorified saints (and one human sinner) was approaching the Etz Cha'im river flowing past the southeast corner of the Temple Mount. They could already see and hear the magnificent waterfall cascading down from the river's source. Rushing water poured out from under the Holy Temple and then fell dramatically over the side of the historic mount, tumbling down some 600 feet into the Kidron Valley below, where it produced a steady crashing sound. It would be dubbed by local residents as *Thunder Falls*.

"Oh, it truly is lovely," cooed Donna as she studied the glorious new addition to the ancient Holy City. "I'd love to get under that water right now!"

Still possessing the playful, curious hearts of young children, Benny and Micah decided they absolutely had to test out the water. Dutifully noting they were gritty from the day's dissolution work, they pointed out it would beneficially cleanse them. "Boys will be boys," shrugged Jonathan as he gave his consent.

Seconds later, Donna was gently lowered back down onto the stone pavement. The two childhood friends undid their gold sashes and took off their white robes, revealing beige linen shorts underneath. After handing the robes to Sarah, in they dove, splashing around a small jetty where the river current was not so strong. Gritty himself, Craig glanced briefly at Ken before saying, "What the heck." Soon he was in the water as well, followed by Ken. The rest watched with delight as the four saints swam and played in the soothing healing water that flowed from underneath King Yeshua's exalted throne.

As the swimmers happily horsed around, dunking each other's heads under the sweet-smelling water, Sarah and Jonathan strolled over to one of the nearby trees sprouting up by the side of the river. "These trees look like they've grown over a foot since we passed by just this morning," Sarah observed as she plucked some of the pale green healing leaves. "And look at the trunks," added Jonathan. "They appear luminescent in the fading sunlight."

In fact, the Trees of Life internally glistened day and night, pleasantly illumining the clear water flowing past the recently-formed river banks. Donna pointed out to Tali that it looked like a scene from one of her favorite movies. "Sweetheart, do you remember that 3-D film I took you to see a few years ago called *Avatar*?"

"Sure, Aunt Donna. It had all those floating mountains and flying creatures."

"That's the one. Well, don't these trees remind you of the glowing vegetation featured in it? There are even luminous butterflies fluttering around the shimmering tree trunks, just like in the film! That's *really* cool."

Donna glanced around with increasing wonder after the brethren resumed their northward journey ten minutes later. As they neared the Temple Mount, she could see and hear hundreds of thousands of jubilant Kadoshim singing triumphant praises to the Son of God as they energetically danced the hora before His hallowed throne.

When the marchers arrived at the new eastern entrance to the Temple Mount through the previously sealed Golden Gate—which had miraculously opened up as the Lord of Hosts approached after touching down with His heavenly army on the nearby Mount of Olives—Sarah suggested that she, Tali and Stacy should take Donna up to the Augusta Victoria hospital, located almost directly opposite the Temple. She urged the rest of the group to enter the sacred sanctuary. Sarah was especially thinking of her former husband. "You need to spend more time with your parents, Jonathan. Apart from very briefly this morning, you haven't seen them at all in almost five years."

"But can you manage carrying Donna up there?" he enquired.

"No problem!" boasted Tali as she effortlessly lifted her gaunt aunt onto her back.

A lofty footbridge, made out of whitish-pink Jerusalem-stone, connected the Mount of Olives with the open Golden Gate. The walkway had also materialized moments after the Messiah's burnished feet touched earth. Located just north of the new cascading waterfall, it was supported by several 600-foot pillars that stretched down to the newly verdant Kidron Valley below.

Sarah hustled across the wide bridge with her two companions and Donna to the small Augusta Victoria medical facility, the only one operating in Jerusalem after the great earthquake leveled four larger area hospitals. Named after the last German Empress and constructed by German Lutherans with thick stone blocks between 1907 and 1910, it was a longtime city landmark due to its high fortress-like tower which rose up in the center of the Mount of Olives. The well-built tower was still visible despite being seriously damaged during the massive earthquake that, among many other things, split the Mount of Olives in two just a quarter mile north of the Lutheran complex.

As they hiked across the footbridge, Sarah noted that the taller Ascension Tower on the southern end of the Mount of Olives was also still standing. It had been built in the 1870s by the Russian Orthodox Church. Featuring the first Christian steeple bell ever allowed to be sounded in the Holy City by Turkish Muslim Ottoman authorities, the tower was constructed over the traditional site of Yeshua's ascension to heaven. Rising over 200 feet into the air, the old structure was severely damaged during the earthquake, partly due to its much greater height. Gaping cracks were visible in several places. To the north of the Augusta Victoria complex, the tall Hebrew University surveillance tower, built in the 1970s by Israeli officials, had collapsed to the ground when the Mount of Olives split open not far south of it.

Soon Sarah was checking her sister into the functioning hospital for some much needed treatment and nutrition. She introduced herself and her companions to the head nurse, writing on a notepad while leaning against the admission desk. The nurse responded that her name was Leah Rabinowitz. This pricked Sarah's memory bank. "Leah Rabinowitz. Did you happen to work at Hadassah a couple years ago?"

"Actually yes, I did. I was the deputy head nurse in the Pediatrics Department. Did we meet there?"

"Yes, I saw you in your ward several times, and we ate together one time in the cafeteria. You told me you'd immigrated to Israel from Dallas, I believe?"

"That's correct. Sarah Goldman, let me think…oh sure, you were the volunteer originally from the Los Angeles area who came a couple times a week to visit with some of our patients, especially children and adults who had no family in Jerusalem. I remember now, you told me all about some elderly holocaust survivor you were especially fond of being cared for in a room on the third floor."

"Dear Yitzhak, that's right. I can tell that you're a redeemed saint now, but you didn't seem to be a believer then."

"I only gave my life to the Lord after that large luminous cross and Star of David appeared in the eastern sky after the Feast of Trumpets last fall. I was among tens of thousands of mostly local Orthodox Jews who fled into the desert after the first massive earthquake destroyed part of the city and split this Olivet Mount in two. I've heard that many people trudged as far as Petra and other parts of Jordan, but I stayed in the Judean wilderness near Ein Gedi with around 200 other souls. We were supernaturally fed by this incredible guy from Tel Aviv who could produce food out of thin air! His name was Danny Katzman. He shared about the Lord with us, and most gave their lives to Yeshua, including me."

"We know Danny!" exclaimed Tali. "He lived for a time with us at a large house here on the Mount of Olives, just a bit south of here. We used to minister together near the Western Wall every day!"

"So you must also know Yochanan and Natan-el" Leah surmised. "We'd all seen them on the news, of course, but Danny told us a lot more about them and their warnings of imminent judgment and the like."

"I'll gladly introduce you to them later on if you'd like," offered Sarah.

"Oh, that would be wonderful," replied Leah as another nurse approached.

"We're ready to admit your sister now," she announced. Donna was sitting comfortably in a wheelchair next to Sarah, listening in wonder to the unusual conversation. Soon she'd be out of her smelly clothes and into a fresh hospital gown after undergoing a full shower. Brief embraces were exchanged, and Sarah's survivor sister was off.

"I think Donna mainly just needs rest and some good food," opined Sarah as they wheeled her younger sister away, noting she had not bathed or slept in a proper bed for over two months, and was only consuming bits of self-rationed canned tuna for the past month. "I doubt she'll need treatment for more than a few days. I'll take her with me to my new home when you release her."

"We'll give her the best care we can, Sarah," pledged Nurse Leah. "It would indeed be good if you can fetch her fairly soon. I understand many of the thousands of Jews who fled into Jordan are making their way back to the city. We're preparing to receive many of them for treatment, and we expect some will be in pretty rough shape. We're short-staffed, but Prince David says we'll be given more help starting tomorrow."

Tali spoke up. "Nurse Leah, do you happen to have a set of twin girls here?"

"Indeed we do. They were brought in by a rescue team this afternoon. Do you know them?"

"My brother and I and his friend actually discovered them under some rubble at my old elementary school earlier today. We were helped by Stacy here and some other friends to free them, and then someone called your rescue team. Their mother was my second grade teacher, and my mother Sarah knew her as well."

"Bless you my dear. Of course, you're welcome to visit them, they're in room twelve. They don't seem to have any surviving family, so I'm certain they'll both be very glad to have you stop by."

"Hello little pumpkins," gushed Tali as she pranced into the twins' room followed by Sarah and Stacy. "Do you remember me? I helped rescue you earlier today. I'm Tali, and this is Stacy, who was there as well, and this is my mother Sarah."

"Yes, I remember you, and her!" proclaimed Dalya as she pointed to Stacy, apparently happy that unexpected visitors had shown up.

"Me too!" added Daniyella, sipping contentedly on cold orange juice.

She paused to say "Thanks so much for saving us, Tali and Stacy."

"It was our great joy girls," replied Tali. "Have they been treating you well?" she enquired while tugging at the bed sheet to pull it up closer to Dalya's exposed shoulders and neck.

"Very well," she affirmed before smiling affectionately, revealing two missing front teeth.

"Girls, do you remember the student in your mother's class who gave you a Mounds chocolate bar nearly three years ago? You were both pretty little then, about four years old."

"Oh yes, we remember that," confirmed Daniyella.

"The student told us her name was also Tali," added Dalya. "She was the nicest girl I ever met! We hadn't had any chocolate for a long, long time. That was the best present ever!"

"Well little sweethearts, that girl was me."

"What?" Daniyella sputtered as she nearly dropped her drink.

"I'll come back and explain it to you both tomorrow. My aunt is also a patient here now, so we'll be in every day. We'll let you rest for now. Shalom, lovely ladies!"

Kisses were exchanged and the three glowing Kadoshim were off.

While Sarah, Tali and Stacy were transporting Donna to the hospital, Jonathan, accompanied by Benny and Micah, had located his parents. He described to them how he and the other workers rescued the twin girls after making the unexpected discovery that Sarah's younger sister was still alive. Then the Kadoshim couple's only son told them he was to serve as Eli's Foreign Minister, and Benny as his Justice Minister. Rebecca Goldman nearly fainted before she blurted out, "My son, the Foreign Minister, and my grandson, the Chief Judge!"

Benny grinned as Jonathan finished his account. Then he noticed an unknown saint slowly approaching them. The stranger was clearly studying Jonathan's profile.

"Dad, someone seems to want to talk to you," Benny informed his father, prompting Jonathan and his parents to swing around.

"Excuse me, I'm so sorry to interrupt, but are you by chance Jonathan Goldman?"

"Yes I am. But I'm afraid I don't recognize you, brother."

"We've never met. I'm a good friend of your wife Sarah. She showed me many pictures of you and your family. My name is Yitzhak Ackerman."

"The Holocaust survivor she visited at Hadassah?"

"One and the same. It's a great pleasure to meet you, Jonathan. Sarah spoke so highly of you, and obviously loved you very much. I've been looking around for her for several days now without success, but just now I spotted you, thank the Lord."

"And I'm very glad you did, Yitzhak. It's an honor to meet you. Sarah is a jewel for sure. She'll be back here shortly. We discovered her sister Donna alive today in the ruins of our south Jerusalem home, so she and our daughter Tali are checking her into the hospital right now. Of course, Sarah has also been anxiously looking around for you."

"It will be great to see her again! But oh my, she told me all about Donna. A real character! And I did meet Tali and Benny. Lovely children, but that didn't surprise me given how sweet their young mother was. Sarah took such good care of me, Jonathan. I was all alone in Jerusalem, no family at all, and most of my friends were either gone or too old to visit me. You know, she led me to the Lord, and at a very high personal cost. She stayed behind in Israel when she sent your young son off to be with your parents in America. I know it was extremely difficult for her, but I came to Yeshua as a result."

"Praise the Lord, Yitzhak. That is in fact my son Benny standing there on the right." Jonathan paused and chuckled. "I guess he's just a tad taller now than when you met him."

"He is indeed! Hello young fellow; so very good to see you again!"

Benny was not looking at him. He was staring down at his feet. "Hello Yitzhak," he said as he slowly raised his head. "Mom will be really glad to see you."

A bit embarrassed over his son's seemingly rude behavior, Jonathan grabbed the mike back and carried on. "Yitzhak, I'd like you to meet my parents, Abe and Rebecca Goldman."

"Hello," Abe said politely.

"Sarah told us a lot about you, Yitzhak, and it's so good to finally meet you," added Rebecca.

"Great to meet you both as well, but I am somewhat surprised. Sarah spoke often of you. Abe, she informed me your father was gassed to death at Auschwitz, and that you were briefly imprisoned there as a boy before they sent you to a work camp. I was also born in Berlin like you, and watched helplessly as the Nazis arrested my older sister Rachel there. I told Sarah many times how much she reminded me of Rachel. They looked a lot alike, even though my sister was about ten years younger than Sarah when they nabbed her. We'd been hiding out in a neighbor's attic. Still, they managed to arrest her, but not me. I came to Israel after the war with my only surviving uncle."

Yitzhak paused and then continued. "I have something important to show you all. If you'll excuse me, I'll be right back."

The gathered Goldmans and Micah starred at each other with puzzled faces. However before they could think much more about Yitzhak's mysterious announcement, Craig Eagleman walked up to the expanding circle of friends, bringing two other saints with him. It was Jonathan's close friend and pastor, Yoseph Steinberg, and his earthly wife Cindy. Jonathan had spoken briefly with them three days before and was looking forward to additional interaction.

"Hey guys, how are you doing?" asked Yoseph as he offered Jonathan and Benny warm hugs.

"Hi Yoseph and Cindy. It's wonderful to see you both again," greeted Jonathan.

"We heard from Craig the fantastic news that your parents are here…is this them?"

"Oh yes, I'm sorry, this is my dad Abe Goldman, and my mom Rebecca."

"You both look a little younger than when we met at Jonathan's funeral," said Rebecca as she exchanged embraces with the Steinbergs.

"And both of you do as well," replied Cindy before Jonathan interjected, "Oh, I forgot you'd already met. I knew you wouldn't recognize them though, since dad and mom have *grown really* young since then!"

Benny couldn't wait to make his own introduction. "Yoseph, we were all so proud of you when we found out you'd risked your life, and lost it, in order to locate and teach those young new believers in south Jerusalem. Well, this is one of them, my best childhood friend, Micah Kupinski."

Micah stepped forward and gave Yoseph a strong bear hug. "Sir, I want to thank you so very much for coming to teach us about the Lord. You gave your life for us, kind of like Yeshua did. We were all so young, although I was the youngest. I didn't know much at all about the Lord, even though I'd read some scriptures from Jonathan's Bible." Micah stopped and pointed to the priceless book that had not left

Jonathan's left hand all day, apart from when he helped lift the slab of concrete entrapping the twin girls.

"I didn't realize at the time that you were Benny's pastor at Beit Yisrael. My dad never allowed me to go there, not even for Jonathan's funeral. Sir, I gave my life to the Lord that night soon after you left. So did two others, a ten-year-old girl and a fourteen-year-old guy. I for one will be totally grateful forever."

"Thanks so much for sharing that with me, Micah. Your testimony makes what I did much more than worthwhile. I know it's also important for Cindy to hear what you said. She confessed to me this week that she was quite upset when I left unannounced to try and find you guys after Yochanan told me some new believers were holed up in the south of the city. I never even uttered a proper goodbye to her. But the Lord was clearly in it. And now we're all reunited for eternity!"

"Amen, thanks so much for sharing Micah, it does mean a lot to me," confirmed Cindy before adding, "By the way, Big Benny is a pretty cool friend to have."

"That's for sure!" exclaimed Micah as he tapped his buddy on his arm.

Ken and Betty Preston showed up a couple minutes later to join the expanding circle of friends who were standing near the back of the Temple. They were followed moments later by Eli, accompanied by his former roommate Moshe Salam and Yochanan Ben-Zevedee, the Apostle who was Yeshua's most beloved disciple.

After greetings were exchanged all around, Jonathan introduced his parents to Moshe and Yochanan. "Eli told us your testimony, Abe and Rebecca, and it is very moving indeed," stated Yochanan.

"Well, it is our tremendous honor to meet you, sir" replied Abe. Rebecca added that "Sarah probably informed you that we spotted her and Tali with you and Natan-el in downtown Chicago on the evening news. We were so thrilled when they showed up with Eli and Craig the next day at our doorstep."

Yochanan then made a confession. "The Lord actually showed me you had been cruelly beheaded by UW murderers later that week after surrendering your hearts to Him while imprisoned. However I never shared that information with Sarah. She and her children were still having a hard enough time dealing with Jonathan's death. I thought it was best to keep that revelation to myself."

"Thank you, Yochanan," said Benny. "I think it would've been too much for me to handle right then. Grandpa and Grandma took such good care of me while I was living with them, and I really love them. It would have definitely been too much to bear."

Betty lightened the mood when she said in her usual drawl, "We saw you all over here and decided to drop by. Ken told me all about finding Donna alive and also about the twin girls. What an exciting day you've all had!"

"And it's not over yet" replied Jonathan. "Sarah's friend Yitzhak turned up a few minutes ago, and then abruptly left to fetch some 'surprise' he said he wanted to show us."

"Oh, I met Yitzhak with Sarah at the hospital one time," recalled Betty. "It'll be great to see him again, and Sarah will be so thrilled."

Benny waved his left hand in the air. "Speaking of mom, there she is now, along with Tali and Stacy."

As the three Kadoshim approached the redeemed group of friends, two other saints were heading arm in arm toward them from the opposite direction.

"It's true!!" shouted out one of them before fainting onto the stone marble floor.

SIX

ALIVE FROM THE DEAD

Benny and Micah rushed over to help up the Holy One who had collapsed onto the Temple floor just ten feet away from them. As they did so, the rest of the group of friends moved closer to the scene.

"Are you alright?" enquired Benny as he thrust his steady arm under one of the fallen saint's slumped shoulders. Micah did the same on his other side. Like all the Kadoshim, the focus of their attention appeared to be about thirty years old. Soon the stranger was alert and back on his feet.

With their inborn medical instincts kicking in, Eli and Sarah trotted over to the unidentified saint, closely examining him with experienced eyes.

By now, almost everyone had noticed the tattooed concentration camp number on his forearm. "Thank you, I'm okay. I was just shocked and overwhelmed, that's all."

"It's my fault, I should've told him in advance," confessed his companion before adding, "Hello, my sweet Rachel."

"Yitzhak! Is that you?"

"Yes Sarah, it is." The two friends embraced.

"I was just about to tell you that Yitzhak stopped by a little while ago after he recognized me from your photos," Jonathan interjected. "We spoke for a few minutes before he excused himself, saying he had some surprise for us and would soon return. I presume this is the surprise?"

"It is," affirmed Yitzhak. "Jonathan, meet your grandfather, Rabbi Benjamin Goldman. Benny, your great grandfather, whom Sarah told me you were named after. Abe, your beloved poppa."

Rabbi Benjamin was still in way too much shock to absorb all this information. His son Abe let out a yelp and nearly fell backwards as he reached out for Rebecca's hand.

"I can't believe it! Is it really you poppa?"

Benjamin moved forward toward the son that he had not seen in many decades, wiping tears from his eyes as he struggled to regain his composure. "It is indeed, if you're Abraham Joshua Goldman from Berlin. And I...know that you are because I read your concentration camp number just seconds ago as I approached you. I knew in an instant it was you, son, which is why I fainted. Yitzhak told me he had a huge surprise for me, and so he did! I still cannot believe it!"

Jonathan quickly realized that his father was simply too stunned to speak. "Grandpa Goldman, I'm Abe's son, Jonathan, and this is my mother Rebecca, and over here is my earthly wife Sarah, and our children Tali and Benjamin—we call him Benny and he was indeed named after you."

The Holocaust victim was astounded once more as he finally comprehended what he was being told. Never in his wildest fantasies had he ever dared to pretend that he would one day meet his great-grandson, let alone one named after him.

"But how...when..." Abe still couldn't speak.

"Son, you're...wondering how I...came to be here," the rabbi uttered, barely able to get the words out himself. He paused once again to wipe his watery eyes. "I was taken to Auschwitz, as you know Abe, since you were with me. However you were soon transferred to a work camp, thank *Ha Shem*. You were only eight years old, but healthy and strong for your age."

The circle of Kadoshim brethren clung to Benjamin's words like plastic wrap, especially Abe, Jonathan and Benny. "You'll recall we only saw each other once while we were both incarcerated there. Then I heard the news that you were taken away, Abe. The murderers didn't even let me say goodbye to my only son!"

"This is indeed my poppa," Abe confirmed as he stretched his hand out and braced it on his father's forearm, the one with the death camp identity tattoo. The entire Goldman family was now unleashing tears, along with most of the rest of the listening saints.

"A few weeks later, everyone in my bunkhouse was told we'd be taken down the next morning to be deloused in some 'special shower.' We weren't stupid, we knew what that meant. So right after the sun came up, I went to the washroom to brush my teeth and comb my hair. I was not going to die like some animal! If I was to be gassed to death, I was determined to depart with as much human dignity I could muster."

Abe paused and turned his gaze up towards the Sovereign Lord seated upon His majestic throne. "And then *He* appeared!" Five Hanukkah flames flickered in front of the Lamb of God. King Yeshua's fiery eyes were directed out over the myriad dancing saints, staring straight in Rabbi Benjamin's direction. The Blessed Redeemer was absorbing every word.

"I was combing my hair when I noticed this shining light reflecting from my small mirror. I turned around and asked, 'Who are you?' The Lord answered, 'I am the slain Passover Lamb. I am Israel's Eternal Messiah and King. I am alive forevermore.' Well, I was completely dumbfounded! Then he added, 'Receive me into your life right now, and your sins will be forgiven you.' Then I spotted the scars in His hands and feet, and realized who He was. I said, 'Lord, pardon my sins. I do receive You.' Then Yeshua proclaimed, 'Today you will be with Me in Paradise.' And just as suddenly as He came, He disappeared."

Rebecca started to sob out loud. Sarah softly placed her hands on her former mother-in-law's trembling shoulders. Jonathan did the same with his weeping father. Benny and Tali moved behind their dad, each grabbing hold of one of his strong arms.

"Twenty minutes later, when I was being herded through the steel door into the crematorium, Yeshua appeared again! He said, 'I will go with you.' I was ashamed, since I'd just been complaining to myself, but I guess really to the Lord, that I was dying all alone, that my family was all gone. That's precisely when Yeshua reappeared! I don't know why, but then I said to Him, 'Lord, if you're going to bear those scars for all eternity, then let me keep this Nazi tattoo as well. I want to remember the evil that was done to me and my Jewish kin here. I want to never forget, even if, with your help, I can one day forgive.' The Lord simply nodded His assent and walked silently beside me as the gas came pouring out of the showerheads. Then, as I was choking to death from the toxins, He said 'I love you my child.' Seconds later, I was standing in King Yeshua's glorious presence before His heavenly throne."

Jonathan now began to weep loudly, recalling his almost identical sudden death-to-eternal-life experience. Eli leaned over and hugged his friend as Tali and Benny joined in.

Rabbi Goldman turned his wet face back towards the Lamb of Life; the One who was slain to take away his sins and those of the whole world. "King Yeshua, I never thought I'd ever see my precious son again. Today I've not only seen him, but also his wife, my grandson and his wife, and my great-grandson and granddaughter! How can I ever thank You enough? I love you so much!" His listeners soon joined in the heartfelt refrain of praise. The Prince of Peace smiled at them all as He blew a gentle kiss their way.

The seven Goldmans and their redeemed friends then burst forth into a spontaneous anthem of adoration and praise. Eli and Moshe quickly recognized it as the very same sacred song that they, as part of the 144,000 sealed Jewish males, had sung when caught up to the presence of the Lord on the heavenly Mount Zion

Victory belongs to our God, who is seated upon the throne, and to the Lamb! Praise and glory, wisdom and thanks, honor and power and strength, belong to our God forever and ever!

After pouring out their grateful hearts for over an hour, Benny skipped over to his great-grandfather and gave him a loving kiss on his cheek. Tali then did the same, followed by Jonathan and Sarah. Then Jonathan introduced the re-born rabbi to Yochanan, Eli and Moshe, telling him briefly the roles each had played during the turbulent end of days. Next he called over Stacy and Craig, Yoseph and Cindy, and finally Ken and Betty, giving a brief synopsis of their lives and relation-ships with Jonathan and his family.

When he finished, Abe asked his father the question on several minds. "Poppa, how is it you came to discover us here today? I realize Yitzhak brought you here, but how did you link up with him?"

"Son, I was gratefully worshipping the Lord out in the Temple courtyard with the other Kadoshim. After a few days passed, I realized most of them were dancing and celebrating with others they knew from the past. I suddenly felt kind of alone. I hadn't the slightest clue you were here or my other descendants, or that I even *had* any other family. Then Yitzhak came over to me. He said he noticed my death camp tattoo, and had himself been persecuted as a Jew by the Nazis in Berlin. I told him I was also from there, and had been murdered in an Auschwitz gas chamber. From that moment on, we became instant friends."

Yitzhak picked up the story. "I was feeling a little lonely myself. Please don't misunderstand me, I was extremely grateful and joyful to be in the presence of the Lord, and so thankful for Sarah's crucial role in that. But I also realized I had no family or friends here at all, apart from Sarah, whom I couldn't locate. And there are countless millions of Kadoshim here!"

Sarah's friend stopped and took hold of her soft hand. "Plus you do look a bit different my dear, but lovely as ever!"

Sarah smiled as Yitzhak resumed recounting his story. "This only happened a few hours ago. Then I asked Benjamin what his family name was, and he said Goldman. I thought, *could he be related to Sarah?* before dismissing the prospect. Then I suddenly recalled she told me Jonathan's father was named Abe, and that Benny was named after his great-grandfather from Berlin who perished at Auschwitz. So I asked, 'Did you by chance have a son named Abe?' Well, he nearly fell on the floor right then! So after I found Jonathan, I went back to get him, and here we all are!"

"The Lord places the lonely in families," interposed Yochanan.

Then Benny spoke up. "Yitzhak, I must ask your forgiveness for something. I sort of…resented you after mom announced she was sending me off to America and staying behind mainly to minister to you. I blamed you for my separation from her and Tali, even though I was glad to spend time with Grandpa and Grandma. I'm so very sorry sir, please forgive me."

Yitzhak walked over and embraced the remorseful young saint. "Oh Benny, you were only a mere lad, just five or six years old when you left. Of course you were upset to be parted from your mother and sister, especially after you lost your dear father. It was a natural reaction, not a sin, son. Anyway, I do forgive you, and thank you big guy for sharing your sweet mother with me. She literally saved my life—forever."

I've made the right choice for my Minister of Justice, thought Eli.

"Benny lost his dear father?" sputtered the puzzled rabbi. "What does that mean?"

Abe answered his poppa's question with thoughtful deliberation. "Jonathan served as a reserve army soldier here in Israel, in the same unit with Eli and Moshe."

Benjamin immediately interrupted his son. "Never in my brightest dreams could I have hoped, as I was walking with the Lord to my death at Auschwitz, that I would one day have a grandson serving in an Israeli army! I'm so proud of you Jonathan!"

"We all felt the same, poppa. I still vividly remember the vow you made me take the very last time I saw you in that death camp. You said, 'Swear to me that if you survive the war, and if the Jews in Palestine succeed in setting up a state one day, and if you have a son, you'll ask him to go and defend it. And poppa; that's exactly what happened!"

Everyone was deeply moved by Abe's words. Jonathan took hold of his father's right hand. "Well dad, you kind of made that a reality. Even though you only occasionally attended synagogue, you were always talking about Israel, about the many enemies that wanted to destroy the country, and how we all needed to support our Jewish state. So it was sort of natural for me to want to move here and do just that."

"You know Jonathan, when I was sent off after the war to live with my father's sister in the city of Leeds in Britain; I swore I'd never darken the door of a synagogue again. How could there be a God if a hideous death camp like Auschwitz could exist? But after I migrated to New York at age eighteen and later married your mother, she talked me into going back to synagogue, especially after your older sister was born. However, you're quite right. I wanted to instill a love for Israel in you, to hopefully fulfill the pledge I made to my dear poppa. I didn't think it was right to tell you what he requested, since I only wanted you to move here if you really wanted to. Still, it's true; I did deliberately encourage that, son. I regretted it at your funeral however, but not anymore."

"So Jonathan, you were killed fighting for your country?" his newfound grandfather asked, adding with shimmering eyes, "If so, I'm even more proud of you!"

"Yes granddad, I perished in a Syrian gas attack up on the Golan Heights over five years ago."

"In an enemy gas attack?" gasped Rabbi Benjamin. "Exactly like I was murdered by the Nazis!"

"The same demonic spirit was at work against the Jewish people once again, grandfather. I was on night watch sitting on a rock when a Syrian chemical shell suddenly exploded nearby. I'd taken off my protective gas mask for a moment to get some fresh late evening air. Eli's told me he came running over from his medical supply tent seconds later wearing his mask and protective suit, but it was highly toxic Sarin gas, so I was already dead."

Eli remembered that spring evening as if it were only last night. "I picked up Yonni's limp body and cried out the refrain that King David uttered when his friend Jonathan was slaughtered in battle: *Your beauty O Israel is slain on your high places! How the mighty have fallen in the midst of the battle! Jonathan is slain on your high places!*"

"I didn't know you quoted that scripture verse," whispered Jonathan in Eli's ear as he again embraced his precious friend.

Rebecca now picked up the story. "It took a few weeks before Jonathan's remains were released by the Syrians, who overran the outpost one day after the gas attack. Meanwhile thousands of grieving relatives like us were heading to Israel in droves after the short war ended, so we were barely able to get a flight to Tel Aviv for Jonathan's funeral. It was held at the Mount Herzl military cemetery here in

Jerusalem. Everyone standing here now was there, except for Yochanan, Micah, Ken and Betty. Eli and Moshe had just arrived back in the city after being released from a Syrian prisoner of war camp, which happened soon after Israel dropped some nuclear bombs on Damascus."

Moshe thrust in a comment. "Eli led me to the Lord in that camp. I was ready by then for *any* salvation I could get!"

Benjamin Goldman scratched his head. "Israel destroyed Damascus with nuclear weapons?"

"I'll tell you about it later on, poppa," Abe promised.

Rebecca continued, "Abe recited the *Kaddish* prayer for the dead at our son's funeral. He was barely able to get out the words. When he finished, he cried out, *'God of Israel, why? My father and my son; both gassed to death by hate-filled madmen!'* We were all awash in tears."

They were all in tears once again, especially Rabbi Benjamin and his grandson Jonathan, who was also hearing most of this for the first time. The Kadoshim did not yet realize that every time they remembered and wept over some painful memory from their past lives, the pain was washed away forever.

Sarah looked straight into Jonathan's teary eyes as she added some information about the post-funeral memorial service held at the Beit Yisrael congregation building on Bethlehem Road. "Yoseph delivered such a moving tribute in your memory, honey, at a special service we held later that day, and he clearly spelled out the Gospel message; I think especially for the sake of your parents."

"It was the first time we heard the good news presented so fully like that," Abe confirmed. "It really touched our hearts, and seeded our brains. Thanks so much, Yoseph."

The former Beit Yisrael pastor bowed his head. "Thank you for sharing that, sir." He inwardly rejoiced anew over the privilege Yeshua had given him to lead dozens of souls to the throne of grace during his earthly existence in Jerusalem. He was hoping many more human salvations lay ahead during the Lord's millennial reign.

Rebecca thought it was time to lighten the mood. "And Eli, you also gave a very moving tribute. You obviously loved and missed Jonathan so much, and that also really touched us. Why, you even helped us to laugh a bit as we remembered our dear son, relating that funny pink underwear story."

"You told them about that?" snapped Jonathan as he turned toward Eli. He was not terribly amused.

"Well Yonni, it was very funny, and I just felt after all the heaviness of the day, it was somehow appropriate to cheer everyone up just a bit."

"I've got to hear this!" Micah exclaimed.

Eli was clearly reluctant to share the story, so Rebecca took over. "Well, it seems that Sarah had accidentally put some of Jonathan's underwear in the washing machine with Tali's red ballet tights. When she later took out the laundry, one set of white boxer shorts and a tank top vest were now decidedly pink! Still, she packed them in Jonathan's bag when he went off the next day with his reserve unit for some training exercises in the Negev Desert, as a back up pair just in case he ran out. Jonathan only discovered them at the bottom of his bag after he used up the other pairs. He came from the shower area with them on that evening while Eli was playing cards with Moshe. They both laughed out loud, as did all the other men in the army tent. Jonathan apparently dove under the covers of his cot as quick as he could!"

Jonathan was finally smiling, so Eli took over. "Moshe was always playing practical jokes on guys in our unit, Micah. He whispered to me, 'I'm going to hide Jonathan's army uniform after he falls asleep!' which he did. So the next morning when Yonni went to get dressed, he had nothing to put on over his pink underwear! He ran about the tent looking desperately for his clothes as everyone giggled. Then Moshe said to him, 'You look like a ballerina this morning, Jonathan.' Everyone cracked up as Moshe went over to a supply chest and pulled out Yonni's army pants and shirt. It really was hysterical."

"Okay guys, I forgive you," stated Jonathan with a chuckle. "I agree it's a funny story, but was it really appropriate to share that at my memorial service?"

"Actually it was perfect," affirmed Sarah as tears appeared again in her eyes. "We were all so...distressed over our tremendous loss, Jonathan. The kids were trying *really hard*, but they were weeping like a waterfall as your father said the *Kaddish*, and then referred to Hitler and the Syrian dictator, Halled Hasdar. I was pretty broken up too, as were pretty much everyone else in attendance. You see, Eli then went on to say that he could imagine you right then standing in heaven with Yeshua in your new white robe, but that it was probably not white, but pink! And then he added, 'I bet when Yonni returns to Jerusalem with the Lord, he'll have on that same pink robe!' Well, we all laughed, but you know what? It was the perfect reminder that you were not really dead, but alive forevermore with Yeshua, standing in glory at that very moment in front of His heavenly throne. Plus it reminded us all that you would indeed be returning quite alive with the Lord one day soon. In fact, Tali and Benni spoke about that wonderful fact almost every day from then on."

Jonathan walked over and gave Sarah a squeeze around her trim waist. Then he winked at Eli and said, "Thank you, dear friend."

"What is all this talk in the Holy Temple about pink underwear?" asked an obviously amused Prince David as he appeared behind Tali's back.

Eli answered. "Oh, we're sorry, Prince David. It's just something I shared at Jonathan's funeral."

"Prince David?" blurted out Benjamin Goldman as he cocked his head.

"Oh Rabbi Goldman, let me introduce you to the new governor of Israel, Prince David, who I guess you would have known as King David." Benjamin Goldman had served many years at his synagogue in Berlin. Of King David he knew quite well.

"The King David?"

"One and the same," the tall Prince confirmed, prompting Benjamin to fall to one knee and kiss his regal emerald ring.

"Please get up, my brother" said David as he turned his gaze toward the Lord perched like a watching shepherd on His royal throne. "He is now our only Sovereign King."

Then Israel's new provincial ruler turned his ruddy countenance back toward Tali. "Are you the young saint who wanted to know about the twins and their mother?"

"Yes I am," answered Tali as a surge of anticipation erupted in her childlike spirit.

"At Eli's request, I checked with King Yeshua about the matter, and I'm sorry to say their mother is indeed deceased, and no other relatives remain alive. She was killed in her partially destroyed classroom where she'd gone to search for some private items in the rubble. She perished in the gigantic ultimate earthquake just one day before the Master returned to the Mount of Olives."

"We must have dissolved her body," observed Eli.

"You did indeed," Prince David affirmed. "The twins will need a good home, and King Yeshua is delighted that you've volunteered to offer them that." Israel's hallowed governor looked around at the assembled band of Kadoshim before adding, "It appears the twins will have plenty of family and friends to support them."

"Thank you Prince David," replied Tali in genuine awe mixed with equal parts of bubbling joy. "I promise we'll take very good care of them."

"I know you will, kind one, and so does your Savior. He told me this is precisely what He's doing all over the earth right now...linking the millions of orphaned humans with older people or Kadoshim to take care of them. The Lord bless and keep you in this most sacred endeavor, dear one."

Six-foot-three and smelling of sweet lilacs, Prince David turned to Sarah and Stacy, standing next to each other. "I'd like to speak to each of you separately tomorrow morning at 10:00. Eli can show you my temporary office."

"We'll be there, your highness," answered Sarah as both friends reverently bowed their heads.

"Excellent, I will see you then. Shalom redeemed ones!"

After Prince David was out of earshot, Rabbi Benjamin scratched his head and asked, "What was all that concerning twins?"

"I'll tell you about it later on grandfather," pledged Jonathan, adding with a broad smile, "Let's just say that you're about to become a great-great-grandfather."

"Oh my!" Once bereft of all family, the rabbi's awestruck heart again overflowed with unspeakable joy.

Eli offered congratulations to Tali before asking if she thought she'd need help in breaking the news to the twins that their mother was dead.

"I'll take Sarah and Stacy along when I inform them, so it should be okay."

Benny requested to join his sister in the planned trip to the hospital, as did Micah.

Tali accepted their offers before adding, "My main concern is that the twins already had their hearts broken when their father was killed in that horrible Hamas terror attack outside the central bus station, which took place the year Mrs. Bernstein was my teacher."

"She talked about that atrocity with my class as well," added Micah. "She said her girls were still not over it, and that was two years after the attack."

"We'll all be in prayer for you Tali," Eli assured the young saint as he kissed her left cheek. Then he turned toward Abe and Rebecca Goldman. "I have an important proposal to make to you Mr. Goldman, and also to you Mrs. Goldman."

"Please call us Abe and Rebecca," said Abe. "We're all now brethren in the Messiah, and anyway we all look to be about the same age, at least externally!"

Eli chuckled as he gently consented. "That's true, Abe. Jonathan told me you ran a travel agency in the northern part of Chicago for over twenty years. Is that correct?"

"Yes, Eli, and it allowed us a cheap way to visit many parts of the world, on top of making us good money. We even took Jonathan and his sister Dinah to Paris and London one time."

Rebecca lowered her head and teared up yet again at the mention of their daughter's name. Dinah and her husband, Bob Hartsfeld, and their three children had all received Andre's implantation and were therefore separated from the Lord—forever.

"Yonni told me about that trip. Abe, would you be willing to serve as my Transport and Tourism Minister? I think it will be a very important position in the place I'm being sent to govern."

"I would be *delighted* to serve with you, Eli, especially since my son and grandson will also be in your cabinet. It's a family affair!"

"I'm so pleased." Eli waited a second while Jonathan's mother brushed the salty water from the corners of her eyes. "Rebecca, I know you were a practicing nurse in New York before your marriage to Abe. Would you serve as my Minister of Health, helping the humans living in my province to recover?"

Rebecca's mood quickly brightened. "With great honor, Governor Eli. It will be a delight for sure."

"This is starting to sound like nepotism to me," Moshe quipped before adding, "Four Goldmans in one government cabinet! Such a deal!"

Eli smiled as he walked over and positioned himself directly in front of Rabbi Benjamin. "Well Moshe, the final total might be more than that. Sir, I know that you served at an Orthodox congregation in Berlin before it was destroyed by the Hitler Youth gang and Gestapo rioters on *Kristallnacht* in November 1938."

The statement sparked a flash of extremely painful memory in Abe's mind, producing copious tears in his brown eyes. The toddler had stood by helplessly as his father desperately attempted to douse the raging flames consuming his mother Devorah's clothing after a homemade firebomb was hurled through a broken window into his synagogue. The entire building was soon on fire, forcing father and son to flee. His beloved mother was burned to death within five minutes. Besides Devorah Goldman, 90 other Jews were killed and over 250 synagogues destroyed on that horrendous night of Nazi rampage and rage.

"Yes Eli, I was a rabbi there, and I think a good one, or at least I tried to be."

"Well sir, I heard from Abe at Jonathan's funeral that you were an excellent teacher who thoroughly knew and taught the sacred scriptures to your flock. Under King Yeshua's good governance, we will be teaching about the Lord in all of our schools. No more will the truth about our God be left outside of the classroom. Will you serve as my Minister of Education and Religious Affairs?"

"To sit in your cabinet with my son and his wife, my grandson, and also my great grandson? Yes, I suppose I could just manage that," replied the rabbi with a twinkle in his eye as he received Eli's tender congratulatory hug. The gesture caused Abe's tears to dry up. The intense childhood pain over the loss of his dear mother had finally evaporated.

"Fantastic sir, welcome on board." Then Eli wandered over to Yoseph and gave him an affectionate thump on his expansive chest. "Yoseph, I actually asked Prince David about the possibility of recruiting you to serve in that position, before I knew Rabbi Benjamin was here with us in eternity. He told me you'll be given your own province to govern, as I sort of anticipated. Congratulations on that!"

The gathered saints echoed the sentiment. Yoseph then revealed that his area of governance would be the unique city he was born and raised in, New York, which produced another round of approving well wishes and a kiss from Stacy, who had also grown up in the Big Apple.

"It will be a challenging position, at least to begin with" added Cindy as the friends quieted down. "Prince David told us the city is fairly decimated, and there are many human orphans in the area to deal with, a good portion of them Jewish. Yoseph already asked me to serve as his Education and Religious Affairs Minister, and I've agreed, but I know it'll be difficult, especially at first. So we do really appreciate your prayers."

"You have them Cindy, and lots of love," replied Sarah as she give her longtime friend a peck on her cheek.

Benny could not stand it any longer. He started to leap up and down in excitement like the little boy that he still basically was. "Uncle Eli, where are we going to serve?"

"Well Big Benny, I know Moshe's been appointed governor of a province centered in Athens, Greece."

Another round of hearty congratulations poured forth from all mouths as Eli shook his buddy's hand and winked. Mostly of Moroccan stock, the Sephardic Jew was looking forward to his new assignment, especially since his maternal grandmother had been born and raised in Athens.

Finally Eli turned to face Benny, still bobbing up and down as if on a trampoline. "So you want to know where we will be sent?" he teased.

"YES, YES!!"

"Well young saint, let's just say we'll definitely need a good Minister of Tourism, and a swim suit."

Jonathan patted his father on the back.

"So, where is it?' pleaded Benny as he clapped his hands in joyous anticipation.

"I've been asked to govern the Greek Isles."

The appointed ministers now joined Benny in squeals of delight.

"My province will encompass all of the Aegean islands, including the big ones of Crete and Rhodes, plus Samos off the coast of the old city of Ephesus, Chios to the north of it, and all of the Cycladic islands, such as Naxos, Mykonos, Paros and Santorini. Some of them were altered in the final earthquakes, but all are still there." Eli turned his head to look squarely at Yochanan, who was still present with the group. "And we'll also govern the island where our dear friend here was once imprisoned, Patmos."

"That's magnificent, Eli, may the Lord grant you great success!" uttered a delighted Yochanan.

Rabbi Benjamin was once more puzzled. "Where Yochanan was imprisoned?"

"I'll explain that to you later as well, Grandpa," promised Jonathan.

"Thank you Jonathan, I have so much to learn. This is almost too much for an old man to take in, even if I now appear fairly young in this wonderful new body! You know, I was originally born in 1916 after all, during World War One. Finding my family alive to the third generation here in the Temple in Jerusalem, being asked to be a government minister by my grandson's best friend, meeting my great grandson who was named after me, and meeting King David, my hero as a boy. I'm entirely speechless!"

"He was my hero as well, great-granddad" stated Benjamin's still hopping namesake. "And since my dad was called Jonathan, I was especially fond of the story of the friendship between Saul's son and the King."

"So was I!" revealed the elated rabbi.

"Jonathan, I think I told you my poppa loved King David and Abraham the most of all the ancient biblical figures, didn't I?" enquired Abe.

"Yes you did dad. You told me that was the reason he named you Abraham and you named me Jonathan."

Rebecca suddenly burst into tears once again, startling everyone and prompting Sarah to rush to her side, and Benny to stop leaping. "What is it mom?" she enquired.

Abe was now sobbing as well. Another excruciating memory was about to be cleansed.

"Jonathan, we're so sorry, your mother and I never told you. We just didn't see what good it would do to add to the trauma you already felt when I explained why your Goldman grandparents were no longer alive."

Embracing his father, he replied, "You can tell me now, dad."

"Jonathan, you actually had a twin brother. He only lived a few hours after you were both born. You were the first one out. His umbilical cord got twisted somehow during the delivery process. Plus you twins were six weeks premature, and both of you were very small and frail. Still, you were a bit heavier than him son, and thankfully you survived. He was immediately placed in an incubator after your mother and I were allowed to hold him for a few seconds."

Rebecca had recovered enough to carry on the account. "I'd found out I was having male twins a few months before, and we knew how much Abe's slain father loved the story of deep friendship between King David and King Saul's son Jonathan. So we named your brother David…and then he died." The bereaved mother was weeping once again. This painful memory would take more than one washing to fully heal.

Eli spotted Prince David passing nearby once again. The governor-designate darted over to speak to him as Jonathan, also now gently crying, silently enfolded his mother in his arms.

"Rebecca, Abe, Jonathan. Prince David has something to tell you."

Israel's new provincial governor moved directly in front of the elder Goldmans before proclaiming, "I'm certain your son David is alive."

Rebecca gasped. Abe threw up his hands. Jonathan and Sarah smiled.

"All of the babies who died in the passing era before they reached the age of accountability were immediately swept into the Lord's holy presence. There is a huge company of them worshipping the Good Shepherd right now near the front of the Temple. They're spiraling up from the floor to the ceiling, rejoicing in their gracious Savior. I'll gladly check into his exact whereabouts for you. After all, he is named after me!"

"I have a brother!!" proclaimed Jonathan as he joined his father Benjamin and son Benny in joyously jumping up and down in sheer delight.

"Oh, and that reminds me, I meant to tell you all something else when I stopped by earlier. I have so much on my mind at present."

The bobbing stopped as the group of friends again became rapt with attention.

"When I asked King Yeshua about the Bernstein twins, he told me that you Goldmans are mainly descendants of the tribe of Benjamin, while both Jonathan's mother and wife are mostly from the tribe of Judah. Of course, I am of the tribe of Judah myself, as is our Sovereign Lord, and my close friend Jonathan, King Saul's son, was from the tribe of Benjamin.

Benny leapt up and down once again. "So Tali and I are descendants of both Benjamin and Judah, as is our dad? That is so awesome!!"

Abe was equally awestruck, as were the rest of the listening saints. "Well, that might partly explain why Rebecca and I wanted to name our twin sons David and Jonathan: One after you, my prince, and the other after your dear friend Jonathan."

"Indeed," replied Israel's governor with a broad smile beaming out between his cropped mustache and beard. "Oh by the way, I just found out today that my Jonathan, who we call *Yonatan* in Hebrew, is willing to serve as my top administrative aid. I'm very pleased with that development, and he is as well."

"Wonderful!" proclaimed Eli as Yochanan and the others nodded in accord.

"Well, I must be on my way; still much to be done. I'll see you in my office tomorrow morning, Sarah and Stacy."

As Israel's renowned prince departed, the astounded saints stared at one another in silence, trying to absorb all of the marvelous things that had occurred so far during this jubilant Festival of Lights.

Sarah Goldman's glistening eyes were darting back and forth as she and Stacy were led by Eli to Prince David's administrative office the next morning. She was looking everywhere for her parents, hoping against hope that they'd given their lives to the Sovereign Lord and were celebrating somewhere with the rest of the redeemed. After two days of searching, she hadn't uncovered any trace of them.

"This is David's temporary office," announced Eli as he led the two friends through a side door into a small chamber on the north side of the Temple. "Over there is Prince David's personal secretary, his second human wife Michal, who was also King Saul's daughter and Yonatan's sister." After introductions were made, Eli excused himself as Sarah and Stacy sat down to wait.

Prince David appeared five minutes later, wearing his saffron robe which featured a beautiful embroidered pattern on the sleeves and along the hem. "Good morning children of the Most High God! Thank you for coming to see me."

"It is our honor," answered Sarah as her longtime friend nodded her accord.

"Stacy, would you please come in first? We'll only be a few minutes."

The Manhattan-born saint pinched herself as she dutifully followed the distinguished Prince into his temporary office; still wondering if she might wake up any moment and find this had all been a very pleasant dream.

"Please sit down, Stacy. First of all, I should tell you the Lord will be assigning Hebrew names to all the Kadoshim of Jewish extraction that were given non-biblical names by their human parents. He informed me you'll be called Shoshel, meaning the Rose of God."

Stacy—Shoshel—was elated with that news, and promptly told Israel's new provincial governor so.

"Now Shoshel, I've been searching for an appropriate saint to administer my palace household. I will be graciously gifted a fantastic new palace by our Mighty King this coming Shabbat, when all of Jerusalem's new housing will appear, along with some other things you'll delight in."

The former starlet's eyes sparkled as she waited to hear Prince David's offer.

"I plan to have a permanent staff of around 200, Shoshel, some Kadoshim but mostly humans. With many foreign visitors coming to Jerusalem for the various annual feasts and other events, I'll be hosting frequent state banquets, so will need a large kitchen and servant staff. I'll also have gardeners, housekeepers, maintenance personnel and many others. Shoshel, I'd be greatly blessed if you'd agree to manage my staff. You'll have an office in the palace. Would you do that for me?"

"Oh my prince, it would be a fantastic honor indeed! But if I may beg to enquire, why me? I've never done anything like that before."

"Maybe not, but your friend Eli tells me you have a most gracious heart, are very hospitable and relaxed in relating to others, so that means you possess excellent social skills. He also mentioned you're a tremendous cook, so you already know about kitchens and what they involve. All of this is exactly what I need in my palace administrator.

"Again, I am honored Prince David, and I gladly accept your offer."

"Splendid! You'll begin the first day of next week. Oh, by the way, you will be living with Sarah in her new home. I would not subject you to private quarters in the palace. You'd be too close to your job and the staff, especially the human beings who'd never let you enjoy a moment's rest."

"Thank you again, kind prince. I promise to work hard and obey your directions," said Shoshel sincerely as David escorted her to his office door and then motioned for Sarah to enter. "Goodbye Shoshel, see you soon!"

Shoshel?, thought Sarah as she passed her radiant friend before sitting down on the velvet couch situated directly in front of Prince David's opulent oak desk.

"Thank you for coming this morning, Sarah. You're probably wondering why I called your friend 'Shoshel' just now?"

"The thought did cross my mind, Prince David."

"The Lord is assigning new names to all those Kadoshim of Jewish descent who were given non-Hebraic names by their parents."

"Oh I see...but I guess I'll still be known as Sarah since that was the name of Abraham's wife."

"You're correct. Sarah, I'll get straight to the point. I want you to administer the three hospitals and several smaller clinics that will be springing up here in Jerusalem this coming Shabbat, along with the promised new housing and other buildings including my new palace where Shoshel will serve as my staff administrator. The medical facilities will only be for the city's human residents and visitors of course, since the Kadoshim are no longer subject to illness or accidents."

Sarah pondered Prince David's words as he continued to speak. "Actually the surviving human race will be much healthier than it was in the old era due to the leaves and fruit from the Trees of Life and the overall vast improvement in the quality of living and diets they'll enjoy, not to mention the stable weather and absence of wars and terror attacks. Still, some will need medical attention at times, especially the children and returning Jewish refugees, plus many of the ingathered Jews who are already beginning to stream to the Promised Land from abroad. Most of the humans will later become quite elderly before they die, and some will certainly need medical attention then as well."

"I will be so pleased to hold that important position, Prince David, and I'm also very happy for my dear friend Sho...."

"Shoshel, the Rose of God. Sarah, I was told by Eli that you're especially compassionate with those who are ill, being quite concerned for the health of the patients you ministered to at Hadassah Hospital. Along with that, he informed me you are very organized and work well with others. So I believe you're an excellent choice for this administrative position. You'll have an office in my palace, and also in the largest city hospital, which will arise where the old Hadassah stood near Ein Kerem."

"Thank you, Prince David. However I hope you realize I possess no formal medical skills."

"Yes I know, but that's not what I am looking for. My medical administrator needs to be able to relate well to the hospital and clinic managers and staff, and also to my Minister of Health, who along with all of the rest of my cabinet will be chosen from among the former ancient kings and queens of Israel."

"Again, thank you. I gladly and humbly accept your wonderful offer."

"Excellent!"

"Prince David, may I ask you a quick question before I go?"

"Of course Sarah, go ahead."

"You just mentioned the healing power of the Trees of Life, as did King Yeshua when He addressed us the other day. I have a living human sister currently hospitalized at Augusta Victoria. I presume she'll be residing with me in my new home. Could you explain just a little bit how these sacred trees prolong human life, and how they bring healing to the sick? That might help me minister to her."

"When Eli enquired about the twins, Sarah, he told me you'd discovered your sister alive in the ruins of your old home. He said she is not yet the Lord's. I should tell you first that while she *will* be permitted to live in Jerusalem, along with other humans who resided here before the Lord's return, she will *not* be allowed to actually see King Yeshua in person unless she surrenders her life to Him. She'll naturally view Him on television, as will everyone on earth, but she cannot enter the Holy Temple unless she truly repents of her sins, which I understand from Eli are not few."

Prince David shifted in his russet leather chair as he continued. "On the matter of the Trees of Life, the leaves and fruit not only act as healing agents, but also slow down the natural aging process in human beings. As our Eternal King mentioned, what formally took one year in their bodies, as far as aging is concerned, will now take ten—that is if they're careful to ingest the leaves and fruit on a regular basis. We'll make sure the world's human population is regularly supplied with all that is necessary to stay healthy and prosper. Anyway Sarah, this means that humans will be capable of potentially living many hundreds of years. In fact some alive now might still be around when the Lord's millennial reign is transformed into His heavenly kingdom in a thousand years time, although they'd obviously be very old by then."

Prince David smiled. "Does that answer your question?"

"Thank you kind prince, yes it does. But may I beg to ask just one additional short question?" Israel's new governor nodded his consent. "If humans will potentially live many hundreds of years, won't women be capable of having dozens of babies, especially if abortion is outlawed, as I presume it will be?"

"You're correct about abortion being banned. Many other things will be different from the previous era, which our Majestic King will explain in due time. The Lord certainly is quite cognizant of the problem you just mentioned. Therefore a new strain of rice will be made available via medical clinics which will act as a natural contraceptive in women who desire to keep the number of their children to a reasonable level. After all, they're still human beings, with all of the limitations in stamina, patience and other resources that implies. It temporarily shuts down the reproductive system, preventing conception. So the Lord will mercifully make the rice available to all women who truly need it. However we'll require they're properly married in order to legally purchase it. Coupling out of wedlock will be against the law from now on."

"Thank you so much, Prince David. I'll pass that news along to my sister."

"Oh, and one other thing before you go, Sarah. Would you kindly inform Jonathan and his parents that I have not yet found time to enquire about their son, David? I've been extremely busy with preparations for this coming Shabbat, and with informing the designated provincial governors about their world postings. There are actually 1,000 of them!

"I'll gladly do so, Prince David, and I appreciate that you are extremely busy right now. Still, I was wondering if, when you get the time, you might also ask King Yeshua if my earthly parents are alive here somewhere? There are hundreds of millions of Kadoshim either inside of, or surrounding, the Temple as you well know. I haven't been able to locate them yet, if they're actually here. I'm not really certain they gave their lives to the Lord, but they told me when we were last able to speak on the phone a couple years ago that they were planning to take my advice to visit a nearby Messianic synagogue in southern California, where they lived. Their names are Ariel and Esther Hazan."

"Certainly, let me write down those names. I'll gladly let you know, Sarah. Godspeed with your hospital visit!"

Sarah and Shoshel eagerly informed the thrilled circle of saints about the new royal managerial positions they'd just accepted. Shoshel also explained her new name to them. Then Sarah told the other Goldmans that Prince David would inform them when he had any tangible news about Jonathan's twin brother.

After another half hour of conversation, Betty Preston pulled Sarah and Tali aside to ask them an important question which had been burning in her heart since she first heard about the Bernstein twins the day before. "I'm sure you'll both remember I told you Ken and I had our own identical twin girls in the United States?"

Sarah and Tali nodded affirmatively before Sarah added, "I recall you said they were in a terrible car accident because the boyfriend of one of them was driving drunk in North Carolina, where you all then lived. He was instantly killed, along with one of your daughters. The other twin, riding in the back seat with her boyfriend, was badly injured, but survived. I think you said they were only 16 when that tragedy took place."

"Yes, that's exactly correct Sarah. Well, I've been searching all around here for our surviving daughter, who would be 24 now in natural terms, but I strongly doubt she's here. She was very rebellious against my Christian faith, like her father had been. Ken now blames himself for that fact. I say all of this because it would mean *so much* to both of us if you'd allow me to help raise the Bernstein girls. It would bring tremendous healing to us both, especially to me."

"Oh Betty, that would be a major answer to our prayers!" Sarah exclaimed as she gave her friend a loving squeeze. "I told Tali yesterday that she'd need some other assistance to raise the girls since the Holy Spirit had already shown me I'd be offered an important medical position here, which as you know has now been confirmed. Your participation in raising the girls would be perfect for her!"

Tali concurred, admitting that, "I really don't know much about raising children, Betty, since I was only just a girl myself when I received my new glorified body; not much older than they are now. So your help and advice would be a real asset for sure!"

"Well it is set then," pronounced Sarah. "You can accompany us up to the hospital to meet the twins later this morning."

Soon after the three friends returned to the larger circle, Eli Ben David approached them all. He stood opposite Abe and Rebecca Goldman. "I've just received some important news from the Prince about your son David."

The former married couple braced themselves in case the news was bad. Then Eli smiled. "He is indeed alive and here in the Temple, and you won't *believe* what he's doing!"

Shouts of joy filled their portion of the sacred sanctuary as Jonathan warmly embraced his parents and grandfather

"So, what's David doing, Uncle Eli?" enquired the ever-curious Benny after joyously leaping up and down yet again.

"I'll let him tell you that…he should be here fairly soon."

A chorus of hallelujahs rose to the Temples vaulted ceilings.

Then Eli slowly strolled over a few paces to where Sarah was standing. He did not relish this next announcement. The change in his expression was abrupt, and immediately caught everyone's attention.

"Sarah, I'm afraid I must inform you I have sad news about your parents. King Yeshua told Prince David that they're not among the saints here in Jerusalem, sweetheart. I'm really sorry."

Jonathan moved closer to Sarah in order to comfort his earthly wife. Tali and Benny embraced their gently weeping mother as well. Her transformed children were quite distraught themselves. As ecstatic as they still were over the surprise appearance of the three older Goldmans just one day before and the revelation that Jonathan's twin brother was also with them in glory, they would apparently only have one set of grandparents around during the Lord's millennial reign. It stung them hard to realize that the other pair would be banished from the Majestic King's glorious presence forever.

SEVEN

The Hills Are Alive

Sarah Goldman wept quietly for nearly five minutes before the pain sparked by the news that her beloved parents were not among the Kadoshim was fully washed away. She'd felt in her spirit that Ari and Esther Hazan *had* accepted Yeshua as their Lord and Savior, even if their daughter Donna remained doggedly rebellious against Israel's conquering Messiah. After Sarah's grief was eliminated, she and Jonathan returned to the circle of friends, who were all eagerly anticipating the imminent arrival of Jonathan's twin brother.

A smiling saint whom Sarah did not recognize was standing close to Shoshel. He had apparently joined the brethren while she was weeping several yards away in Jonathan's arms.

Shoshel Pearlman was literally glowing. "Sarah and Jonathan, I'd like you to meet my father, Amos. He's been celebrating in the Temple courtyard with some friends from his old Manhattan synagogue who came to know the Lord during the great tribulation, as he did."

Sarah already knew that Shoshel's father, who'd managed a bank on Wall Street for many years, was among the Kadoshim, and she was looking forward to meeting him.

Still, she felt a tinge of jealousy when Shoshel introduced her father, coming so soon after Eli delivered his distressing news about her own parents. However given that her emotional pain was already washed away, Sarah felt increasing joy for her longtime best friend, prompting her to clap her hands in delight before embracing Shoshel and eagerly shaking her father's outstretched hand.

113

After warm greetings were exchanged with Amos Pearlman by all of the assembled saints, Sarah explained to Jonathan how Shoshel and her father had been martyred by the demons who served Emperor Andre, the Antichrist. "I was in New York City with Eli, Craig, Yoseph and Cindy, and of course with Yochanan and Natan-el as well. We were ministering over a period of several days in Central Park, where some Android gang members attempted to assault us. Shoshel had left Israel some time before in the American government's secret evacuation of US citizens, in order to be with her elderly father who was quite ill. After we got to Manhattan, she told me on the phone she'd somehow managed to avoid Andre's forces since arriving in the city."

"I stayed inside dad's apartment as much as I possibly could," Shoshel interjected.

Sarah continued relating her difficult story. "Jonathan, we were all really looking forward to seeing Stacy again, especially me, and had planned a reunion at a restaurant near Wall Street. She didn't show up, and I just knew something was wrong. Yochanan later told me the Lord showed him precisely what happened. A group of Androids broke into the Pearlman's apartment and arrested Stacy and Amos. They were taken to a nearby church that had been converted into an Android center, and ordered to bow down and worship before Andre's demonic nude statue. They both refused, and a column of fire poured out of the statue's mouth. The flames instantly killed them. It was such a blow to me, Jonathan, coming so soon after your death, but now they're both here with us, alive forevermore!"

As Sarah was speaking, Eli went to search for David Goldman in order to help him find his family and their friends in the midst of the thousands of saints swirling around in celebration on the Temple floor.

Soon after Sarah finished her moving story, Yoseph Steinberg pulled Amos aside to ask him an important question. Given his strong financial background, would he be willing to serve as Yoseph's Finance Minister in the province of New York City? The experienced banker immediately answered in the affirmative. The newly-appointed provincial governor then asked him if he knew of any other suitable candidates for several positions he still needed to fill (this came after

Yoseph realized that his friend Eli had already recruited a number of eligible candidates from his former Beit Yisrael congregation for his Greek Isles province).

"It's interesting you ask me that just now, Yoseph. I ran into an old friend only this morning that I believe would make a great Housing and Construction Minister. His name is Leo Scarcelli. He was the CEO of a large construction company his father founded, based in western Connecticut. They built business skyscrapers and apartment buildings all over Manhattan. I got to know him when his company put up a new headquarters building for the bank I managed in the early 1980s."

"He sounds like a real possibility, Amos. Since you spent all your life in the city, while I lived here in Israel for over 35 years, does any other New Yorker come to mind for the position of Transport Minister? It's a vital job in a place like New York, which will need bridges and tunnels rebuilt and mass transit for the human residents, so I prefer someone who already knows the area well. I'm also looking for a good Health Minister; preferably also someone from New York City or nearby parts of New Jersey.

"Interesting timing again, Yoseph. Leo's father-in-law, who was with him when we met this morning, told me he worked for many years as a district manager for New Jersey Transit, which I'm sure you'll recall ran a network of trains and buses throughout the state. He was responsible for the Newark district just across from Manhattan. His name is Giuseppe Marino. I also met Leo's earthly wife this morning. Her name is Teresa. I remember he told me some years ago that before they got married, she briefly managed the ER at the Beth Israel Medical Center in Newark. I could arrange for you to meet all three of them if you like."

"That would be great!" proclaimed Yoseph before Amos moved away to inform Shoshel about his exciting new appointment. The former actress was elated for her earthly father.

Soon the redeemed believers spotted Eli Ben David approaching with a handsome companion in tow.

"Look abba! He's almost a carbon copy of you!" gushed Tali as the two saints drew near. Like his twin brother Jonathan, David Goldman possessed short dark brown wavy hair and perfectly rounded eyebrows framing deep-set turquoise eyes. His face featured high cheek bones set above slight dimples. A four day old growth of coffee-brown hair sprouted above his lips and on his square chin. An eighteen-inch neck with a prominent Adam's apple connected his head to his broad shoulders and muscular body. However his white silk robe was markedly different from Jonathan's. It featured dozens of six-inch menorahs made out of golden threads stitched along the hems of the sleeves and gown. Small silver bells, alternating with golden pomegranates, hung from the bottom hem just above his calves. Like all of the Kadoshim, his footwear was a pair of sandals.

"My brother Jonathan!" cried David Goldman when he spotted the saint that was obviously his twin. As deep emotions erupted simultaneously inside both brothers, they embraced with gusto and then kissed each other's respective foreheads.

"I didn't even know that you existed this time yesterday morning, David," revealed Jonathan as tears of joy flooded his sparkling eyes.

"I knew about you, my brother. King Yeshua revealed that information to me after I appeared before His heavenly throne soon after we were born in America some four decades ago."

David loosened his hold on Jonathan and slowly looked around at the other gathered Kadoshim. It took only a second to guess which ones were his earthly parents. Free-flowing tears of joy gave them away.

"Son, I am your father Abraham, and this is your mother Rebecca." David said nothing as he enfolded his earthly parents in his long arms. Despite being constantly in the hallowed presence of his wonderful Savior, he had nevertheless longed for this day for nearly forty years. All three were overwhelmed with God's goodness.

After giving the long-separated parents and prematurely-born son a few minutes to speak privately, Jonathan introduced Sarah to David, who greeted him enthusiastically. Then he said, "Brother David, meet your niece Tali, and your nephew Benny, who is named after our grandfather, Rabbi Benjamin Goldman, standing right over there." This news took a few seconds to digest. Eli had deliberately not told David that he had a nephew and niece, or that his grandfather was among the Kadoshim, wishing to surprise him. It worked.

"Tali and Benny! How absolutely fantastic to meet you! And Granddad Goldman! I did not know *any* of you were here in the Temple, or that I even *had* a nephew and niece." All three embraced David at once, who felt like he had died again and gone back to heaven. As the eighth day of Hanukkah approached at sunset, the eight Goldmans lovingly stood together in the sacred Temple as Rabbi Benjamin noted that eight is the Hebrew number symbolizing wholeness and completion.

Jonathan introduced the rest of the gathered Kadoshim one by one, noting in particular that Yoseph had been his pastor in Jerusalem, and that Yochanan was the Lord's beloved Apostle who held the role of one of the two end-time witnesses that he himself had written about in his book of Revelation. Then Jonathan informed his twin brother that he and Eli had searched for him the evening before, standing for over an hour near the spiraling columns of celebrating infants—all of course now in youthful adult bodies—which Prince David had spoken of. "We thought we could locate you, David, assuming you probably looked quite similar to me, and indeed you do. Still, we didn't succeed in identifying you."

Yochanan then revealed that he'd actually spotted the tall saint the day before while David was practicing lighting a candle. "He was clearly your twin brother Jonathan, but I didn't say anything to you. I thought I'd let him tell you what he was doing and why."

Jonathan's new-found brother then revealed his tremendous calling to his extended family and new friends. "You and Eli didn't spot me because I wasn't in any of those spiraling columns. I was lying prostrate with a large group of former Jewish male babies who are at this moment still surrounding the platform where the Sovereign Lord is seated on His majestic throne. All of us had either been aborted, were stillborn, or we'd died as babies under the age of two. You see, Yeshua had told us in Glory that we'd form a special priestly branch after His triumphant return to Jerusalem. He revealed that because we only possessed the original sin of Adam which all humans inherit at the

117

moment of conception, and no further sin of our own, we'd actually be the purest redeemed priests serving in His Holy Temple. We will serve the King of Glory night and day in the sacred sanctuary. It's a most holy calling."

Benny was trying hard to control his bubbling joy, but it burst forth anyway. He began to clap his hands almost hysterically as he giggled with delight. The other Goldmans and their brethren were simply in awe, although Jonathan was also wondering how his brother's news might affect something which occurred in California during his former human life. It had been tremendously traumatic to endure at the time, and still hung like a decaying skeleton in his mental closet. Finally Benny calmed down somewhat as his newly discovered uncle continued to speak.

"And there's more. I was told by an angel last Shabbat, the morning after we all touched down with the Lord on the Mount of Olives, that King Yeshua had chosen me to head up the division in charge of keeping the sacred flames lit on the Golden Menorah that will appear in the transformed Temple tonight. Every evening before sundown over the next thousand years, I am to make sure that seven members of our band—and our numbers are quite substantial—are appointed and ready to ceremonially rekindle the flames before the Son of David makes His evening entrance to be seated afresh upon His exalted throne. It's a great honor indeed to be asked to carry out such a sacred task."

Now even Benny was too awed to react. Yochanan stepped up and congratulated David Goldman on behalf of all who were gathered there. Then, with a glint in his eye, he patted him on his broad back and said, "Tell them about your role tonight."

Jonathan's twin brother bowed his head in genuine humility as light tears appeared in his beautiful eyes. Here was a saint asked to perform such a solemn action whose earthly father had barely escaped Hitler's hateful clutches as a boy in Nazi Germany, whose grandmother had perished in a synagogue fire on Kristallnacht, whose grandfather had been gassed to death at Auschwitz, and whose twin brother had met a similar end via a Syrian gas attack. All of these terrible things had been revealed and explained to David in heaven during a very tender time of sharing with the Lord while seated next to Him on His illustrious throne—the only Father that David Goldman had ever known.

"I was told by His Majesty, King Yeshua, that He wished for me to light the eighth candle of Hanukkah this evening, signaling the onset of Shabbat and of the last day of this joyous Festival of Light. It's a tremendous honor indeed."

Benny went back to jumping up and down with joy. His great-grandfather soon joined him, followed by Abe, Rebecca, Jonathan and Tali Goldman. Seconds later, all of the brethren were leaping like deer as they rejoiced ecstatically in the immeasurable goodness of their beloved Redeemer and Lord.

One hour later, Tali was ponderously making her way east across the new stone footbridge that connected the Temple Mount with the Mount of Olives. Sarah, Benny and Micah accompanied her, along with Shoshel and Betty. Sarah and Tali stopped halfway to quietly discuss how they might best break the news of Dafna Bernstein's death to her newly-orphaned daughters. They began their deliberation after the other four saints halted midway to gaze at the cascading Thunder Falls just to the south. Mist rising up from the crashing, healing waters 600 feet below formed a continuous soothing facial bath for anyone traversing the bridge.

Ten minutes later, they arrived at the Augusta Victoria hospital. "Shalom girls, have you been resting and eating well?" enquired Tali cheerfully as she greeted the young twins, who were now connected to IV drips. The doctors had determined the previous evening that the two young sisters were more dehydrated than they'd earlier suspected.

"Hi Tali," said Dalya as she threw out her arms to receive her new friend's warm embrace. Sarah and Shoshel followed with their own hugs as Tali moved on to greet Daniyella. The others watched in silence.

"Sweethearts, I want you to meet my brother Benny, and this is his best friend Micah, who picked you up the other day, Daniyella, when you and Dalya were rescued. You already met Stacy, now called Shoshel, who was also there with Benny and Micah, and this is our

119

dear friend Betty." The four Kadoshim issued their own greetings as the children welcomed them with toothy smiles.

Micah then spoke up. "Girls, do you remember the student in your mother's class last year with thick glasses and teeth like this?" He thrust out two fingers from his ruby lips.

"Do you mean the boy who helped us paint that picture of the school building? Ima thought it was wonderful, and she put it on our 'frigerator' door," stated Dalya, as Daniyella added factually, "His name was Micah, just like you."

"Well little bunny rabbits, that actually *was* me! I grew up really quickly."

"Huh?" they both uttered in perfect synchronization.

"Lovely ones, I'll explain that to you very soon after you're released from hospital," promised Tali.

"Okay," they both replied with the innocence of young children, apparently satisfied with this answer.

Tali gently tugged Betty a bit closer to their reclining beds. "Dalya and Daniyella, Betty here had twin girls just like you in America. She's going to help us take care of you in our home here in Jerusalem." Sarah and Tali had thought this was the gentlest way possible to introduce the difficult subject at hand.

"Oh that's nice," said Daniyella, before adding "But what about Ima?"

Standing between their two beds, Tali reached out and took hold of their small hands. "Dear ones, we learned from the authorities yesterday that your special Ima was killed in an earthquake. So she won't be able to raise you, I'm really sorry to say. She was my favorite teacher; and Micah's too. We both really loved her, like you do."

The girls were remarkably calm, apparently old enough to have already concluded their mother was probably gone. Each began to weep softly as the Kadoshim surrounded them to minister comfort and love as best they could. Sarah was instantly reminded that her mother and father were dead as well, but somehow she could now ponder that reality without the previous gut-wrenching pangs of sorrow. Still, she knew she had to break the news to her sister Donna, and was not looking forward to that task.

After several minutes of tears, Dalya wiped her eyes and then startled the saints with her comment. "Did we tell you that a tiny angel visited us when we were stuck under that wall?"

"A tiny angel?" replied Tali with a gargantuan question mark in her voice.

"Yes, he was only *this* tall." Daniyella showed a length of no more than two feet between her outstretched arms, which was challenging the IV line above her left wrist.

Dalya added more details. "He suddenly appeared soon after the wall fell down on us. He said his name was Michael, and that he was an angel who helped the Jewish people. He brought us some bananas. We hadn't had any for a real long time."

The girls both giggled as Tali and Micah glanced at each other. When they helped rescue the twins, they'd noticed some rotting banana peels lying next to their prone bodies.

"He picked the bananas up one at a time from a big pile he brought with him and dropped them near our trapped hands," added Daniyella. "They were almost bigger than he was!" The tickled twins giggled again at the humorous memory.

Dalya added additional details as her mood continued to brighten. "There was no room for us to stand up or move under that wall, so he carried the bananas over to us. He had these cute little wings! Then he filled our water bottles—we're not sure how—and told us to sip them real slowly since the water had to last a few days. He said we should only eat one banana each morning after we saw the sun had woken up. Then he disappeared. He was really sweet."

The Kadoshim smiled at each other as they again inwardly rejoiced at the goodness and mercy of their God.

Just then, Prince David unexpectedly popped his head in the door, accompanied by Head Nurse Leah Rabinowitz and two other Holy Ones.

"Shalom brethren, may we come in and say hello to the twins?"

"Of course Prince David," answered Sarah, glad to notice Yochanan right behind him along with one other saint she didn't know.

Sarah quickly introduced Israel's new governor and Yochanan to the girls, deciding she would leave out the details of their biblical backgrounds and current roles for the time being. Then Prince David introduced his dear friend, Yonatan, to the Kadoshim and the twins before explaining to Sarah and Shoshel that he was touring Yochanan around different parts of the capital city, adding that King Yeshua had asked His beloved Apostle to act as His liaison with Prince David, among other things. "And guess what else the Master said," interjected Yochanan with a broad smile. "He's invited me to live in His new palace, which will appear not far from here this evening. Several other redeemed saints will reside there as well, including His mother Miriyam."

"Oh that is more than marvelous, Yochanan," Sarah cried with sheer delight. "Can we visit quite often?"

"Of course!" the great Apostle replied as he winked at young Benny.

Sarah had been studying Yochanan's face as he spoke. She still could not fully accept that this very handsome, youthful saint before her was the elderly, sackcloth-wearing prophet that she and her children and friends had ministered with not so long before. Yochanan's formerly long gray hair and beard were now jet black. His glowing eyes, always soft and tender, were now a sharper shade of their original amber brown. He wore a shimmering silk robe embroidered with alternating golden lambs and lions. His voice had always been resonant and strong, but now it seemed to have an extra layer of richness to it.

Shoshel—whose own appearance was lovely like Sarah's, each with radiant faces set off well by flowing silk robes embroidered with red roses and apples—was busy examining Yonatan and Prince David. A bit taller than his companions, she noticed that King Saul's son had reddish highlights in his auburn colored hair, as did Prince David, although his hair was a tad darker. Both sported short beards whose colors matched their hair. David's eyes were also darker than his dear friend's, although each revealed hints of burgundy streaks mixed in with brown. Muscle-bound with strong straight backs, Shoshel thought both David and Yonatan held themselves in a manner quite befitting for royalty. She especially loved the golden-thread embroideries around the hem of Prince David's sleeves and lower robe. They pictured smiling sheep sitting on their rumps while happily playing harps with their front hoofs.

The dignitaries soon exited the hospital room, needing to get back to the Holy Temple. The other saints then issued goodbyes to the twin girls and headed for Donna's nearby room. However Sarah decided to stay behind a few minutes to talk with Leah Rabinowitz. She asked her if she would head up the Pediatrics Department at the new Hadassah Hospital, and the former Texan replied she'd gladly do so. Leah added that Prince David just informed her anyway that the Augusta Victoria building would no longer serve as a medical facility after three fully-equipped area hospitals began operating soon after the end of Shabbat.

Sarah realized that she was stalling for time. How would Donna react to her news? It was time to find out.

"Shalom sister, how are you today?" enquired Sarah brightly as she entered Donna's small room. The other standing saints cleared a path for Sarah to reach the recovering patient and greet her with a kiss on her forehead.

"I'm so much better, Sarah, I can hardly believe it. Thanks for bringing me here folks. I'm pretty sure I was nearing the end of the road at our destroyed house, least that's what the doctor told me. But that natural herbal medicine they're giving me is simply wonderful! It's the same thing you put in my coffee, Sarah, very effective!"

"There's even more to it than that, Donna, but I'll tell you the details after you're released from here."

"Aunt Donna, we brought you a Hanukkah present," announced Tali as she reached into the cloth bag hanging from her golden sash, pulling out an eight-branched silver Hanukkiah and eight candles.

"Oh that's really lovely Tali, thanks so much! I'll light it at sunset."

"Our dad's brother David is going to light the one in the Temple fairly soon," Benny casually revealed without any elaboration as his eyes danced with glee.

"What?" Donna nearly dropped her gift on the tiled floor.

Sarah grabbed hold of her sister's right hand. "Jonathan has a twin brother named David, and he showed up to meet us all today. David died right after their birth in Illinois, and Jonathan's parents decided not to tell him about it. He met us all today after his grandfather Benjamin, who as you know perished at Auschwitz, appeared with my friend Yitzhak, and that was right after Jonathan's parents showed up."

"Jonathan's parents and grandfather and brother all turned up? What in the world is going on Sarah?"

"Well, it's actually happening in the re-born world, Donna. It's quite a long story, honey. I'll relate it to you next time I visit. We need to head back to the Temple for the onset of the Sabbath. As Benny noted, Jonathan's brother has been asked to light the final candle of Hanukkah and we don't want to miss that ceremony."

Sarah turned to her companions and asked them to wait for her in the hall. After goodbyes were exchanged, she told her sister the news that their parents were apparently deceased. Not really expecting to ever see them again, given all the upheaval that had recently rocked the earth, Donna Hazan-Svenson took Sarah's news in stride, failing to shed even one tear. Somewhat put off by her rather cold reaction, Sarah said her own farewell after promising to return as soon as possible.

When the hospital visitors arrived back at the Jerusalem Temple, they found their brethren in animated conversation about what might occur that evening. The hints dropped by Prince David, Yochanan and David Goldman, not to mention the earlier comments by King Yeshua, had ignited everyone's imaginations. All realized that a very special evening was about to begin.

Within ten minutes of their return, a chorus of trumpets sounded. It was time for the Sovereign Lord to speak. The Kadoshim inside the Temple and those out in the courtyard immediately prostrated themselves as Yeshua the Messiah slowly rose up from His throne. The millions of Holy Ones wafting in the air around and above the sacred sanctuary reverently bowed their heads.

"Shalom to all My precious children! This week of hallowed celebration has been a time of great blessing to Me, as it has also apparently been for each of you as well. This evening we will enjoy our first
Shabbat meal together. It will be similar to the wedding feast that we
shared last week in the clouds before our descent to this Holy City. As
occurred then, tables will appear filled with sumptuous food, some of
them in the Temple itself and many others surrounding it on the outer
courts and in the air. You will each know where your assigned seats are
located."

The Word of Life stepped forward several paces in the direction
of the large Hanukkiah resting in front of the platform to the left of
His throne. "However before that wonderful feast takes place, we will
light the eighth and final candle of Hanukkah, and this Holy
Temple—defiled by the devil in the form of his Antichrist—will then
be officially rededicated to the Father of Lights, for whom there is no
turning or shifting shadow. Do not be disturbed at what will take place
immediately afterwards, my beloved sheep. This hallowed hall has
been cleansed, yet it was still constructed by Satan himself through the
aegis of his Man of Sin. A new Holy Temple will be formed out of the
atomic energy in these walls and ceiling, along with other energy
poured out by our Eternal Father from the heavens. Your new homes
and other buildings will appear soon afterwards, along with My
glorious palace up on the Mount of Olives. Another palatial home,
this one housing Israel's new provincial governor, Prince David, will
appear near the southeast base of this Temple Mount, where King
David's original palace stood in ancient days."

Joyous anticipation glistened from every eye. The saints of all the
ages were together forever with their Good Shepherd, the Lover of
their Souls.

"I have still more to tell you, my dear lambs. The Shenikah Glory
of the Father will return this very evening to this, His resting place on
earth. His brilliant enduring light will shine day and night from this
very spot upon the City of Elohi—-the footstool resting place for Our
feet!"

Exhilarated gasps of joy sprang from the lips of the Kadoshim
before the Sovereign Lord resumed His message.

"And now, lift up your heads as My dear son and Temple priest, David Goldman, kindles the eighth candle of Hanukkah."

The Kadoshim on the Temple floor and those lying face down in the outer courtyard all rose to their feet. The circle of friends had been positioned by Yochanan just in front of the large golden Hanukkiah so they could be close to David as he performed his sacred task.

All Goldman family faces radiantly beamed as their close relative strolled solemnly to the front of the Hanukkiah. Rabbi Benjamin Goldman was especially moved when he saw that his earthly grandson was wearing a beautiful Jewish prayer shawl with the name YESHUA embroidered in Hebrew around the collar. He had not seen even one prayer shawl since before his incarceration at Auschwitz. Now he watched with awe and wonder as his glorified grandson prepared to light the eighth candle of Hanukkah inside the sacred Temple in Jerusalem.

David Goldman reverently approached a silver stepladder positioned directly in front of the middle *shamesh* candle used to light the next additional Hanukkiah light at sunset during each evening of the eight-day Jewish festival. He carefully lifted it out of its holder and descended back down the small stepladder before moving quickly to an identical ladder placed in front of the eighth unlit candle.

After ascending the four steps, the honored saint touched the shamesh wick to the flickering seventh candle. Then he lit the eighth candle as the Lord pronounced a sacred blessing over the glistening lights. A shout of joy, which collectively sounded like mighty rushing water, burst forth out of every saint's mouth. Millions of angels rejoiced in the heavens above.

Then it began. Myriad trumpets sounded again, signaling the onset of the weekly Shabbat and the final day of the sacred festival. Suddenly the walls and ceiling of the Holy Temple started to burn with a glowing red light. The atomic particles forming them were swirling about like whirling dervishes. The existing sanctuary was instantly dissolved as its kinetic particles rushed to their new pre-assigned locations. Two fiery columns of energized atoms poured out of the sky, mixing like cement with the ones already assuming their new positions.

Within half a minute, the nascent Holy Temple was formed. It was ten times wider on the ground, and twenty times higher than the sanctuary the Lord and His Kadoshim had just been celebrating in. It would accommodate far more worshippers at any one time.

The reconstructed Holy Temple was similar to its predecessor in that it was made entirely of marble, and box like in overall appearance, with straight walls and a flat roof.

However the saints in the air above could immediately see that it was formed in the shape of a large cross similar to the medieval cathedrals of Europe. At the center crossing on the marble roof sat a glistening gold-covered dome 200 feet in diameter at its base. Rising nearly 100 feet into the air, it was viewable from all over Jerusalem. Directly underneath the towering dome, the central crossing became the new Holy of Holies where the Lord's hallowed blue throne was instantly situated on an elevated *bema*, or platform.

The reconstituted Holy Temple ran north and south along the entire length of the Temple Mount. At the northern end was the Apse, the area equivalent to the top of a cross where the Temple priests and sacred choirs would be positioned. At the eastern end was the Sunrise Transept, equivalent to the right side of the lateral cross bar. Running from the central crossing to the western edge of the Temple Mount was the Sunset Transept. The upper walls of the two transepts contained the only exterior openings in the renewed Holy Temple, featuring two large, perfectly round stained-glass windows that would let in shafts of the morning and evening sun. Four weeks out of each year, two in early spring and two in early autumn, the brilliant shafts of sunlight would fall directly onto the Lord's sublime throne.

Two-thirds of the space inside the new Holy Temple was taken up by the Nave, which ran horizontally from the central Holy of Holies all the way to the south Temple wall, which abutted the southern border of the Temple Mount. Two massive cedarwood doors were positioned like giant sentries on that end of the new sanctuary. Saints exiting the Temple could easily see all the way south to Bethlehem from the new passageway. The thick stained doors, featuring dangling golden handles inside and out, opened up to a long set of exquisite marble stairs which descended through a new opening in the Temple

Mount's southern wall. The broad stairs sloped gently down to the original City of David just below the sacred mount, where the Prince's new provincial palace would soon appear. The stairs were positioned directly over the ancient stone steps used by the Jewish priests to enter Solomon's Temple, ascending as they sang and recited the psalms. The same practice would begin again the following evening, with thousands of King Yeshua's priests parading up to the new Holy Temple each afternoon from then on, beginning exactly at 4:00 PM.

Seconds after the reconstructed Holy Temple was complete, a river of energized particles cascaded down onto the nearby Mount of Olives, rapidly forming the new palace for the eternally reigning King of Kings. As the energy made its initial contact with the ground, it instantly melted the damaged Ascension Tower, incorporating its atomic particles into the new palace. With an appearance somewhat similar to the American White House, but made out of marble, the palace's center-point was positioned directly over the spot where the tower had stood. The grand four-floor structure had two wings on the north and south where various royal offices would be located. The splendid front entrance faced west toward the Temple Mount.

The Lord's private chambers would occupy most of the top floor, with a large balcony on the western side overlooking the majestic new Temple enabling a clear view of Thunder Falls and the beginning of the Nahar Cha'im river that flowed from it. A large balcony on the eastern side afforded a fantastic long view of the river as it descended down the hills of Judea and then into the Jordan Valley ten miles away before emptying into the Yam Cha'im sea. The hills that rise east of the Jordan River were also easily visible. The former country of Jordan above the valley was now part of the Holy Land ruled by Prince David, as foretold in several sections of the Hebrew Bible. The southern portion of Lebanon, much of Syria and most of the Sinai Peninsula were also now within the land's formal boundaries, as was the western section of Iraq up to the Euphrates River.

The millennial sunrises would be spectacular from the eastern side of the new royal palace, with the golden sunsets equally breathtaking from the west. Yochanan would have a private chamber on the north side of the top floor, with a spacious balcony jutting out over the north office wing below it. The balcony offered a clear view of the head of the Nahar Yehuda river that flowed out from the northeast corner of the Temple Mount before rushing west down the Judean hills toward the Mediterranean Sea.

The Risen Messiah's private office would be located on the south side of the top floor, featuring another expansive balcony positioned over the south wing facing in the direction of Bethlehem and Hebron. The Sovereign Lord's public office would be on the second floor opposite the Temple Mount, along with other government offices, including one designated for Yochanan. The main floor featured a spacious dining hall with scenic pictures gracing solid oak walls. Towering rectangular windows faced the Temple Mount, framed by gold-threaded silk curtains. Elegant crystal chandeliers hung from the ornate high ceiling. A beautiful 15 foot high fireplace was centered on the east side of the hall with a marble mantle above it. Two doors on either side of the fireplace led into an adjacent large kitchen and other work rooms, plus restroom facilities for human guests. A large sitting room occupied the southern third of the main floor, designed for guests to rest in before entering the dining area, or before ascending a flight of curved cedar stairs that rose up inside the front foyer to the public offices on the second floor.

Three large apartments were situated on the third floor. Each had two separate bedroom chambers located next to each other on the east side of the palace featuring adjacent private offices and restroom facilities. The apartments each contained a private kitchen with an adjoining small dining room. The living rooms featured built-in fireplaces and large picture windows facing the Temple Mount. The bedrooms had comfortable beds in them, even though the Holy Ones no longer needed to sleep, or even to rest. However if they wanted to do so, in order to dream, pray, relax, or just to have some quiet time alone, they were able to do so.

Restrooms in all of the Kadoshim sections of the royal palace contained a large Jacuzzi, a spacious shower and a marble sink with a magnificent mirror positioned above it. However there were no toilets in them since the new heavenly spiritual bodies the saints possessed didn't need to process liquids or solid foods in the former earthly manner. The Kadoshim could and would eat and drink at times, but they no longer needed to do that in order to survive. Blood no longer carried nutrients and waste to and from the various organs in the body. In fact, the resurrected bodies had no blood in them at all; and only one internal organ. They still had hearts, which did not beat anymore but instead acted as the seat of all emotions and memory. Bathing was strictly for pleasure. It was no longer mostly designed to rid the skin of sweat residue, since the glorified bodies did not feature that need or function anymore.

The southernmost third floor apartment would belong to the Lord's earthly brother Ya'acov, known in English as James, residing with his father Yoseph. Along with Yochanan, they would act as senior aids to King Yeshua as He governed the restored world. The central apartment housed Shimon Kefa, Simon Peter in English, along with fellow Apostle Shaul, who was also called Paul. Shimon Kefa would also become a top aid to the King of Kings while Shaul would serve as Yeshua's Foreign Minister, meaning he would be gone many nights.

The northern apartment, which was slightly larger than the other two, belonged to Miriyam, the Lord's earthly mother, who would oversee all official functions at the palace. She had a large private office and bedroom chamber with a similar view to that of Yochanan's quarters just above her own. Sharing the living room and kitchen spaces with her would be another Miriyam, the sister of Marta, who ministered greatly to the Lord during His human sojourn.

As soon as King Yeshua's palace was completed, the two columns of atomic energy glided slightly to the southwest where they began pouring down onto David's City, producing an instant palace for Israel's new Governor-Prince. It was a smaller version of the royal palace perched up above it on the Mount of Olives. Prince David's private chambers would be on the top floor facing north, with a peaceful view of the Temple Mount just above and of the Nahar Cha'im that flowed down between its verdant banks not far from the palace. David's dear earthly friend Yonatan, King Saul's son, would inhabit the southern third of the floor. Other biblical figures including David's son Solomon, Natan-el, the lawgiver Moshe, King Yeshua's cousin Yochanan Ha Matbil (John the Immerser), Elijah, Avraham,

Yitzhak and Ya'acov, and several ancient Israeli kings and queens including Batsheva, would reside on the two floors below Prince David's chambers. Most would be serving on King Yeshua's new 24 member council, sharing their opinions and thoughts with David's Greater Son. Shoshel and Sarah would have assigned administrative offices on the northern end of the palace complex, which contained two office wings similar to the Lord's royal palace on the Mount of Olives just above it. Their office windows faced west toward the glistening new marble stairs leading up to the Temple Mount.

After the princely palace was formed by the creative hand of the Almighty, dozens of shafts of radiating energy began to pour out of the sky all over the expanded Promised Land. They formed millions of single dwelling homes, townhouses, apartment towers, school and medical facilities, and many other buildings in every portion of the land. Public parks with lush lawns and vegetation surrounding swimming pools and other recreational facilities instantaneously appeared amid the new buildings, as springs of living water burst to the surface all over the land. Small streams and lakes formed everywhere. The Kadoshim hovering in the air around the Holy Temple marveled as they watched this awesome creative procedure in the fading western twilight, as they'd done moments before when the reconstituted Temple and the two royal palaces swiftly appeared. A new day had dawned in the Lord's special Holy City and Holy Land, a unique day like none other before it.

EIGHT

SHEKINAH GLORY

Wrapped in utter astonishment, the excited Kadoshim eagerly examined the majestic Holy Temple that the Father of Lights had just graciously gifted to His redeemed children. As was the case in the previous sanctuary, the thick marble ceiling and walls were completely translucent to the eyes of all who were gazing from outside, allowing them a clear view of the magnificent interior and of the Eternal King seated upon His majestic throne.

Seconds after the Creator of the Universe completed the homes and other new buildings stretching from the Sinai Peninsula to the Euphrates River, the golden dome perched high over the hallowed sanctuary began to spin around like a top. The scene reminded most of the Jewish Kadoshim of a spinning Hanukkah dreidel. Then the dome sprang open like a huge jack-in-a-box lid attached to a hinge. The stunned Holy Ones watched the unexpected action with hushed anticipation.

The Shekinah fire of their loving Father God began to descend from the evening sky like a speeding train. The flaming column soon entered into the nascent Temple. Like the ancient glowing pillar of fire that led Moses and the children of Israel through their desert exodus from Egypt, the blazing spiral of flames lit up the sky for hundreds of miles all around. The pillar appeared to the Kadoshim to be comprised of millions of thin fiery strands whizzing about in a sacred celestial dance, weaving in and out and swirling about all at the same time. It was an amazing and glorious sight to behold.

The front end of the fiery column, about twelve feet in diameter, soon landed on a fifteen-foot round fire pan made out of pure gold that had appeared just to the front-left of Yeshua's lapis lazuli throne during the Temple transformation. When the Holy Fire reached the pan, the golden dome immediately returned to its closed position. The spinning column of brilliant light stretched down from the inside center of the dome to the glowing fire pan below. The Shekinah presence would remain in that exhilarating position for 1,000 years before being spread out to illuminate the New Jerusalem which the Bible foretold would descend from heaven after the final Great White Throne judgment.

Only the Kadoshim would be allowed into the newly formed Holy Temple. The iridescent Shekinah light would instantly blind any human eye that might inadvertently look upon it. Beyond that, no flesh—still bearing the original sin of Adam—could survive in the sacred presence of the Eternal Light. The swirling pillar was so incandescent that it literally made the marble walls and ceiling of the Temple shimmer inside and out with an illustrious glow. This would brighten the night sky all over Jerusalem with the intensity of ten full moons, and be visible as well from every part of the expanded Holy Land, which now encompassed the wide dimensions promised by the God of Israel to Abraham before his son Isaac was born.

What happened next is actually impossible to adequately describe in human terms. The inside of the Holy Temple instantly took on the spiritual dimensions of the Third Heaven written about by the Apostle Shaul in Second Corinthians, chapter twelve. In other words, it truly became an inexpressible paradise. Every single saint hovering outside—and their numbers were well over one-billion—instantly found themselves whisked inside the Holy Temple. It was as if they'd suddenly merged into one giant organic Body which filled every inch of the re-born Temple, with the Sovereign Lord, strategically seated at the center of the sanctuary, as its Holy Head. Indeed Shaul, in his indescribable vision, had been caught up in his spirit to this very time and place, as had Yochanan and several other ancient Hebrew prophets before them.

Every day from now on at exactly 5:00 PM Jerusalem time, this same exhilarating spiritual dimension would be experienced by all of the Kadoshim, the Body of Messiah. The glory would last for around two hours until most would depart the hallowed place. However it would be a permanent feature for the hundred-million or so fulltime Temple priests, who would remain night and day inside Immanuel's consecrated sanctuary in a state of utter bliss. When the other redeemed saints were absent, they formed a single organic Body that filled up the entire Apse from the back wall to the towering ceiling and polished marble floor. Many had been murdered by the Antichrist during the Great Tribulation or martyred for their faith in earlier times, while others were unborn or stillborn babies, or children under the age of two. All would remain in this state of utter bliss for 1,000 years.

The perpetual priests were positioned just behind the four-foot-high cedar platform supporting the Lord's majestic blue throne, along with the golden fire pan, a marble altar, and 24 smaller thrones. The eight-branched Hanukkiah sat by itself in front of the platform. It would be replaced after Shabbat ended with the seven-branched golden Temple Menorah. Individual priests could and did emerge out of the larger corporate Body from time to time to perform certain specific functions, as David Goldman would do on a daily basis from now on. They'd also join family and friends for the weekly Shabbat meal. Otherwise the blessed members of the spiritually-merged priestly band would sing unending praises or recite worshipful psalms to the merciful King of Kings.

It is impossible to describe in words the rapturous ecstasy the Kadoshim felt when fully united as one consecrated Body with their Messiah King. What each experienced in their beings was a continuous, euphoric sense of joy far more intense than any earthly pleasure or feeling they'd previously known. This was combined with a constant feeling of overarching awe that they were directly attached to their Head, the King of Glory, and worshipping in the presence of the Heavenly Father's glistening Shekinah fire. Each individual saint literally felt the Chief Cornerstone as if He were their very own head. They'd merged into one celestial spiritual Body with the Lord, and nothing else even remotely compared to it. Truly, the Bridegroom had become one Body and Spirit with His Holy Bride. On top of that, each saint sensed the presence of the other billion plus Kadoshim as an intimate part of their own singular being. It was an awesome, exhilarating and ecstatic experience that would certainly be the towering summit of every day from now on.

Two seconds after the golden dome returned to its closed position, the united Kadoshim began singing magnificent songs of worship and praise as they recognized in their spirits that they now inhabited the Lord's Temple united as one redeemed Body, with Yeshua Himself as their Head. The powerful harmonious voices were entirely beautiful to the ear. The sound of their symphonic singing carried throughout Jerusalem, prompting Donna Svenson, the Bernstein twins and other human beings positioned nearby in the city to listen in captivated wonder.

After two hours of passionate celebration, Israel's Eternal King slowly rose up from His elevated throne. With every eye focused on the Monarch's incandescent face, the Bright Morning Star spoke tenderly to His united servants. As in the book of Genesis, He now employed the royal "We" in His short address to His beloved followers.

"Shabbat shalom, dearest saints of the Most High God! My heavenly Father and I are enraptured by your presence with Us. We are filled with inimitable joy, knowing that We will spend this glorious time with you every single day in this Holy House over the next thousand years. We have loved you with an everlasting love! Therefore We have called you Our friends!"

The Kadoshim responded to the Godhead's limitless love by bursting forth once again in highest praise, melodiously singing in perfect unison the song of Moses and the song of the Lamb: *Great and marvelous are Your works, oh Lord God the Almighty! Just and true are all Your ways, oh King of the Nations! Who will not fear and glorify your Name, oh Lord? For You alone are holy! All the nations will come and worship before You, for Your righteous acts have been revealed!*

When the exhilarating anthem ended, the smiling Lamb of God blew a loving kiss using both of His nail-scarred hands toward the long Nave of the sacred sanctuary, then turned and did the same in the other three directions, finishing with the holy priests in the Apse behind His throne. All hearts were filled with overflowing joy. Then the Word of the Father spoke again.

"We will now begin to share the weekly Shabbat meal together, followed by a night of hallowed celebration. However with the dawn, you will each begin a period of solemn reflection. At noon, you will individually appear before My holy Judgment Seat to review your earthly life. The only exceptions will be miscarried or aborted babies and anyone who did not live beyond their second year. We are righteous to render to each one of you according to what you have done. Now, let the feast begin!"

Thunderous blasts of ceremonial trumpets sounded as most of the Kadoshim again found themselves outside of the vastly-enlarged Temple. Elongated oak tables appeared inside the Temple, in the outer courtyards, and suspended in the air all around and above the sacred sanctuary. White linen table cloths with golden tassels hanging from their four corners covered the tables. Silver candelabra were positioned every ten feet, radiating soft light onto the white bone china plates with gold trimmed rims positioned near tall crystal goblets, which contained succulent red wine. Polished silverware rested on cherry-colored linen napkins. Elegant water and wine crystal decanters and silver serving utensils were centered between the candleholders. Plush lavender velvet-covered chairs were positioned near the tables.

Within seconds, the thrilled Holy Ones were supernaturally stationed behind their assigned seats. At the center of the head table located on the dais in the Holy of Holies was a ten-foot-high royal chair with large white pearls embedded across the top. This is where the King of the Universe would sit. Standing behind their chairs to His left were the twelve Hebrew saints who would serve on the Lord's 24-member ruling council. Positioned next to King Yeshua was Prince David, followed by the three Jewish patriarchs, Abraham, Isaac and Jacob. Next to them were Moses, Elijah, Samuel and Solomon, followed by the prophets Isaiah, Jeremiah, Ezekiel, and finally Daniel. To the Lord's immediate right was the Apostle Yochanan, then his brother Ya'acov, followed by the nine other Apostles who served with Yeshua during His earthly ministry, beginning with Peter, Shimon Kefa. At the very end was Shaul, the self-professed 'least of the Apostles.' Yochanan's earthly mother gasped with delight when she spotted the seating arrangement, satisfied that at least half of her declared wish to see her two sons seated on either side of the Lord's throne had actually come to pass.

Directly across the table from the Lamb of Life were His beloved earthly parents, Yoseph and Miriyam. Standing next to the Jewish couple was the Lord's brother Ya'acov and other siblings, plus his cousin Yochanan the Immerser, his mother Elisheva, Natan-el, Miriyam and her sister Marta, their brother Lazarus, and other Kadoshim including Joshua, the matriarchs Rachel and Leah, Yoseph and his brother Binyamin, Job, King Hezekiah, Devorah, Elisha, Zechariah, Batsheva, Ruth and several others.

The Messiah King lifted His silver chalice into the air, prompting all to raise their crystal goblets as well. Then Yochanan turned to face his Lord as he pronounced the sacred Hebrew blessing over the wine *"Baruch Ata Adonai, Melech ha Olam, boreh pree ha gaffen."* Blessed are You, oh Lord, King of the Universe, who creates the fruit of the vine. All then drank the wine, which no longer had any affect upon their bodies since they could not absorb any alcohol.

Next Prince David picked up a loaf of fresh *challa* bread from a silver platter positioned in front of him on the banquet table. He raised it up as he turned toward his Greater Son. *"Baruch Ata Adonai, Melech ha Olam, ha motzi lechem min ha aretz."* Blessed are You oh Lord, King of the Universe, who brings forth bread from the earth. He broke the challa bread and passed it around, giving the first piece to his beloved Sovereign. Others shared loaves positioned on all the tables.

After consuming His delicious morsel of bread, the Universal King sat down on His regal chair, followed by all of the Kadoshim. Silver platters piled high with sumptuous roast beef, lamb and chicken appeared on all tables, along with large ivory bowls filled with all sorts of cooked vegetables and salads. However the "meats" were actually not the real thing. They were made out of a new substance akin to tofu, yet they featured the exact texture and taste of actual beef, lamb and chicken.

The protein-rich faux meats would soon be made available to the entire surviving human population. Some people would still raise cattle, goats and chickens, but only for their milk and eggs. However when the animals eventually died a natural death, their owners were permitted to consume their meat. However, there would be no more mass slaughterhouses where frightened animals were put to death in order to produce food for human consumption, nor war zones where human soldiers were killed or wounded while defending their countries. The wolf would dwell with the lamb and the cow would graze with the bear. There would be no sanctioned human or animal killing, war or destruction on the Messiah's restored earth, which would be filled with the knowledge of the Lord as the waters cover the sea.

The reunited Goldman family, including David, sat at a table not far from the elevated dais. Eli Ben David, Craig Eagleman, Moshe Salam, Micah Kupinski, plus Shoshel Pearlman and her father Amos, feasted along with them, as did Ken and Betty Preston, Yoseph and Cindy Steinberg, and several other Kadoshim. Micah was sitting next to Danny Katzman, who, as one of the 144,000 sealed Jewish males, had led him and his band of young new believers into the desert before the earth's final judgments began to unfold. After thanking Danny profusely for his heroic action, Micah informed him that he'd spoken earlier in the day with Leah Rabinowitz, the nurse who was also part of the group that fled the city under Danny's good guidance and protection and later came to faith as a result of his anointed biblical teachings in the wilderness.

Many of the brethren discussed the events about to unfold, especially their individual appearances before the Savior's judgment seat in just over sixteen hours time. "I must admit I'm glad I don't have to go through that," stated David Goldman as he cut up a thick juicy piece of tofu roast beef—the first "beef" he'd ever tasted. "I guess there was some benefit in not living very long on earth."

Jonathan was sitting directly to his left. "But brother, based on the Lord's words over the past few days, it sounds like He's not intending to pass judgment upon our lives in order to condemn us, but only to reward us or not, as the record allows. He's already forgiven our sins." Jonathan was desperately hoping his assessment was correct, knowing he'd be forced to confront a serious sin that he'd never even confessed to his earthly wife Sarah.

"Yes, that's my understanding as well," added Eli as he spooned some buttered corn onto his plate. "Still, it'll be difficult to review some of the questionable or awful things we did while living in the flesh, despite out redemption."

Jonathan cringed inside as Sarah added, "That's for sure. I was not exactly Mother Teresa before I accepted the Lord, although I was certainly much better behaved than my sister Donna."

The feast ended two hours later after platters of cakes and bowls brimming with fruit and ice cream appeared following the main meal. When the plates, bowls, goblets and utensils were no longer needed, they simply vanished into the air. This caused Eli to quip that he didn't know who to tip for the fantastic service they'd received. "I think you just increase your offering to King Yeshua this month Uncle Eli," joked Benny with a twinkle in his eye.

Following the divine banquet, the Kadoshim returned to their joyous celebrations before the Lord's royal throne. Since they were not digesting any of the food and drink-which was dispensed as raw atomic energy from their glowing skin—they were able to move into immediate dance just seconds after finishing their meals. The saints were spinning more vibrantly than before, since all now possessed a deeper understanding of the Paradise of God that they would be part of for all eternity.

As the first golden shafts of dawn rained down upon the restored Holy Land, the Kadoshim halted their joint celebrations and began individual periods of inner reflection. No one uttered a word or sang one note of a song for the following six hours. For some saints, like Benny and Tali, the introspection was not terribly disquieting, given they'd barely sinned in their short human lives. However for others like Prince David and Jonathan, it was more troubling, wrestling with the vivid memories of their roles in deliberately ending the lives of fellow human beings. The Apostle Shaul was dealing with his recollections of this as well, having persecuted and killed many saints before his Damascus Road transformation. Although each of them had repented and been fully forgiven of their sins, they anticipated that even the recounting of them before the Lord's throne of grace would be a difficult experience.

In Jonathan's case, his great sin involved ending the budding life of his unborn son. At age seventeen, he'd gotten a sixteen year old teenage girl pregnant during a drunken party at a friend's house in Chicago. When Heather Petersen, who was raised a Lutheran, informed him she was with child, he insisted she get an abortion despite her reluctance to do so. Just two days after she caved in to his constant pressure, he broke up with her. Jonathan could not bear seeing her pretty face, which only served to remind him that he was responsible for cruelly ending his offspring's life.

At noon, trumpets again sounded inside and outside the Holy Temple. It was time for judgment to begin with the household of God, as foretold by the Lord Himself, and also by the Apostle Shaul in his book of Romans and second letter to the saints in Corinth.

The Messiah's Judgment Seat was separate from His royal throne. Placed directly in front of the towering blue throne, the seat resembled the high back leather chairs found in many courtrooms across the world.

The Judge of All the Earth slowly walked over to His imperial seat. The moment King Yeshua sat down, every single one of the Kadoshim was instantly standing five feet in front of their Merciful Savior. This was possible since each had been transferred to another dimension beyond space and time. So even though in earthly terms it appeared that they were all being judged simultaneously, this was not at all the experience that each one had. In their own perception, and in actuality, each was standing alone before the King of Kings, who was granting every single saint His undivided attention. Of course, such a remarkable feat could only be accomplished by a powerful God for whom absolutely nothing is impossible.

Benny's time with the Master was short and fairly sweet. He had only three sins to review: He'd lied to his mother, fought some with his sister, and nurtured resentment against Sarah's elderly friend Yitzhak.

The young saint's first conscious sin was telling his mother that he'd accidentally dropped a chocolate chip cookie behind the living room sofa while waving goodbye out the picture window to Tali, heading off to school. This took place just six months after his father's untimely death. Benny related how he'd quickly consumed the delicious cookie and craved an immediate replacement. He knew Sarah only baked six cookies that morning with rationed chocolate Eli brought her the evening before. One cookie was for Benny, another for Tali's lunch box, and one each for Sarah herself, for Donna and for Stacy, who all gobbled down their special treats right after breakfast. A sixth cookie would be kept all day for Eli, who was expected over for supper.

"I'm sure mom knew I was lying, King Yeshua. I mean, she could've just moved the couch and rescued the cookie if she really believed it was down there. Instead, she went in and got Uncle Eli's cookie and gave it to me. It tasted sweet in my mouth, but was bitter in my stomach. That evening, I couldn't look Eli in the eye; I was so consumed with guilt."

"Your mother indeed realized you were lying to her, Benny, but she also understood that the punishment she gave you—to rob the sweet gift-giver whom you loved of his own chocolate chip cookie—would be far more effective than any other penalty you might incur. Even the memory of your lie is now washed away."

After Benny reviewed his two other sins, the Great I Am restated the pardons He'd already granted the young boy when he confessed his sins in prayer while still residing in his earthly body. Then the Sovereign Lord detailed the many good and holy things that the youngster had done, including sharing the gospel with dozens of people when he ministered with his mother and sister alongside the two witnesses.

After that, Israel's Messiah said something that few other penitent saints would hear that special day. He called Benny to come and sit with Him for a minute on His royal Judgment Seat. "Son, you will play a very important role during the second half of My millennial reign on earth. You have been chosen for this task because of your pure and honest heart. Our ancestors Avraham and Prince David will be very proud of you, along with your family and many others; even as I already am."

Just before Benny's session was finished, the Lord handed the ransomed saint a white stone with a new name written on it that only he and his Savior would ever know. This would occur as well with all the other Kadoshim. When Benny heard in his spirit his new name being uttered by the Lord in the future, he was to immediately come into the presence of his Eternal King. Finally, the Wonderful Counselor grasped Benny's large hands and said, "Well done, good and faithful servant! Go in peace and prosper, dear child of Mine! Enter into your eternal reward!" Benny felt the nail scars on the Lord's wrists as tears of joy welled up in his bright eyes.

Benny Goldman received the Savior's warm departing embrace with unspeakable joy as he pondered what his Heavenly Father's unexpected words might mean. As Yeshua's mother Miriyam had done after the Angel Gabriel foretold before the Lord's birth the sacred role she would play in history, Benny would cherish the Redeemer's mysterious prophecy in his heart.

Jonathan's session before the Judge of all the Earth was, needless to say, quite different than his human son's had been. It was focused on his high school years in particular, the time when he plunged into deep rebellion against his Jewish parents with heavy drinking and illegal drug usage. Then with tears in his eyes, the redeemed sinner spoke of Heather Petersen's out of wedlock pregnancy and abortion, taking full responsibility for it. "I know you have forgiven me for that, King Yeshua, but I have not fully forgiven myself. I'm not sure I ever will."

"You will, my son. This evening you will meet the holy saint your seed created 23 years ago. I raised him Myself in heaven. I gave him the name Jesse after our ancient ancestor who was Prince David's father. He is now serving alongside your brother David as one of my fulltime perpetual priests." Although this news was not a total surprise, it touched Jonathan very deeply, causing him to weep sorrowful tears mixed with thanksgiving which would finally wash away his guilt and pain forever.

"King Yeshua, what will my punishment be for this great sin?"

"My son, there is no punishment for the Kadoshim, only differing levels of reward. Some will barely receive any rewards at all; some will receive many. As for you, I paid the ultimate price for your sin long ago, but you paid the penalty of being separated from your beloved family for nearly five years, made more difficult by the fact that your wonderful children were so young and needy." More tears flowed from Jonathan's beautiful eyes, washing away the residue of that painful separation forever.

After restating the pardon He'd granted Jonathan when he first confessed his sins while still in his human body, the Blessed Redeemer recounted the many good things that the former Israeli soldier had done; commending him in particular for how careful he'd been to raise his children in the admonition of the Lord. Then the Messiah handed him his secret name and bid him great success in his new governmental role before proclaiming, "Well done, faithful servant! Go in peace and be a blessing to many!"

When the personal judgment sessions all came to an end, the Kadoshim were called by their Savior into one united Body of jubilant praise and worship, celebrating the goodness and mercy of their much-loved Messiah King. This went on for five hours until well after Shabbat ended, marking the end of the eight-day Hanukkah festival and the start of a new week, and indeed, of a new millennium.

When the justified ones were again visible in their individual spiritual bodies, Jonathan quickly found Sarah, Tali and Benny. He had something important to tell them. However before Jonathan could speak, Tali and Benny made clear they each had their own announcements that absolutely could not wait. Tali spoke first: "The Lord thanked me for adopting the Bernstein twins and gave me a white stone with my private new name on it. And after that, He told me from now on all would call me *Talel*! Of course 'El' is Hebrew for 'God' so I was very honored and thrilled!"

"That's wonderful honey," said Sarah as she squeezed her earthly daughter's hand.

Benny jumped right in. "And King Yeshua told me I would play a major role during the second half of His millennial reign! He didn't tell me what it would be, but isn't that just too cool for words?"

"Amen son, it is," confirmed Jonathan as he patted Benny's back while his beaming mother took his other hand.

Then Jonathan bit the bullet. "Dear ones, I hate to break this sublime mood, but I have a sad confession, but also a happy revelation, to make to you. Sarah, I especially apologize for never telling you this before now. When I was just seventeen, I got a teenage girl pregnant. She was only sixteen. I naturally reviewed it with King Yeshua today. I forced her to have an abortion, for which I've been extremely remorseful ever since."

Sarah bowed her head as a teardrop formed in her right eye.

"Our precious Redeemer already forgave me when I confessed this awful sin after surrendering my life to Him in college. I'm most grateful for His abundant mercy. But there's more. Benny, Talel, you have a new brother! His name is Jesse and we'll meet him very soon. He's serving with my twin brother David as a perpetual Temple priest."

Benny's eyes turned wider than a button. "I have a brother like you dad? That is just so awesome!"

"For sure it is son, and it's a mighty act of redemption by the restorer of our souls."

The two transformed children embraced their earthly father as Sarah slowly joined in. It would take her a few more minutes to fully process this news.

Abe and Rebecca Goldman arrived with Abe's father five minutes later and were informed by Jonathan what was soon to take place. Jonathan's parents were not overly surprised to learn that their then-rebellious son had fathered a child out of wedlock which he'd not allowed to come to term. They had spent many sleepless nights waiting for Jonathan to come home from what they knew must have been drinking parties, at the very least. They confiscated his car keys several times as punishment when he'd not returned home at all, but it failed to curb his rebellious behavior. Only their wayward son's subsequent salvation during his sophomore year at the University of Illinois in Chicago had done that.

Benny was the first to spot David Goldman walking arm in arm with someone toward his extended family. His companion was a handsome blond saint with ocean blue eyes. Jesse had apparently picked up more of his mother's looks than his father's, although he clearly inherited Jonathan's high cheek bones and dimples.

Jonathan rapidly lost his composure. Although the tremendous guilt and pain that had long dogged him had been entirely washed away earlier in the day, he was immediately overwhelmed by the tender mercy of his Lord in transforming murderous death into eternal life. He wept tears of elation as he bear-hugged the son that he never dreamed he would ever see. The tears were quickly reflected by Jesse, and then by Talel and Benny.

When the weeping subsided, David introduced the rest of the Goldman family to Jesse, who was six-foot-four and built like a linebacker—about the same dimensions as Benny. The two new-found brothers embraced as Benny pronounced how tremendously blessed he felt to have an uncle and a brother serving the Alpha and Omega as perpetual Temple priests. "You must join us for Shabbat meals from now on," he insisted as Talel nodded in agreement.

"I've asked Jesse to serve on my menorah lighting team, and he's agreed," added David with a sparkle in his eyes. Like Jonathan, he was just an inch shorter than his earthly nephew. The two priestly saints were obviously quite close in spirit, sharing both human lineage and a similar background in heaven. In fact, they'd been informed of their family connection by Yeshua soon after Jesse arrived in the Lord's presence. David then revealed that he'd actually helped 'raise' Jesse, filling him in about his earthly father and grandparents, and teaching him what he himself had learned about the world from the Master Builder. David also told Jonathan he'd decided not to previously mention Jesse's existence to him after being told by the Lord that the forgiven sinner needed to first clue in his earthly wife and children about his past actions and their consequences.

Eli soon showed up with two friends in tow. Before Jonathan could reveal who the blond saint standing near him was, the governor-designate blurted out, "Hey guys! Look who I found!" Although the elder Goldmans and the two priests didn't recognize the two saints, the others did. Jonathan greeted them first. "Sampson Baker! How wonderful to see you brother! And Tom McPherson, it's great to see you as well!"

Sampson had been an economics major at a university in his native Lagos, Nigeria before taking a year off to study Semitic languages at the Rothberg foreign students program at Hebrew University in Jerusalem. Son of a Christian pastor with a thriving Nigerian church, he'd attended services at the Beit Yisrael congregation during his short time in Israel. "You still look like that handsome actor Denzel Washington, but even more so now!" exclaimed Sarah before her former children gave the African saint their warm greetings.

"I've asked Sampson to serve as my Minister of Finance, and he's agreed," announced Eli. "And Thomas will become my new Industry, Trade and Agriculture Minister. Tom will be an excellent trade representative I'm sure, aided by the fact that his earthly mother was born on the Greek island of Crete. I expect once we get everything up and running, we'll see many humans move to the Greek Isles and want to do business there, which I'm told by Prince David is still one of the most beautiful places on earth."

"That's wonderful Tom, congratulations," offered Jonathan, before commending Eli for the strong team of government ministers he'd assembled.

From Melbourne, Australia, Thomas McPherson was of mixed Scottish and Greek extraction. Six-foot-one in height and bulky, he retained the ruddy complexion of his father and the soft green eyes of his mother. The itinerant preacher had stopped off to tour the Greek islands after spending a semester studying theology at Jerusalem's Holy Land Institute on Mount Zion, where he first heard about the Beit Yisrael congregation.

Jonathan took the new provincial governor aside to share his news. "Eli, do you recall that I told you I'd committed a major sin when I was a teenager that I was too ashamed to even speak about?"

"Sure Yonni, when we were sitting outside on the Golan Heights just before sunset the evening you were killed. But you didn't tell me the details."

"Well, there is my sin!" He pointed to Jesse who was animatedly conversing with Benny and Talel. "I got a girl pregnant and insisted she abort the baby, and there he is! His name is Jesse, and he's serving as a perpetual priest with my brother David."

"Oh my goodness, Yonni! You Goldmans are sure full of surprises! Every time I show up there is another one of you!"

"What the enemy meant for evil, brother, the Lord has turned to good."

The native Israeli smiled at his best friend before quoting from the New Testament book of Romans. *"We know that God causes all things to work together for good to those who love God and are called according to His purpose."* Then he added, "Prince David just informed me all the governors and their ministers will hear a message tomorrow from King Yeshua that will greatly aid us with our coming assignments. I'm so excited I can hardly breathe! Actually I guess we don't need to breathe anymore!"

The two friends laughed as they embraced, rejoicing anew in the goodness of their Holy King.

NINE

THUS SAYS THE LORD

Throughout the night in and around the Holy Temple, the Kadoshim celebrated the Mighty God of Israel's tremendous goodness and enormous mercy. An hour after dawn, shofar trumpets sounded, signaling that the Lord of Lords was preparing to speak.

With a radiant smile on His lightly bearded face, King Yeshua rose up from His royal throne, prompting the glorified saints to humbly bow before the Firstborn of all Creation. He was still wearing a golden silk vest and breastplate draped over His substantial chest and abdomen—partially visible under His shimmering white robe which had been dipped in sacrificial blood.

"My dear children, it has been an enormous joy to celebrate the festival of Hanukkah and the weekly Shabbat with you! As you already know, we shall all spend every Shabbat together here in this sacred sanctuary from now on, along with our daily times of worshipful celebration beginning each afternoon at 5:00 PM."

His Majesty stepped down from the square platform surrounding His throne and slowly walked forward ten paces on the Holy of Holies dais. His nail-scarred hands were clasped tightly together. The Sovereign Lord's skin was glowing like burnished bronze. His crowned head was so effervescent that His dark brown hair appeared to be almost white. His riveting regal eyes still blazed of fire

"Precious ones; today will be counted as Day One of your Savior's thousand-year reign on this revitalized earth. With all of you now fluent in Hebrew, which will also become the new universal language taught to all of humanity, we will employ from today on the Hebrew names for each weekday. So the first day of each week will be called Day One, the second Day Two and so on, ending with Day Six, known in the old era as Friday. This is of course how the days were called at the beginning of creation, as recorded in the book of Genesis, and also by ancient and modern Hebrew-speaking Jews. As prophesied in the Bible, we will call this new era the Day of the Lord, which actually began when We poured out the final judgments upon the earth, but today will be counted as the start of the millennial Year One. Like Shabbat, each weekly Day One will be a time for additional rest around the world. All shops and businesses will be closed on Shabbat, and most on Day One as well, but some, such as food outlets, may operate on a limited schedule, along with places of light entertainment."

The Kadoshim were listening carefully, cherishing every note of the magnificent Word of the Father's resounding voice.

"Over the next thousand years, I will share a weekly message with all of you on Day One in the morning. Until My official millennial coronation takes place in just over one month's time, it will only be heard by you, My beloved Kadoshim, who will be concentrated here at the sacred Temple for the address. From then on, it will also be broadcast around the world for all of humanity to absorb, and replayed several times during the week so that the entire human population has a chance to listen to it. At first it will be translated into the various national languages until everyone becomes fully fluent in Hebrew. I will speak often about your Heavenly Father, recount Bible stories and teachings, and maybe even share a parable or two." The Lord turned His hallowed head to the right and winked as He smiled in the direction of His faithful Apostles, seated in a row next to Him on seven-foot-high ivory thrones stretching out from His taller blue throne. All twelve lovingly smiled back at their beautiful Master and King.

"At least once in their life, every human living on earth will travel from their provincial homes to Jerusalem in order to worship before the God of Israel. Most will come soon after reaching adulthood. They will not enter into this Temple lest they die, but they will gather before Me at a magnificent new outdoor pavilion that runs up and down the cleansed Hinnom Valley, just south of this Old City. Like Moses coming off of Mount Sinai, My glory will be somewhat veiled to allow them to gaze in my direction without harming their human eyes."

King Yeshua's expression turned solemn. "Dear ones, as I have already informed you, there are some thirty million human beings who survived the final judgments of the devil and his dark kingdom. One-third are children too young to have received the mark of the beast. A large portion of those are orphans. It will be our top priority to minister to them as quickly as possible." The Good Shepherd glanced in the direction of the Temple priests who'd perished as small babies or been aborted in the passing era.

"In fact, throughout our time of celebration here, Jehovah Jireh has been nightly providing manna to people all over the world, apart from here in Jerusalem where some of you have been kindly ministering food directly to the few people left alive in the city. In the mornings, men and women, boys and girls have been gathering nourishing manna from the ground. This will continue until My formal coronation. By that time, we will have established other food resources for the needy human race. Many of you will help with this process, overseeing workers who will harvest the leaves and fruit from the Trees of Life, which will then be shipped all over the planet.

"When the Creator gave you your new homes and this glorious new Holy Temple, We also fashioned a series of canals down in the Jordan Valley. Living water from the Nahar Cha'im is even now flowing through these canals before entering the restored Yam Cha'im. Millions of additional Trees of Life are already growing along the verdant banks of the canals." Sarah turned and smiled at Talel, both thinking of the healing power that the leaves were already bringing to Donna and the Bernstein twins.

"The fruit and leaf harvesting will mainly be done by returning human Jews and Arabs who wisely refused the mark of the beast—many because of the warnings issued by Our dear friends Yochanan and Natan-el. These people were later guided to safety by many of the 144,000 sealed Jewish males, heading either into the Judean Desert wilderness or to Petra and other locations in the former country of Jordan. Numbering almost two-million souls, they have been walking back towards Jerusalem since My return. Many will begin arriving today, and the rest will be here by the end of the week. Some are unwell, but most are fine. Capable adult males and females will begin working on the harvest right away. Later on, laborers will come from the nations to take over most of their jobs, but only human workers who have already sincerely received Our gift of eternal salvation, issued through My shed blood." Sarah thought about her still unrepentant sister Donna, wondering what sort of job she might end up doing.

"The Israeli Jews will soon be joined by nearly one-million additional Jewish men, women and children from around the world who survived the end-time judgments. As foretold via the pen of Our servant Ezekiel thousands of years ago, We will leave none of them in exile any longer. Many sons and daughters of Ya'acov are beginning to come back even now on horses and any other means of working transportation they can find. Overseas Jews with close Kadoshim relatives living in Jerusalem will be allowed to reside here in new housing We have already provided for them. However most will live along the coastal plain and other parts of Our Holy Land. They will plant vineyards and sit in safety under them, and no one will make them afraid."

The Beginning and the End paused for a second and smiled. His last comment—confirming what was revealed by the prophet Isaiah over 2,500 years before—brought intense joy to every listening heart, as the Lord of course knew would be the case. Apart from a brief period of time at the very end of Immanuel's millennial reign, there would be no more famine or war to kill off humanity, nor muggers or thieves to rob and steal.

The King of Kings continued His informational inaugural weekly address. "Most of those Jews coming from Asia, Australia, Iran and other places to the east will travel on the new Highway of Holiness which begins on the expanded eastern border of the land of Israel that runs along the Euphrates River. The highway's eastern entrance is located not far from the old southern Iraqi port city of Basra. A new fully-equipped seaport has been created near there on the Persian Gulf. Others will travel to the Holy City via the western section of the same highway, which runs to Jerusalem from our newly expanded Sinai border with the province of Egypt. Ships from Europe and the

Americas will bring many Jewish immigrants to a new Mediterranean port that the Father and I have created near that end of the sacred highway. The western port and highway will later be used by African and European pilgrims, along with people from South America and the eastern portion of North America, all coming by ship to worship during the annual feasts. The eastern port and highway will bring up worshipers traveling from the western half of North America, Asia, Australia, New Zealand, Japan and other Pacific island nations. Our new main international airport, to be located in the northern Negev Desert near Beersheva, will also channel many visitors to and from this special land."

Benny gently poked his elbow in Micah's side as both friends eagerly pictured in their minds' eye the future streams of international pilgrims heading up to Jerusalem to worship the Lion of Judah.

"By ingesting the fruit and leaves of the Trees of Life, the many Jewish human children who are even now beginning to make their way to this, their Promised Land, will still retain their youth at the age of 100. As your Holy Father foretold through Our faithful servant Isaiah, any who do not reach that age will be thought accursed. Most people all around the world will in fact live many hundreds of years, as in the days of old. Those of you going out this week to begin your government service in the nations will receive more information about the surviving human race later today when you meet with Prince David."

Jonathan winked at Eli as King Yeshua turned His radiant head in Prince David's direction and gently smiled. Israel's new provincial governor, seated with Avraham and ten other elders immediately to the left of the Lord's glorious throne, smiled back. Then the Mighty One of Israel continued His initial weekly address to His beloved Kadoshim.

"We will immediately require millions of volunteers to go and work in the nations. Most of these will be temporary positions until the devastated human population gets back on its feet. We especially desire help from any of you who had prior experience in construction, medicine, utility work and childcare. We will be immediately putting in place basic medical aid as food distribution begins this week. Childcare facilities must also be quickly established to minister to the many abandoned orphans. All volunteers will return to your new homes here in Israel when it's evening in the locations you are going to, heading back to your labors the next morning. And of course, you will each be here for our delightful late-afternoon daily meetings, and for all of Shabbat. My dear children, any of you willing to volunteer to help Us with the sacred task of ministering to the nations, please raise up your right hand now."

Millions of qualified Kadoshim gladly lifted their arms to signal their willingness to serve their Messiah King in the needy nations.

"Splendid! Thank you so much, Holy Ones. May you be blessed by the Father as you serve to build up Our kingdom. You will each receive a notice in your spirit later today where you are to report, with all work commencing tomorrow. Now sweet saints of the Most High God, go in shalom to tour your wonderful new homes. We will meet here together this evening for another time of joyous worship and praise!"

Before they exited the sacred sanctuary, the grateful redeemed of all the ages joined their beautiful voices together in one parting song. The words were from Isaiah, chapter 35: *The ransomed of the Lord will return, and come with joyful shouting to Zion, with everlasting joy upon their heads. They will find gladness and joy, and sorrow and sighing will flee away.*

After the prophetic song ended, Eli Ben David gathered his embryonic cabinet together to inform them that all newly appointed governors and cabinet ministers would be meeting with Prince David at noon inside his royal palace. Later they'd also gather together with some of the new volunteer helpers at a beautiful city park that Eli would escort them to.

Just then, a saint walked up who was instantly recognized by those cabinet ministers who'd been congregants at Beit Yisrael. "Shalom Miri, thanks for coming along," said the governor-designate as he gave the newcomer a welcome hug, followed by the others who knew her. Miriyam Doron, known by her Israeli nickname Miri, had been raised in her native Tel Aviv. She began attending the Jerusalem Messianic congregation while studying as a young adult in the Holy

City. Eli quickly introduced Miri to Jonathan's parents and grandfather. Then he revealed that she'd agreed to serve as his personal administrative assistant in the Greek Isles, managing his residential and office staffs. Craig Eagleman, who dated the affable brunette while they were both students at Hebrew University, was especially pleased with this news.

Eli then revealed that four city apartments had been provided for the ministers to use on business trips to Jerusalem, plus during the annual feasts and private visits to the city. Prince David had given him the addresses an hour before, prompting Eli to quickly pop over to locate the building. He was happy to discover the adjoining dwellings were on the twenty-second floor of a forty storey apartment building standing in the lower Judean foothills alongside the Nahar Yehuda river. "The views are fantastic from the places," he added, noting that the towering dome of the new Holy Temple to the east and the Mediterranean coast to the west were clearly visible from the front apartment windows.

Since the Jerusalem flats would only be occasionally used, he clarified they were fairly small, yet quite comfortable. Jonathan and Eli would share a room with twin beds in one apartment, along with Micah and Benny in another room. Craig and Ken would stay in the second apartment with Sampson and Thomas. He added that both apartments featured a common living area and small kitchen for use by all four occupants. The third apartment next door would house Miri Doron and Rebecca Goldman, along with Abe, who would share his room with another Transport and Tourism Minister that he'd often be working closely with, Kostas Karamilis, who would hold that position in Moshe Salam's new province of Athens. Rabbi Benjamin Goldman would receive a private room in a fourth apartment that he'd share with Sarah's friend Yitzhak Ackerman, who would be the only fulltime resident of the four apartments and would keep an eye on things when all the others were out of the Holy City. Eli added that Sarah had asked Yitzhak to work with her at the new Hadassah Hospital, overseeing the mostly human kitchen and laundry staffs.

After the governor-designate finished speaking, Jonathan announced that Sarah had invited them all to come and see her new home in the afternoon after she, Talel, Betty and Shoshel settled Donna and the twins in there. Sarah and Talel had briefly gone over to Augusta Victoria the previous evening after Shabbat ended, where they happily learned from the hospital staff that all three patients would be ready for discharge by early the next morning.

As Eli spoke, Sarah and her earthly daughter were on their way with Shoshel and Betty to fetch the three human females. "How are my lovely young ladies this fine morning?" enquired Talel cheerfully as the four saints entered the Bernstein's hospital room. The fair-skinned twins were sitting in chairs dressed in clean pink jumpers that Nurse Leah had gifted them. "We're feeling really good, and ready to go!" proclaimed Dalya as Daniyella nodded her assent."

Sarah then grabbed hold of Talel's and Betty's warm hands. "Sweet ones, I have some nice news for you. My daughter Tali was given a new name by the Lord yesterday, Talel! And our dear friend Betty has just told us that she's decided to slightly alter her name since she's now fluent in Hebrew and will be living with us here in Jerusalem. So say hello to Talel and Bet-el."

"Hello Talel. Hello Bet-el," chirped the identical twins in identical voices, before Dalya added, "Those are really good names."

"Thank you children" replied Bet-el as her heart rejoiced over God's enormous goodness in giving her a vicarious replacement for her eternally-lost twin daughters. "My new name actually means 'the house of God' as you might already realize."

After scooping up the twins in their arms, the small crew then marched down the hall to Donna's room. She'd met the Bernstein girls the night before when Sarah and Talel stopped by for a short visit. Donna was clad in a pair of faded blue jeans and a cotton blouse that Nurse Leah had kindly given her. Along with a plastic bag containing a toothbrush, toothpaste, a bar of soap and a comb provided by the hospital staff, the new clothes were her only possessions. The twins carried similar care packages in their petite hands.

The three female humans and four redeemed saints rapidly exited the old German hospital and began strolling to Sarah's new home less than two miles south of the Old City. They gazed in amazement at the restored Jerusalem all around them. Upon leaving the small hospital, the young Israeli twins were immediately impressed by the steep waterfall gushing out from under the central section of the eastern Temple Mount stone wall, located less than a quarter mile across the narrow Kidron Valley. While laying in their hospital beds, they could hear the cascading water crashing onto the valley floor, but Thunder Falls was not quite visible from their narrow window. However they *were* able to see the renewed Holy Temple towering above the falls, and had been repeatedly awed by the splendid sight.

Soon the happy hikers were nearing King Yeshua's exquisite palace. Sarah briefly explained to the twins who He was as they sauntered along the Jerusalem-stone sidewalk. All marveled at the magnificent new structure, noting in particular how beautiful the polished marble walls and tall picture windows looked in the reflected morning sunlight.

The majestic palace was surrounded by a park featuring lush green lawns dotted with dozens of oak, cedar, apple, cherry and date palm trees. Scores of pink marble fountains flowing with living water were scattered about, surrounded by redwood benches. Hundreds of robins, blue jays, cardinals, purple finches, wrens, larks, and sparrows chirped merrily in the morning light as they either bathed in the fountains or hung out in the trees with the bald eagles and condors. Parrots and cockatoos were busy shooting the breeze with one another on the dangling branches, while dozens of storks, peacocks and ostriches wandered about on the lawns. Squirrels darted about the trees and well-kept lawns, looking for nuts and fallen fruit to consume. Deer and ibex drank from a stream that flowed west down the hill to the Nahar Cha'im. Its source was a gurgling spring in the middle of the park directly in front of the grand palace entrance.

"Let's just stay put here today," sighed Talel as they merrily breathed in the tranquil scenery.

Soon they could make out Prince David's smaller palace just southwest and below King Yeshua's royal home, which had a similar park surrounding it. "That's the new home of the tall man with the silver crown that you girls met the other afternoon in your hospital room; the one named Prince David," said Sarah, explaining he was the new provincial governor of Israel who would be watching over the children and every other human citizen of the land. She added with a chuckle, "That's where I'm going to take my daily walk." Talel's mother was pointing to a footpath made out of pure gold which straddled the north side of the palace garden.

"Oh that's right, you told me you're going to have an office there," recalled Donna, adding she would love to visit whenever Sarah desired a walking companion.

There were no buildings taller than five storeys anywhere in the vicinity of the walled Old City. The view of the majestic Holy Temple would be unobstructed in the center of Jerusalem's greatly expanded municipal boundaries. However the seven strollers could make out the tops of some high-rise buildings located about ten miles to the west in the foothills of the Judean range, which had been refigured in many places due to the recent gigantic earthquakes. Similar skyscrapers were visible to the east in the low hills rising just above the Jordan Valley. Portions of the new canals mentioned by King Yeshua were also identifiable in the distance—with the air now pure as the driven snow.

The mixed group of humans and saints crossed over another new stone footbridge that straddled the Nahar Cha'im river flowing below it. The bridge ran from the south end of the Mount of Olives west to the biblical City of David, just over the northern section of the old Arab neighborhood of Silwan. The heavy structure was supported by 400-foot high stone columns. Immediately after they passed Prince David's illustrious palace just north of the footbridge, the Kadoshim marveled at the new outdoor pavilion the Lord also mentioned that morning. Located off to their right, it was a quarter mile long, stretching up the entire length of the sloping Hinnom Valley gorge— where children were idolatrously sent to their sacrificial fiery deaths against the Lord's command in ancient times—to Sultan's Pool southwest of the Old City. Linear columns of carved marble benches covered the steep valley walls. The benches would seat tens of thousands at any one time.

Situated on the lower eastern end of the biblical valley was a 55-foot-high elevated marble stage where the Messiah of Israel would address visiting human pilgrims every year during one of the three pilgrimage Jewish feasts, especially during *Succot*, the Feast of Tabernacles. It sat just in front of the Ein Rogel spring which gurgled up from underneath the Nahar Cha'im river. The view of the river behind the elevated dais was breathtaking on its own. However when the King of Glory would make appearances on the stage, the combined scene would be indescribably spectacular to the assembled pilgrims. Those sitting in the northeast-facing seats would also have a wonderful view of the restored Temple on the top of the nearby, elevated Mount Moriah. Special musical concerts and other performances would be held from time to time at the sprawling outdoor site, especially during the jubilee celebrations which would take place every fifty years during the millennium.

As the small group neared Sarah Goldman's new home, Donna noted they'd not seen one single car on the cobblestone streets, which she also observed were actually quite narrow. "Eli told me no vehicles will be allowed anywhere in the center of Jerusalem from now on," Sarah revealed, adding "Only small electric service carts will be permitted to transit when necessary. However, Eli said the city has a fantastic new underground public transport system designed mainly for human use. Actually we could've taken the subway today, but I thought we'd all want to see what our restored city looks like. Eli said there's a subway entrance just outside of Jaffa Gate, with stops in all the neighborhoods including ours. Prince David told him all about it."

"You said it's meant for human transport...so how will the Kadoshim get around?" asked Donna as she scratched her fading blonde hair.

"All we have to do is simply picture where we want to be, sis, and we instantly appear there, in the twinkling of an eye! That's how Jonathan and Eli and the others will 'travel' back and forth between the Greek Isles and Jerusalem every day. No more airport delays for us! So these streets are really mainly designed for bicycles, walking or jogging."

"How about for pet-walks?" enquired Dalya before adding "I really want to get another dog."

"And I want another cat!" proclaimed Daniyella, prompting the Kadoshim and Donna to chuckle.

"We'll see about *that* later on," replied Talel as she shared a knowing glance with her earthly mother.

"Our new house should be in this upcoming block," revealed Sarah as she looked again at the address Eli had given her. The homes on both sides of the stone path were all semi-detached three storey townhouses finished with mauve marble walls and red ceramic roof tiles. Set back about eight-feet from the narrow cobblestone street, they had small nicely landscaped yards in front featuring a water fountain surrounded by blossoming violets and lilies.

"There it is!" exclaimed Sarah, prompting the wound-up twins to dart forward.

Sarah reached into her beige cotton bag and pulled out a metal ring containing house keys, which she would soon distribute to the other adult residents. After unlocking the large oak door, the saints and humans all squealed with delight as they took in the meticulously furnished interior, with aqua granite tiles on the floor, ceiling to floor silk indigo curtains, matching couches and recliners, cedarwood coffee and end tables, brass lamps with crimson velvet shades, a large red brick fireplace and an opulent kitchen and dining room.

Sarah was delighted to discover that the wide, silver-plated refrigerator was already stocked with fresh food and drink. After downing some sweet orange juice, the seven residents went upstairs to check out the six fully-furnished bedrooms, three on each floor. Sarah, Shoshel and Donna quickly dibbed rooms on the top floor of the immaculately clean house. Talel and Bet-el would each have a room on the second floor, with the twins sharing a third. A broad, covered balcony fitted with lounge chairs and a round glass table and padded chair was located under the back section of the pitched roof.

Donna marched the hungry twins back down to the kitchen to find something yummy to munch on. Sarah and her three Kadoshim companions then bowed their heads as they offered heartfelt thanks to their Eternal Bridegroom for providing them with such a gorgeous new home, which seemed like a mansion to them.

Governor Eli Ben David and his cabinet companions oozed excitement as they entered the grandiose front entrance to Prince

David's sublime palace, located on the west side of the extensive complex. Ceremonial guards wearing cobalt-colored silk robes with navy-blue waistbands stood at attention on either side of the twelve-foot-high main entrance doors. Thousands of Kadoshim were streaming into the palace where they were guided toward a set of broad carpeted stairs situated on the right side of the opulent foyer. They quickly descended in orderly fashion to a massive basement hall designed to hold up to 12,000 visitors.

Exactly 1,000 newly appointed governors were being seated by dozens of ushers next to their 10 hand-picked cabinet ministers, meaning 11,000 Kadoshim were gathering in the great hall. Lively conversations rumbled through the august venue as the Holy Ones looked around to see who they might recognize in the large general assembly. All of the designated governors and their cabinets would gather together at the beginning of each year from now on, meeting every five years in Jerusalem, and during the intervening years at rotating locations around the world.

Eli and Jonathan spotted New York City provincial governor Yoseph Steinberg coming up the main aisle with his earthly wife Cindy. His nine other new cabinet ministers were right behind them, including Leo and Teresa Scarcelli and Giuseppe Marino. After exchanging greetings, Yoseph announced that Cindy had been given a new first name by King Yeshua for all to use—Zinel. He explained that she was being named after the northern Negev area known as the Wilderness of Zin, due south of Beersheva, now a well-watered zone containing newly-created residential neighborhoods, fertile farms and magnificent parks.

With a proud smile on his handsome, dimpled face, Sampson Baker began waving at two saints seated three rows behind him to his right. He then informed Micah and Craig, perched on either side of him, that they were his earthly father and mother from Lagos. Clearly delighted to have spotted them, the designated Finance Minister with milk chocolate-colored skin explained that his pastor father, the Reverend Nelson Baker, had been appointed by the new governor of the Lagos province to serve as his Religious Affairs Minister, while his mother, Shantiya, who had headed up the Christian school that their large church operated in the sprawling West African city, would serve as Education Minister.

Of Eli's ten cabinet ministers, only Jonathan Goldman, his father Abe, his son Benny and Sampson Baker were settled in eternity with at least one of their human parents. All of the other forebears had sadly refused to surrender their fleeting human lives to the Sovereign Lord during their short human sojourns, or perished before they could do so. Rebecca Goldman's Orthodox Jewish parents had died during the 1970s in Crown Heights New York; her mother Pearl from a brain tumor and her father Samuel from a heart attack five years after his wife passed away. Eli's beloved father Yishai had been killed in the 1982 Lebanon War, dying of asphyxiation during a fierce tank battle with Soviet-backed Syrian forces in the Bekaa Valley. His mother Rivka, a kibbutz member from her youth who was raised a dedicated socialist, had reacted to her husband's unexpected death by becoming even more secular, telling Eli until her death from lung cancer that she had absolutely no interest in any form of religion.

Ken Preston's parents in Richmond Virginia were even more agnostic than the TV cameraman-reporter had been until the day he finally surrendered his life to Yeshua after his wife Betty's violent death at the Western Wall plaza. Craig Eagleman's mother, Cynthia, had actually pranced up to the base of a football stadium stage with thousands of others during a Billy Graham crusade in Orange County, California in 1985, but had not followed up her action with a true repentance that had any lasting effect on her subsequent daily life. Her husband Bill, a non-practicing Catholic, had scoffed at her public profession from the start, terming it a meaningless emotional outburst, which did not exactly help her to take hold of her newly professed faith.

Thomas McPherson's Australian mother was raised by immigrant parents doggedly loyal to their ancestral Greek Orthodox Church. Still, they had not passed along to their attractive daughter Annette any genuine connection to the Lord that proved strong enough to successfully withstand her husband Ian, who had totally rebelled years before against his childhood Church of Scotland upbringing. So when

Ian basically ordered his wife to accept Emperor Andre's economic mark or get out of their Melbourne home, she had rapidly caved in.

When every saint was seated on their green cushioned chairs, sonorous shofar trumpets sounded as Prince David walked regally to the gray and white granite podium, which bore the new official seal of the Messianic Kingdom picturing King Yeshua on His lapis lazuli throne with a colorful rainbow stretching above Him. Israel's new provincial governor was accompanied by a small entourage that included the Apostles Yochanan and Shaul, the Lord's earthly brother Ya'acov, Batsheva, and Solomon. For the first time, Israel's anointed administrator was wearing a purple cape with golden fringe draped over a saffron-colored silk robe. The other provincial governors would later be supplied with similar capes and robes to don on formal occasions.

"My dear friends, welcome to my new home! It is a modest home, but I think I'll keep it." Giggles erupted throughout the exquisite hall as the charismatic prince smiled broadly. "We will all meet here every five years from now on; and each provincial governor and their cabinet ministers will be my individual guests from time to time."

As Benny's glance met Micah's, he instantly thought of Shoshel and her exciting assigned work position in the new palace. Sheer delight danced in his vibrant eyes. Here were close childhood friends who were mere Israeli lads constructing small Lego buildings and putting together puzzles not so long ago. Now they were government ministers in the Messiah's millennial realm, listening to an address by the former King David in his glorious new palace in rebuilt Jerusalem. When would they wake up from this humongous dream?

"On King Yeshua's behalf, I will now explain to you some of the rules and regulations of our royal government administration, and outline the general conditions you will face. As you all know by now, the earth has been divided up into 1,000 provinces, each ruled by a governor assisted by 10 cabinet ministers. There will be no other national elected or appointed leaders during our Messiah's millennial reign, just you governors. This will eliminate the possibility of future outbreaks of rapacious national and ethnic conflicts which plagued the earth so frequently in the old era. That is the reason why no defense ministers are included in any of your cabinets—there will be no more war until the very end."

Egypt's new provincial governor, Yoseph Ben Ya'acov, who saved ancient Egypt from starvation during a seven year drought, smiled at Israel's new governor-prince from his front row seat.

"Many of you resided as human beings in the areas that you will be administering, along with quite a few of you cabinet ministers. Others have some human ancestry from your zones of control. The rest have no previous earthly connection to your newly-formed provinces, yet you were chosen for your administrative skills and backgrounds, which will quickly aid you to excel in your areas of responsibility."

Sitting next to the central aisle in the third row back, Eli glanced briefly at his chosen ministers seated immediately to his right. Although only Tom McPherson had any Greek heritage, he was certain they'd all do a marvelous job in fulfilling their auspicious new roles.

"As King Yeshua outlined this morning, our first order of priority will be to minister to the many orphaned children and wounded or ill human beings that we will immediately encounter in our provinces. You'll each be transported to your assigned provinces as the local dawn commences in them tomorrow morning—apart from those places where daybreak coincides with our daily service in the Holy Temple, which is actually only in Hawaii and a few other Pacific Ocean locations and in Northwest Canada and Alaska. Teams of Kadoshim volunteers will go with you to assist in setting up critical infrastructure to carry out your holy assignments. Health Ministers will immediately begin overseeing medical treatment in makeshift facilities. Emergency medical teams, comprised of both Kadoshim and qualified humans, will begin operating out of large, fully-equipped field tents that will be instantly transported to your provinces tomorrow, along with rescue vans and other supplies."

Prince David paused as he turned toward the dignitaries seated near him on the podium. "King Yeshua's new Foreign Minister, the Apostle Shaul, who you'll all be seeing on a regular basis, gave us some very good advice over the past week as we designed the new tents. Apparently he's done some of that work before." The affectionate quip drew another ripple of animated chuckles from the assembled government officials.

After winking at his illustrious colleague, Prince David continued. "Housing and Construction Ministers, you'll begin assessing the needs in your provinces and assigning urgent projects to the volunteer building teams which we've established. Whenever possible, local human laborers will be employed. Transport and Tourism Ministers will naturally focus on the transport side of your responsibilities for the time being, assessing your urgent needs and employing volunteers and local workers to quickly begin to meet them. Meanwhile Finance Ministers will commence setting up essential currency and banking services which your human citizens will soon require."

Craig patted Sampson Taylor on his left knee, glad his Hebrew University friend was on board Eli's ministerial team.

"I was informed just one hour ago by the new Mayor of expanded Jerusalem, my earthly son Solomon, that a quick study by our scientific teams of our divinely provided city homes and other buildings has already unlocked some advanced technologies which will benefit all of mankind. In particular, I'm told fossil fuels will no longer be needed to produce electricity, or power vehicles, apart from rockets and airplanes. Solomon has requested that all of you Transport, Construction, and Communications Ministers, and any others who are interested, return here this evening right after our daily worship time together in the Holy Temple, when the wise Mayor will deliver the important details." The remark prompted Ken Preston to wonder what new technologies might be employed in his area of expertise.

"To all you Justice Ministers, you must rapidly oversee the setting up of police forces in your respective provinces, later focusing on courts and other related services. Although there should be little crime or other vestiges of the former era in your cities and towns, there will still be a need for rapid and visible law enforcement. After all, we are still dealing with fallen human beings. They still possess the sin-prone natures inherited from the passing era; even if we hope and assume most will become loyal followers of our Messiah King, if they're not already."

As Prince David was making these comments, Benny was warmly receiving encouraging pats on his shoulder from his earthly father Jonathan, seated between him and Governor Eli.

"Holy Ones, in our service to Israel's Messiah King, we will firmly rule the earth with a rod of iron. This means we will strictly enforce our new rules and laws; benevolently designed for the prosperity and wellbeing of every person residing on earth. All governors and ministers will be given printed copies of our royal constitution and laws as you depart this hall. However, please permit me to highlight a few social items right now.

"We shall in many ways return to the moral standards that prevailed upon much of the earth before society became utterly corrupt in most localities over the past century or so. We will no longer allow unmarried couples to live together in a carnal manner. Anyone caught doing so will be subject to prosecution. Divorce will only be permitted if proven infidelity has been committed by one or both partners. If a faithful couple does not wish to remain together for some reason, they may separate, but not formally divorce or remarry. The erosion of this biblical standard, even in the Lord's professing Body, caused much heartache and grief in the previous era, especially to children. You may have noticed that some well-known church leaders and preachers from the last century are not with us in glory today because they led many astray by their unbiblical personal example in this regard.

"Abortion will be outlawed, although the use of natural contraceptives by licensed married women will be permitted, given that most will now be physically capable of bearing many children over several centuries. Fortunately, humans regularly digesting the leaves and fruit from the Trees of Life will not only age much slower internally and externally than before, but the onset of puberty will be delayed until around their eighteenth year. This will obviously help eliminate unwanted teenage pregnancies."

Jonathan squirmed a bit in his chair as he mulled over this good news.

"In the passing dark era, the widespread use of growth hormones and other chemicals had so speeded up the puberty process that girls as young as eleven or twelve were becoming physically capable of bearing babies. With the introduction of much purer diets and the healing leaves and fruit, this will thankfully no longer be the case.

"During our upcoming millennial reign, human marriages will generally be much stronger than before. This welcome reality will partly be the result of the absence of serious financial problems and tensions which tore apart many unions in the passing era. As we emphasize purity of heart over an unreachable Hollywood standard of beauty in women and men, we will find much more contentedness among couples. We'll also eliminate pornography in the media, on the internet and in movies and television programs, which will help to strengthen marriages and reduce immoral urges and behavior. Gratuitous media violence, which helped to promote rape, plus spousal and child abuse, will also be banned in all entertainment movies and programs." Rebecca Goldman vigorously nodded her head in approval of this revelation.

"On a related, more personal note, all of you must keep your holy robes on at all times while in public. You may take them off as desired in your private dwellings or while swimming in designated areas. You must all understand that lust continues to operate in the human race, and we Kadoshim, in our glorified bodies, are the pictures of perfect health and tremendous beauty, which they will obviously notice. So please respectfully keep this in mind, since we do not wish to put any stumbling blocks before our human brothers and sisters."

"I guess we *are* a pretty good looking bunch now," whispered Eli to Jonathan with a glint in his eye.

Prince David took a step forward and then carried on with his informative address. "Let me return to some additional legal issues. Cigarette production will be banned in our world dominion. Along with distilled diets, abetted by the leaves and fruit of life and pure water and air, this ban will help the human plague of lung cancer to virtually disappear."

Remembering his chain-smoking mother, Eli glanced with melancholy at Jonathan, who laid his right hand on his longtime friend's upper arm.

"The strictly-controlled production and sale of beer and wine will be permitted, however the legal alcohol content of beer will be reduced to around two per cent, and of wine to four per cent. People will be allowed to produce their own beer and wine at home, but not for public sale or consumption. No stronger alcoholic beverages will be permitted. The legal worldwide drinking age limit will be set at twenty-one. On top of this, no roadside pubs or bars will be allowed to operate anywhere on earth. It was one thing in my time for someone to get drunk at a public location, which I'm afraid I did more than once myself. They would mostly only hurt themselves if they fell down while heading back to their private dwellings. However with the invention of automobiles, the number of innocent victims of drunken recklessness soared. During the Antichrist's rule alone, over ten million people were slaughtered around the world as drunken debauchery flooded the roads. Wine and beer sales will be permitted in some roadside restaurants, but only if served with food. If the customer has no designated driver, the number of drinks allowed per patron will be limited to two, even with food." This last comment drew another firm nod of approval from Rebecca Goldman, who was hospitalized for over one month after an inebriated driver from Chicago struck her in a crosswalk when Jonathan was just 11 years old, breaking her collarbone and left arm in the process.

"On a happier note friends, the Sovereign Lord has asked me to inform you that magnificent regional temples will be constructed in many of your provinces. They'll be smaller versions of the one perched just above us on the Temple Mount. In most cases, they'll be jointly built and shared by several provinces. For instance, one will arise in Athens Greece, to be constructed with two other participating provinces, the Greek Isles to the east and Macedonia, located due north of the new province of Athens. The Construction Ministers of the three provinces will jointly oversee the hallowed building project."

Benny smiled broadly at his buddy Micah who was euphorically dizzy with this news.

"The regional temples will not be created supernaturally, as occurred here in Jerusalem. They are to be built by the donations and hands of your resident-citizens. In this way, your human populations will cherish their local temples in a more personal manner. A one-percent sales tax will help finance the illustrious projects. However people will also be encouraged to give freewill offerings on top of their taxes and tithes as the Lord prospers them. Tithes will mostly be used to help maintain the temples and pay for all road building and maintenance, hospitals, schools and other community services. A new worldwide currency featuring our Messiah King's portrait on one side and the Holy Temple on the other will soon be introduced in various denominations."

Sampson Baker nudged his two seating companions over this news.

"As for your residences abroad, all of you governors will be gifted a mansion and offices similar to this one, albeit in smaller versions. Tomorrow you can begin scouting out your preferred locations. Where ever you decide to locate your capital will automatically become your provincial seat of government. When you're ready, you need only ask of the Father and your office mansion shall instantly appear. Any of you ministers who wish to reside in the royal government houses may do so, with the consent of your governors of course. If you want to live in a separate location, you may do that as well, and housing will be immediately provided for you in your preferred location."

Several of Eli's cabinet ministers had already informed him they wanted to stay in his new headquarters: Jonathan, Benny, Micah, Craig and Ken. The three elder Goldmans indicated they preferred to live a bit further away from their working offices. Eli had not spoken about the matter yet with Sampson or Tom.

Prince David issued a warm farewell to the new government ministers and governors after asking Foreign Minister Shaul to utter a prayer of dedication and prosperity over all of them. Just before departing the large hall, they joined their winsome voices together in a hymn of praise and thanksgiving to their gracious Messiah King, with the lyrics taken from Isaiah, chapter nine.

For a Child will be born to us, a Son will be given to us. And the government will rest upon His shoulders. And His name will be called Wonderful Counselor, Mighty God, Eternal Father, Prince of Peace! And of the increase of His government, there shall be no end, on the throne of David and over His kingdom, to establish it and to uphold it with justice and righteousness, from then on and forevermore!."

TEN

POWER FROM ON HIGH

After Eli Ben David and his ten cabinet ministers exited the grand basement hall in Prince David's exquisite palace, they sat down together on a couple of redwood benches to enjoy the verdant new garden surrounding the grand structure. Pink and yellow roses were in full bloom below a large crystal water fountain situated in front of them. Several silver-lined puffy white clouds wandered by in the brilliant blue sky as warm early afternoon sunlight poured down upon their contented faces. No longer would they have to worry about acquiring sunburns or skin cancer from the rich celestial rays, not to mention premature wrinkles. All was at peace in their souls. All were at rest forever in their Lord.

After a few minutes of relaxed conversation about the administrative address they had just eagerly absorbed, Jonathan Goldman suggested it was time to head over to Sarah's new home for a scheduled lunch. The Kadoshim joined hands together in a circle as Eli spoke out the house address. The saints were instantly standing in front of Sarah's south Jerusalem townhouse, taking a few seconds to admire the edifice and yard before Jonathan rapped gently on the cedarwood door.

With a broad smile on her glistening face, Shoshel Pearlman swung open the door to usher in all ten visitors. Benny Goldman offered immediate praise for the highly skilled Carpenter who had created the elegant home as the others vigorously nodded their accord.

Soon Donna Svenson strutted into the living room with the two young twins in tow. All three humans had visible evidence of food preparation either on their hands or around their mouths, especially the children. Abe and Rebecca Goldman greeted their son's former sister-in-law before Jonathan introduced her to Rabbi Benjamin. Donna was flustered when she noticed the Auschwitz tattoo on his forearm, but she quickly regained her composure and issued a warm hello. The twins were then introduced to Sampson Baker and Thomas McPherson and to all three elder Goldmans, who gave them friendly hugs. Talel had entered the living room just in time to witness this scene, which brought light tears of joy to her sparkling eyes.

Sarah waltzed in from the kitchen right behind Talel, carrying a platter full of hot spice cakes fresh out of the oven. Bet-el followed with some fruit drinks. "This place is absolutely beautiful Sarah," opined Jonathan as he grabbed a proffered cake. "Indeed it is," Sarah concurred as she continued to make her way between the now-seated saints. "And the rent is really good...it's free!" quipped Donna as she hoisted Daniyella onto her left knee.

"Well, not exactly," replied Sarah before adding, "The cost to be here today was actually quite high, paid for by the precious blood of the Lamb."

"In My Father's house there are many dwelling places..." said Eli softly, quoting the Lord's comforting words as recorded by Yochanan.

Sarah then announced that two other guests would be joining them for lunch—Miri Doron and Yitzhak Ackerman—prompting Rabbi Benjamin to proclaim that "Yitzhak's going to be my roommate, at least part time. And Eli tells us our new places have tremendous views!"

The designated Greek Isle provincial governor then detailed the housing arrangements made for himself, his ministers and Yitzhak on the western edge of Jerusalem. "Oh that's wonderful!" responded Shoshel, adding, "We can do lunch here, and dinner in Yitzhak's apartment with its gorgeous view! is, if he invites us, which I'm sure he will. He's obviously still very fond of you Sarah."

"Well, Aunt Shoshel, don't forget that you and mom will be having lunch in a governor's mansion most days, just like we cabinet ministers can do in the Greek Isles if we want to," observed Benny, who was actually very much looking forward to imminently partaking in his natural mother's home cooking even if he no longer actually felt hungry in his substantial spiritual body.

Yitzhak soon arrived and greeted all the saints he recognized before exchanging pleasantries with the twins, Sampson and Tom. Miri Doron quickly followed. All twelve guests were then led out to a long picnic table resting on soft green grass in Sarah's serene back yard. A stained wooden fence surrounded the area, which featured a pecan tree in one corner and a soothing rock-laden waterfall in the other one with fish moving about in its basin underneath floating water lilies. After giving thanks for the wonderful new house and the ample food, the hosts and guests eagerly passed around faux fish, roasted tofu lamb, stewed tomatoes, and steaming corn on the cob, along with a brimming bowl of potato salad and loaves of freshly baked rye bread.

With her newly-dyed hair tied in a bun, Donna mentioned how amazed she was that absolutely no bees, flies or other winged creatures were buzzing about, apart from a few colorful butterflies, as they enjoyed the outdoor feast, given that ten days before the city was covered with rotting human and animal carcasses infested with vermin. Eli ceased chewing his food before stating, "That reminds me. Prince David told me this morning that specially equipped squads of returning Israeli soldiers will be asked to go out and gather up decaying bodies in the outlying portions of the expanded Holy Land. He said official estimates are that it may take up to seven months to dispose of them all. The bodies are apparently mostly the remains of the millions of international soldiers who attempted to invade Jerusalem in the final battles over the past few months. Their weapons will be gathered up and burned as well."

Talel noticed that Dalya had stopped eating so she quickly changed the subject, commenting how absolutely scrumptious everything was. Bet-el brought up the rear by noting that Talel had prepared some of the food herself, adding how nice it would be to share meals together in their new home from now on.

Eli later apologized to Talel over his untimely comments, saying he had momentarily forgotten that three humans who had somehow managed to live through the terrifying end-time judgments and upheaval were eating with them at the table, including two children. "Don't worry about it, Eli. I've already been thinking how I'll need to be careful what I say and do around the twins. They're outwardly fine, but I suspect inwardly quite fragile, having lost their father in that horrendous Hamas terrorist attack just a few years back, and now their precious mother, not to mention their pet animals and home."

An hour later, Eli and his ten ministers, accompanied by Talel and Yitzhak, were exiting Sarah's front door, on their way to check out their new digs on the western edge of Jerusalem and to get ready for a scheduled late afternoon meeting with the Kadoshim volunteers in a public park near their gifted apartments. As they were departing, Shoshel informed them that Prince David had offered to personally tour Sarah and herself through his royal palace after Temple services that evening, adding that both saints would begin working in their offices located there in the morning. Benny then revealed that he'd accompany his grandfather, Micah, Ken, and maybe a couple other ministers for a palace visit at the same time, where they'd hear Jerusalem Mayor Solomon speak about some new technology that would reportedly revolutionize the restored world.

Governor Eli then took a democratic vote (a dictator he would not be) and all agreed that it might be fun to ride the new subway to their destination, just to test it out. Free to the public, the saints were delighted to discover that the underground trains floated on air instead of riding on tracks, and featured plenty of comfortable passenger seats, with toilets and water fountains in each section. Of course, the trains didn't have many human riders since most evacuated residents were just beginning to return to the Holy City. The journey from Sarah's neighborhood to the new central subway station, located just one block from where the old Jerusalem bus station had stood, took only eight minutes. After a quick change of trains, it was another ten minutes before they arrived at their destination in the western Judean foothills.

After discovering that their apartment tower was a mere one-minute walk from the subway exit, the twelve saints entered their building's main foyer, which would later host a human doorman. A bank of eight high-speed, gold-plated elevators would whisk passengers up to the apartments, although of course the Kadoshim inhabitants could also simply will themselves to their homes if so desired. Benny and Micah, who'd been major Star Trek fans as young boys, would later prove to prefer the latter option (which they had already dubbed *twinking* since they were literally transported in a twinkling of an eye), always preceding it with one of them enthusiastically proclaiming, "Beam us up, Scottie!"

Rebecca Goldman pointed out a notice in the lobby revealing there were food and gift shops and other public facilities on the bottom and 20th floors, with a recreation area featuring a swimming pool and a gym for human residents on the 39th floor and an exclusive Kadoshim recreation facility on the 40th floor. A rooftop balcony with an outdoor restaurant was open for all to enjoy. After the saints quickly toured their assigned Jerusalem digs, Yitzhak kindly promised to watch over any personal possessions the traveling government officials wished to leave in their apartments in the future.

The Holy Spirit notified Eli's 3,000-plus Kadoshim volunteers when and where to meet up with him and his chosen cabinet ministers. At 3:30 PM, all were dutifully gathered in the lush local park that straddled the wide Nahar Yehuda river just west of the government minister's spiraling apartment building. Similar staggered residential skyscrapers, surrounded by sprawling green public parks, were spread out on either side of the rushing river until it emptied into the Mediterranean Sea south of Tel Aviv, some 20 miles to the west.

As the late afternoon winter sun cast its golden hue upon the assembled saints, Governor Eli profusely thanked the volunteers for offering to serve overseas. Then he introduced his ten ministers to the workers, asking each volunteer to gather around the minister whose area of governmental responsibility most closely matched their own skills and qualifications.

Rebecca Goldman garnered the largest number of Kadoshim helpers, nearly 950, which was excellent given she was Health Minister with the most urgent human needs to fulfill. Micah Kupinski came next with 822 construction-related volunteers—equally positive since another pressing task was restoring human infrastructure virtually from scratch. As both Education and Religious Affairs Minister, Rabbi Benjamin Goldman had the next largest pool of workers, 643. They would help him establish schools on all of the Greek islands and open public places of worship.

Benny was pleased to have 486 Kadoshim with some sort of security background gathered around him. A similar number would aid Ken Preston in rebuilding communications networks, with 345 volunteers assisting Abe Goldman to restore transport systems. Sampson Baker would be aided by 278 volunteers as he set up a financial network for the province, and around 95 former captains of industry and trade and farm owners would aid Tom McPherson as he put together the framework for future economic and agricultural expansion.

Very few volunteers stood near Jonathan; which was fine with him since his Foreign Ministry would only really come into play once a normal functioning society was re-established. The same was true for Craig Eagleman, the new Culture, Sports and Music Minister. Both had actually already offered to assist Eli in setting up his overall governmental body in the near term, and to aid any other minister who urgently needed their help.

The various ministers spent several minutes ascertaining what type of skills and experience their volunteers brought with them. Rebecca was pleased to learn that she had over 400 former doctors and 520 registered nurses in her crowd. Micah had 310 building foremen and 245 contractors, along with many architects, building engineers and construction workers. Rabbi Benjamin had over 400 former professional educators in his group, including 83 university professors and 124 school principals. He discovered that many of the teachers had taught courses about the Christian faith in private schools, so they could also aid him in establishing worship centers. Nearly 200 of his volunteers had served as pastors in their human incarnations. Benny had 295 former policemen in his volunteer batch, including nearly 80 police chiefs, along with 118 special army forces personnel, navy seals, ex- marines, and government security agents, along with a few former lawyers and judges.

After the cabinet ministers outlined pending projects with their groups of willing workers, Eli announced that all would meet at the same park at 8:00 AM the next morning to head over to the island of Crete, their first stop of the day. After briefly joining in prayer, the new provincial governor again thanked his volunteers and wished them all much success.

In a split second, most of the assembled Kadoshim willed themselves over to the base of the Temple Mount to join millions of others on the ground and in the air who were gathered to witness the inaugural parade of priests ascending the long southern stairs in preparation for the evening celebratory worship service at 5:00 PM. Eli and his cabinet ministers appeared as requested near Sarah and Shoshel, who were standing with Talel and Bet-el near the north office wing of Prince David's palace. The human twins were resting back home with Donna.

"Shalom friends," greeted Sarah after the five Goldmans and the others materialized near her. "These are our new office windows behind us; this one is mine, and there is Shoshel's. We'll be able to watch tens of thousands of saints entering and exiting the Holy Temple all day long while working at our desks, and also this majestic procession each evening before the Temple service. Isn't that simply marvelous?"

"It is a tremendous site to behold," concurred Rabbi Benjamin. Marching in unison before the gathered saints were row after row of perpetual Temple priests; some vigorously shaking cymbals or tambourines, others blowing shofars or waving colorful banners. Precisely 100 per row, all but the shofar-blowers were singing lilting psalms of praise in ten-part perfect-pitch harmony. "I recognize those lyrics," the rabbi added, noting they came from Psalm 150: *Praise the Lord! Praise God in His sanctuary! Praise Him in His mighty expanse! Praise Him for His mighty deeds! Praise Him according to His excellent greatness!*

Governor Eli added some thoughts as the Kadoshim listened in reverence to the powerful voices while their gleaming eyes followed the enchanting holy parade. "I don't know about all of you, but as exciting and invigorating as this day's events have already been—highlighted by the addresses from King Yeshua and Prince David, and a fantastic lunch at Sarah's new home—I've been longing all day to gather again with all the Redeemed into one sacred Body in the Temple at sunset, with the Lord Himself as our Head. Has anyone else felt that way?" Without exception, all either answered "yes" or nodded their affirmation.

"Look! There's my brother Jesse!" bellowed Benny after spotting the blond priest marching about half way up the 150 steps. The stirring sight brought instant tears to Sarah's eyes, washing away the last vestiges of sorrow still lingering after Jonathan's surprise revelation of his secret sin the evening before.

"Now they're singing lyrics taken from Psalm 147," announced Rabbi Benjamin as he watched in awe while his second great grandson and thousands of other sanctified priests ascended up to the Holy Temple. In reality, all of the billion plus Kadoshim were fulfilling priestly roles every day when they gathered as one unified Body in the sacred sanctuary. But Jesse, along with Jonathan's twin brother David, were especially privileged to serve in that hallowed position night and day, as they would do for all eternity.

Praise the Lord! For it is good to sing praises to our God, for it is pleasant and praise is becoming. The Lord builds up Jerusalem. He gathers the outcasts of Israel. He heals the brokenhearted, and binds up their wounds.

After another exhilarating two-hour praise and worship session before the King of Glory—seated as the Great High Priest upon His matchless throne—most of the Kadoshim dispersed to their homes. However Sarah and Shoshel invited Jonathan and Eli to accompany them on Prince David's scheduled private tour of his elegant palace. The government officials gladly accepted the kind offer.

"Ah, my new palace administrator!" proclaimed Israel's royal governor as he greeted his guests in his opulent main foyer. "And welcome as well to you, sweet Sarah, but who are these two bums?" he joked as he eagerly shook Eli and Jonathan's hands.

"We're just here to make sure our friends are working in sanitary conditions with adequate job benefits," Eli quipped back as the second handshake ended.

The four Kadoshim were overwhelmed at the sheer beauty of the Prince's stately palace. Shoshel couldn't believe that she would be moving around this magnificent regal home every day but Shabbat; bumping into the likes of Queen Batsheva and the ancient Jewish patriarchs and matriarchs while supervising the mostly human palace staff. Although Sarah would often be out at one of Jerusalem's hospitals or clinics, she too found it exhilarating beyond words to think that she would have an office in such a noble complex.

After the five entered the north office wing, Prince David informed Shoshel that she would report directly to Batsheva on a daily basis, alerting his former queen to any special problems or needs that arose and coordinating all public functions in the home, including in the basement grand hall. "Batsheva will have an office not far from yours, at the northwest corner of this wing, right over there" the Prince informed her. "Tomorrow you can begin interviewing human applicants for the staff positions we need to fill," he added while escorting the four saints past a northern entrance that would be used by palace and office workers like Sarah and Shoshel. "You'll also select a private secretary for yourself Shoshel, as will you Sarah."

"Can I apply?" asked a poker-faced Jonathan as he inwardly rejoiced at the superb servant positions that the Great Provider had assigned to his beloved earthly wife and her longtime closest friend.

As Shoshel, Eli and the Goldmans were being escorted around Prince David's fabulous palace; Benny sat riveted in the basement hall with his grandfather Abe, his dear friend Micah, Craig, Ken, Tom McPherson and Sampson Baker. Prince David's celebrated earthly son Solomon stood tall on the stage wearing a golden-colored Jerusalem-stone necklace visible at the top of the opening of his flowing beige robe, which was embroidered with alternating pictures of the Holy Temple and the Trees of Life. Seated on the dais right behind him was his earthly mother Batsheva, along with Prince David's chief advisor, Yonatan Ben Shaul.

Solomon's ruddy skin glowed as he employed his erudite wisdom to explain some important technological breakthroughs to around 5,000 gathered international government ministers. "My dear colleagues, welcome again to our family's Jerusalem palace. Let me get straight to my topic. A team of royal Kadoshim scientists went to work immediately after Shabbat ended last evening. Their goal was to study the new buildings and homes that our merciful Savior provided for us here in His Holy Land. Actually they examined this palace first, at Prince David's suggestion. Attached to the flat roof, they came upon dozens of solar panels. Some are designed to heat water, and others to gather energy from the sun for electrical purposes.

"As for the solar water panels, they feature same basic simple technology that was widely employed in Israel in the passing era to heat water in homes and offices, as was also the case to a lesser degree elsewhere around the world. However the system's ability to meet all home needs was limited by the fact that clouds occasionally obscured the sunlight for days on end, especially during the winter months. Now that the climate of the entire world has been altered, giving us uninterrupted sunlight every day, apart from an occasional passing cloud, we can meet all global hot water needs with this technology. The solar panels designed to produce electricity will in a similar fashion be far more effective due to the wonderful climate changes that we'll all enjoy in every part of this restored planet."

Benny nudged Micah as he whispered "I can't wait to go for a swim with you in Greece."

"And maybe some deep-sea diving as well," added Micah softly back to him.

"On top of this, our scientists discovered an incredible gift from the Father that will spell the end of most fossil fuel use from now on. No longer will oil spills spoil our oceans or noxious automobile emissions poison our air. Nuclear and coal power plants will no longer be needed at all, no matter how large the earth's population grows. The breakthrough is this device that I hold in my hand."

Mayor Solomon moved from behind his granite podium and held up the small item for all to see. Benny and the other assembled ministers deployed their zoom eye lenses to study the object up close. Flat and rectangular like a cellphone or digital music player, it was only two inches wide and four inches long. Built in to one of its narrow sides was a series of small copper prongs that looked like they were meant to connect with some other device.

"This, my friends, is a new divinely-created battery that can store enormous amounts of solar produced electricity inside of it. Our scientists determined that each battery can power an automobile for over 1,000 hours of operation on the road. It can also power an average household for at least two weeks. In fact, this entire palace is only using up one per day, and we have dozens of fully charged batteries in storage. Of course, public and home energy needs have already been greatly reduced due to the moderate temperatures now being enjoyed all over the globe, meaning winter heating and summer air cooling are no longer required in most locations."

"Cool!" exclaimed Benny just loud enough to be heard by all those seated around him.

"When not in use, the fantastic new batteries will be slotted into a designated space on a large receptacle where the solar energy flows into them from an attached converter box. The receptacles hold a dozen batteries at a time. They're attached to the boxes and solar panels via traditional power cords. We intend to set up thousands of giant charging farms all over the globe. For a very cheap price, human beings will be able to purchase dozens of batteries at a time for their personal needs. They can also install home charging devices and panels to meet their own energy requirements. It only takes a few days of sunlight to fully recharge each battery. Our new solar panels are able to capture much more energy from natural sunlight than the old panels in the previous era.

"The car batteries can be conveniently stored in vehicle glove compartments and similar places. Two batteries will be inserted into a slot on the front panel at any one time; one for current use and one set on reserve mode, which will kick in automatically when the first battery runs out of juice. The same principal will apply in homes and all other buildings. Electric panel boxes in any undestroyed private homes will be replaced with new ones that can hold four batteries at a time, three on reserve. In public buildings, the number of panels and batteries will be increased to meet internal energy requirements. Aircraft will continue to utilize fossil fuel, but vastly improved engine designs and lighter building components will significantly reduce the amount of fuel needed to power them."

Benny winked at his grandfather Abe, who he recalled loved to fly business class during his frequent airplane forays when he owned his travel agency in Illinois.

Mayor Solomon turned around and placed the small battery on the nearby podium before sharing more information. "Employing the luminous star in the sky that our planet orbits every year, the eternal Son of God will transform energy use on earth; eliminating all pollution and national strife connected to the use of fossil fuels, coal and nuclear energy which sullied the previous era.

"My dear colleagues, your provinces will each be provided with thousands of these batteries by the end of this week, along with hundreds of recharging platforms and solar panels. Production of them all has already begun in two factories down on the coast north of Tel Aviv. Our scientific teams were amazed and thrilled to find out this morning that the factories had been graciously prepared in advance by our Heavenly Father, making the discovery of this breakthrough technology rather easy and inevitable."

Solomon turned and smiled at his radiant earthly mother and his father's beloved friend Yonatan before he continued with his informative address. "Each of your provinces will be provided with similar production factories in the coming weeks. Meanwhile you should have enough supplies to meet essential energy needs in your respective zones of governance.

I have some additional information of special interest to all of you Communication Ministers." Ken sat up straight in his seat at this notice of coming attractions. "Our scientific teams also came upon a fully-equipped factory near the energy production complex designed to produce telecommunications satellites. Not far away was yet another factory that will produce the rockets needed to propel the

181

satellites into space. As stated earlier, the rockets will utilize fossil fuel. You may not realize that almost all former communications and spy satellites were destroyed when magnetic firestorms ripped through the heavens in the days just prior to our Lord's return. We shall send up dozens of solar-powered communication satellites before King Yeshua's glorious Millennial Kingdom coronation ceremony here in Jerusalem in five weeks time, giving people all over the planet the opportunity to view it live."

Despite possessing a photographic memory like all the Kadoshim, Ken was busily scribbling notes on a pad of paper. He thought this was just too good to be true.

"Around two weeks from today, relay stations and equipment will be shipped by boat to all of your provinces, which you can then set up in time to download the international broadcasts for viewing by your human populations. We'll also provide large flat-screen television sets to be placed in public places. Individual television set production is not a high priority at present. Mobile cellphone and internet services will take awhile to reestablish as well, but they're frankly not a high government priority either since we Kadoshim have other means of communication to employ." Craig Eagleman, who'd disdained hi-tech gadgets in the old era, smiled at Benny over that last remark.

"I trust this presentation has been helpful and encouraging to all of you. We who are serving here in your world capital, Jerusalem, pray that the Lord of Hosts will grant you much success as you go out tomorrow to begin your sacred assigned tasks. Remember that we're always here to support you in whatever manner you may require. Godspeed dear friends and colleagues, and much shalom from the Lord on high!"

ELEVEN

BRING THE CHILDREN TO ME

Eli Ben David spent the night in corporate prayer with Jonathan and their four other Jerusalem roommates, interspersed with times of private prayer and reflection alone on the spacious apartment balcony. Just after 3:00 AM, he received a call in his spirit to return to Prince David's palace for an important meeting. He invited Jonathan to join him. In a flash, the longtime buddies were there.

Eli and Jonathan materialized right in front of the main palace entrance. Although it was the middle of a winter night, the temperature was a pleasant 65 degrees. The glowing Temple walls above the palace, reflecting out the Shekinah Glory within the sacred sanctuary, produced enough light to easily make out everything around them without the use of streetlamps or any other artificial light. It was as if the Holy City was bathed all night in a perpetual dawn.

A single saint was standing just inside the open door next to a ceremonial palace guard. Eli and Jonathan immediately recognized him as they moved toward the entrance. "Shalom Governor Eli and Foreign Minister Jonathan," he said as he thrust out his right hand.

"Shalom to you, Foreign Minister Shaul," Eli shot back as he shook the Apostle's strong hand. Shaul was nearly four inches shorter than Jonathan and three inches less than Eli, which meant he measured almost six feet—significantly taller than his human incarnation. His closely cropped straight hair and eyes were dark brown, and he no longer needed anyone to act as his scribe because of poor eyesight.

"Eli, I have some old friends who would like to join your volunteer work party later today. And by the way, I'll probably drop by at some point; the Greek Isles being one of my favorite places in the entire Mediterranean basin. Come, I'll introduce you to my friends."

Kingdom Foreign Minister Shaul led his intrigued guests into a small sitting room just off of the main palace foyer. "Friends, this is Eli Ben David, the new provincial governor of the Greek Isles, and this is his Foreign Minister and chief advisor, Jonathan Goldman." The two government officials smiled politely as their names were uttered.

"Gentle ones, this is my good friend Doctor Luke, and that is Aquila, and next to her Prisca, who served the saints in the old era in what later became known as western Turkey. This fine young man is Stephanas, and next to him are Fortunas and Achaicus, and Crispus from Corinth. That is Jason from Thessaloniki, and this is my dear friend Timothy."

"We're honored to make your acquaintance," proclaimed Doctor Luke on behalf of the others.

"The feeling is quite mutual," replied Eli, half wondering if he was not experiencing a sweet dream after a late-night read though the book of Acts.

The Apostle Shaul got right to his point. "Governor Eli, my friends are mostly of Greek extraction, as you undoubtedly know, and they—like me—have a tremendous burden for their former homeland and its human citizens. Doctor Luke would like to join your health team in the morning and assess the needs on the ground, assisted by most of the others. Timothy and Jason are interested in helping out your Religious Affairs Minister to assess your province's spiritual needs."

"We're honored beyond words," replied Eli. Jonathan nodded his concurrence before revealing that "My human mother is actually our new Minister of Health, and my grandfather, who served as a rabbi in Berlin before World War Two, will be our Religious Affairs Minister."

"Wonderful, then it's settled," stated Shaul with a toothy smile on his stout face.

Nearly as tall as Jonathan with olive colored skin and reddish-brown curly hair, Doctor Luke asked where and when the provincial governor was meeting with his ministers and volunteers. After Eli spelled out the details, the physician-historian said "We'll wait a little while until you plot your courses with your ministers and volunteers in Crete. When you're ready for us, just let the Holy Spirit know and we shall appear."

"Splendid, brothers and sisters, we'll eagerly await your arrival. Thank you so much for offering to serve your wonderful people in this important endeavor."

After the two delighted Greek Isle officials bade their farewells and departed the palace, Jonathan asked Eli if he'd noticed what language he was just fluently speaking. "What do you mean, Yonni? Wasn't it Hebrew?"

Jonathan laughed as he answered his friend in flawless Greek. "No Eli, you were all speaking Greek, as I am right now. I guess this is another gift from on high, even though I did study a little Greek after becoming a Christian at university."

"It's a gift that will come in very handy I suspect, Yonni. Our Lord is so good!"

Just after sunrise, Jonathan asked Eli (both talking again in Hebrew) if he could break the exciting news to his mother, father and grandfather before all eleven government officials walked over to the adjacent park, where they were scheduled to meet up with their volunteer workers before heading to the Greek Isles. "Sure Yonni, I think they'll be very blessed."

Jonathan knocked on his parents' adjacent apartment door and was quickly let in by Miri Doron, who directed him to the kitchen where his earthly parents and grandfather were enjoying some morning coffee together. "Mom and dad, Grandpa Benjamin, I know you didn't have time to read the New Testament after you gave your lives to the Lord in that Illinois United World prison cell, and certainly not in Auschwitz, but I think you probably all know that one of the Gospels was authored by a man named Luke."

Benjamin Goldman stated he'd heard of the Gospel while a student at a rabbinical seminary in Berlin before Abe affirmed, "We know about Luke as well, son," prompting Rebecca to add, "We actually took up Benny's offer to lend us his Bible soon after he arrived in Skokie. He was really pleased. We took turns reading it out loud to each other over several evenings after Benny went to bed."

"I especially liked the Gospel of John," Abe confessed. "It was so…Jewish, and so was the book of Hebrews. But we were totally puzzled by Revelation, which I guess Yochanan also wrote."

"He did dad, and the island where he recorded his end-time vision will actually be part of our province. Hey, I have a nice surprise for all three of you. The author of the biblical books of Luke and Acts, Doctor Luke, will be joining us today, along with a team of mostly Greek saints who are either mentioned in his books or by the Apostle Shaul, who sort of 'stars' in Acts, grandfather. Luke's a physician, mom, and wants to assist your ministry in setting up hospital facilities this week. And two others who are Jewish want to help you, Granddad, set up worship facilities on the populated islands. One is named Jason, who headed up a synagogue in Thessaloniki, and the other is Timothy, whose father was Greek. You must've read Shaul's letters addressed to him."

"Oh that's fantastic news!" exclaimed Abe, adding that he'd explain to his rabbi father who these saints were during their short stroll to the park.

At exactly 8:00 AM, Eli was standing in the warm morning sunshine before his new cabinet ministers and their eager Kadoshim volunteers. He had already decided to break the riveting news of who would be aiding them only after they all arrived in Crete. The governor asked Rabbi Benjamin to lead them in a brief prayer for the day ahead. When it was finished, Eli said, "Lord, please take us to Iraklion Crete." In a twink they were there.

Before the Lord's final judgments began to rock the earth, Iraklion had been the largest city on the island of Crete, and the fourth most populated in all of Greece. An ancient city dating back to some 2,000 years before Messiah's birth in Bethlehem, it was home to over 140,000 residents when the last government census was taken. With a thriving port and an international airport, it had been the biggest city in Eli's new sprawling island domain.

Crete itself was by far the largest of the over 6,000 Greek islands, whose numbers were reduced by nearly a thousand during the final tectonic upheavals. Measuring 160 miles across and 37 miles at its widest point, the mountainous island was the fifth largest in the entire Mediterranean Sea. The center of the Minoan civilization, the oldest and most advanced in Europe dating back to nearly 3,000 years before Messiah's birth, it had a year-round population of over 650,000 people. However this number would swell greatly every summer as many Greeks fled the hot mainland for the cooler islands, joined by tens of thousands of Germans, Brits and other Europeans who maintained holiday homes in Crete.

Iraklion was centrally located on the northern coastline of the elongated island. It faced all of the other eastern Greek islands, which themselves numbered well over 4,000, stretching from Crete some 150 miles southeast of Athens to the island of Thassos, due east of Thessaloniki, which was located nearly 400 miles to the north. Most of the islands in Eli's new province that managed to survive the final world judgments were very small and uninhabited, but at least 60 had year round communities and most had been popular tourist destinations in the old era. All of the remaining islands had physically moved about 10 miles to the southeast, meaning they were now a bit closer to Israel, which was located less than 500 miles east of Crete.

Gathered with his cabinet ministers and volunteer saints near the virtually destroyed seaport, Eli outlined the general program for the day. The ministers and their workers would spend several hours on Crete, assessing its most urgent needs and setting up medical facilities. Judging from the devastated condition of the city located directly behind him, he noted that a lot of elbow grease would be needed to rebuild the infrastructure of the large island. However before that could commence, the medical teams would be assisted by most of the other volunteers in setting up immediate-care facilities in Iraklion and four other island towns. He revealed that the Holy Spirit had shown him during the night exactly where they were located and what their general needs were.

The new provincial governor explained that after leaving behind half of the volunteers on Crete, he would accompany most of his cabinet ministers and the rest of the saints to the second most inhabited island under his rule, Rhodes. They would visit several other large islands after that, leaving volunteer crews in every location.

Eli then requested that the Holy Spirit alert Doctor Luke and his crew to appear, which they did moments later. All the gathered Kadoshim, but especially those who'd been Greek Christians in their earlier incarnations (at least 800 fit that description, which is why the Lord assigned them to Eli's group) were awed to meet the saints who had ministered with the Apostle Shaul. Rebecca Goldman was especially pleased to have such an eminent physician on board her substantial medical team.

The Kadoshim were increasingly shocked as they set out to tour the nearly annihilated city of Iraklion. Portions of concrete buildings and homes littered the cracked streets. Fires had swept through most areas, leaving charred remains in their cruel wake. The putrid stench of dead bodies—some appearing to have been in that condition for several months—hung like rotting rags in the air. The saints were thankful their new noses had the ability to block out the odious smells after sampling a short whiff.

As the stunned saints wandered around the rubble in the streets, Eli instructed Micah to set up crews who would immediately begin dissolving the ruined city's remains, along with all the decaying bodies. After enough space was cleared, Rebecca Goldman would call out for medical tents and equipment, which would be instantly delivered from Israel via angelic couriers. Then building volunteers would assemble the tents before the trained doctors and nurses went to work. Any surviving Greek medical personnel would be recruited to aid the Holy Ones.

Micah had been doing a fine job sending out cleansing crews until his bud Benny spotted the children. The Construction Minister—who'd been a mere lad when the Sovereign Lord returned to earth—was busy discussing the dissolution program with his childhood friend and Rabbi Benjamin when Benny noticed the orphans. Numbering some 220 helpless souls, they were clustered 55 feet away underneath the still-standing remains of an aluminum warehouse several blocks from the port. Some of the children were completely naked, others wore torn dirty rags. Most displayed wounds of one kind or another. Like half-starved wild dogs, they were rapidly downing morning manna that they'd apparently just gathered in the area. Behind them lay several dozen children on soiled blankets, presumably too sick or wounded to sit up and eat. Sweat stains and vomit were visible everywhere.

Jonathan noticed the startled look on his son's face before he too spotted the children. He quickly went over and put his arms around both Benny and Micah. Eli walked over to check out why the four saints had stopped walking. He bowed his head low after Benny pointed toward the clustered children, most seemingly under age five or six at best.

Rabbi Benjamin started to daven back and forth as he asked the Lord to assist them.

Eli rushed back and fetched Rebecca and Doctor Luke, who were discussing medical plans as they strolled thirty feet behind most of the other ministers. After viewing the jarring discovery, the Health Minister immediately called out for an angelic medical delivery, which appeared seconds later. Micah then snapped back into action, ordering qualified construction volunteers to immediately begin assembling the large tent, utilizing the tools that were part of the special delivery. Similar scenes would occur throughout the city and elsewhere all day long as the Kadoshim began to spread the Messiah's visible rule of mercy and grace to the entire world.

As the medical tent was being erected, Rebecca joined Doctor Luke and other physicians in evaluating the children's conditions and urgent needs. They quickly ascertained that well over 100 displayed open wounds, 42 had broken limbs, 16 showed symptoms of concussion, several appeared likely to have internal bleeding, and all were emaciated, although the manna was helping greatly to alleviate that condition. Indeed, if the supernatural food had not been provided by the Heavenly Father, none of the children would have survived at all. A subsequent analysis by several of Eli's volunteer scientists determined that the sweet wafers contained all of the essential daily vitamins and minerals needed for healthy human existence.

Tom McPherson was the only government minister who'd seen Iraklion before it was destroyed. Indeed, his maternal grandparents, Alexander Palamis and his wife Dianna, were born and raised in the city. The new provincial official had walked silently ten paces behind Rebecca Goldman and the other ministers, not able to speak at all. Despite his best efforts to appear governmental, he could not stop the tears from flowing down his cheeks. However the sight of the desperate children jolted Tom back to today. He rushed over and picked up one of the little Greek girls who was sobbing the loudest. "Calm down honey, it'll be alright. We're here to help you." Although he knew quite a bit of Greek from his human upbringing, he was now fluent like the rest of the cabinet ministers and volunteer workers.

One of the tallest boys explained to Tom and Eli that they were staying near the port because of its abundant drinking water. The less injured older boys would take turns lugging filled buckets from the purified sea to bring water back to the others. Several dozen lads were healthy and strong enough to do this job, he added, noting it also gave them an opportunity to take a swim and clean up. Benny then asked the boy his name and how old he was. "I'm Nikos, and I'm nearly eight years old!" he proclaimed with a proud smile. It was almost exactly the age that Benny had been when he received his new body, sparking an instant bond of love for the boy that would endure forever.

As they toured Crete's other main centers, the saints discovered thousands of children in similar conditions, along with hundreds of adults who had somehow managed to both avoid Andre's mark and survive the final judgments which fell upon his devilish kingdom. Four were qualified doctors who'd been working day and night to save the children's lives under the harrowing conditions they found themselves in. Three gave their lives to the Lord on the spot when told who the saints were and why they'd come to help, while the fourth had already done so on her own.

Craig Eagleman offered to stay behind with Tom to visit other towns and oversee the day's operations in Crete. Governor Eli gladly accepted the suggestion and then accompanied his other ministers and crews to their next destination, the island of Rhodes, located 11 miles southwest of the Turkish coast. The fourth largest Greek island with a pre-tribulation population of 120,000, its main city was also called Rhodes. The urban center was in similar condition to Iraklion. Over 4,000 children were discovered alive, along with a few hundred adults. Doctor Luke, who'd visited the island with the Apostle Shaul in biblical days, offered to stay behind with a group of volunteers to supervise medical operations on the once beautiful isle.

The other Kadoshim moved on to the third biggest Greek island, Lesbos, which had a smaller permanent population than Rhodes. Located just a few miles off the western Turkish coast near where the ancient city of Pergamum once stood, it had been a popular tourist destination for many international lesbians since one of its most famous local poets in antiquity, Sappho, was a woman who wrote poems of love about other women (which became the root for the modern 'lesbian' moniker). Its main city of Mytilene—also visited by the Apostle Shaul on his journeys through the region—was totally destroyed. The island's tallest peak, Mount Olympus, had collapsed, going from over 3,000 to just under 850 feet high. Around 1,800 children remained alive, along with 127 adults.

The next stop was on the fifth largest Greek island, Chios, also located off the Turkish coast, but west of the ancient city of Smyrna. With a permanent old-era population of just over 50,000 people, only a few hundred children remained, along with 43 adults. After leaving behind a volunteer crew at the stop, the dwindling number of Kadoshim visited the next largest island in Eli's domain, Samos, located one mile from the Turkish coast. Although the ninth biggest Greek island, it was less than 200 square miles in size. Its year round population had been just over 35,000, and very few remained alive.

Eli and his accompanying cabinet ministers were very pleasantly surprised to discover that on the next largest Greek island in their province, Naxos—which would be their last stop of the day—the number of survivors was much greater than any other island they'd visited except Crete. This welcome fact was initially an enigma to Eli since he knew from his research that its pre-judgment permanent population was just over 20,000 people, although it was also a very popular tourist destination with many European Union and Greek summer residents. Located in the middle of the surrounding Cycladic islands, which was also not far south of the geographical center of Eli's sprawling new island province, the tenth largest Greek island was much closer to Athens than Crete and the other islands they'd visited near the west coast of Turkey. Like several surrounding islands, it had been serviced daily by high-speed passenger ships from the port of Piraeus which could make the journey from nearby Athens in just over three hours.

The mystery was later resolved when Eli and associates learned that many of the over 3,200 surviving children and nearly 400 adults had fled the mainland metropolis in the last months of Andre's world-wide rule, landing mostly on islands within a hundred or so miles from the Greek capital city. Naxos fit that bill, as did Mykonos just a few miles to the north, and Paros, five miles to the west. The saints would discover the next day that those adjacent islands, plus Ios, Sikinos, and the lovely island of Santorini—all viewable south of Naxos—also had proportionally far more survivors than any of the other islands they'd visited in the sprawling province. They quickly learned that another draw to Naxos was the fact that, with verdant fields nestled in mountain valleys and along the coastal plain, it was considered the potato growing capital of Greece, and therefore a good source of food as famine swept the earth.

Governor Ben David had been keeping an eye out for a possible capital as they visited the biggest islands in his new province. While pondering the question in Jerusalem the day before, he'd thought he would probably settle for Iraklion, since Crete was by far the biggest isle under his rule and would certainly have the largest population once again as the number of human beings grew over time.

Now the nascent government official was leaning towards Naxos. For one thing, he loved its natural beauty, noticing upon arrival that unlike Crete with just a few nearby small islands, the views of the surrounding hilly islands from Naxos were utterly spectacular. Plus its highest granite peak, Mount Zas (named after the ancient mythological Greek god Zeus, who was supposedly raised in a cave on the mountain), had remained basically intact during the final earthquakes, still standing at well over 3,000 feet high. Eli would later find out that

Naxos had been the seat of a regional government established by the Roman Catholic Church in the wake of the Fourth Crusade, comprised mainly of Italians from Venice. What little remained of the old era architecture in the island's main port-town still bore that out.

Eli also liked the geographical location of Naxos in relation to the rest of the spread-out islands under his administrative authority. It would take a human traveler many hours to reach Iraklion by boat from Thassos in the far north of the Aegean Sea, but one-third less time to arrive at Naxos. On top of that, Naxos was much closer to the province of Athens where the regional Holy Temple would be built with Micah Kupinski's assistance.

Now fully convinced of his choice, Eli informed Jonathan before telling him that they would go scouting together in the morning to determine an exact location for their shared mansion. The government leader then bowed his head and asked the Lord to bring Craig, Tom and Doctor Luke to him to report how things were going on Crete and Rhodes. The summoned saints appeared just seconds later. Both Craig and Doctor Luke revealed that they'd been able to recruit very few human adult assistants to help care for the children, so they asked if Eli would check with officials in Jerusalem to see if a skeleton crew of Kadoshim could remain behind during the two-hour worship service set to begin in just forty minutes time. Eli promised to immediately submit their request to his superiors in the world's new capital city. He asked Craig and Tom to stay put for a couple minutes while letting Doctor Luke return to his posting. Then Eli called for Benny and Micah to join them. After the childhood friends arrived, the governor informed the four ministers of his decision to place his provincial capital in Naxos, and asked them to accompany him and Jonathan the next morning to scout out a site for their new government mansion. All replied they were pleased with Eli's decision and would gladly help him pick a suitable location.

Seconds later, Governor Eli Ben David appeared outside of King Yeshua's Jerusalem palace. He was entering the beautiful building for the first time. It was similar to Prince David's palatial home, but significantly larger and definitely more ornate. After stating his name and governmental role and what his business was at the imperial residence, Eli was escorted by a guard up to Yochanan's second-floor office. He repeated his information to the Apostle's secretary before being let into the inner office.

"Eli, how good to see you! I was hoping to come visit you and your team with Foreign Minister Shaul today, but we've had a larger influx of returning Jewish and Arab refugees than expected, so we've all been very busy helping out with that. Hopefully we can head over tomorrow."

"That would be delightful, Yochanan. We'd all be tremendously honored to have you and Shaul see the work we're doing. The needs are very great, but we have a dedicated team helping us, and so far all is going smoothly. But I do have one issue to discuss with you. Doctor Luke and Craig Eagleman asked me for permission to leave behind small skeleton crews during our two-hour worship service this evening; and probably all week long. They've only managed to recruit a few human adult helpers so far and we've discovered many orphaned young children today on the islands. Quite a few seem to be from the mainland who escaped with their families. Many of the children have told us their parents were Andre's followers, and so they perished during the Lord's final judgments of the Beast's evil kingdom."

"I'll check on that immediately, Eli. The Lord's office is right next door. Just give me a minute and I'll let you know what He decrees."

"Thank you, kind brother."

Yochanan returned moments later with a positive answer. "King Yeshua says it will be fine to leave behind small volunteer crews. You know Eli, He has a very soft spot for young children. Plus He asked if you'd join several other governors in His royal procession into the Temple in just thirty minutes time. The others have already been told to meet downstairs in the main sitting room at 4:50 PM. Bring along your new purple cape."

"Thank you so much Yochanan. What a tremendous blessing it will be to watch the Holy One of Israel parade into the sacred sanctuary."

"Oh, you won't just be watching, Eli," Yochanan said with a twinkle in his beautiful eyes as a smile appeared on his face.

"What do you mean?"

"You'll find out soon enough, my dear friend. Now I better get back to work; and you as well. See you here again soon!"

Sarah and Shoshel's day had been similar to their Kadoshim friends hard at work on the Greek Isles. They'd arrived together outside the north office wing of Prince David's palace at 8:00 AM. After inspecting their marvelous new offices, which contained large mahogany desks and matching bookcases, two comfortable arm chairs for visitors and decorative fish tanks teeming with bass, trout and other aquatic varieties, they quickly begun preparing printed applications for the human workers that each would need to recruit later in the day. Sarah planned to head over late morning to the largest new hospital in her district, Hadassah. Twelve floors high, it had been created in the exact location where the renowned old-world medical institution previously stood, just above the village of Ein Kerem in southwest Jerusalem which was once home to King Yeshua's second cousin, Elizabeth, known in Hebrew as Elisheva. After meeting with Batsheva, Shoshel would tour the palace again and make note of specific needs there.

However their plans changed when Prince David unexpectedly entered Shoshel's new office.

"Good morning, dear one. You look radiant today, as usual."

"Thank you, kind prince, you do as well."

"Bless you. Shoshel, I've just received a note from Mayor Solomon who is heading up a team of volunteer Kadoshim workers in the great hall downstairs. He informed me the number of refugees arriving in the city this morning from the eastern deserts is significantly greater than anticipated. He enquired if you and Sarah would be willing to go down and assist him and his team in processing some of them this morning. You'll hopefully find some qualified applicants for the positions you need to fill at the same time. Batsheva has prepared a detailed breakdown of our expected palace needs which you can pick up on your way downstairs."

"We'll be honored to assist in this effort, Prince David. I'll let Sarah know right away."

Shoshel and Sarah stood with amazed expressions on their radiant faces. They had just arrived at the west foyer main entrance after passing through the substantial palace from the north government office wing. Seven lines of returning Jewish and Arab refugees stretched beyond the palace doors for as far as they could see. The two friends quickly concluded that the broad stairway leading down to the great hall was far too crowded for them to successfully navigate it. They would later learn that a small stairway designed for use by the royal family was tucked away inside Prince David's office in the north wing. At any rate, they simply willed themselves downstairs and they were instantly there.

Packed with people of all ages, the great auditorium reeked of human sweat. Most had been walking for almost one week, eating fresh manna every morning after camping overnight. They'd only stopped a few times a day to drink water from one of the new springs that had sprouted up all over the transformed desert, and to relieve themselves behind rocks, trees and bushes.

Thousands of sealed Jewish males had been ministering to the last-days refugees in the desert, many for several years. However all of the redeemed saints had disappeared as soon as King Yeshua's feet touched down upon the Mount of Olives. The sealed Jews had previously informed their human charges they would be transported to meet Him when He returned to earth, making clear that this would be the signal for them to pack up their meager belongings and begin their arduous journeys back to Jerusalem and other parts of Israel. They were also told that food and drink would be provided for them along the way.

A survey being handed out by the volunteer Kadoshim workers would later reveal that over half of the returnees had either already been believers when they fled the besieged Israeli capital city, or had given their lives to the Jewish Messiah under the guidance of the sealed males. Another quarter had done so after the Lord's supernatural sign first appeared in the eastern sky the previous Rosh Ha Shana, called in the Bible the Feast of Trumpets. The rest were either too young to make such a spiritual decision or still not certain where they stood in relation to Israel's Eternal King.

A majority of the Jewish refugees came from Orthodox backgrounds, while some of the Arabs—about twenty per cent of the total returnees—still labeled themselves as observant Muslims. Neither indigenous religious community had exactly welcomed Emperor Andre's spurious claims to be some divine savior who would unite the world in worship of himself. Between the two ancient religions, their numbers had initially been large enough in Jerusalem to successfully resist attempts by Andre's United World security personnel to force them to accept his mark, although in the end most had found they could only sustain their resistance by fleeing to the desert.

Sarah and Shoshel quickly spotted Mayor Solomon and reported for duty. He sat them down in some open chairs at one of several eighty-foot-long tables where hundreds of Kadoshim were taking down names, handing out surveys and assigning housing to the refugees. Then King David's most famous son informed Sarah he had just heard that dozens of doctors and nurses had already been registered, adding that their names and addresses would be given to her later. In the meantime, the municipal ruler would gladly have her application forms handed out to all of the other volunteers, who'd pass them along to any person reporting previous medical experience. The esteemed mayor told Shoshel he would also see to it that the forms she'd drawn up would be given to the Kadoshim workers, designed to help find qualified maids, butlers, gardeners, chefs, waiters and waitresses, kitchen workers, doormen and security guards.

In the end, Sarah and Shoshel spent all day in the grand hall. The people just kept coming, and so they quickly realized that their help was desperately needed. More than that, other volunteers kept sending a stream of returnees over to them whom they felt might be good candidates to fill their work positions. By the end of the day, both Shoshel and Sarah had scheduled hundreds of appointments with eager applicants who were more than ready to get back to work.

Before each individual returning refugee left the downstairs palatial hall, they were given a small care package that contained healing leaves from the Trees of Life. This would help the many not feeling well to rapidly recover. Despite this, Sarah could see that there were many urgent medical needs to fill. She also realized that the sheer numbers of human beings streaming back into the land—a large portion of them children—would mean the hospitals and clinics under her supervision would hardly be empty. She decided to ask Prince David to give her a handful of Kadoshim volunteers to conduct scheduled job interviews while she toured all of the new facilities the next day. Sarah would also put in a request for additional qualified volunteers to labor in the facilities until she could get her human staff in place. The immediate care needs would obviously be great, as Nurse Leah Rabinowitz had anticipated. Leah was actually already working at the new Hadassah Hospital, along with most of the rest of the volunteer Kadoshim doctors and nurses who had helped heal the sick and injured in the shut-down Augusta Victoria medical facility.

Governor Eli showed up at King Yeshua's palace as requested at 4:50 PM. He'd dropped by his west Jerusalem apartment to pick up his new governor's cape, which he was now proudly donning. When the provincial ruler entered the large south-side sitting room, he was thrilled to see Yoseph Steinberg, Moshe Salam and Danny Katz seated together, along with eight other governors whom he did not know. Danny had been assigned to oversee a province in the western half of England centered in the city of Birmingham. It stretched from Chester to Swindon. His parents immigrated to Israel from a Birmingham suburb in the 1980s, and his family had returned there annually to visit his two sets of grandparents and other relatives.

Eli greeted his fellow administrators with glee shining out of his gentle eyes. "Shalom governors! It's wonderful to see you all." He then sat down in an empty chair next to his former pastor, Yoseph.

After introductions were made all around, Eli leaned over and quietly asked Yoseph if he knew what was up. "I'm really not sure Eli, and neither are any of the other governors here with us, but it seems we're going to play some sort of ceremonial role in the Lord's entrance into the Holy Temple today. I'm basing that guess on the fact that we were all asked to wear our new purple capes, which by the way you look great in." Eli blushed as Yoseph spotted Yochanan waltzing into the spacious sitting room, and so added, "It seems we'll find out soon what's in store, brother."

"Shalom, shalom to all of you fine governors! I bring you greetings as well from Yeshua, our revered Messiah and King! Brethren, every day from now on, His Majesty will select twelve different governors to assist in His ceremonial entrance into the sacred Temple. He told me part of the reason you've been chosen first is that all of you are physical descendants of King David, and thus closely related to our wonderful Savior, as I am myself." This was news to most of the governors, especially to Eli whose secular parents had absolutely no idea what their Jewish tribal backgrounds might have been, nor the slightest interest in finding out.

"Today you will each have the tremendous privilege of holding up the train of the Lord's High Priestly cape as we parade from the royal palace to the Eastern Gate of the Temple Mount and then into the sacred sanctuary. Millions of our fellow Kadoshim will be watching from the ground and air. I suspect we may have quite a few human observers as well, since thousands are even now streaming through the gorge in the Mount of Olives that the earthquake created, just north of the new stone footbridge we'll be crossing over. So come with me now to the main foyer where we'll witness the Master's descent from His private chambers upstairs."

Before they rose up from their comfortable seats, Eli and Yoseph gazed at each other for several seconds in astonished delight. They had not expected this honor. They were humbled beyond measure to be asked to perform such an awesome task.

Yochanan positioned six of the governors on each side of the marble floor at the bottom of the staircase that wound up to the second floor above. King Yeshua soon appeared wearing His glorious new cape. Made out of what appeared to be crushed velvet, it was crimson in color with small golden tassels hanging down every few inches from the sides. It was held in place over His broad shoulders by a golden chain with a polished sparkling diamond dangling down from the middle. The chain was attached to the cape from the inside front of each well-rounded shoulder.

Underneath the majestic cape, the Great High Priest wore a new silk vest the color of a sunflower. Like the breastplate worn by the high priests in the ancient Jewish temples, it featured twelve precious stones embedded in it, placed in four rows of three gems each. The top row was comprised of a ruby, an opulent topaz and an emerald stone. The second row contained a turquoise gem, a sapphire and another glistening diamond. The third row displayed a jacinth, an agate and a large amethyst stone, while the bottom row featured a beautiful beryl stone, an onyx, and a jasper stone. Below the breastplate vest, which was attached to the Lord's chest under His armpits and below His waist by thin golden ties, the Lamb of God wore what resembled a Scottish kilt made of pure white wool, stretching down a few inches below His glowing knees.

When the Shining One reached the bottom of the winding staircase, the Kadoshim could see that the crimson train of His cape was equal to the long stairway's entire length. In matching sets of twos, they lifted up the train on Yochanan's cue as the King of Glory proceeded out of the open front doors. Yochanan then joined up with the eleven other Apostles and twelve Jewish elders who were marching in two rows behind His regal train.

What happened next utterly astounded the twelve governors, along with the Kadoshim and angels watching from the park in front of the palace and from the sky above. A palace ceremonial guard, leading a docile donkey by a rope, slowly approached the risen Son of God. The Lord then handed the guard His shimmering crown to give to one of the elders before mounting the beast of burden. As the King of the Universe climbed on, His cape lifted a few inches off of His bare back. Eli and the other governors gasped when they spotted the scars of the lashes which the Roman governor Pilot had ordered inflicted on the Son of Man just before He was crucified.

A steeple positioned on top of King Yeshua's new palace began to emit festive sounds, with hundreds of bells simultaneously ringing out their praises to the Lord of Life. A thick bed of palm branches then appeared all along the stone pathway. Thousands of Kadoshim standing near the path, including Sarah, Shoshel, her father Amos, Bet-el, Yoseph's earthly wife Zin-el, Talel, Miri, and Eli's entire cabinet-who had all been summoned to the scene by Yochanan-picked up some of the branches and began vigorously waving them in the air as they cried out in Hebrew, *"Hoshanna! Hoshanna! Hoshanna, la Ben*

David!! Baruch ha ba beh Shem Adonia!" Hosanna! Hosanna! Hosanna to the Son of David! Blessed is He who comes in the Name of the Lord! Soon all were joining in the joyous refrain.

The Goldman family and their dear friends were standing right next to the footpath's west side. Marching behind the Messiah, Eli winked at his close friends when he spotted them in the crowd. Benny and Micah began giddily leaping up and down as they hoisted their palm branches high in the air. Rabbi Benjamin, Abe and Jonathan were standing together waving palm branches right next to the footpath, with Sarah and Rebecca near to them, and the others positioned just behind. As the Lord of Hosts passed by, He spotted the Auschwitz tattoos on Abe and Benjamin's forearms. He raised His right hand to His lips and blew the two a loving kiss. As the Son of Man was lifting up His strong arm to perform that tender action, His cape rose up just enough to reveal the scourging scars lining His back.

Like a powerful lightning bolt striking them from the sky, Jonathan, his father and grandfather were each immediately overcome with deep emotion. They had either been gassed to death by the minions of manic anti-Semites or beheaded by the same. Yet at least they had died quickly. Their people's merciful Messiah, now passing humbly before them, bore the weight of the sins of the whole world on His back and shoulders; suffering gruesomely for several hours in the process. Now the world government was upon the scarred shoulders of the eternal Prince of Peace, and they were to play a significant role in it. As they joined in the procession behind the twenty-four elders, their hearts were bursting with awe and thanksgiving for what the Lord had done.

Eli and his fellow governors were also moved beyond description to be holding up their Savior's royal train as He rode astride a donkey toward the Temple Mount. Their hearts were overflowing with an exhilarating intoxication that was far stronger than anything they had ever felt before.

As the Sovereign Lord neared the new footbridge that crossed the Kidron Valley, many noticed a group of around 150 wide-eyed human refugees standing near the walkway watching the holy procession. Included were around 25 young children. Like toddlers will sometimes do, most broke away from their families and ran up to the Good Shepherd, eagerly touching His donkey and the tassels of His royal robe.

Shimon Kefa quickly stepped out of the group of parading Apostles to prevent the children from interfering with the procession. With a wide smile on His glistening face, King Yeshua gazed down at His beloved friend and said, "Shimon, Shimon, you have such a short memory. Let the children alone, and do not hinder them from coming to Me; for the Kingdom of Heaven belongs to such as these." The youngsters then picked up some of the palm branches from the foot-path and began waving them ecstatically in the air. Israel's Messiah-Monarch had returned home to Jerusalem, never to depart His restored people and world again.

TWELVE

HIDDEN TREASURES

The holy procession that set out from the Sovereign Lord's royal palace ended at the Temple Mount's Golden Gate at 4:58 PM. The winter sun was just setting to the west of Jerusalem, signaling that the third "evening and morning" of the new millennial era was about to begin.

King Yeshua dismounted from His blissful, tail-wagging donkey. His burnished crown was then carefully placed upon His glowing head by His dear friend Yochanan. The joy-filled children and other human beings following the Lord of Life would not be allowed to proceed beyond this point into the Holy Temple, lest they die.

Eli and the other governors continued to hold up the Lord's majestic train as the Mighty One of Israel marched the short distance to a solid gold door with a large brass handle. Allowing entrance into the sacred sanctuary through the eastern Sunrise Transept, the door was eight feet wide and twenty feet high, and arched along the top. The entrance was exclusively designed for use by the King of Kings and His daily entourage.

The Alpha and Omega stood at the door and ceremonially knocked three times. A pre-assigned perpetual Temple priest then solemnly pulled open the golden door, allowing the King of Glory to come in. When the heavy door was fully opened, hundreds of shofar trumpets sounded. The millions of surrounding Kadoshim on the ground and in the air were then whisked in a single second into the recreated sanctuary, where they literally became Immanuel's united Body once again.

The Bright Morning Star paraded slowly into the holy chamber. Every eye was upon Him. As He did so, the brilliant light from the Shekinah fire lit up His crimson cape and train as if they were in flames. The conjoined saints all instantly thought of the precious blood of the Lamb shed for their transgressions. King Yeshua proceeded to the central crossing point of the Temple, with the governors and elders following just behind. The elongated train of His regal cape filled up two-thirds of the eastern Transept. The holy fire reflecting off it sent beams of crimson light flashing throughout the mammoth house of worship.

Then the Great High Priest stopped parading and turned toward His glorious throne rising high up in the center of the Holy of Holies. Two magnificent seraphim measuring twelve feet tall and draped in glistening white robes appeared above and behind the throne on either side, their translucent wings touching each other. Above them arched a shimmering rainbow aglow with brilliant colors.

The party following behind the King of Kings turned to face the Holy of Holies as David Goldman signaled for the day's chosen crew of perpetual priests to begin lighting the seven-branched golden Temple Menorah, which was situated at the base of the elevated dais just in front of the swirling Shekinah fire. Standing tall directly behind candle number four was Jesse Goldman.

Positioned on the platform directly behind the beautiful silver Menorah, the seven priests took deep breaths and then blew out the flaming wicks that had been lit the previous evening. Holding pairs of large golden scissors, they then trimmed the wicks directly in front of them, which were resting in twenty-inch candle basins filled with fresh olive oil. After finishing that task, the anointed priests walked over to a nearby golden altar, put down their scissors and picked up seven long-handled silver rods with cotton wicks attached to their ends. They stretched out the rods toward the edge of the spinning Shekinah fire and lit the wicks. Next they positioned themselves on the dais five feet behind the menorah and simultaneously lowered their rods to light the seven trimmed candle wicks. Three-foot-high flames danced resplendently as if they were living creatures, adding more glowing light to the Sovereign Lord's hallowed house.

The Merciful Savior then resumed His procession toward His sky-blue throne. He elegantly made His way up four mahogany steps in front of the center of the Holy of Holies dais and then walked the short distance to the base of the elevated square platform which His exalted throne was resting upon. The Lord of Hosts paused facing the throne. Upon Yochanan's signal, the 12 governors then slowly lowered the regal train and stood at the base of the dais. The 24 elders reverently strode up to their respective thrones. The train of the Messiah's crimson cape draped down the mahogany steps and onto the marble Temple floor, closely resembling a stream of blood flowing from a sacrificial altar basin.

Two perpetual priests approached from behind the royal throne and stood on either side of the Giver of Life. One undid the golden clasp holding the luxurious velvet cape over King Yeshua's shoulders before they jointly removed the regal garment, laying it gently down on top of the front end of the train. The action instantly revealed the Suffering Servant's scarred back, which was incandescent as internal light flowed out of His powerful body. The brilliant light from the nearby dancing column of glorious Shekinah fire further illuminated the scourging stripes crisscrossing His broad back. The united Kadoshim immediately remembered the high price that the slain Lamb of God had paid to take away their personal sins and the sins of the whole world. This same action would trigger fresh reminders of His life-giving crucifixion every day from then on.

Israel's Messiah then stepped up to His illustrious throne, slowly turned around, and sat down on the mauve silk cushions placed upon it. His magnificent torso then began to radiate internal light more intensely than ever before. It illuminated His golden vest and white wool kilt with such luster that a human eye could not behold the sacred garments without going instantly blind. The piercing light shot through the twelve, three inch round precious stones embedded on His breastplate, casting off dazzling beams which were colored turquoise, ruby red, emerald green, plum purple, and other shades of light that delightfully danced all over the Holy Temple. As the God of the Universe's eternal light flooded the sacred sanctuary like never before, the Third Day's worship service began.

Ten minutes after the tremendous two-hour Temple service ended, the Kadoshim were finally coming back down to earth. Eli Ben David then gathered his cabinet ministers together in the southern courtyard, including Craig Eagleman and Tom McPherson who had missed most of the service after returning to the Greek Isles to supervise the ongoing rescue operations. All expressed enormous pride that their esteemed governor had been selected to help carry the train of their Savior's crimson cape on His first day of public procession. "I thank you all so much, dear friends," Eli replied before humbly pointing up to King Yeshua's palace on the nearby Mount of Olives. "He's our all in all."

After a few seconds of quiet contemplation, the new governor requested an update on the current situation in his province. He was happy to learn from Craig that the Kadoshim doctors and nurses on the island of Crete had already healed most broken bones and many diseases simply by means of prayer. However, widespread dehydration and emaciation would apparently take more time to fully repair, he reported. Despite this, Craig estimated that most of the orphaned children and adult patients would probably be back to good health within a few days, although he reminded everyone that there were still others to minister to on the remaining Greek islands they planned to visit in the morning. Eli thanked everyone for a job well done, especially Rebecca Goldman and Micah Kupinski, before dismissing them all for the evening, adding they would meet again at 8:00 AM the next day before returning together to the province. The governor then revealed he would accompany Craig and Tom back to the islands that evening to check on the current situation.

While the government ministers were convening, Shoshel went with her father Amos and Sarah to talk with Yoseph Steinberg. She was made aware by Amos, Yoseph's new Minister of Finance, that the New York City provincial governor and his cabinet were returning to the devastated metropolis soon after the magnificent Temple service since it was only just after noontime on America's east coast, and there was still much urgent work to be done.

After expressing how thrilled she and Sarah were to see their former pastor carrying out his exalted processional role, Shoshel popped her question: "Yoseph, I was wondering if I might accompany you back to New York this evening? You know I grew up there, like you, and it would be really good to see the Big Apple again before you begin your main cleanup work."

"Well Shoshel, there's much shocking death and destruction to behold, but of course you're more than welcome to come along. And you too Sarah, if you want."

"I actually do Yoseph, thank you. Would it be possible to bring along Jonathan and his father and mother. You know Rebecca grew up in the Crown Heights neighborhood of Brooklyn, and that's also where she and Abe were married, so I think they might want to see it again as well."

"That's fine Sarah. I'll introduce you to my other cabinet ministers after you arrive in New York. Invite Talel and your son and his friend Micah along as well if you'd like to, and also Rabbi Goldman, who I presume never made it to America during his earthly life. You won't be in our way, and it'll be good to spend a little time with all of you."

Sarah approached Jonathan and the other cabinet ministers just as Eli's short consultation with them was ending. After greeting her family and friends, she pulled Jonathan aside to see if he'd accompany her and Shoshel to New York. "Sure, I'll be glad to come along. I know it might be hard to see the reported devastation, but on the other hand it would only be a larger-scale version of what we've already experienced on the Greek Isles today."

"What about your parents, Jonathan? Do you think they'd like to visit Crown Heights before the rubble is removed? Yoseph says we can also take along your grandfather and the kids, plus Micah if we wish to."

"Hmm...that's another matter, Sarah. It might be too hard for mom and dad to go back there, especially mom who you know grew up in Crown Heights. But let me check with them, and if they want to go,

207

let's take along the kids and Grandpa Benjamin as well. It might be good for Benny and Talel to see where their grandmother originally hailed from, even if the area is in ruins. They'll appreciate it more after Yoseph restores the city. And I suspect it might actually be encouraging to Micah…he'd see firsthand that he hasn't nearly as much rubble and rebuilding to deal with as they undoubtedly do in New York."

Abe and Rebecca Goldman mulled over the proposed visit for several minutes. By that time Yoseph and his ministers had disappeared, but the new governor already informed Sarah he'd be stopping first in lower Manhattan. Abe was all for going while Rebecca was understandably more reluctant. "I think it might do you good, Rebecca. I know there's significant pain involved, but this might be an opportunity to let the Lord wash it all away."

"I guess you're right Abe, and I *do* have deep concern for my home area. So okay, let's go. The Lord will be there with us, I know."

After informing Jonathan of their decision, Sarah twinked back to her house to invite Talel to come along with the family. Meanwhile Jonathan invited Benny and Micah, who eagerly accepted, while Abe asked his father to come along. Having never been to the United States, let alone to the famous city of New York, Rabbi Benjamin was eager to accompany them.

Sarah returned quickly with Talel, and then all held hands together as Jonathan said, "Lord, please take us to Yoseph Steinberg in lower Manhattan." In the twinkling of an eye, they were there.

Jonathan had underestimated the initial impact of seeing America's greatest city in utter ruin. The piles of debris in lower Manhattan were a quarter mile high in some places. Thousands of crushed and rotting bodies could be seen everywhere the saints looked, with hundreds of thousands of others surely buried underneath the crumbled buildings. Fires still smoldered in many places. Flood damage was also evident from the tidal waves which struck the area several times. Water now permanently covered some lower parts of the island due to the heightened level of the Atlantic Ocean. A comet had landed near Central Park, carving out a deep crater that almost divided Manhattan in two.

Despite its pre-judgment population of over one and a half million residents, Yoseph's cabinet ministers and 10,000 volunteer workers had only found a few hundred people alive in Manhattan so far, most of them children. Dissolution crews had begun working in the northern Harlem section of the renowned island a few hours before the evening Temple worship service began, making their way block by block south to the former financial district.

Yoseph led his guests from the decimated stock exchange on Wall Street, where they had met up, to the base of the destroyed Freedom Tower. The rubble was so immense on the cracked sidewalks and streets that they soon discovered they could not possibly walk there. Instead, they willed themselves to the base of the ruined skyscraper after holding hands in a circle.

Although the tallest building in America had collapsed over three months before, columns of smoke still wafted from embers smoldering underneath the debris. Some of it smelled of burning flesh. Amos and Shoshel Pearlman, who had tearfully watched from the roof of their east-side apartment building as the World Trade twin towers collapsed in September 2001, were especially shaken by the horrific sight. Harry Berman—the closest friend Amos ever had—was among those killed in the Al Qaida terrorist attack. He'd been working in his law office on the 54th floor when the second hijacked airplane struck. They were heartened when they spotted the iron rod cross that had been part of the collapsed towers still standing amid the rubble.

Most of Yoseph's cabinet ministers, except his earthly wife Zinel and Shoshel's father Amos, were currently on the north side of the island working with the volunteer crews. The new governor decided to call them in for a brief consultation to see how things had progressed from the time they all left for the Temple service almost three hours before. Yoseph bowed his head and asked the Holy Spirit to bring them to him, and all quickly answered His summons.

Governor Steinberg introduced his newly arrived ministers to his visitors before introducing the Goldmans, Shoshel and Micah to them. Talel was intrigued to hear the name of Yoseph's new Culture, Music and Sports Minister, Carmella Bernstein. Later Talel pulled her aside and enquired if she was perchance related to the late New York Philharmonic conductor, Leonard Bernstein. "He was a second cousin, or maybe a third, of my deceased husband's father," she answered. This answer worried Talel, although she said nothing more. She knew her adopted twin's slain father was also a distant relative of the famous conductor and composer, having moved to Israel from the Soviet Ukraine, where Leonard Bernstein's father was born.

Construction Minister Leo Scarcelli—who was actually named Leonard after his socialite mother's most admired conductor, and also in honor of his father's favorite artist, Leonardo Da Vinci—gave a brief update report to the governor and his assembled deputies. However the burly saint first admitted that he was finding it hard going since his former company, Scarcelli Construction, founded after World War Two by his father Giulio, had built many of the skyscrapers that were now piled in pieces on the ground. "We're moving very slowly with our dissolutions, Governor Yoseph, since we're concerned there may still be trapped victims alive in many of the collapsed buildings. Most of our workers are actually busy removing rubble by hand. It's a good thing we possess supernatural strength to do that. I'm finding very few buildings even partially intact. It's a real disaster for sure, although the Prophet Yochanan did warn the city residents that this was coming, and that they needed to repent and turn to the Lord."

"We were actually part of Yochanan's team that ministered here in Central Park," interjected Sarah as she placed her arm around Talel's shoulders.

"Oh bless you!" blurted out Leo's earthly wife Teresa, serving now as Yoseph's new Health Minister. "That's where Leo and our daughter, Angelica, gave their lives to the Lord! I was already a believer and took them to the park that day to hear Yochanan and Natan-el share their message. I recall it was a very hot summer afternoon. We were almost killed when a large group of Android thugs attacked the gathering."

"Of course we remember that very well, Teresa," stated Sarah as she moved her arm to Talel's trim waist. Her earthly daughter's eyes were revealing that she was revisiting that day's terror in her memory bank.

"What exactly happened there, Sarah? You haven't shared any details with me yet," noted Jonathan. It turned out to be a divinely ordained question.

"Well, Yochanan was issuing warnings of looming judgment to about 10,000 people gathered in the park. Then a group of New York-based reporters approached us and began asking him and Natan-el pointed questions, which actually allowed the two witnesses to tell millions of people across America in English exactly who Emperor Andre really was, and what would happen to all who received his insidious mark. Suddenly a group of around 200 Android gang members strutted up, waving nude statues of the Emperor and chanting slogans against us like '*Kill the Jewish Pigs.*' They told us to get out of what they called 'their' city before hurling homemade firebombs and hand grenades at us. Most of the onlookers ran like rabbits in a race, but thankfully none of us in the ministering party was hurt. It was as if an invisible wall was protecting us, Jonathan. Still, it was a very frightening experience, especially for young Talel."

Sarah's last statement was confirmed by the copious tears now flowing out of Talel's eyes. Jonathan walked over and put his arms around his earthly daughter as Israel's gracious Redeemer washed away the last vestiges of fear and pain from her tender heart.

Teresa Scarcelli then revealed something that immediately added to Talel's healing. "It was precisely the fact we'd just witnessed an obviously miraculous act of divine protection which convinced Leo that Yeshua was Israel's Messiah; and Andre nothing but a lying demigod. He and our daughter gave their lives to the Lord that very afternoon." This statement prompted Talel—who had shrieked in terror as the explosions went off all around her that terrible day—to smile warmly as she wiped away her remaining tears. She now realized more than ever before that whatever the personal cost had been of ministering with the two witnesses during the final tribulation period, it had been well worth paying.

Teresa Scarcelli later admitted to her colleague Rebecca Goldman that, like her previous-era husband Leo, she was struggling with her emotions as she fulfilled her new role as New York provincial Health Minister, given there were so many dead bodies and so few survivors, and the latter were generally in very poor condition. Rebecca then affirmed that she too had found the same to be true while carrying out the identical ministerial role on the Greek Isles earlier in the day.

Abe Goldman was busy comparing notes with New York City's new provincial Transportation and Tourism Minister, Giuseppe Marino. "My biggest challenge is that our province is spread out over hundreds of islands, with a distance between some of them of around 400 miles. I've been talking to my new roommate in Jerusalem, Kostas Karamilis, who is the Athens provincial Transport Minister. He's going to see if we can get some passenger ferry boats up and running fairly soon, hopefully using the new long-life electric battery technology."

"I used to be a district manager for New Jersey Transit, Abe, and my top priority is to get the subways cleared and prepared for a resumption of underground service. But my initial survey shows there's a huge truckload of work to be done. The tunnels have totally collapsed in many places, others are flooded, and all are littered with smashed trains and debris. I'm forming crews out of my 1,000 volunteers who'll start dissolving the rubble as soon as we get the surface ground cleaned up. I also need to get to work on new bridges and roads…it's a monumental undertaking for sure."

A volunteer foreman suddenly appeared directly in front of Leo Scarcelli. "Minister Leo, we need as much help as we can get right away! We just discovered a group of children under the rubble of what looks to have been a school in Harlem. They're trapped and crying out for help." Leo quickly informed the other New York and Greek Isle ministers and all decided to head up-island with him and Governor Yoseph to assist at the scene. In a flash, they were there.

"It sounds like dozens of kids are trapped in there, maybe more" reported a volunteer contractor who was organizing the rescue operation. Governor Steinberg then ordered Leo to call in some of his cleansing crews to help with the heavy digging and lifting. Jonathan and the other Greek Isle ministers jumped right into the rescue effort, with Benny and Micah leading the way. Within 20 minutes the work crews had removed enough wreckage to spot the first of what turned out to be nearly 300 children crammed into what had apparently been a lunch room in the school basement. Mostly African-Americans, all but a handful appeared too young to have been students at the school, having apparently only taken shelter there.

While the rubble removal was going on (the workers could not simply dissolve the debris without potentially harming the trapped victims as well), Leo organized a construction crew to set up a freshly delivered medical tent in a cleared area directly across the street from the decimated school. Rebecca, Sarah and Talel joined Teresa, Zinel, and others in patching together a medical team to serve in it.

Working as if there was no tomorrow, Benny and Micah were the first to actually touch any of the children; a boy and girl who looked to be about four years old. Micah asked them if they were injured. The boy shook his head no. Then Benny asked if they were hungry and thirsty, naturally assuming the answer would be yes. "We still have some of this food that God has been giving us every morning," the toothy boy said as he pulled out some drying manna from his torn pocket. "And we get these drinks too," added the little girl as she pointed to a half-empty plastic water bottle lying on the cracked tile floor next to her. Benny smiled and said "Thank you Lord" as the husky saints effortlessly picked up the two children and carried them across to the medical tent.

When the rescued children were all safely brought out, Yoseph offered to take Abe, Rebecca and his other guests over to the Crown Heights neighborhood, located in the north-central part of Brooklyn just above Flatbush. Abe gave him an address, and they joined hands and instantly arrived there. It was the old apartment building that the Goldmans had moved into after their marriage was sealed at her father's synagogue four blocks away.

When Rebecca's parents, Samuel and Pearl Silverstein, were growing up in the New York neighborhood, it was still a posh bedroom community for many of Manhattan's social elite, especially Jews. However by the time she started in school, Crown Heights had a growing population of African-Americans who mainly moved there from the south of the country, along with others who immigrated from Jamaica and other Caribbean island countries. Growing racial tensions between the different communities would later explode into three days of fierce racial clashes in 1991. This was partly the reason Abe moved his family to Skokie Illinois soon after Jonathan's older sister was born.

Like pretty much everything else in the borough of Brooklyn—which alone had a pre-judgment population of around two and a half million people—the Goldman's old apartment building was completely wiped out. As difficult as this was for them to witness, it was nothing like the impact Rebecca would feel a few minutes later when she saw the condition of her childhood home, a townhouse three blocks south of Atlantic Avenue. It had burned so severely that absolutely nothing remained. Tears immediately welled from her turquoise eyes, flushing away the remaining sorrow she felt that her parents were not among the Kadoshim.

The saints gingerly walked around rubble to arrive at the synagogue that Samuel had served in as a rabbi for several decades. While they carefully moved along, Jonathan explained to his earthly offspring that he'd often traveled to Crown Heights as a young boy with his parents to visit his grandfather after his grandmother died. Rabbi Goldman was listening closely to the conversation. "Grandpa Samuel was still ministering in his synagogue until the day he had his massive heart attack. I cried all day when we got the news. I'd lost two grandfathers, both of them rabbis. But now I have one back." Jonathan turned and smiled at the Greek Isle Education and Religious Affairs Minister, who he thought was looking younger and fitter every day.

Being a solidly-built one storey structure, the synagogue was still partially standing. Abe and Rebecca held hands as they stepped over rubble to reach the spot on the bema where they were married under a *huppa*, with Rabbi Samuel presiding. Yoseph then uttered something that immediately brought tears again to Rebecca's eyes, as it did to Abe, Rabbi Benjamin and Jonathan. "I think I've just found the site where I'll place my gifted governor's mansion. This shall be a thriving neighborhood once again."

Benny had wandered over to the wooden ark behind the elevated bema. It had tumbled face down in one of the final earthquakes, and was covered with chunks of concrete from the partially-collapsed ceiling. With the strength of a seasoned weightlifter, the Justice Minister easily pushed the toppled ark back up into its original position. After gazing inside, he slowly walked over to his family and friends, cradling his sacred discovery in his arms. Then he handed it to his startled grandmother. It was the Torah scroll her father had personally purchased for his congregation while on a trip to Israel after the 1967 Arab-Israeli war. He had found it in a shop in the Old City's Jewish Quarter. He was told by the shop owner that it had been salvaged from a destroyed synagogue in Germany.

"Oh Benny, thank you so *much!* You don't know what this means to me!" cried Rebecca as she clutched the precious parchment scroll to her chest.

Rabbi Goldman fell backwards as she finished speaking—barely caught before he hit the littered floor by Jonathan's swift-acting arms. Benjamin blinked back tears as he was helped back on his feet. "That...that is the very scroll the Nazis tried to confiscate from my congregation! I hid it in a fireproof basement vault right after my wife was burnt to death on Kristallnacht. I recognize the embroidered velvet cover. Your mother made that, Abe. I haven't seen it since the night she was viciously killed." Rabbi Benjamin raised his right hand to his lips and kissed his fingers before he reached out and reverently touched the velvet Torah scroll cover, which to him was almost like touching the Holy Face of God.

Governor Yoseph began quoting some verses from one of his favorite psalms: "For in the day of trouble, He will conceal me in His tabernacle; in the secret place of His tent He will hide me. He will lift me up on a rock, and now my head will be lifted up above my enemies around me."

As Yoseph was speaking, the Goldmans fell into tearful hugs with the revered scroll at their center. Then Rebecca smiled sweetly as she handed the parchment Hebrew Bible to Rabbi Goldman, who gently took it from her as fresh tears flooded all eyes. Meanwhile Yoseph ordered the rubble on the floor to disappear. The holocaust victim then began dancing with his beloved scroll, just as Rebecca's father had often done during Shabbat services in that very synagogue. He joyously hoisted the 450-year-old scroll in the air while shouting out praises to Israel's Mighty King. Soon everyone was gleefully joining in the chorus of praise as they formed a hora circle around the ever-living rabbi.

Some twenty minutes later, Yoseph noticed his earthly wife Zinel standing in the doorway, a broad smile creasing her youthful face. He waltzed over and explained why their dear friends were rejoicing. After expressing her extreme delight, Zinel informed the governor that Leo and Teresa Scarcelli and Teresa's father Giuseppe had asked her to check if they could all head over to Newark to survey the situation in that portion of Yoseph's new province. "Teresa told me they especially want to visit some orphanages in the area. She said one of Leo's volunteer construction engineers and his team report there are still quite a few children alive in a couple of them; one in Newark itself, and another in the nearby city of Elizabeth, where Giuseppe and his wife Catrina lived."

"Tell them yes, they can head there. In fact, I wanted to go over myself today and assess the situation, so maybe we'll join them. Leo mentioned to me that Teresa's sister Gina announced to them she was pregnant just a few days before they were both killed by UW forces in Connecticut, along with their daughter. So I assume they're hoping to find the baby alive, although the chances of that seem pretty slim to me."

"Thanks Yoseph. I'll go tell them it's okay to go. In fact, I might join in as well."

"That'd be fine, Zinel. We'll transit over in a little bit. I want to give the brethren a few more minutes to celebrate the goodness of the Lord." Yoseph smiled as he turned his gaze toward the jubilant saints. "I've never seen a rabbi dancing with such gusto and joy in my entire life!"

The party of four New York City provincial ministers appeared first just outside an orphanage near downtown Newark. It was situated only a couple miles northwest of the Marino's former apartment building where their daughter Gina had been living with her husband

George Kirintelos. Giuseppe was hoping and praying that maybe they would find a baby boy or girl there that bore his son-in-law's family name. He knew the baby would be just under one year old since his daughter Gina had only been pregnant for two months the last time he saw her. That was just three days before he and Catrina were beheaded by UW forces in July, two years before. Leo, Teresa and their daughter Angelica had been martyred for their faith the following week.

When Gina had informed her thrilled parents that she was expecting, Giuseppe and Catrina went straight out to a local department store to buy her a baby shower gift. While there, Giuseppe decided he might as well go ahead and purchase a highchair, anticipating many happy days with their visiting grandson or granddaughter in the future. Catrina bought a large sand-filled baby rattle and a new set of crib sheets and pillows. She knew the sheets would fit the baby's bed since Teresa had already informed her she'd pass on her used mahogany crib to her younger sister. Teresa and Leo had not lived long enough to hand down their gifts to Gina, but their son Chad later made the delivery.

The downtown orphanage was supervised by the Roman Catholic Diocese of Newark. The Marinos had regularly attended Sunday Mass in a nearby church until they moved to Elizabeth. The cabinet ministers discovered that 231 children were sheltered inside the south end of the orphanage, the only portion of the large two-storey building still standing. Kadoshim volunteers were assisting several human adults in supervising food distribution to the orphaned children. The ministers were told there were a few babies among them, although most were older children ranging up to age twelve.

While Leo checked on the structural soundness of the remaining walls and ceiling, Giuseppe and Teresa were joined by Zinel in going through a registry listing the names of the children. They'd been told that most of the orphans only arrived in recent months, and not all of the youngest ones had yet been identified. The names of three babies were unknown. Teresa enquired if they might take a peek at them.

"What do you think dad, do any of them look to you like they might be Gina's child?"

"It's so hard to tell with kids this age, but I think only that cute baby girl is a real possibility. The male looks to be only about six months old and the other female maybe twenty months old. Gina's baby would be just under one year old now."

Teresa Scarcelli clasped her earthly father's hand and then informed the orphanage director that she would return with more medical and food supplies later in the day. She'd also pursue her important personal matter at that time.

As the saints exited the children's home, they discovered Yoseph and his friends waiting outside. The group appeared only moments before. Leo and Teresa gave the new provincial ruler a brief overview of the situation inside the orphanage. It was then decided that a rein-forced medical tent would be provided to shelter the children, since the badly damaged ceiling looked to Leo like it could collapse at any time.

The Kadoshim, who also now included Shoshel's father Amos, then moved on to the second orphanage they'd been told about in the city of Elizabeth, due south of Newark. The Construction Minister was glad to discover that the old stone building, a converted parsonage, appeared to be fairly sound apart from missing all of its shattered windows.

Upon entering the orphanage, the saints were greeted by a friendly woman named Julia who looked to be about 65. She told them she'd worked at the orphanage before Andre rose to power, but left during his reign, only recently returning from her self-imposed exile. Julia added that she'd become a follower of Yeshua soon after seeing His sign in the eastern sky, just over three months before. Always suspicious of Andre's claims to divinity, the widow explained that she had hidden out in an old family cabin in the hills of eastern Pennsylvania for several years, and so successfully avoided receiving the mark of the beast.

"Julia, this is our new provincial governor, Yoseph Steinberg, and some of his cabinet ministers," stated Zinel, adding that the others were friends from Jerusalem.

Teresa was sensing an inner excitement she couldn't rationally explain. She went straight for the jugular. "Julia, can you tell us how many children you have here, and especially if there are any babies around one year old?"

"We have 24 children, most of them fairly new arrivals. There are five babies, but only a couple of them around the age you mentioned."

Just then Giuseppe spotted the familiar highchair through an open kitchen door. Without excusing himself, he rushed into the kitchen and turned the chair over. There under the seat were his initials and phone number. It had become his policy to carve his ID on all his possessions following a break-in at his Newark apartment soon after Teresa moved out to study nursing at a university in Connecticut.

Giuseppe grabbed his chest over his heart as he whistled with hopeful delight. The others moved like speeding bullets toward the kitchen to find out what was going on. "Teresa, this is the highchair I bought for Gina's baby! My initials are on the bottom of the seat where I put them."

"Oh, that seat belongs to a baby boy named George Kirintelos," revealed Julia, adding factually, "He's exactly the age you mentioned, Teresa."

The Scarcellis hugged each other and then embraced Giuseppe, who was now shedding full-blown tears.

"It's my sister's baby, and Giuseppe is his grandfather" explained Teresa after she regained her composure. "Could you take us to him?"

Like bald eagles chasing their flying prey, the saints followed Julia into a nearby living room where they spotted a young woman seated with her back to them. She was sitting in a rocking chair next to a plastic Christmas tree, quietly singing to a baby in her arms while gazing out an open door into the back garden, which had been severely burned. "Maria, is that you?" asked Giuseppe as he sped to her side along with Leo and Teresa.

"Yes sir; that is my name. Excuse me, do I know you?" As she said this she spotted Leo, whom she instantly recognized.

"I'm Giuseppe Marino—only a little younger looking than before. Oh Maria, it's so good to see that you're still alive!"

Maria was instantly drenched with emotion, which was actually the common denominator in the now-crowded room. She said nothing as she lifted the contented baby up toward his grandfather's waiting arms. Giuseppe kissed little George Junior on the forehead and then grasped him close to his chest. Teresa pecked her nephew on the back of his smooth neck and then kissed her father on his left cheek, which was wet with tears.

Following several seconds of blissful silence, Leo asked Maria Alvarez how she had survived and come into possession of Gina's baby.

"After Giuseppe and Catrina disappeared, Gina kept coming over to their home, desperately hoping they'd show up there one day. She asked me to continue cleaning the house even though there really wasn't very much to do, and she paid my salary. So I got to know her quite well. She was of course pregnant. Gina told me that you and Teresa and Angelica had been murdered by Andre's forces. She actually thought your son Chad had turned you in."

"He did," confirmed Leo as fresh tears formed in his eyes that would wash away this excruciating pain forever. The same thing was occurring in Teresa's torn heart, which was receiving its final healing from this gaping sore wound.

"Oh I'm so sorry," said Maria as she rose out of her rocking chair and folded her arms around Teresa. "Anyway, the little one was born just after Christmas last year. Gina actually bought the tree you see here and set it up in your house, Mr. Marino. Well, I remembered that you told me you'd hidden a baby highchair behind some clothes in your bedroom closet, so I went and got it out and put it next to the tree after she left your home on Christmas Eve. Gina was so surprised when she and her husband George walked in the next day. She really cherished that gift, Mr. Marino, although it took her a while to stop crying. She'd asked me to cook a Christmas Day dinner, and we had such a great time. We really became like family."

Giuseppe gratefully grasped one of her warm hands as he held the baby close to his heart with his free hand. "You will be part of our family forever, Maria. And you can call me Giuseppe by the way...I don't appear to be much older than you anymore!"

Maria smiled and said thank you before carrying on with her story. "Gina and George were quite worried about me, Teresa, because I'd taken your advice to avoid Andre's mark, as your parents obviously did as well. The claims the Emperor was making just didn't seem right to me. And I definitely didn't like the way his Android bullies were lording it over the city. After the baby was born, Gina came over less frequently. Then her husband was killed. I went with her and an older woman from her apartment building to his funeral. Gina was a real wreck."

"What happened to George?" enquired Leo, not certain he really wanted to hear her reply.

"He was killed by two Android gang members after he apparently resisted their attempts to rob him while buying some cough medicine for little Georgie at a local pharmacy. The baby was only a few months old at the time." Leo and Teresa lowered their heads as they absorbed this sad news.

"And what about Gina?" asked her earthly father, who already realized his daughter could not have survived since she and her husband had previously accepted the evil identity implant chips that marked them out as Andre's followers.

Maria began to weep softly as she replied. "Just after those two Jewish prophets who visited Central Park rose from the dead in Jerusalem, we had this massive earthquake and then a huge tidal wave. My parents were killed along with my two sisters and younger brother. Fortunately I was outside relaxing on a bench when the quake hit, or I would have been killed as well since our apartment building was totally destroyed. I was able to avoid the subsequent big wave by rushing upstairs in a nearby partially-standing apartment building where a friend of mine lived."

Sarah thought about her sister Donna's similar ordeal in Jerusalem as Maria related more details of her story.

"Late that same night, I decided to go over to your home, Giuseppe, to see if any canned food was still stored in the pantry. I hadn't been there in a couple months after Gina finally gave up hope that you and Catrina would come home. It was becoming too dangerous for Gina to drive there as well. Thankfully, I still had a key.

When I entered the front door, I heard a baby crying in the kitchen and discovered it was Georgie. He was actually hidden inside the oven…I guess to keep debris from falling on him since we were having some pretty strong aftershocks." The mention of the word "oven" brought an instant shudder to Rabbi Goldman's spiritual body.

"Then I spotted Gina's body on the kitchen floor. Part of the collapsed ceiling was lying on her shoulder. She was…face up in a pool of her own blood. It was a…horrible sight." Maria was now sobbing, as were many of her listeners, especially Teresa and Giuseppe. More cleansing healing was taking place in several hearts.

After a couple of minutes passed, Leo asked when Maria had arrived at the orphanage.

"I'm a little bit ashamed to tell you, Leo. I pulled little Georgie out of the oven and fed him his bottle, which was sitting in a pan of water on the stove, and then brought him here. I just left him on the front steps and knocked on the door. I didn't…know what else to do. There was only a little food in the badly-damaged house. I am so sorry. I felt really guilty for just abandoning him like that, so I came back two days later and knocked on the door. But this time I stayed put, and Julia let me in. I told her I'd dropped off the baby, and I've lived here ever since."

Teresa embraced the weeping maid. "You did what you could, Maria, and you rescued Gina's son. He would surely have perished otherwise. We're grateful beyond words, kind servant of our Father.

"Maria has been like a mother to him," added Julia proudly.

Giuseppe gently handed the baby to his aunt and quickly stepped out of the room. He then asked the Holy Spirit to inform his earthly wife Catrina and granddaughter Angelica that they should immediately appear at the orphanage. They both showed up less than one minute later.

"Where are we, Giuseppe? We were resting in our west Jerusalem apartment when we sensed a call to come see you."

"We're in an orphanage in Elizabeth, our old hometown. Catrina, you have a living grandson! His name is George after his father. He's in that room with Maria Alvarez."

Catrina nearly collapsed before Giuseppe grabbed her right hand and led her into the sitting room. She leapt to her earthly daughter's side like a deer hurdling over a high fence. Then she carefully took the smiling baby in her arms. After Leo briefly filled her and Angelica in on what Maria had just shared—apart from the details of Gina's horrible death—Catrina thanked her former maid profusely and then kissed her right cheek.

"It's been a real joy to take care of him, Catrina. I will miss that."

"Oh no you won't!" exclaimed Giuseppe. "You're not going anywhere, Maria. We'll need your help to raise him. From now on, you are part of our family."

As the visiting Greek Isles ministers took turns congratulating the Marinos and Scarcellis, Governor Yoseph made up his mind. He soon placed his offer on the table. "Giuseppe, you've already asked if you could live in my new government mansion, along with Leo and Teresa, and as you know I gladly said yes. Why don't you join us Catrina and Angelica; along with you, Maria? You can all help raise the boy there. I think it might be…quite interesting having a young human lad running around the mansion. It should liven things up a bit."

"Oh that would be *wonderful*, Governor Steinberg," declared Catrina as Giuseppe and the Scarcellis nodded their eager consent. Maria was simply in a state of shock. "Live in a…governor's mansion? I, uh…don't know what to say."

"Just say yes, dear," Catrina advised with a Cheshire grin on her radiant face.

Benny walked over with a Christmas present in his hand, carefully wrapped in yellow paper picturing big fuzzy brown bears merrily munching honey out of tan clay jars. "It's got the baby's name on it," he pointed out as he handed it to Catrina.

"That's the rattle you bought for little Georgie, Catrina. I found it hidden away on your top shelf in the closet when I went back over last month to pick up the highchair. It's the only Christmas present we have for the baby this year."

Catrina squeezed Maria's hand. "Not anymore. He has all of us."

Yoseph recited more scripture, this time as recorded by Doctor Luke: "For unto us is born this day in the City of David a Savior, who is the Messiah, the Lord."

THIRTEEN

ON OUR WAY HOME

Three human females were riding on the thirsty mule that was cautiously making his way around deep potholes and large cracks in the asphalt pavement. Seated in front was the widowed mother, enfolding her five-year-old daughter in her arms. The little girl in turn was cuddling her pet dog, a tan-colored male Miniature Pinscher named Pookey. Straddling right behind them was the gray-haired grandmother with her arms around the young mother's waist. Grandpa, nearing sixty, was walking a few paces in front of the mule, holding reins attached to a throat latch at the top of the mule's short mane. In a wicker basket inside the open saddle bag was the little girl's pet cat, a blue-eyed Siamese female named Ginger.

The four humans and three animals were traveling as fast as they could on Interstate 40, nearing the central Arizona city of Flagstaff. Grandpa was a bit nervous as they approached the city—the first urban center they would encounter since they got on the shattered highway several days before. Apart from the poor road conditions, their only major problem so far had been crossing the Colorado River, since the bridge was completely down. However they were able to cautiously make their way across the waterway by carefully balancing themselves on chunks of concrete and asphalt that littered the river, which was anyway almost dry due to the collapse of much of the Rocky Mountains at its headwaters, along with Hoover Dam upriver. The mule had fallen into the shallow water twice, but he actually seemed to enjoy the cool down.

It was nearing nightfall, so the adults decided to stop just outside the town of Bellemont, some 15 miles west of the outskirts of Flagstaff. The travelers spotted a few campers huddled near a bonfire by a stream and decided to head there. It was a big mistake.

A badly-wrinkled man in his late seventies grabbed his prone rifle as the traveling party approached a group of six adults and four children. *"Don't come one step closer or I'll shoot your fricken brains out!"* he shouted.

"We mean you no harm," Grandpa said calmly as he wiped sweat from his brow. "We're heading back East, and have our own food and water supplies." The water was from the Colorado River, the food was mostly that morning's manna.

"Are you Jews heading to Israel?" he spat out as he waved his rifle barrel at them.

"Yes we are, but how could you possibly know that?"

"Because that's about all the folk we've seen passing through these parts in the past week, beginning a few days after that massive earthquake. Nut-ball Jews on their way to the Zionist nut-house state! Well, we don't talk to any Jews, so get your fat butts out of here right now!"

The rude speaker was Oscar Schmidt, founder of a small neo-Nazi group called *The Aryan National Identity Movement*. He and two dozen followers, including his wife Sheila and grandson Brock and his family, had fled from central California into the Kaibab National Forest in the early days of Emperor Andre's global rule. There, they set up a new operations base not far from Humphreys Peak, the highest point in Arizona, due north of Flagstaff. Everyone in Oscar's extended family, except his grandson and one great-granddaughter; had perished during the tribulation period, along with 15 other group members.

Brock had his lustful eyes fixated on the widowed mother. Appearing to be in her mid-twenties, she was a voluptuous knockout, he noticed. The shapely brunette had shoulder-length hair under her ruby-red baseball cap, with thick rosy lips that matched it. Wanting to run over and give her a moist kiss on the spot, Brock instead sat still as the wandering Jews turned away. They ended up camping under one of the few evergreen trees still standing a quarter mile downstream. This would help their tent stay dry during the nightly soft rains which were beginning to bring fresh life to the entire planet. Each day just before dawn, manna would cascade down like snow soon after the rainwater was absorbed into the ground.

After a quick manna and raisin breakfast, the three females were mounting their strong mule when Brock suddenly appeared near them. He'd been hiding amid some fallen burnt trees next to their camp. Grandpa stepped forward to block the intruder. "What are you doing here?" he demanded before adding "Please just leave us alone!"

"Don't be afraid, old man; I just want to go with you! I know that God is with the Jewish people, and He's calling you back to your ancient homeland. I want to visit it too before I die."

Although not terribly religious, the shaken grandfather recognized this startling statement as being a nearly verbatim proclamation of a Messianic-era prophecy found in the biblical book of Zechariah, which speaks of many individuals and nations heading up to Jerusalem to entreat the favor of the Lord in the Holy City.

"I don't expect you to immediately trust me, sir, but I'm honestly no longer a follower of my grandfather's strange theology. He hates the Jewish people; always has and always will. But we all saw that sign in the sky a few months ago. Grandpa thought the Star of David with the cross inside was just another trick performed by Andre, who he believed was secretly controlled by an international Jewish cabal. But to me, such talk had already become total nonsense. I now realize we've been worshipping a false god in his small cult. I want my God to be your God, and likewise for my five year old daughter."

The widower now turned his eyes to the beautiful young woman sitting astride the snorting mule. He smiled at her, and she smiled back. Susan had already noticed the evening before that he was extremely handsome, even if a bit on the thin side. She especially liked his square jaw, brown curly locks and amber eyes. He in turn instantly liked absolutely everything about her; a fact he was not hiding very well, nor wanting to.

"What's your name?" enquired Susan in her sultriest voice as she swished back a strand of brown hair from her daughter's tranquil face.

"I'm Brock Schmidt, originally from Bakersfield California" he eagerly replied as he moved closer to the three females on the mule. "We headed over here about 35 months ago, soon after Andre was crowned Emperor. I must say, I did agree with that part of my grandfather's theology—that Andre was not divine, and we should resist getting his economic implant chip."

"I'm Susan Levinson, and this is my daughter Justina. We also came from central California."

Before she could introduce the other adults, Brock blurted out "Wow! My daughter is named Tina, almost the same as your little girl!" He blushed with excitement when Susan reacted to this news by coyly cocking her gorgeous head to one side while enticingly brushing back her silky hair. Still, he forced himself to get back to his important argument while turning to face Grandpa. "I have my own horse, sir, which I can bring with me. You can ride with me and Tina, instead of walking." Or better yet, *Susan can ride right behind my back, he thought,* but did not articulate. "I have my own gun and supplies. You'll make much faster time, sir, if you're all riding instead of one of you walking. I really want to see the Lord's land before I die. Please, let me go with you!" As he again presented his entreaty, Brock reached out his long right arm and gently touched Grandpa's beige tee shirt.

"Okay, I guess we can give it a try. However, if there are *any* problems at all, we'll separate immediately. Do you understand?"

"Yes sir. Thanks so much; you definitely won't regret it."

Now Justina was smiling broadly along with her tantalized mother.

"What do you think?" asked Governor Ben David as he gazed at the quarter-mile long narrow peninsula stretching out toward the southwest sea in front of him. Gentle waves lapped onto the nearby shoreline as several seagulls glided in the light breeze overhead.

"I definitely like it the most of the four spots we've looked at today," replied Jonathan.

"I agree, dad. It's a super location," opined Benny just before Micah added, "I love it too."

"You got my vote," piped in Sampson as Tom stuck his right thumb up. Craig and Ken nodded their accords.

"Okay guys, here goes!" The new provincial ruler stood back and ordered the rocky terrain to be instantly cleared of several large boulders and dozens of smaller ones. Then Eli humbly bowed his head and asked the Lord to deliver his gifted new mansion to this scenic spot, which had previously been a place for sheep to graze and for local and tourist hikers and joggers to enjoy.

The splendid government mansion appeared seconds later. It was quite similar to Prince David's palace, as Israel's royal governor had promised it would be. However it was about half the size. Still, it offered more than sufficient space for most of the Greek Isle ministers to live in, and for all to work in.

Eli's new elongated mansion was spread out east to west on the short peninsula, which was located at the westernmost point on the island of Naxos jutting out into the crystal-blue Aegean Sea. It featured a grand main entrance facing south toward the islands of Ios and Sikinos about 20 miles away. The governor's private chamber on the top floor had a balcony directly facing the hilly island of Paros; the twentieth largest Greek island located less than four miles west of the narrow peninsula. From his expansive balcony he could see at least four islands lying to the south, Ios being the largest of them. Paros and part of Milos southwest of it were clearly visible to the west. To the north on a clear day, which was everyday, he could make out Mykonos and Delos, where the mythological Greek god Apollo was supposedly born. However the new provincial ruler could not see the thirteenth largest Greek island, Andros, located about 20 miles northwest of Mykonos. That was actually fine with him since it had been a favorite summer vacation spot for the Emperor Andre.

The energetic redeemed governor and his seven resident ministers sprinted into their new shared home like Olympic athletes competing in a race. Eli was naturally deferentially granted the large governor's chamber on the fourth floor. Jonathan dibbed the smaller quarters on the east side of the mansion's top storey, with a large balcony facing Mount Zas and several smaller hills on Naxos located about six miles away.

On the third floor, Benny and Micah claimed a self-contained two-bedroom apartment on the east side, right underneath Jonathan's quarters. Tom and Sampson staked out another pad in the middle, while Craig and Ken took the only other remaining unit, on the west end, which was fine with them since it had the same spectacular views as Eli's did right above it. Magnificent water scenes, dotted with picturesque islands, were actually visible in every direction the brethren looked from any window inside the sprawling mansion. And even though much of the natural island vegetation, including pine trees and tall reeds, had burned up in the end-time fires which ravished the earth, hints of fresh greenery were already appearing due to the nightly rains and moderate temperatures.

After they quickly toured the fantastic facilities gifted to them by the gracious God of Israel, the eight ministerial saints decided to take a late afternoon swim on a private south-facing beach located near the point of the narrow peninsula. Benny in particular had been anticipating this prospect all day. The provincial officials had toured ten islands in the morning and early afternoon, including Ios, Mykonos and Paros, dispensing medical aid and meeting other urgent needs as they assessed future projects. Around 7,000 young children were alive on the islands, along with nearly 3,400 teenagers and adults. Eli was disappointed, but not overly surprised, when a messenger appeared mid-day to inform him that the Apostles Yochanan and Shaul could not make it yet again for their hoped-for visit, due to a continuing huge influx of human refugees into Jerusalem.

After sharing a quick mid-afternoon lunch on an eastern bay in Paros featuring feta cheese sprinkled on Greek salads and a glass of local Retsina white wine, the officials had twinked to Naxos to select a permanent location for their government offices and home, zipping to several spots on the island suggested to Eli by some local human residents. The eight brethren almost picked a splendid site on the southwest corner of the island. A remote forty-room hotel had been located there before an earthquake and subsequent fire destroyed it. The area featured a beautiful marble sand beach and a stunning view of Santorini and other islands to the southeast. However it was over 20 miles south of the main town on the island, also called Naxos, which was just a mile north of the peninsula location they finally chose. Eli later recommended the southern spot to Jonathan's parents and grandfather, along with Miri Doron, who all decided that evening to place their shared gifted house there. Like Prince David had counseled his new administrative assistant Shoshel Pearlman, Eli recommended to Miri that she not live in the governor's mansion lest she be hounded by the human staff night and day.

Needing to head to Jerusalem for the daily worship service in a half hour, the dignified government leaders slipped into silly mode as they whipped off their robes and laid them on a nearby rock before jumping like greased fish into the clear warm water. The sun was drifting low in the southwestern sky, casting a beautiful beam of reflected light on the sea waves gently washing onto the beach.

Benny was hysterically happy as he quickly confirmed what he'd already suspected: the Kadoshim could dive underwater and stay put for as long as they wanted since they no longer needed to breathe. He held onto his cotton boxer shorts as he dove like a lead balloon to the bottom of the sea, with his companions paddling close behind. The jubilant friends spent 20 minutes examining the rich aquatic life that had miraculously reappeared in the world's oceans and seas the minute the healing waters flowed into them from underneath the Temple Mount. Colorful coral and other ocean plants were perched upon boulders scattered on the seafloor. Clean white sand lay like a wool carpet between them. Before the eight saints exited the refreshing water, they playfully built a Kadoshim pyramid, with Benny on the bottom, Micah standing on top of his strong shoulders, and so on until it ended, appropriately, with Governor Eli on top just below the sea surface. A good time was had by all. This would become part of Benny and Micah's regular routine from now on, and just a bit less frequently for the other ministers as well.

When Sarah and Shoshel arrived at their private offices in Prince David's palace that same morning, they were pleased to discover each had been assigned ten Kadoshim volunteers who would conduct job interviews for them. The workers would hand a narrowed-down list of potential employees to the two executives by early afternoon; who would then choose final staffs from the recommended candidates.

In the meantime, Mayor Solomon offered to escort Sarah over to Hadassah Hospital for a short tour. Shoshel decided to go along as well. Sarah was thrilled to discover that the divinely-gifted medical facility was spotless and bright, with large windows looking out over the newly reforested hills and parks all around the sprawling complex. The pediatric ward was the largest in the new hospital, with over 800 beds. Department head Leah Rabinowitz met the three guests at the main desk with a big grin, expressing straight away how absolutely delighted she was to be working in such a wonderful, fully-equipped facility. The next largest department was the maternity ward, since it was expected the human race would grow rapidly in the coming decades as the substantial number of surviving children became adults and got married. The geriatric ward was the smallest, although it would be expanded in the coming centuries as its patient load rose.

Sarah was pleased to see that all essential medicines and other supplies were already fully stocked, having also been gifted by the Lord. However from now on, the mostly human staff would facilitate the acquisition of additional supplies. There was also a large quantity of leaves and fruit from the Trees of Life. Dried leaves would be served in teas and as spices on many foods, and fresh fruit would come with every meal. Mayor Solomon pointed out that the special rice that acted as a natural contraceptive was kept under lock and key in a room off of the main drug dispensary. It would only be made available under a doctor's prescription if the government-mandated conditions were met.

When the visiting party entered the spacious kitchen facility, Sarah was pleased to run into Yitzhak, busy checking on food supplies in a large pantry. "I've been doing all sorts of odd jobs this week, Sarah," he revealed after greeting his friend and Shoshel with affectionate hugs; and Mayor Solomon with a deferential handshake. "Until you get your human staff in place, it seems I'm the main run-around guy!"

"Well, bless you Yitzhak. It's just so good to have you on board, whatever you're doing! We should have a full staff operating here by the end of this week. I have volunteer saints interviewing qualified candidates as we speak, as does Shoshel, to help select her palace staff."

"That's great Sarah, but I really don't mind doing whatever I can. I mean, the last time I was in Hadassah, I was a crotchety old patient knocking on death's door, as you'll recall. Now I feel like a spring-chicken who could run around the complex 50 times and not get tired, which of course is actually quite the case!" Yitzhak was beaming as Sarah grabbed hold of his left arm, a warm smile on her lovely face.

"Well Yitzhak, I'm glad to hear of your restored stamina, but we'll send you some human help anyway."

"I could send over some of my ex-wives," quipped Mayor Solomon with a wink. "There are enough of them to staff this whole facility!" Then the Jerusalem Mayor turned serious, noting that his many wives had caused him to sin before adding, "The Lord was so gracious to forgive me when I repented of that, but the consequences were severe for my people, just like they were from my father's great sin before I was born."

Sarah was moved to tears when she and Shoshel, Mayor Solomon and Yitzhak entered her new private office in the administrative wing on the tenth floor. Positioned there on her mahogany desk was a large framed picture of the former widow with her family. In fact, it was a blown-up version of the Polaroid snapshot that Jonathan had taken the night before he went off to war. He had apparently beaten her to the new office. Next to the photo was a beautiful bouquet of red roses in a pink crystal vase with a note that she read out loud: "I'm so proud of you, Sarah. May you have abundant prosperity and great success in your new position, bringing many human patients to health, happiness and everlasting life in our Savior and Lord. Eternal love, Jonathan."

Shoshel put her arm around her close friend as the four saints studied the picture. Then following farewells all around, Yitzhak returned to his go-for job while the visitor's zapped back to the provincial government palace.

Sarah was surprised to find her wayward sister Donna sitting on a comfortable burgundy leather couch when she entered her outer office. "Hi Sis, I thought I'd drop by to see your new work place. It's really something!"

Thanks Donna, it is indeed. I've just seen my smaller office at Hadassah and it's wonderful as well. And guess what…Jonathan left me a bouquet and a framed family picture over there. I'm heading back later this afternoon after I finish going over some staff applications here."

"Jonathan's a love. Speaking of applications Sarah, I actually wanted to check if you could use my help around here. I'm already getting pretty bored at home, and until the schools get going again, the girls are around all the time. Don't get me wrong, I enjoy their company, but not everyday, all day. I'll keep watching them while you all go off to your evening Temple services of course, but otherwise I thought maybe I could help you out here during the day."

"That's very kind of you, Donna. Actually I *could* use a secretary right away, and I know you did a bit of that before you dropped out of college and moved over here from the States five years ago."

"Great! Just point me in the right direction and I'll get started."

Well, you can begin right there," said Sarah as she pointed her thin index finger at the reception desk, which was near a slightly larger one designed for her executive secretary.

After the two earthly sisters went over some job details, Sarah brought up the delicate issue she'd been wanting to discuss in private with Donna since she discovered her living in the ruins of her former home just over one week before. "Let's go into my inner office for a few minutes, Donna. I'd like to talk to you about a personal matter."

The saint and sinner sat down next to each other on a russet leather couch near Sarah's large desk. She didn't waste any time. "I've been wondering if you've thought about surrendering your life to the Lord, Donna. I know you had great doubts about my faith when you lived with me in my home. But surely now that you've seen us Kadoshim in our glorified bodies, including Jonathan and his parents and Rabbi Benjamin alive from the dead, not to mention the spectacular new Temple, King Yeshua's marvelous palace and this one, and our fabulous new home and all the other miraculous things that have appeared here in Jerusalem, you cannot deny the reality of the Lord's great goodness and mighty power."

"You're right, Sarah. I can't deny that some pretty fantastic stuff is going on. I'm still quite dazed over it all. But...I just need a little more time to adjust to all these incredible changes. I'm certainly very open to what you're saying, sis. I suppose I'd have to be a real idiot not to be. Just give me more time to work things out in my mind."

"Okay Donna, that's fair enough. I can't imagine what it must be like for you to have gone overnight from the terrors of the pervious era to what you see today. All I ask is that you keep your heart open to King Yeshua. He loves you very much, as demonstrated by the fact that you're still alive. I just want to see you alive forevermore."

"How exactly does that work Sarah? Like, when would I get this 'eternal life' that you always talk about?"

"Yochanan's book of Revelation tells us the Lord will reign on this earth for a thousand years, Donna, which has obviously just begun. At the end of the millennium, Satan will be released for a short period of time to lead some sort of an attack upon us here in Israel. Thankfully, it will not succeed, and the adversary will then be banished to hell forever, along with all of his followers."

Sarah gazed at an open Bible on her desk before she went on. "All of the dead will be resurrected at that point, both from the former era and any who die during the millennium. Then all but the Kadoshim will be judged, each according to their deeds. Those who have not surrendered their lives to the Lord and followed His commands will be thrown into what is called the 'Lake of Fire,' also known as the 'Second Death.' Yochanan quoted the Lord as telling him it will be a place that burns forever with fire and brimstone, designed for the unbelieving and idolaters, for murderers and immoral persons and for liars and the like. So not exactly a place you want to make your eternal home, to say the least!"

"Fine Sarah, that's enough for now. You're scaring the...you know what out of me!"

"Sorry Donna, but that's exactly what I hope will happen to you! I'm just telling you what the sacred scriptures say."

"Do you really believe in all that hellfire and brimstone stuff?"

"Actually the Lord spoke the most about it of anyone whose words are recorded in the entire Bible. So yes, I do believe it, since I obviously very much believe in Him."

The pilgrims heading toward Jerusalem were making good progress, mostly due to the fact that they were all now either seated on a fairly fast-moving mule, or on a horse that felt itself somewhat constrained in its potential speed by its half-breed cousin. The six humans and four animals had made their way through devastated Albuquerque five days before, and then passed through the ruins of Amarillo, Texas. In each city, they encountered few signs of life apart from an occasional group traveling one way or the other on the highway. Severe fire damage was evident everywhere. Several times a day they had to detour off of the asphalt pavement either because the cracks were too large to traverse, or bridges were out.

The two men were getting along better now, although there'd been a brief moment of friction the first night when Grandpa made clear to Brock that he would be sleeping next to his young daughter Tina in his small pup tent, not anywhere near the attractive young Jewish mother whom he quite obviously craved. Later, the men decided they would head off of Interstate 40 at Oklahoma City, and cut up on Interstate 44 to St Louis. Then they'd take Interstate 70 through Indianapolis, Columbus, and keep on it south of Pittsburg. When they got to Harrisburg, Pennsylvania, they would decide on their final route into New York City after assessing conditions on the scene.

Instead of riding into St Louis, the adults decided it was much safer to spend the night near the tiny town of Mosselle some thirty miles west of the metro area. They set up camp along the banks of the Bourbeuse River, just a few miles south of the much larger Missouri River, whose path had been significantly altered by the devastating earthquake which struck the Midwest two years before Andre came to power. The mighty river was further diverted from its original course during subsequent tremblers.

While gathering weeds to feed his horse, Brock spotted a young camper nearby with a horse similar to the Appaloosa stallion he owned. He went over to chat with the fellow who seemed to be traveling alone—a spur of the moment move he'd later deeply regret.

"Hey man, that's a fine looking horse you have. Is it your own?"

"Sure is. It's a filly from Philly! Well, not exactly, but from central Pennsylvania. But *I'm* actually originally from Philadelphia. My cousin had a ranch near Kansas City, and he asked me to bring over a couple horses from our uncle's farm outside of Lancaster a few years ago. I moved out to Kansas City to take a job at a law firm there."

"Oh, so you're a lawyer?" enquired Brock with a smirk on his face.

"Well, I was until all the proverbial manure hit the fan. Now I'm on my way to New York, and then on to Israel, I hope."

"Far out man! That's exactly where we're heading; Israel I mean, picking up a boat first in New York, we hope."

"Yah, that's my plan as well. My name is Aaron Feingold." The swarthy 28 year old Jewish attorney thrust out his hand, which was quickly captured in Brock's firm grip.

"I'm Brock Schmidt, originally from central California. I bought my colt in Arizona a couple years ago. I was living there with my young daughter and some others up in the mountains, and it sure came in handy to own him. Hey man, there are six of us riding together to New York, four adults and two girls, including mine. My daughter and I joined up with the others near Flagstaff. I'm sure you'd be welcome to ride along."

"Thanks Brock. It does get a little lonely traveling on my own, plus I know it'd be safer with others around. I almost got mugged two nights ago west of Columbia, and would have if I didn't have this." Aaron reached into his bag and pulled out a different kind of colt than the one Brock was preparing to feed.

"I've got a forty-five almost like that one in my bag. So far, haven't had to use it, thank God. Anyway, look, I'll check with the others and get back to you about riding together. The more the merrier, I say."

"Thanks guy, I appreciate that."

Brock began to realize he'd made a huge mistake soon after the party of seven human travelers passed through St. Louis and forded the Mississippi River, which was nearly bereft of water. Whether he wanted to or not—and he did not—Brock could see that Susan was easily as attracted to Aaron as she had seemed to be to him just a couple days before. At the very least, she was flirting hard with Feingold in order to make him jealous, he surmised. If so, it was working.

Although Brock was hardly the type of man that regularly assessed the looks of other men, he had to admit that Aaron was fairly handsome, and definitely better built than he was. Adept at hunting, fishing and splitting wood, Brock had been in top shape until he fell ill with a severe case of swine flu the winter before. It had nearly killed him.

Three days before, the blond widower had finally convinced Grandpa it would be considerably more comfortable for both men if the older man rode with his longtime wife on the mule, while the Californian carried Susan and her daughter on his steed. Tina and Justina sat happily in front, Brock in the middle and…as in his dreams…Susan snuggled in right behind him. However now she rode with her daughter astride Aaron's filly! The logical lawyer had suggested the arrangement, saying it made more sense for each horse to hold two adults and only one child.

The rival studs had their first fistfight just before the pilgrims crossed the Ohio-Pennsylvania state line. Brock claimed Aaron started the confrontation, even if indirectly. What seemed to set it off was the stress Aaron kept putting on Jewish themes whenever he chatted with Susan, which was as frequently as possible. Brock was certain that the not-too-subtle subtext was 'Schmidt may not be gay, but he is definitely a goy.' Grandpa was forced to jump up from the campfire to break up the scuffle; not an easy task at his age. Susan was outwardly quite disturbed over the brawl, while inwardly thrilled to have two handsome young hunks wrangling like rival cockatoos over her. It had been three years since her husband Evan was killed when the San Andreas Fault gave way soon after Andre first claimed the vapid title of god incarnate. She had missed the attention of a besotted man.

Two more fistfights broke out before the party of seven arrived several days later outside of New York. After the second clash, Grandpa threatened to take his original crew away from both men.

The horrifying prospect of no longer having Susan along as a traveling companion had instantly transformed the dueling titans into tranquil angels—at least on the outside.

By the time the human party and animals arrived on the outskirts of the new province of New York City, the sprawling metro area had been cleared of most of the rubble that had been piled everywhere only a couple weeks before. However, there was still enough junk around for them to get a pretty fair idea of what it must have looked like before the Kadoshim volunteers and ministers began working in the area.

The pilgrims could not reach any of the New York area islands since all bridges and tunnels were still out. However they were informed by some kind human police officers in Newark that transit docks were already being set up in Great Kills Harbor on the nearby Jersey shore, where thousands of Jews from the area, and indeed from all over the United States and Canada, were gathering in hopes of hopping aboard a ship to Israel.

With thousands of Jewish refugees joining many local sons and daughters of Abraham in expressing their keen desire to head back to the Promised Land, Governor Yoseph Steinberg had realized he needed to begin organizing a ship or two that could depart soon to the Jewish homeland. He ordered his Transport Minister, Giuseppe Marino, to head up the emergency operation. The minister in turn asked his granddaughter Angelica if she would volunteer to begin registering the burgeoning number of Jewish refugees; a request she gladly complied with.

"Welcome folks! My name is Angelica Scarcelli. We are repairing and upgrading a large passenger ship at present, and hope to have you on your way to Israel within one week. So if you could just give me your names, ages and where you're from, I'll be happy to place you on the growing list."

"Thank you," said Brock, who had rushed to the head of the small line. He liked being first in everything. "My name is Brock Schmidt, and this is my darling daughter Tina. We're from Bakersfield, California. I'm 27 and Tina is just five."

"Thank you Mr. Schmidt. And who is that lovely girl behind you?"

"My name is Justina, and I'm almost five and a half!" said the enthusiastic girl with four missing front teeth. "I'm Jewish, and we're going home to God's land!"

"I actually share an apartment in Jerusalem with my mother, honey, although we recently moved to the Governor's new mansion here in New York after we discovered my baby nephew was alive and living in an orphanage near Newark. We're raising him in the mansion."

"Wow, that's neat!" said Justina with dimples imploding. Then she proudly held up her pets. "This is Pookey and my cat is Ginger. I hope they can come with us!"

"I'm sure that can be arranged sweetheart."

"I'm her mother, Angelica, Susan Levinson, age 25." The latter statement was not exactly correct since she had recently turned 26. "We're from Santa Monica California. That's a wonderful story about your baby nephew."

"Thanks so much, Susan, God is so good. Okay, you're both registered. Next."

"My name is Aaron Feingold, and I'm originally from Philadelphia. I'm a spry 28. I had an uncle living in Tel Aviv, and hope he and his family are still alive."

"I hope so too, Mr. Feingold. Next please?"

Grandpa and Grandma stepped up slowly to the portable desk underneath the green tarp.

"I'm Ariel Hazan and this is my wife, Esther. She's a young 57 and I'm nearly 60. We're from Santa Monica as well. Susan is our niece."

Esther took over the conversation, as was her wont. "We're on our way to see our daughters and grandchildren in Jerusalem, who we pray are all still alive. Our daughter's names are Sarah Goldman and Donna Svenson."

FOURTEEN

SWEET REUNIONS

Angelica Scarcelli scratched her head as she looked again at the names in front of her. She had been briefly introduced by her mother Teresa to a saint from Jerusalem named Sarah. That occurred a few weeks before; the same day her cousin, George Kirintelos, was discovered alive. Angelica had not caught Sarah's last name. However, she was later told by Teresa it was Sarah's son who spotted the Christmas package with the baby rattle in it. *Wasn't his name Benny Goldman?* She scratched her head again and then called out to the retreating pilgrims.

"Excuse me, Mr. and Mrs. Hazan! Would you come back here for a minute please?"

The five other humans stayed in place while the couple returned to Angelica's portable desk.

"Is there a problem?" Ari enquired.

"No sir, it's just that I briefly spoke to a saint from Jerusalem a couple weeks ago named Sarah, the same day we discovered my nephew alive. I didn't catch her family name, but I'm pretty sure I also met her son, whose name I'm quite certain was Benny Goldman."

Esther clutched Ari's arm as she let out a loud cry of joy. This brought the other humans scrambling back to Angelica's desk. "What's going on, Aunt Esther?" exclaimed Susan as she grabbed hold of her hand. Susan's deceased mother Stella was Esther's younger sister.

241

"Your cousin Sarah and our grandson Benny are alive! Angelica met them a couple weeks ago here in New Jersey. Thank you Heavenly Father!!"

Both women were now in tears, along with Sarah's father. "Oh, and I'm pretty sure she was with her earthly husband, whose name I didn't hear, and also her daughter. They are all saints like me living in their glorified new bodies. I think mom said the father is a senior government advisor in a new province in Greece, and Benny is the new Justice Minister there."

"My grandson, the judge!" shouted Esther as the others bristled with delight.

Young Justina was slightly puzzled. "But momma, didn't you tell me Benny was now eight years old and Tali eleven? How could he be a 'just-us' minister?"

"It's 'justice' honey. Like Angelica said, they're all now in some sort of glorified new bodies. I'm guessing adult ones."

"Indeed, we all appear to be around 30 years old, despite whatever ages we actually reached in the old era. Benny's like six-foot-four and strongly built, Justina. I suppose you won't recognize him Mr. and Mrs. Hazan. Oh, and mom told me Sarah is managing the health care system in Jerusalem. She has an office in Prince David's palace, who is the 'King David' from the Bible."

Even though he didn't know Sarah from Eve, Aaron Feingold let out a whistle over this fantastic news. "My daughter, the healer in King David's palace!" exclaimed Esther as Ari scratched his nearly bald head.

The last time the Hazans had seen Sarah and her family was six months before Jonathan was killed on the Golan Heights. They had flown on a direct El Al flight from Los Angeles to Tel Aviv to celebrate the Feast of Tabernacles with the Goldmans in Jerusalem. Benny was not even four yet. However the couple did speak by phone to Sarah as often as possible until they fled to the Sequoia National Forest northeast of Bakersfield two years after Jonathan's death. They were not able to attend their son-in-law's funeral since Esther was having another round of serious heart problems.

Until they escaped to the mountains with a group of Jewish believers from a congregation in Thousand Oaks, they spoke to Benny every week while he was living with his paternal grandparents near Chicago. Plans were in place for him to visit their California home over the Christmas school break, but Sarah had suddenly decided to take him with her back to Jerusalem after Jonathan's parents were arrested a few months earlier in Skokie. It was actually just after Sarah told them about the senior Goldmans incarcerations that Ari decided it was time to head for the hills where many of the congregants had already taken shelter, assisted by a sealed Jewish male from Long Beach.

The welcome surprises just kept coming. "If you'll all just wait here a few minutes, I'll go inform our provincial governor that you're here. His name is Yoseph Steinberg, and he just returned here after living for many years in Jerusalem."

"The New York provincial governor is Yoseph Steinberg?" asked an astonished Ari rhetorically. Esther smiled and squeezed his hand before adding, "We met Yoseph and his wife Cindy when we visited Jerusalem. Sarah and Jonathan took us with the kids to a meal at their home during Succot. They were lovely people."

"Well, they're still quite lovely, but not exactly 'people' anymore. Cindy is also living here, and is a cabinet minister in Yoseph's New York government. She now goes by the name Zinel, by the way. I'll go see if one or both of them can come and meet you."

"Splendid dear, you are such a saint," said Esther, which caused Brock, Aaron and Susan to break out in gentle giggles.

"Oh, one other thing before I dash off. Don't be alarmed when you see me disappear. We 'saints' can now travel in an instant to anywhere on earth that we want to visit. So it really will just take me a few minutes to go speak with Governor Steinberg."

The provincial ruler dropped everything from his busy schedule as soon as Angelica walked in with her mother Teresa and related her tremendous news. Teresa volunteered to go fetch Zinel, whose office was in the west wing of the new mansion in Crown Heights, Brooklyn.

When all four Kadoshim were present in Yoseph's study, they held hands in a small circle and away they went.

Although the Steinbergs were considerably younger looking than the last time Ari and Esther saw them, they immediately recognized Yoseph, if not Zinel. After hugs and warm greetings were exchanged and introductions made between the other human pilgrims and the Steinbergs, Zinel added some details to what Angelica had already shared. "Your granddaughter Tali is now known as Talel. She's just adopted twin girls a bit older than Tina and Justina. They're all living in Sarah's new house in southeast Jerusalem. If you'd like, I'll pop over and inform them you're here. I'm sure they'll want to see you right away."

"That would be *wonderful*," gushed Esther.

If Sarah and Talel look anything like Susan, this will be wonderful for sure, thought Brock before chiding himself for entertaining such thoughts about two Jewish mothers.

Zinel showed up in Sarah's palace office just two seconds later. She was rather surprised to find Donna Svenson staring at a computer screen. "Shalom Donna, I didn't know you worked here."

"Hi Zinel. I've been helping Sarah out for a couple weeks already. She's just hired a fulltime administrative assistant, but I'll probably stay on anyway for awhile. Setting up an entire health care system virtually from scratch is quite a huge undertaking. I like keeping busy and it fills up the time."

"That's great Donna. Say, is Sarah here?"

"Yes, but she just stepped out to talk with Batsheva about something. I'll go let her know you're here."

"Thanks. I have some very important news for both of you."

"Concerning what?"

"No, I want to tell you both together."

Donna returned four minutes later with her older sister in tail. After greetings were exchanged, Zinel advised the two siblings to sit down. "Sarah, Donna, I have some fantastic news for you both. Your parents are alive! I've just been speaking with them at a port in New Jersey. They're planning to come by ship to Israel."

Sarah gasped as tears of joy flushed her wide eyes. Donna was the first to verbally react; pointing out that Sarah had told her they were deceased. "You're right, I did say that Donna, because Prince David told me they were not among the Kadoshim. I guess I jumped to the wrong conclusion, as I'd earlier done about you too. You'd think I'd learn." Smiling broadly, Sarah then turned back toward her longtime friend and dried her eyes. "So how are they, Zinel?"

"They seem fine, especially considering they told me they'd crossed the States riding on a mule the past few weeks."

"What? They traveled across America by mule?" spluttered Donna as she grimaced and patted her behind while giving Sarah a warm wink.

"That's what they told me. Hey, there's more good news. Your cousin Susan is with them, and her daughter Justina."

"My old drinking buddy!" blurted Donna, who was just a year younger than her first cousin. "I'll finally have another human to hang with!" The comments prompted Sarah to frown.

"They're traveling with two young men; one a blond Gentile widowed father with his five year old sweet daughter, and the other a single Jewish attorney from the Midwest. They both seemed a bit smitten with Susan, although I was only with them all for a few minutes."

"Are they cute?" enquired Donna, whose excitement level was rising by the minute.

"Um, they're not bad looking."

"Yummy! I can't wait for them all to arrive here. How soon do you think that will be?"

"Yoseph is working on arranging a ship with a goal of sailing by next week. So maybe about a month from now I'd guesstimate. I'm actually not sure how long such a journey might take."

Sarah stood to her feet. "Well, I'm going to go get Talel and head over to the States right away. In fact, I think I'll stop off in Naxos and see if Jonathan and Benny are free to come along. Donna, can you go find Shoshel and see if she wants to accompany me? And can you go back with me, Zinel?"

"Certainly Sarah, I've already cleared my schedule for this sweet reunion. I don't want to miss a thing."

"Can't you pop *me* along?" queried Donna, even though she knew the answer would be no. She'd already learned it was against the rules for humans to be transported supernaturally, unless there was a medical emergency or the like.

"Sorry, sis, but I'll sure pass along your warmest greetings. It won't be long until they're all here. Bless you Lord!"

Jonathan and Benny Goldman were both hard at work in their Naxos government mansion when the Jerusalem saints appeared in the main foyer. Jonathan was initially nonplussed by the totally unex-pected news, but quickly joined Sarah, Benny, Talel and Shoshel in free flowing tears of joyous thanksgiving. Eli heard the commotion and entered Jonathan's office, soon followed by Micah and Craig. Rabbi Goldman, Abe and Rebecca also noticed something was up from their nearby offices and went to investigate. When all were told the fantastic news by Zinel, Eli led the assembled saints in a spontaneous hora dance of jubilation. Then they all nipped off to New Jersey.

Ari and Esther were sitting on two folding chairs in the shade of a dark green tarp, soaking up more information from Governor Steinberg about the Lord's Millennial Kingdom and the Goldman family. Teresa Scarcelli sat next to him, and then Susan Levinson. The rival bulls came next. They had locked horns again over who got the seat right next to the beautiful babe. Brock won the battle, since his daughter in his arms wanted to sit next to Justina, seated half asleep on her mother's lap.

Suddenly Zinel materialized with ten accompanying Kadoshim in front of the semicircle of chairs. Justina quickly revived and clapped excitedly while Esther nearly fainted.

Apart from Zinel whom they had just met, Ari, Esther and Susan instantly recognized only one saint: Jonathan. All three leapt to their feet and hugged his neck. Then they spotted Sarah, standing right behind him with moist eyes. Although taller and stronger than she had been in her previous body, she still had her father's sparkling russet eyes and her mother's silky auburn hair—Esther's locks were actually no longer dyed that same natural color since she'd been forced to stop enriching her mane after fleeing with Ari, Susan and Justina to the mountains north of Bakersfield.

"Sarah, we didn't dream we would ever see you or the family again," stated Ari after he gave his oldest daughter an affectionate kiss on her left cheek. Now weeping, Esther enfolded her baby in her arms; hugging Sarah so tightly it might have squeezed the air out of her if she still had lungs.

Susan then got into the act, giving her cousin kisses on both of her cheeks. "This is my daughter, Justina." Sarah took the smiling girl in her arms as Esther eased her embrace. Her cousin had given birth to the baby girl several months before the Hazans visited Jerusalem, and Sarah had only seen photos of her. "And these are our new friends Brock Schmidt and his daughter Tina, and Aaron Feingold."

Oh my, 'they are not bad looking' was truly an understatement. There's going to be trouble ahead for sure, thought Sarah as she smiled politely and used her free hand to shake the two men's sweaty paws.

"So which of you are my lovely grandkids?" queried Esther after she wiped her tears with a handkerchief to better study the faces of the remaining assembled saints.

"I'm Tali, Grandma—now Talel—and this is Big Benny."

Esther gasped with delight as she flung her arms around her two descendants, which was rather hard to do given their newly expanded sizes, especially Benny. Grandpa Ari then joined the embraces, noticing right away that Talel was probably two inches taller than he was, and Benny at least half a foot.

The new Justice Minister then introduced his childhood friend Micah to them. "Grandpa and grandma, I think you'll remember the toothy kid in our neighborhood I played with a lot, named Micah?" The Hazans both nodded. "Well, here he is!"

Sarah stuck to the theme. "Dad, mom, this is my best friend, Stacy Pearlman, who you also met when you visited Jerusalem. We call her Shoshel now, the Rose of God. And I think you'll be very surprised to learn who these three youngsters are." Sarah was pointing toward Rabbi Benjamin, Abe and Rebecca. The last time Ari and Esther saw Jonathan's parents was when their daughter took on the Goldman family name at the Hazan's plush country club. The outdoor wedding ceremony was held on top of a cliff just above the Pacific Ocean. Minutes before the Kadoshim materialized from Israel and the Greek Isles, Governor Steinberg informed the Hazans that Abe and Rebecca were beheaded by Andre's forces after undergoing arrest in Skokie. He did not add that they were now ministers in Eli's new provincial government.

"I'm afraid I haven't a clue," said Esther after she cleaned her glasses to more carefully examine their faces.

"This is Jonathan's father, Abraham, and his mother Rebecca, and that's your grandchildren's great grandfather, Rabbi Benjamin Goldman, after whom Benny's named."

"The one who perished at Auschwitz?" blurted Ari, his aging mind not even close to processing this startling information. Esther was utterly astounded as well, but recovered more quickly. "You look pretty good for your advanced age, sir, no older than Benny actually! It's a great honor to meet you sir, and to see you again Abe and Rebecca. You're looking pretty nimble as well!" Embraces were then shared all around.

"Dad and mom, Zinel told me you already heard about the new government positions Jonathan and Benny have been assigned to in the Greek Isles."

Esther beamed. "Yes, we're so proud of you both, and of you too Sarah...the health department head in Jerusalem! And Tali, taking care of twin girls! We can't wait to see them, and of course your new city of Jerusalem. Yoseph's been telling us all about it."

Jonathan spoke up. "I think you'll recall meeting my best friend there, Eli Ben David. He's our new provincial governor, so now he's my boss!"

Eli faked a stern countenance and then smiled sweetly. "It's wonderful to see you both again."

"I thought you looked familiar," Ari stated as he patted Eli on the back. "We heard from Sarah how good you were to the kids after...Jonathan was killed in the war. Benny told us all about you over the phone when he was living in Chicago." Ari then walked over to Jonathan and put his arm over his shoulder. "Son, you were killed in a

Syrian gas attack, and now you are alive! And Abe and Rebecca, we just learned you were beheaded by Andre's goons, and now you're alive! And Rabbi Goldman, you…" Ariel Hazan could not go on.

Brock and Aaron were following the emotional reunion in utter amazement, both choking back tears. The guys were each thinking as well how much they would love to become a member of this extended family.

Twenty minutes later, the Greek Isle governor and his cabinet ministers returned to their postings, as did Shoshel. Talel then informed her mother she wanted to accompany the Steinbergs and Teresa Scarcelli back to Crown Heights for a few minutes. She had someone she needed to speak to there. Sarah promised to wait for her earthly daughter to return before heading back to Jerusalem. Anyway, she wanted to talk to her parents in private. Susan had taken her young daughter to sit on a ledge overlooking the port, accompanied, of course, by her two salivating suitors.

Sarah was eager to hear more details about how her progenitors had survived the final judgments. More than that, she wanted to determine whether or not Ari and Esther were believers in Yeshua, and also check on the spiritual status of her cousin Susan, who had an infamous pre-marital reputation that easily matched her sister Donna's.

As usual, Esther did most of the talking. "We took up your advice to visit that Messianic congregation in Thousand Oaks, Sarah, going there for the first time soon after Jonathan's parents were arrested. We decided it was just too dangerous for us as Jews to remain in the Los Angeles area, especially since we were holding out on getting the Emperor's identity implants in our right hands; again per your advice. You remember you told us the congregants might be able to offer us some physical protection. However we weren't believers in Yeshua. Nevertheless, we became friendly with some of the ones who remained behind when the others fled up to the mountains, and a couple months later we joined the believers up there, taking Susan and Justina along with us. Of course, that was already more than a year after my sister Stella and your Uncle Jack were killed in that terrible San Andreas earthquake, along with Susan's husband Evan."

"Okay, let me cut to the chase. Are you all believers now?"

Ari cleared his throat. "We only became fully convinced that Yeshua is the promised Jewish Messiah after that supernatural sign appeared in the sky," he stated factually. "But yes, we do believe in Him now, and have entrusted our lives to Him."

Sarah bounced up out of her folding chair and gave her parents fresh embraces. "I'm so thrilled to hear that, dad and mom...you'll inherit eternal life in the end, just like us!" After yet another set of hugs, Sarah added, "And what about Susan?"

"I'm afraid that's another story," sighed Esther. "You know, she was pretty heavily into men, drugs, booze, and that 'new age' stuff. She doesn't let us say too much about our new faith, at least not yet. Still, we believe she'll come along, especially now that she's seen all of you and the power of God up close."

"Is either of those two guys a believer? They seem to be quite interested in Sue for sure."

Ari grunted. "Let's just say I've had to separate them a few times already, and I'm a much older man than they are. Plus we still have a long journey ahead of us. They fight over her like two love-starved wolves. Then again, there aren't many eligible women of her age around right now, nor many men for that matter. And she is rather good looking, and I guess they are too, but I'm not really sure about their spiritual beliefs."

"What do you think about the idea of me inviting Susan to live with us in my Jerusalem home, along with Justina? I think the twins would be elated, and I know Donna would be. Sue would see me, Talel and Bet-el, the friend I told you about, up close every day. I think it might be very good for her."

"That'd be fine with us," Esther affirmed, adding "We'd frankly rather not live with her. And Justina would definitely enjoy having other Jewish girls around to play with. So go ahead and give it a whirl. I'll speak to her about it if you'd like."

"That would be great mom, but do let her know there would be rules in the house, like no men in bed. I want to keep the twins away from that sort of behavior."

"We'll pass that along, Sarah," her father pledged. "What about Donna? Where is she at spiritually?"

Sarah rolled her eyes and lifted her shoulders. "She says she's open to the Lord, but not yet clear where she stands. Still, I have to admit she's gone through quite an ordeal. She has an incredible survival story actually. I think that difficult experience has impacted her a lot, but I'll let her fill in the blanks."

"We have quite a story as well," stated Esther while wiping droplets of sweat off her prominent brow.

"Well, you'll certainly be our dinner guests as soon as you arrive in Jerusalem. Donna and I will want to hear all the details. I see that Talel has just returned, and we need to get back to Jerusalem for our daily Temple service. It's way beyond description by the way, but I'll try to explain it to you next time we meet. I'll pop over again tomorrow to check on you. Yoseph told me he'll have a couple nice tents erected for you later today where you can stay until your ship heads out. Shalom dad and mom, we love you!"

Talel Goldman had gone to the New York governor's mansion to make the confession she was secretly dreading. "Minister Scarcelli, can you direct me to your Culture and Music Minister's office, Carmella Bernstein? I have something important I need to discuss with her."

"Why of course, Talel, and please call me Teresa. It's the second door down that hall, on the right. Would you like me to introduce you?"

"I actually already met her, the day we rescued the kids in Harlem and then discovered your baby nephew alive. She was with you and your earthly husband, Leo, down at the One World Trade Center, along with Governor Yoseph, his other ministers and my family. I met her briefly there."

"Oh sure, I recall that now. Well tell her I said hello. It was so nice to meet your other grandparents and your cousins by the way, and to see the rest of your family again today. I hope we can meet up more often. You have a blessed family for sure."

"Thank you, Teresa. Yours is as well."

Still fairly petite for a transformed saint, Carmella Bernstein rose from her tidy desk as her secretary escorted Talel into her office. "It is so good to see you again, Talel. I remember meeting you near the destroyed Freedom Tower. You asked me if I was related to the conductor, Leonard Bernstein, and I told you he was a second or third cousin of my deceased husband's father. I often get asked that question when people hear my last name. Leonard was a real icon in this city, and beyond."

"Indeed, as a girl I loved the musical score he wrote for *West Side Story*. Mom had that CD and we listened to it quite often. Minister Bernstein, there was actually more to my question than I let on, and I've felt guilty about not saying anything to you at the time we met. I've just adopted twin girls recently orphaned in Jerusalem. There mother was my second grade teacher. Her name was Dafna Bernstein. I recall she told us once that her husband, Uri, whose father immigrated to Israel from the Soviet Ukraine, was distantly related to Leonard Bernstein's father. I also remember she said Uri met some of the family when he visited New York one summer with Dafna and the twins."

Carmella's eyes had already lit up. "Yes, we all had lunch together at the Waldorf Astoria. It was marvelous to meet them. My husband was still alive then, and I was a music instructor at Julliard. That's where I met my husband many years before, and also Leonard for that matter. The girls were around five years old I believe, and adorable. Then Uri was killed in that horrible suicide terrorist attack near the Jerusalem bus station. I only spoke to Dafna twice by phone after that."

Talel sat up in her chair, hands folded on her lap. "Well Mrs. Bernstein, even though I've already adopted Daniyella and Dalya, you were part of their actual human family. So I want to give you the opportunity of caring for them, if you so desire."

The poised government minister rose again from her desk and shuffled over to the humble young saint who was clearly nearly in tears. "Oh Talel, that is so sweet of you. The girls are delightful, as I said. But I'm the new Minister of Culture, Music and Sports for the province of New York City, as you well know, which entails a lot of responsibility as we rebuild the once-thriving human civilization here. I want to re-open Julliard in some form, bring back the famous theatre life, although with cleaner shows than we often suffered through in the old era, and build up healthy sports facilities for the residents. I will be quite busy with all that. Plus the girls' home is Jerusalem. That is all they know. I'm sure you will do a fine job raising them, especially with the help of that lovely family you're part of. I would naturally be thrilled to visit them very soon, and often after that, and have them come here for a visit after we get things up and running."

Talel was back on cloud nine. "Thank you so much, Mrs. Bernstein. I was kind of hoping you would say that."

"I gathered as much, but it's from my heart, dear one. Oh, do please call me Carmella."

"Can you come over after Temple service this evening? I'm sure the girls would be delighted to see you again. I think they're a bit over-whelmed at times with all the dramatic changes around them. It would bless them very much, I'm certain."

"Splendid! Let's meet up after the service and I'll gladly go with you. I'm so excited to hear that they're alive and living with you and Sarah."

Just then, Teresa Scarcelli appeared at the office door holding a baby dressed in tiny denim overalls. George Jr. was happily flailing his arms in the air as a gurgling stream of dribble made its way out of his smiling little mouth. Talel and Carmella scooted over to coo. "Look, he's going to be a conductor like Leonard!" proclaimed the New York Music Minister as the other saints chuckled with glee.

The reunion that evening in the world's capital city was a tender one. Carmella Bernstein was greeted at the front door with affec-tionate hugs and kisses by her late husband's distant young cousins. In her heart, Carmella was almost as happy to discover some human rela-tives still alive as the twins were thrilled to see her again. As far as she knew, no one else was still around in the flesh, or among the

Kadoshim, from either her Jewish mother's extended family or from her Irish-Catholic father's kith and kin. None of her three siblings or their mates or children had accepted the Messiah's free gift of eternal life, nor had her husband or their grown son and his male lover. All were gone now except these two young cousins distantly related to her dear deceased husband.

Talel invited her new friend to visit whenever she wanted to, and Carmella assured her and the twins that she would. Donna watched the happy reunion while thinking mainly about the upcoming meeting with her parents, first cousin and her daughter. She especially wanted to find out more details concerning their male traveling companions, so as soon as Carmella popped back to New York, Donna beckoned Sarah out to the backyard for a grilling.

"So how did dad and mom and the others look?"

"Actually better than I expected, Donna. They've begun eating fresh fruit from the Trees of Life delivered to the area every day by some of Yoseph's Kadoshim volunteers, and mom said it seems to have quickly helped lower her blood pressure and renew her strength. Sue looked as stunning as ever, and it was great to meet her young daughter Justina—full of vinegar, she was."

"And what about the boys? Are they gorgeous hunks?"

"Hmm...I guess you could use that term. They're both quite love-struck for sure. Brock is blond with blue eyes, quite handsome with a rugged square jaw, while Aaron is muscular with dark hair and olive skin and seems very intelligent. Susan seems happy enough to have their full attention, but dad said he had to break up several fist-fights between the guys." Sarah chuckled. "He called them 'wolves' actually."

"Well, I can't wait for them all to arrive here in Israel, and Sarah, I was thinking, maybe Sue could bunk with me, and her young girl with the twins. What do you think?"

"I already proposed that to dad and mom, and they think it's a fine idea. They were going to speak to Sue tonight and let me know what she says when I 'twink' back over there tomorrow, as Benny would say. I'm also going to check with Mayor Solomon about getting dad and mom a place in the apartment building that Jonathan and the others have units in. Aaron told me he's going to see if his uncle and family are still alive in Tel Aviv, and if not, he asked if I could arrange a place for him here in Jerusalem as well, and Brock requested the same. I think maybe Mayor Solomon will bend the rules a bit and allow that. They want to be closer to Susan, which is fine with me, although I don't want any hanky panky in this house as I've already told you, especially with the youngsters around."

"I'm being good, sis. Who knows, maybe Sue will get one guy and me the other one!"

"That would be nice, but please, no sex in this home unless you're legally married. I asked dad and mom to make that clear to Sue as well. I don't want her coming here unless she understands and agrees to that essential condition."

"It all sounds a bit puritanical to me, Sarah, but it's your house and the twins are almost your grandchildren. Imagine, my sister a grandmother at 33…isn't that the age you'd be if you were still in that old clunker body?"

"Yes, that's about right. I was over eight years older than you, and you are now almost 25, I think."

"Right on the mark, Sarah."

"Donna, have you thought any more about the spiritual issue I brought up a couple weeks back?"

"Not really. I've been pretty busy at your office, and here with the children. But I'm keeping my mind open. Are dad and mom and the others believers like you?"

"Dad and mom are, but apparently not Sue; and they're not sure where the men are at."

Whatever they believe, I sure hope at least one of the guys will want to play catch ball with me, thought Donna as she and Sarah headed back into the kitchen.

FIFTEEN

CORONATION DAY

Governor Eli Ben David was standing with his chief advisor, Jonathan Goldman, and Communications Minister Ken Preston. The provincial government officials were busy inspecting the new flat-screen television that had just been erected by local workers in the city of Iraklion on the island of Crete. The screen stood twelve feet tall and fourteen feet wide. Manufactured at a divinely-gifted factory in Tel Aviv, it was brought by ship to a portable dock that local male workers had just erected in the old destroyed port in the Greek Isle city. The large screen was positioned in the middle of a newly-built covered stage in the center of a former football field not far from the port. Similar deliveries were in progress all around the world.

It was only five days before King Yeshua's formal millennial coronation in Jerusalem. The planned ceremony, beginning at sundown on Shabbat, was scheduled for exactly seven weeks to the hour from when the Magnificent One returned to earth to rule and reign as King of Kings and Lord of Lords. Eli wanted to make sure the surviving human population in the Iraklion area, especially the orphaned children, would not miss viewing the elaborate ceremony live via satellite transmission. Kadoshim volunteer workers had taken thirty other flat screen sets to the remaining population centers in Eli's new province.

Over the previous month, remarkable progress had been made in restoring human, animal and plant life all over the globe. Scientists in Israel quickly ascertained that the nightly rains which gently bathed the earth contained many minerals and medicinal components that significantly aided cellular health and reproduction. Destroyed flora and fauna were reappearing with remarkable speed. Fruit and leaves from the Trees of Life were helping the human population to rapidly recover from illnesses and injuries, while also markedly slowing down the natural aging process in both human beings and animals. Dogs and cats and other household pets would now be able to live with their owners for many decades instead of just a relatively few short years. Cows and goats would produce milk for much longer periods of time.

Eli was elated to have been asked to appear with the other world governors in a majestic parade of saints who would follow the King of the Universe into the Holy Temple at the start of the special coronation service. They would all ascend the grand stairs that led to the main entrance just before Shabbat began at the end of the week. David and Jesse Goldman and many other perpetual priests would also take part in the glorious procession. This time, it would be they who would carry the Lord's regal train, which Eli learned would be five times longer than the one he and eleven other governors had been privileged to elevate over one month before.

During the intervening weeks, Governor Ben David had finally been able to host his dear friend Yochanan and Foreign Minister Shaul on a half-day tour of his new island province. Following two weeks of non-stop propulsion, the flood of returning human refugees into Jerusalem had ebbed to the point where the two Kingdom officials could carry out the planned visit, which they'd both been pining to undertake. During their brief stay, the Apostle Shaul was saddened to see the harrowing condition of several Greek Isle towns he'd visited in New Testament days to spread the good news of Israel's Eternal Messiah, Yeshua from Nazareth. The spiritual envoy to the Gentiles had been to Rhodes three times, during both his second and third Gospel expeditions, and on his final sailing to Rome when he also stopped in Crete. He had sailed past Samos twice, visiting the main town by the same name on one occasion. He'd also been to Mytilene on the island of Lesbos during his third voyage after sailing along the coast of Chios. During Shaul's second journey, his ship had passed just north of Naxos on its way to the city of Ephesus, located on the west coast of Asia Minor east of Samos. Later he sailed very near to Patmos on his way back to Jerusalem.

For Yochanan, the stop in Patmos obviously carried the most emotional weight. The small rocky island, covering a mere 13 square miles, is located some 60 miles east of Naxos, where the Jerusalem-based officials ended their short visit by sharing a meal with Eli and his cabinet ministers.

After arriving earlier on Patmos, Eli revealed there were only a dozen humans discovered alive on the small island when his volunteer Kadoshim team conducted an initial inspection a few weeks before, all but three of them children. Yochanan took Shaul, Eli and his cabinet to the exact spot where he'd been incarcerated by the Romans around 50 years after the Redeemer's resurrection in ancient Jerusalem. He explained that even though he was already quite elderly by then, he headed up the thriving church in Ephesus that Shaul helped to establish before his imprisonment and death in Rome. Yochanan related he later learned that the Roman Emperor Domitian, who came to power in the year 81 AD, had personally ordered his arrest in a renewal of persecution which began under the reign of Nero two decades before.

"I was too old to work in the quarry where most of the other prisoners were busy laboring every day," Yochanan recalled as he examined the area where he'd been confined. "I was kept in leg chains in a stone hut, which was extremely hot in the dry summers and terribly cold when the winter rains fell and the blustery sea winds blew. I pleaded with my Roman captors to remove the chains, pointing out I had virtually no chance of fleeing this isolated island. I could hardly walk towards the end of my time here, let alone escape to somewhere else. Still, my hands were free and I was allowed some books and parchment to write on. I used the parchment to record the incredible, end-time vision the Lord gave me while meditating on His word alone in my prison hut."

Benny grasped the beloved Apostle's hand and stated, "Yochanan, I've never told you this before, but you really are my hero. I was so awed when you and Natan-el ministered so powerfully in the Old City and elsewhere in the last days. In fact, I still am." The great Apostle smiled and warmly thanked his young friend.

Governor Eli then revealed his surprise. "Yochanan and Shaul, you are princes of our faith who paid such heavy personal prices to bring the good news to people all over the world. I intend to erect monuments to both of you here in the Greek Isles—right here on Patmos for you Yochanan, and for you Shaul, on Rhodes. I'd be so honored if you would come for the dedications, probably in about one year's time."

"Thank you dear friend, I'd be delighted to attend such a cere-mony, although the honor really belongs to our Master and Savior alone." Yochanan then shed a few tears, washing away the last remaining vestiges of sorrow from his traumatic imprisonment. "The same goes for me, Eli, thank you very much," added Shaul as he turned his gaze in the direction of the coast of Asia Minor some 30 miles to the east, where he had established and ministered to many church congregations.

Doctor William Morgan was thoroughly bored. The physician from Long Island was mostly spending his days with his feet up on his uncluttered desk, reading some old medical journals and a non-riveting novel he found on board set in Tahiti. His two nurses were equally under-worked. The Atlantic Ocean crossing had been completely uneventful. None of the passengers traveling on the large cruise ship were suffering from seasickness since there were no longer any storms on planet earth, or even significant winds, and therefore very few waves. Two small siblings who caught colds had been brought to the infirmary by their guardian in order to get some prescription cough medicine. One man just wanted to buy antacid pills, while an older woman showed up suffering from gout. That occurred just before the 1,800-bed ship stopped in the Azores to pick up 14 passengers and fresh food supplies.

However exactly one day after the electric-powered vessel passed through the Straight of Gibraltar into the Mediterranean Sea, a woman had a serious heart attack. Ari was in the small en-suite bath-room shaving when he heard Esther scream. He rushed to his wife's side as she clutched her left breast and then passed out. Sarah's father yanked opened the drawer by the bed and pulled out the phone list before pressing the number six, which was a direct line to the medical office. Dr. Morgan had just sat down behind his desk with a cup of morning java, ready for another boring day. It was not to be.

In his mid-forties, the New York family physician grabbed his medical kit and dashed up the hall to a door marked *Emergency Exit*. He then descended swiftly down two flights of metal stairs. Ari was anxiously waiting in the hallway with Susan Levinson, whose room was just one door down. Dr. Morgan rushed to Esther Hazan's side and went right to work. A nurse walked in briskly a couple minutes later. She had stayed behind in the infirmary to gather up additional supplies. Ari had meantime told Dr. Morgan that his wife was suffering from Arteriosclerosis, adding she'd suffered two previous heart attacks in California, both thankfully fairly mild. A stretcher soon arrived carried by two human orderlies. Esther was placed on it and rushed to the elevator, held open by another nurse.

Susan's young daughter was sound asleep in her cabin, with Brock's little girl resting right beside her. The besotted men were four doors down, reluctantly sharing a room. The young Jewish mother decided to dart down and alert the guys to the situation so Brock could come and watch the girls as she rushed upstairs to be with her stricken aunt and uncle.

The men's cabin door was slightly ajar. Susan knocked hastily, which only served to push the door further open—just enough so she could see the frightening scene inside. Brock was holding his forty-five Colt in his right hand. It was pointed at Aaron's hairy wet chest. The young attorney was wearing a damp towel, having just returned from the male shower facility down the hall.

"What in the world is going on here!" shouted Susan as she rushed to Brock's side. "Put that gun down right now!"

"I'm going to kill him!" Brock avowed with anger blazing out of his aqua-blue eyes.

"He read my journal notes about you Susan. It's none of his damn business. And now he wants to shoot me dead."

"Where is the journal?"

"It's over there," Brock said as he pointed his barrel toward the nearby desk.

Aaron felt hot even though he was shivering. "It's my private thoughts about you Susan."

Brock grunted. "It's an outline of his plan to get you to marry him! Well, I met you first, and he's way out of line!"

"Put that thing down now!" Susan again demanded. "I came here to tell you both that my Aunt Esther is right now having a heart attack."

"Oh Susan, I'm so sorry," said Brock as he lowered his weapon.

Aaron grabbed his white tee shirt from the back of a nearby chair. *I think I could handle marrying him*, thought Susan as she watched the muscular male effortlessly pull the cotton shirt over his damp head and well-rounded shoulders.

Susan addressed the jealous father more calmly than before. "Look Brock, settle down and help me out. I need to head up to the infirmary where they've just taken Esther. Go to my room and stay with the girls please."

"I'll go up to the clinic with you," volunteered Aaron before racing to the small washroom to jump into his jeans. He wanted to appear as sympathetic as possible, and also to talk with the exhilarating young woman alone—not to mention get away from the crazy Californian.

Aaron and Susan were sitting quietly next to each other in the reception office. Ari was inside Dr. Morgan's emergency bay holding an oxygen mask over his wife's mouth. "Sue, I'm really sorry you had to witness that stinking episode. Brock is off his rocker sometimes. Plus I'm really riled you had to hear about my plans to ask you to marry me in that manner."

The tall Jewish lawyer rose from his chair and then went down on one knee in front of the beautiful widow. The young nurse sitting behind the reception desk stopped working on her computer as Aaron reached out and took hold of both of Susan's soft hands.

"Susan Levinson, will you make me the happiest guy on earth and marry me?"

"Oh Aaron, I think you're a wonderful man. I *will* probably marry you, but I've got a lot on my mind at the moment, as you know. Let's talk some more about it later."

Although he felt a bit dejected, the swarthy attorney, who'd graduated near the top of his class from Princeton law school, was trying hard not to show it. "Okay, that makes sense. Look, I'll head back downstairs and check on Justina. I don't trust that hothead with her." *Show your concern for her little daughter...that should win you some points*, thought Aaron as he sprang to his feet.

"Thanks Aaron. I think she should be fine, but it'll indeed ease my mind if you check on the girls. I want to be here when Uncle Ari comes out."

"If everything's in order down there, I'll come right back up." Aaron bent down and gave Susan a gentle kiss on her forehead. She then lifted her head in a clear invitation for him to move his kiss to her lips, which Aaron eagerly did, and for several seconds.

Twelve minutes later, the athletic American returned to find Susan standing near the clinic's entrance door. He quickly reported that all was well with the girls. They'd not yet been told about Esther's heart attack, only that Susan had gone off with her aunt to buy some items. "Sue, Brock asked me to head out with him to the hallway for a second, and then he apologized profusely for pointing his gun at me. He seemed fairly sincere so I accepted it. We even shook hands."

"That's great Aaron. I have enough stress to deal with right now." This time she initiated the prolonged kiss. The love-struck man, who had lost his longtime girlfriend Yvonne when a measles pandemic swept through Kansas City, put his muscular arms around Susan's waist. He felt like he was getting his desired answer in a much nicer way than mere words could have ever afforded.

Susan opened her sparkling eyes to check who was coming out of the inner infirmary door. She was pleasantly surprised when Sarah appeared, followed by her father Ari. Susan tenderly pushed Aaron away as she greeted her cousin and asked about Esther's condition. "Mom is going to survive, praise the Lord. Dr. Morgan says she'll probably need to undergo bypass surgery as soon as possible, but he doesn't have the necessary facilities or proper operating experience to treat her here. So I suggested I go alert a Kadoshim rescue team to whisk her and dad back to Hadassah in Jerusalem. I'm going to do that now, but I should be back soon."

"Can Justina and I come along?" enquired Susan as Aaron suppressed a frown.

"No, I don't think they'll allow that. But I'm pretty sure dad can go back with her. Anyway, I'll pop over tomorrow to give you an update."

"How did you find out about Esther's heart attack today, Sarah?" enquired Aaron, relieved that his intended was staying put with him on the ship.

"Well, one of the nurses on board is a glorified saint like me, and she appeared at my office in Jerusalem after dad told her where I work." Sarah gave her cousin a brief hug. "You know, Sue, the communications satellites are back up now so you can actually keep in touch with me by phone from now on. I'll write down my number after I return." In a split second, Sarah was gone.

"I better head down and pack a few clothes for myself and Esther," said Ari as he moved quickly to the door. His stricken wife's niece offered to help him, and away they went.

Three minutes later, the medical rescue team materialized with Sarah just outside the clinic reception room. As the four Kadoshim medics went to work loading Esther into the ambulance—which had no tires or engine and was taking up most of the hall space in front of the health center's entrance door—Sarah twinked down to fetch her father. She briefly assisted Ari and Susan as they finished a quick packing job, and then all three walked briskly to the elevator. Five minutes later, Sarah and her parents arrived at one of the new operating theaters at Hadassah Hospital.

Sarah Goldman held her father's hand as they waited for the cardiological surgeons to finish the emergency operation. She had only hired Dr. Yoel Leventhal, a heart specialist originally from Kiev, and Dr. Eliza Stern, a saint born in an Israeli kibbutz near the Gaza Strip, one month before. She never dreamed at the time that the highly qualified pair would ever be working on her human mother at Hadassah.

Donna Svenson and Talel Goldman paced into the spotless reception room and made a beeline for Sarah and Ari. Donna leaned over and gave her father a kiss as she flung her arms around his double-chinned neck. "I'm so glad you're alive dad, but I sure never thought I'd be greeting you at a hospital in Jerusalem. How is mom? Talel told me what happened."

"It's wonderful to see you too Donna, alive and looking healthy. The surgeons are performing a bypass operation on your mother as we speak. I'm just praying it will go well."

"We're waiting for word any minute," added Sarah. "These cardiologists are real experts Donna, and say they're quite hopeful she'll get through this alright."

Several minutes later, Dr. Stern walked into the reception area to deliver her report. "Esther is going to be fine, but she'll need plenty of rest." Sarah embraced her relieved father, who wiped a tear from his eye. "Thanks Dr. Stern, you're due for a raise!" the health official proclaimed to concurring smiles all around.

"I'll gladly accept that, Sarah! However, I estimate your mother will have to stay in our hospital for at least a week. She suffered a pretty serious cardiac arrest." This news disappointed Ari, knowing how much Esther was looking forward to being with her human family in the Temple courtyard to watch King Yeshua's formal coronation on the big outdoor screen that Sarah told them was being erected there. At least his beloved wife of 37 years was alive, so he could hardly complain.

The two sisters stood together near the metal walkway at the port in Ashdod. Although designed for cargo ships, Prince David had approved Sarah's special request that the large cruise liner from America, dubbed the *Millennial Exodus* for this special voyage, be allowed to utilize the commercial port instead of the new passenger facility on the northern Sinai coast. She had learned that most of the passengers wanted to attend the Lord's coronation ceremony that afternoon at 5:00 PM, and would have been hard pressed to get to Jerusalem in time from the northern Sinai port.

"There they are!" Donna exclaimed when she spotted her favorite cousin carrying her young daughter Justina over her shoulder. Right behind the ladies strode two studs whose appearances made Donna whistle like a barmaid discovering a hundred dollar bill in her tip jar.

"Now behave, Donna!" scolded Sarah as she waved briskly at the disembarking party.

Introductions were soon made all around, with Donna kissing her two cousins before making a point to squeeze each of the handsome men as if they too were long lost friends. Susan scowled ever so slightly as Donna embraced Aaron. "I have some news for both of you. Aaron and I just got engaged two days ago! It happened when our ship was passing just south of the island of Crete. It was a beautiful moonlit evening and Aaron proposed while we were on deck."

"Oh that's *wonderful* news," gushed Sarah, not noticing that both Brock and Donna were now slightly scowling.

"So I guess that means you won't be living with us, cuz?" asked Donna, unhappy with that prospect.

"Well, it'll be a few months before the wedding, so Justina and I would still love to be your guests until then."

"Excellent!" said Sarah, pointing out that "The twins would've been very disappointed. You should've seen their faces when Talel informed them you'd be staying with us."

Donna laughed at the fresh memory. "When she told them you had a dog and a cat Justina, they were so excited they nearly wet their pants! Dalya had asked Talel if she could get a dog, and Daniyella wanted a cat, just like they had before that last major earthquake struck. So you'll have to allow them to visit often after you move out."

Susan glanced back at the ship. "Speaking of the pets, we were told we needed to go to a special office inside the port to collect them. We'd better get moving, it's already nearly 2:30 in the afternoon and I promised Uncle Ari over the phone that we'd try to be at the Temple courtyard by 4:00. I also told him about my engagement, and he's very happy for us."

Brock was frowning again, but not as much as before. He strongly suspected that the bogus blonde bombshell staring studiously at him would act as a fair consolation prize.

Jonathan, Benny and Talel Goldman and the Bernstein twins were waiting with Ariel Hazan in a teeming crowd of saints and human beings near the bottom of the marble steps that lead up to the Temple Mount. Standing near them was Eli Ben David, Shoshel Pearlman and her father Amos, Rabbi Goldman, Abe and Rebecca, Micah Kupinski, Craig Eagleman and Eli's three other government ministers. Yoseph Steinberg and his entire cabinet were positioned just behind them, including Zinel and Leo and Teresa Scarcelli.

After stopping by their south Jerusalem home to drop off the traveler's luggage, Sarah and Donna waded through the excited crowd with Susan, Justina, Aaron, Brock and his daughter Tina, who were all boggled at the incredible sights around them. After spotting the Goldmans and their friends, the newcomers to Israel were soon introduced to those they had not met in New Jersey. Ari heartily congratulated the newly-engaged couple, thankful that his gorgeous niece had apparently not fallen under the spell of the ex-neo Nazi from Bakersfield.

The Bernstein twins eagerly embraced the two human girls from America and then giggled with merriment when Justina opened her wicker basket to reveal a tail-wagging little dog standing next to a slightly annoyed Siamese cat. "My cat's named Ginger, and this is Pookey the Pincher," said Justina. This revelation produced more chuckles from the twin sisters even though their English was limited and they had no idea what a Pincher was.

Sarah had already explained to her human companions during the subway ride from Ashdod that they could ascend the long flight of Temple stairs after the ceremonial procession was over. She and the other Kadoshim would already be called into one corporate Body inside the holy chamber. The huge outdoor television screen was located on the southeast corner of the Temple Mount, where a marble courtyard adjacent to it could hold about 4,000 human souls.

Therefore the sooner they ascended the stairs, the better chance they had of securing a good spot in the courtyard.

Susan Levinson gazed up at the corner of the glistening Holy Temple that was clearly visible from the bottom of the stairs. "It is simply majestic," she noted as she squeezed Aaron's hand. Sarah then pointed out that her and Shoshel's offices were located just behind them inside Prince David's palace. Susan swung around to study the lavish royal home, instantly struck by its graceful appearance. With some consternation, Brock quickly noticed that the air all around the area was simply awash with saints, all clothed in flowing white robes. He felt very small and helpless at that moment, even if quite intrigued. Donna noticed his puzzled countenance and took his hand into her own—which instantly changed the subject on Brock's mind.

As thousands of trumpets sonorously sounded, the royal coronation procession got underway. Parading in front of the participants were twelve ceremonial guards wearing purple sashes draped around their golden robes. Each hoisted high a royal standard emblazoned on cloth banners attached to golden rods. The emblems pictured the Lion of Judah, the High Priest's precious gems, the Holy Temple, the Lamb of God, a wooden cross, and seven other regal Kingdom symbols.

Miriyam and Yoseph Ben Ya'acov, the earthly parents of King Yeshua, marched just behind the ceremonial banner contingent. The Lord's beloved mother was now wearing a turquoise robe with gold trim, with a simple beige scarf over her long dark hair. Aware that she had been falsely portrayed, and even worshiped, as some sort of demigod by many people over the centuries, the humble Bondservant of her Lord wanted to make clear she was not sharing the Son of God's divine glory and power in a manner different from any other redeemed saint. Still, her tender heart was bursting with wondrous joy. Her baby boy, born amid straw and animal dung in Bethlehem so many moons before, was about to be formally crowned as the King of the Universe.

Yochanan and the eleven other Apostles came next. The Son of Thunder was positioned directly behind Miriyam, whom he'd taken care of following the crucifixion of his precious Savior and Friend. Kingdom Foreign Minister Shaul and Ya'acov Ben Yoseph, the Lord's brother, paraded on either side of him. Behind the Apostles were many well known saints, including Yeshua's other siblings, his cousin Yochanan the Immerser, Natan-el, Marta, Miriyam and their brother Lazarus, Stephen, Doctor Luke, and many others who had served the Messiah during His earthly incarnation.

The twelve Hebrew saints on the Lord's ruling council, save Prince David, followed right behind them, with Father Abraham and his son and grandson at their head. A host of other biblical figures strolled close behind them, including Job, Joshua, the prophets Zechariah, Malachi, Joel and other seers, Mayor Solomon and his mother Batsheva, Prince David's close friend Yonatan, his earthly father King Saul, Ruth, Samuel, King Hezekiah, Devorah, the twelve sons of Ya'acov, the Jewish matriarchs Sarah, Rebecca, Leah and Rachel, and many others.

Striding behind the biblical saints was Prince David, marching all alone. He was not wearing royal robes or a crown, but a simple cotton shepherd robe. A bleating lamb was draped over his shoulders. A sling-shot hung from his plain cloth sash.

When the 540 children watching the coronation procession on the big television screen in Iraklion spotted the little lamb, they began to cheer. Nikos, the eight year old boy who spoke to Benny and the other Greek Isle ministers after the orphans were discovered in the devastated city on the island of Crete, whistled loudly and then shouted out in Greek, "Glory to the Lamb of God!" Dozens of children clapped elatedly in response.

Just behind Prince David came a host too numerous to count, but Sarah estimated it to be comprised of around 700 souls. They were believing martyrs from the ages—representing all those who had willingly given up their lives for the Lord in the face of violence and persecution, in identical fashion to most of the Apostles and others marching in front of them. Many had been tortured, not accepting their release, in order that they might obtain a better resurrection. Some had experienced mockings and scourgings, or they had been placed like Yochanan in chains while imprisoned. Others had been stoned like Stephen and Shaul, others sawn in two. Some had been put to death by means of a sword. They had wandered about in deserts and mountains, wearing only sheepskins or goatskins. Many had been forced to hide in cold caves or holes in the ground. They were Kadoshim of whom the world was not worthy.

Right behind the martyred saints, walking all alone, was the Savior of the World. About twenty feet behind Him, the perpetual Temple priests were carrying the train of His robe. It had not yet been attached to the robe. The Redeemer of the World was wearing a heavy hooded wool robe that hid most of the incandescent light which shone out of His glorified body, thus allowing the mostly adult humans in the crowd to behold Him. The thick hood was pulled down so that it covered His forehead and eyes, which were nearly shut. His glorious head was hung low as He walked, with His holy hands clasped humbly near His waist.

Prince David stopped walking and pulled a wooden whistle from his sash. He blew strongly into it, catching everyone's attention. *"Shield the eyes of the children!"* he commanded in a loud voice before adding "We will now recall what the Light of the World has done for us."

Suddenly a twelve-foot-long wooden cross appeared right behind the Jewish Messiah, lying prone on the marble pavement. The Sovereign Lord's robe flew off of Him, revealing a bludgeoned human body clothed only in a bloodied loincloth. The Lord of Life fell backwards onto the cross as three Roman soldiers appeared with hammers and nails in their hands. As the soldiers began piercing Yeshua's extremities, the marchers in front of the King of the Jews morphed into human form as well as they turned around to face the Lamb of God.

Miriyam and Yoseph, who had reached the twelfth set of stairs leading up to the Temple, were bent over with grief. Yochanan rushed up to Miriyam's side in a vain attempt to comfort her. The prophet Daniel was cowering in the center of a ring of flames at the bottom of the steps as two hungry lions circled around him. The Apostle Shaul was bound in chains on the steps just above him, as were several other saints. Shimon Kefa was hovering in the air upside down on a Roman cross. The Lord's brother Ya'acov was lifeless on the ground next to his severed head, as was the Lord's cousin Yochanan the Immerser. Stephen was dead under a pile of stones. The bodies of King Shaul and his son Yonatan were strung up on a fence. Yoseph of Egypt and the prophet Jeremiah were screaming for help from deep inside of a pit. Job was clothed in sackcloth and ashes, wailing for his slain family.

The other marching saints all appeared in the conditions in which they too were tortured, tormented or slain. Those who were able to cried out in agony as the Suffering Servant's cross was hoisted into the air by the three Roman soldiers. An Orthodox Jew named Shimon standing with the crowd of stunned onlookers was sternly ordered by one of the soldiers to help prop up the blood-stained cross. With copious tears flooding from his eyes, he reluctantly obeyed.

Holding her daughter's face firmly to her chest, Susan Levinson screamed when Rabbi Benjamin Goldman, his son Abraham and earthly wife Rebecca and grandson Jonathan suddenly fell to the marble pavement near her, all writhing in agony. Benjamin and Jonathan were grasping their throats. They appeared to be choking. Abe and Rebecca appeared headless. Micah Kupinski was bound by chains. Shoshel and her father Amos were lying on the pavement with putrid smoke rising from their charred bodies. Bet-el was face up in a pool of blood, riddled with shrapnel. Behind them were more headless bodies belonging to Leo and Teresa Scarcelli and their daughter Angelica, along with Giuseppe Marino and his earthly wife Catrina. Yoseph Steinberg was crumpled on the pavement with a bullet hole in his left temple.

Aaron Feingold quickly grabbed Justina and hoisted her into his arms, burying her head in his chest. Brock had already done the same with his daughter Tina after Prince David spoke, as had Talel with the twins. Susan Levinson screeched again in panic and sprang forward out of the crowd. She yanked on the strap of a lined cooler bag draped around her neck which carried a plastic water bottle inside of it. The strap snapped in two. She then hurled the water bag through the wall of flames surrounding Daniel, who barely caught it with his left hand. The lions were startled by the sudden movement and began growling at Susan. Aaron then handed Justina to Sarah and rushed out of the crowd to grab hold of Susan's arm before dragging his bewildered fiancé back into the crowd.

The Crucified Lord appeared to be dying from asphyxiation on the tree. He pushed up His torn body via His bleeding feet to allow in some air, which sent spasms of intense pain reeling up His bruised legs and spine. Three seconds later, a voice like the sound of pealing thunder boomed out from the cracked lips of the King of all Kings: "IT IS ACCOMPLISHED!"

In a flash, all was as it had been just a couple minutes before. However now the Bright Morning Star was clothed in the same jeweled breastplate and crimson cape He had worn every evening while processing into the Holy Temple. The light from His head and arms and His sandal-shod feet was so brilliant that Susan, Aaron and the other human beings in the crowd had to quickly shield their eyes. The perpetual priests carrying the Lord's elongated train then marched up to their Sovereign Savior before several of them attached the velvet garment to Yeshua's glistening cape.

The Goldmans were all back on their feet, quite alive in their glorified bodies, as were the other saints of all the ages. Every eye was fixated on the Risen Lord as He resumed His regal procession up to the Holy Temple. Prince David waited on the sidelines for the King of Glory to reach his position. Arm in arm, he joined his Greater Son in His processional ascent to the sacred sanctuary.

"There they are!" shouted Benny as his brother Jesse and Jonathan's twin brother David appeared, holding the royal train while positioned about thirty priests behind King Yeshua.

"Are they the ones you were telling me about?" enquired Susan, who was stroking her daughter's hair in order to help calm her back down. She had quickly regained her own composure when the Goldmans rose back up on their feet, rapidly realizing that she and the other onlookers had just witnessed a shocking, yet entirely accurate spiritual reenactment of what the Kadoshim and their slain Restorer had endured in their human habitations. The intense impact would later help lead Susan and millions of other still-unrepentant sinners to the eternal Throne of Grace.

Sarah waved at the marching priests as she answered. "Yes, the first one is Jonathan's twin brother David, and the blond priest right behind him is his aborted son, Jesse."

"I can see the resemblance, especially between Jonathan and David," remarked Susan as Aaron and Brock nodded their agreement. Benny and Micah began leaping up and down in utter joy. The King of Life was alive forevermore, and so were His chosen ordained children.

Esther Hazan was chewing on some peanuts, eagerly watching the live transmission from her hospital bed. The television cameras had not transmitted the headless saints or other similar sights, or the Lord being nailed to the cross, since many viewers around the world were human children. However, they had briefly broadcast the Rose of Sharon hanging from the Roman execution stake, and shown pictures of His weeping mother Miriyam bent over in grief, with Yochanan vainly attempting to console her. Otherwise they focused on Prince David carrying the bleating lamb over his shoulders; his eyes filled with tears as he watched his afflicted descendant recreate His severe crucifixion, including the excruciating gasp of His last breath.

Esther was elated when she briefly spotted her family in one of the crowd shots. She also noticed who she was fairly certain must have been a beaming David Goldman carrying the hem of Yeshua's train. The resemblance to her earthly son-in-law was striking, she thought, and she suspected she was also looking at his aborted son Jesse marching next to him, matching the description Sarah had shared with her. Esther still could not quite believe that her daughter's devoted husband had fathered an aborted baby, but she appreciated more deeply than ever before that Israel's Merciful Savior was slow to anger and quick to forgive, if the human repentance was genuine. This gave her hope as she recalled her own secret sin that her loving life-partner still did not know about.

Maria Alvarez rocked baby George in her arms as she watched the riveting coronation ceremony live on the large television screen recently set up in the New York City provincial government mansion in Brooklyn. She was awestruck by the images before her. The former housekeeper had just spotted with great pride and joy Giuseppe and Catrina Marino in the crowd, along with the Scarcellis, Governor

Steinberg and Zinel, Abe Pearlman and other provincial cabinet ministers, and the Goldman family and their friends.

Maria longed for the day when she could visit Jerusalem and see the Holy Temple in person. She yearned for the hour when her eyes would behold her King in radiant splendor. She thanked the Lord with all her heart for the high price He paid to take away her sins, and for sparing her life during earth's frightful end-time judgments. She looked forward to the time when the baby boy in her arms would begin to understand the Bible stories she was already reading him every evening before bedtime.

The royal coronation procession came to a formal end as the last of the selected marchers—10,000 perpetual priests singing melodious songs of ascent while waving banners or banging tambourines—passed through the Temple's main entrance doors. They were preceded by Eli Ben David, Yoseph Steinberg, and the other provincial governors who joined the procession from their places in the crowd after the Lord's royal train had passed by.

Shofar trumpets blared, calling all of the Kadoshim into one sacred Body inside of the Holy Temple. Susan quickly gathered her daughter into her arms after giving the wicker basket with the pet dog and cat to Aaron. Donna then offered to take the pets home with her, saying she preferred to watch the coronation ceremony on television in the comfort of her bedroom. Susan gladly accepted the proposal before herding her young charges up the long flight of stairs.

The Bread of Life had marched all the way to the crossing point of the Temple, halting like a statue just before the Holy of Holies. The train of His cape reached almost to the southern end of the Nave, just a few 100 feet from the south Temple doors. The elders who paraded in front of Him had parted to either side, with half now standing in the Sunrise Transept and half in the Sunset Transept. All but a handful of the remaining Kadoshim were no longer individually identifiable, having merged into one Body that filled every inch of the sacred sanctuary.

David Goldman gave the signal, and the seven assigned perpetual priests ceremonially lit the Golden Menorah at the base of the raised

Holy of Holies dais. The Shekinah fire swirled about just behind them with a luminescence that transcended anything seen before. Among the seven priests participating on this special coronation day was the first son of King David and Batsheva. He had perished as an infant in ancient Jerusalem after the God of Israel turned down the King's intercessory request that his baby's life be spared.

The Son of God prostrated Himself before His Father's Shekinah Glory. The shimmering holy light then intensified even further. Susan and the other humans gathered in the outdoor courtyard noticed with awe that the Temple walls were now glowing like hot coals in a fire, lighting up the early evening sky above Jerusalem to the point where the rising full moon was barely visible.

Discreetly positioned television cameras mounted on the Temple walls zoomed in on the Eternal Light as He rose to His feet and walked to the bottom of the steps of the raised dais. Several temple priests then undid the train from His crimson cape. Meanwhile the 24 elders made their way up to their thrones, positioned on either side of the Lord's majestic blue throne. As silver crowns appeared on all heads, seven large Cherubim with their wings stretched out materialized above the thrones.

In New Jersey, Maria Alvarez fell to her knees with the baby sleeping soundly in her arms. "Yeshua, you are Lord of all!" she proclaimed. Six other humans seated in the mansion's theater room with her also bent down in worshipful adoration of the unmatchable Lord of Glory.

Esther Hazan had been joined in her hospital room by Dr. Leventhal and two human nurses. The Jewish American grandmother voiced her thanksgiving that she lived to see this illustrious day: "Oh Lord, bless you for keeping me alive! Thank you for the doctors and nurses ministering to me here in Your Holy City! Thank you for granting us the gift of eternal life!"

The Messiah King moved forward several more steps toward His regal throne before other priests unclasped His gold-trimmed cape.

274

Camera lenses were tightened even further to broadcast close up shots of His scarred bare back, which was radiant with light.

The Prophet Isaiah, standing in front of his side throne, opened a leather-bound Bible and began reading in a powerful voice from chapter 53 of the prophetic book he was privileged to record for posterity: *"Surely our griefs He Himself bore, and our sorrows He carried. Yet we esteemed Him stricken, smitten of Elohim and afflicted. But He was pierced through for our transgressions. He was crushed for our iniquities. The chastening for our well-being fell upon Him, and by His scourging we are healed. All of us like sheep have gone astray, each of us has turned to his own way, but the Lord has caused the iniquity of us all to fall on Him."*

The Great I Am then turned toward the Nave and sat down upon His lapis lazuli throne. The precious gems on His dazzling breastplate were shimmering with light, sending out colorful shafts all over the hallowed sanctuary. A brilliant rainbow appeared 70 feet above the Lord's radiant head, arching high over all 25 thrones and the Cherubim hovering directly over them.

Yochanan and Prince David walked to the marble altar on the far side of the brilliant Shekinah fire. Each took hold of a handle attached to a silver tray where a beautiful three-tier golden crown was positioned upon a purple velvet cloth. The royal crown had diamonds, rubies and other superlative gems embedded around its circumference. The two saints carried the tray to a small cedar table positioned next to the Lord's majestic throne. They placed the tray on the table and took hold of the crown. King Yeshua bowed His head and the crown was placed upon His glistening hair.

Trumpets again sounded as the 24 elders cast their silver crowns down in front of the Author of Life. Then they proclaimed in a unified voice: *"To Him who sits on the throne, and to the Lamb, be blessing and honor and glory and dominion forever and ever!"* The elders fell on their faces and worshipped the Shining One, whose incandescent light would never fade again. The Kadoshim burst forth in a jubilant song of worship with lyrics that repeated the elders' ecstatic proclamation. The eternal King of Kings would reign forevermore!

SIXTEEN

YEAR OF JUBILEE

Anticipation was growing in Jerusalem as the first fifty-year Kingdom Jubilee celebration drew near. A spectacular program had been put together for the month-long festival, scheduled to commence at the end of the annual Feast of Tabernacles holiday. The highlight would be a reenactment of the Lord's splendid formal coronation five decades before, although on a smaller scale.

George Kirintelos was busy preparing a lavish repertoire for his upcoming concert at the outdoor amphitheatre just south of Jerusalem's walled Old City. By the time he turned seven, both his grandmother Catrina Marino and Maria Alvarez noticed that the young lad was gifted with an exquisite singing voice. Catrina then asked New York Music Minister Carmella Bernstein if she would organize professional singing lessons for the talented boy, which she gladly did. George later studied music composition at Julliard, along with other related topics.

At age 22, George gave his first public concert at a plush theater in Manhattan. He had previously decided to use *Yourgos*, a Greek version of his given first name, as he embarked on his budding singing career. The debut performance was attended by all of Yoseph Steinberg's cabinet ministers, along with most of Eli Ben David's government colleagues. Several humans flew from Israel to New York City for the gala event, including Aaron and Susan Feingold who'd been married in Jerusalem in the millennial year 2 DL (Day of the Lord). The couple brought with them their two teenage children along with Susan's daughter Justina, now in her late twenties and engaged to a nice young Jewish immigrant from France.

Still single and sassy, Donna Svenson traveled to New York with her cousin and family along with the Bernstein twins, but mainly, she averred, to tour the city. Not a big fan of operatic music, she confided to Susan she would go to the tenor's concert mainly to gawk at some of the handsome guys dressed to the hilt in their fine tuxedos. However, Donna was more than thrilled to discover that Yourgos Kirintelos was a very handsome and muscular young man with a golden voice that would subsequently propel the budding performer to international stardom. Although over 20 years older than him (she did not look it due to the retarded aging process), the transfixed female fan would closely follow the singer's burgeoning career from that day onward.

Donna had dated Brock Schmidt on and off over the previous two decades. She even clandestinely moved in with the tall American for a couple years after his roommate Aaron married Susan Levinson and then secured a larger Jerusalem apartment to accommodate his bride and her daughter. Donna's departure from Sarah Goldman's home came soon after one of the Bernstein twins surprised the Jewish beauty by coming home early from school, only to discover her adopted great aunt in the backyard in a carnal position with Brock. Sarah then asked her rebellious sister to leave the house, at least until the girls grew up a little more. The saint's periodic attempts to persuade her sinning sister to repent had so far come to nothing. Now she would find herself issuing warnings to Donna that living out of wedlock with the American widower was strictly against Kingdom law, prompting the fake blonde to conceal from Sarah that she was doing so.

Brock later managed to get himself placed on Sarah's no-go list for a second time due to his pernicious actions at Hadassah Hospital. Within one month of his arrival in Israel, Sarah had hired the supple Californian to act as one of the hospital's security guards, a job Brock relished. However suspicions of illegal activity surfaced just two years later when some of the anti-fertility rice supplies, kept locked up in the hospital's walk-in cooler, disappeared. Brock was one of eight

Hadassah employees who possessed a key to the pharmacy cooler, along with Sarah's friend Yitzhak who spotted the security guard walking out of it late one evening with two bags of rice stashed under his armpits. Sarah then confronted Donna, who admitted that Brock had been stealing the prescription rice for her use. "I don't like the guy well enough to have a child with him," Donna said dryly at the time after reluctantly admitting to her part in Brock's thieving scheme. Brock was fired from his job and quickly sentenced to six months in jail for his crime. Donna then moved her things out of his apartment, heading for a rented room in her Cousin Susan's three-bedroom home. That arrangement lasted just under two years before Susan gave birth to a baby boy. Donna was then allowed back into Sarah's house, but only on the strict condition that she refrained from having any more trysts there.

Some ten years later, Donna Svenson found herself in hot water with her older sister once again. She'd become quite close to Daniyella Bernstein as the twin girl grew with her sister into attractive young women. Still feigning she was a natural blonde, Donna had secretly shared some contraband cigarettes with Daniyella who enjoyed smoking them with her while sipping a glass of bootleg vodka and orange juice. Donna then began taking the shapely twin with her to illicit drinking parties held in a northern Tel Aviv suburb. It was not long before Talel's adopted daughter began engaging in immoral acts at the gatherings, as her great aunt had been doing for several years. After discovering the nefarious activity via photos the young woman had carelessly stashed under her bedroom mattress, Talel grounded Daniyella, then 24, for one month. Growing deeper in love with her Sovereign Lord every day, Daniyella's identical sister Dalya was shocked when news first surfaced of her sister's escapades.

Brock dated two other women before deciding he'd devote his full energy to getting his daughter Tina ready for adulthood. After completing three years of probation, he acquired a new job delivering fresh bread from a bakery operating out of a south Jerusalem industrial zone. As the Jubilee celebrations drew near, Brock was still single and driving a truck to earn his living.

In the summer of 38 DL, Brock traveled with his daughter Tina, Talel, Donna and the Bernstein twins to visit the island of Naxos. They were hosted by Jonathan and Benny Goldman in Eli Ben David's government mansion, which contained four guest bedrooms. Sarah was not thrilled when she learned Brock would be traveling with the four human females and Talel to Greece, but Donna pledged she would not fool around with her occasional boyfriend during their shared summer vacation.

It was the third time Donna visited her relatives living and working on the island of Naxos. During her first visit in the year 12, she was especially impressed by the comfortable home Jonathan's parents and grandfather lived in with Eli's administrative assistant, Miri Doron. Featuring six bedrooms and three full bathrooms, the seaside house had been incorporated into a new gated community several years before known as *Summerset*. New homes were being constructed every year as the worldwide Kingdom economy grew stronger, spreading prosperity to human residents all over the globe.

During the vacation visit in 38, Dalya Bernstein, now nearly 45 years old but looking more like 22, had taken an immediate liking to a slightly older man living in Eli's mansion. Named Nikos Cozantine, he was the human orphan that Benny had made an instant heart connection with on the island of Crete many years before. The Greek lad was officially adopted by Benny in the millennial year 14. A small bedroom had been created for Nikos in an unused office next to Benny's room. During Dalya's visit, it soon became clear that the swarthy Greek bachelor, who managed the mansion's landscaping staff and passionately loved the Lord, was equally captivated by the appealing Israeli woman. Benny thought it was cool that his adopted son and his sister's adopted daughter were showing a keen interest in each other.

Towards the end of her vacation trip with Brock and the other women, Donna brought up with Talel an idea that had been brewing in her mind since her second visit to Naxos in the year 23. Noticing how much Tina and the twins enjoyed swimming in the Aegean Sea, she pulled her niece aside to suggest they collectively purchase one of the new homes in the gated community where the elder Goldmans lived.

"Sarah might want to join us in buying a place there as well," Donna opined. "We could all take turns using it, and arrange for everyone to be there together at certain times. Benny tells me the new homes in Summerset sell for around 200,000 shekels, which I'm sure we can come up with if we all pool our financial resources."

"I'm willing to give it a try," replied Talel, who was anxiously looking for more opportunities to spend time with Daniyella outside of Israel, where she had proved overly prone to find and fall into trouble. A vacation home on the island would also give her other daughter Dalya a chance to more easily pursue her blossoming relationship with Nikos. Talel would make sure that it was only an extremely rare occasion when they would be at the Naxos house together with Donna.

Sarah liked the idea of having her own vacation bedroom on Naxos, which she'd long been visiting every month or two given that she, like Talel, only needed to will herself to the beautiful island in order to see family and friends living there. It took the humans around four hours to fly from Tel Aviv to the island; less than two hours to Athens and then, after transferring to a smaller jet, another forty minutes to Naxos. There was also a daily passenger cruise ship that set sail from Haifa port and took around sixty hours to reach Rhodes, where another boat would ferry travelers to Naxos and other Cycladic islands.

Donna Svenson had a hidden reason for wanting to acquire a place in Summerset. She learned from Greek Isle Housing and Construction Minister Micah Kupinski that her favorite musical artist, Yourgos Kirintelos, was purchasing a recently-built small mansion in the gated community. She'd met the tenor briefly at a reception following his stupendous Manhattan concert debut many years before, and it was love (or at least lust) at first sight. Donna had later read in a magazine article that the American performer wanted to buy a place somewhere in Eli's province in order to reconnect with his father's Greek heritage. Beside that, the famous vocalist noted that the two other renowned tenors he frequently performed with, Benito Geovinelli and Carlos Menendez, were both Europeans—the former from Florence Italy and the latter from Seville in Spain.

280

Sarah Goldman and Talel had twinked over to Naxos in the spring of 39 DL to complete the property transaction. Each had designated 50,000 shekels for the home purchase, with Talel's portion coming mainly from her work as a private seamstress for several prominent residents who lived in the two Jerusalem royal palaces. Dalya and Daniyella each officially paid out 20,000 shekels for the home acquisition. However in reality, Dalya contributed the lion's share since her imprudent twin sister wasted most of her earnings as a chef at a local pastry shop on illegal cigarettes and booze.

Donna put nearly 80,000 shekels into the home buying project, using her savings from many years of working for her sister in Prince David's plush home (Sarah had relieved Donna of her duties soon after she ordered her out of her home, but rehired her after she returned some years later). The unsaved woman had not informed Sarah that 10,000 shekels of that investment money had come clandestinely from Brock, who wanted to occasionally use the shared vacation house himself with his daughter Tina and her family. Tina had married a young Jewish man in the year 34, and was already pregnant with her second baby. During the month-long summer vacation that Brock took with the other women in the year 38, Tina's husband Rami, who worked as an architect for an international firm based in Shanghai, stayed behind in Jerusalem with their two young children.

In the winter of 39, Sarah popped over with Talel to discuss which Summerset house to purchase, with four exquisite new dwellings then on the market. After previously finding out from Micah exactly where the New York tenor's vacation home was located, Donna began lobbying her relatives to purchase an available house two lots west of his small mansion. She claimed she liked the nearly completed new home because of its stunning views south toward the blue Aegean Sea. In reality, it was mostly because the four bedroom dwelling was located near her hoped-for paramour's vacation home. The elder Goldmans' dwelling was conveniently located on the other side of the now 42 home community. In the end, Sarah signed a contract to purchase the house Donna wanted, having no particular preference herself.

From the year 40 DL onward, Donna Svenson managed to get at least one month off work each summer, a bit more vacation time than Sarah was taking. Donna always spent most of her free time at the new home on Naxos. She especially enjoyed showing off her swimsuit-clad toned and tanned body at the nearby community beach. A few enquiries to Maria Alvarez in New York had given her a fair idea of the talented tenor's annual Greek vacation patterns, meaning the love-struck fan was usually relaxing in Summerset during sweet juxtapositions that took place when the crooner was on Naxos for his yearly summer visits.

Before her first solo vacation, Donna was able to persuade her sister and niece to give her two weeks alone on the island before the others joined her in Summerset the middle of August (the month was actually now known by its Hebrew name, Av). She'd already ascertained from Maria that Yourgos would be staying at his Naxos residence during the first ten days of the month. Clad in her tightest jogging outfit, Donna began running daily on the road in front of his house, passing by the Kirintelos mansion no less than four times the first morning while jogging in circles around the well-manicured neighborhood.

Donna learned from Miri Doron that the tenor usually spent the better part of his mornings reading an English-language newspaper by his private pool. Later in the day, he normally headed to that section of the Summerset beach designated solely for human use. Usually on his own, he brought with him a large yellow umbrella and an ice cooler filled to the brim with cold beer (it took at least three beers to equal the alcohol level found in just one beer during the old era). Although drinking legally-produced beer or wine was not allowed on public beaches on the island, it was permitted on private community beaches, but by residents only.

After sunning herself for two hours, Donna was dying of thirst. Or at least that's the line she used to re-introduce herself to the popular tenor.

"My, it's a lovely warm afternoon, don't you think? A hot girl sure could use a cold beer about now." Decked out in a two piece bronze-colored bikini, Donna deftly moved closer to the American singer who was wearing turquoise swim trunks which covered most of his solid upper thighs. "My name is Donna Svenson, and we actually met before, but many years ago. I spotted you sitting over here a few minutes ago."

"Well Donna, have a cold one on me!" Yourgos handed the enticing blonde an amber beer. "So where and when did we meet? It seems I would have remembered such a pleasant encounter."

"It was nearly 20 years ago in Manhattan, at a wonderful reception held right after your debut concert ended. You'll recall the place was packed, so I was just one of many people you were introduced to that evening. I'm the aunt of Benny Goldman and his sister Talel, who adopted the twins related to Carmella Bernstein."

"Oh yes, I do recall meeting you, Donna. I just needed to get my memory jogged. You were with Talel and Benny and other members of your family who were with my grandparents when they found me alive as a baby in New Jersey. By the way, I thought you looked fantastic at the reception, as you still do today."

Donna was savoring the star's rich speaking voice, and especially his complimentary words. "Thank you, Mr. Kirintelos. The Trees of Life sure help us ragamuffin humans stay young, don't they?"

"They do indeed; and please call me Yourgos." The talented singer crossed his arms in a deliberate move to add more visible girth to his sinuous biceps. "Say Donna, are you free to join me for dinner this evening?"

"Why yes, I actually am Yourgos, thank you. I'm here by myself for the first half of the month, then my sister Sarah, Talel, the twins and others are coming to stay at our new jointly-owned home right here in Summerset. In fact, I *think* it's located not far from your place."

"Well, welcome to our community, Donna. I'm normally here on Naxos for a few weeks every summer, and occasionally at other times of the year when I'm performing in the region. I really like your relatives who live and work here by the way, especially that Benny-what a joy he is. I hear he's doing a wonderful job as Justice Minister."

"That's what I understand as well, Yourgos. We're all very proud of him, and of course of his father and the other Goldmans serving here too. Speaking of achievements, your musical career is really outstanding. I'm probably one of your biggest fans on earth. I've been following your work ever since I heard you sing so beautifully at your debut concert. I was elated when your premier disc rose to number one on the international music charts in the mid 20s. I bought all my friends copies."

"So you're both beautiful and a big fan of mine? It must be my lucky day!"

With these tender words floating like listless clouds in the sultry late afternoon air, Donna took a bold step forward, placing her arms around her potential lover's trim waist as she gave him a brief squeeze. To her delight, Yourgos replied by resting his bulging biceps upon her petite shoulders, allowing her to prolong her warm embrace for almost one minute. Her fantasy dream was seemingly coming true. She would be the girlfriend of a worldwide superstar stud; not some ordinary buffoon from California.

Donna Svenson was standing by her ornate front door wearing a light summer dress featuring bright floral patterns of alternating red roses and purple lilacs. She had mainly picked out that dress due to its dangerously low neckline and mid-thigh hem. Yourgos turned into her driveway seconds later in his silver convertible sedan, which like all millennial automobiles, ran solely on electricity. He jumped out of his flashy sports car to politely open the passenger door for his dashing date, commenting while doing so how magnificent Donna looked in the form-fitting floral dress. She in turn commended the singer's attire, especially his black leather slacks and matching shoes. Although she didn't mention it, the American-born woman was even more impressed by the musical star's snow-white silk shirt which clung to his hefty chest and ripped abs-bodily features she'd immediately noticed when spotting Yourgos sitting under his umbrella on the beach. The sleek shirt featured six buttons that appeared to be made of pure gold.

The couple made their way to a faux fish restaurant located on a hill overlooking the sea not far from Eli Ben David's government mansion. The summer sun was just setting in the western sky above the adjacent island of Paros. Seconds after the Greek waiter brought over a metal bucket containing a bottle of locally-produced Retsina wine, Benny and Micah sauntered into the restaurant, to Donna's undisguised chagrin. She did not want word to go around that she was dating the hunky superstar, who loved to work out like his father had done, at least not until she was certain it was more than a one time occurrence.

"Aunt Donna and Yourgos! What a nice surprise to see you here!" Benny exclaimed as Micah smiled politely. "I heard you were both on the island, and here you are...together!"

"Donna recruited a beer from me at the Summerset beach this afternoon and then reminded me we met years ago at my first public concert in New York. I think you were both there as well."

"We were indeed," replied Benny, adding "Begging a beer; that sounds like my Aunt Donna for sure!"

"That's enough Benny," scolded Donna, which did not stop the tall Justice Minister from noting that "She is your biggest fan on earth Yourgos—a lady who really goes gaga over you."

Donna scowled at her cheeky nephew as she bit her lower lip. However, her souring mood improved dramatically when the handsome singer reached out and gently placed his large right hand on her resting arm. "Having a devoted fan as gorgeous as you are is quite fine with me, Donna." The blushing female was feeling like she needed to consume some special rice right away.

"Benny, I talked with your grandfather on the way to the beach the other day and he told me you've implemented one of the best judicial systems found anywhere on earth. He said you'd handpicked great judges for your courts and that your police forces are well-trained and compassionate. I heartily salute you for those fantastic achievements."

"Thank you Yourgos. It's a great blessing to serve our Lord and His Kingdom in such a capacity, and we're really honored to have such an artist like you as an annual resident on our provincial capital island."

"And now your Aunt Donna vacations here as well," Yourgos pointed out as he flashed a broad smile her way. "I suspect we'll become good friends."

If he only knew what a snake she can be at times, thought Benny as he patted his friend Micah on the back. "Yourgos, have you heard about the new Temple that Micah is building over in Athens? It's half completed and already looks quite extraordinary. Micah is doing a wonderful job with that hallowed project."

"Well, thanks brother, but I'm actually only the co-coordinator of that outstanding building project. I'm working with two other Construction Ministers on it; one from the province of Athens and another from Macedonia. We hope to have the Temple finished before King Yeshua's Jubilee celebrations in 10 years time. He's promised to visit each of the 330 regional Temples currently rising up all over the planet. Ours is scheduled to be one of the first sanctuaries He will appear in. We can hardly wait for that."

"Speaking of new buildings, how do you like your new home in Summerset, Aunt Donna?" Then Benny added wryly, "It's very close to your place, isn't it Yourgos?"

"Indeed it is, just two doors down in fact. I'm definitely enjoying my island dwelling more and more each day."

Donna blushed again before stating that, "I love our new home, Benny, and yes, the neighbors are very nice." Donna smiled warmly at the studly star who had inched his substantial body even closer to hers during the short conversation with the two Kingdom government officials.

"Would you care to join us for supper?" enquired Yourgos as Donna suppressed a squirm.

"No, we'll leave you two alone to get better acquainted," Benny shot back quickly, loath to face the wrath of his promiscuous aunt if he dared to answer affirmatively.

At the end of the evening, Yourgos planted the first of many kisses on Donna's eager lips. It would only be two days before they were under the sheets together at Yourgos' fabulous mansion. That sordid scene would be repeated many times over.

The Master of the Universe was delivering a special Jubilee address in Hebrew from His majestic throne inside the Holy Temple in Jerusalem. It was being broadcast live around the world.

"We have so much to be thankful for, dear children of our loving Father God. We have shared 50 years of peace and tranquility under

My rule. The human population on earth has grown to nearly half a billion souls. I will begin visiting all international Temple cities after our Jubilee celebrations here in the world capital come to an end in three weeks time. It will be so good to see many of you during those stops, especially the little children who are sprouting up like verdant green grass everywhere on our restored planet earth."

Watching the royal address on the large television screen in her south Jerusalem home, Sarah Goldman warmly hugged her baby grandson who was seated happily on her lap. Bright-eyed with just a wisp of dark hair on his shiny head, the baby's name was Yochanan—born to Dalya and Nikos Cozantine just three months before.

"I am so very pleased with the devoted work my government officials are carrying out here in our international capital, Jerusalem, and also in My Kingdom's provinces. The earth has truly been transformed into a paradise over the past 50 years with the help of their dedicated efforts."

Jonathan Goldman gave a hi-five sign to Benny, Eli and Micah who were stretched out comfortably next to him on his long office couch. All four Greek Isle provincial officials were eagerly taking in every single word uttered by the King of Kings during His long-anticipated special Jubilee televised address.

"I am also pleased that most of the adult human citizens of My Millennial Kingdom have pledged their faith in Me as Savior and Lord, as have many of their sweet offspring. Although free will is still in operation amongst you, you have each made the right choice in entrusting your lives to the Lily of the Valley, the lover of your souls."

Donna was ignoring the Lord's broadcast comments as she sipped red wine perched on the night stand next to her bed in south Jerusalem. She was engrossed in clothing and makeup preparations for her lover's outdoor concert scheduled for later that evening in the outdoor amphitheatre just south of the Old City. Yourgos Kirintelos would be crooning both alone and with his two polished tenor companions, singing traditional ballads, hymns and a few contemporary favorites in Hebrew, English, Spanish and Italian.

Sarah had actually made an appointment two years before with Prince David to inform him that the planned Jubilee concert involved a tenor who, she was convinced, was carrying on an illicit sexual relationship with her sister. She had previously re-fired Donna as her receptionist after learning from Benny of the annual trysts on Naxos. Donna had not spoken to her nephew ever since. After consultations with King Yeshua, Prince David told Sarah that the concert would take place as planned, with the Lord stating to him enigmatically that the apparent out-of-wedlock clandestine relationship would "ultimately serve Our divine purposes."

Most of the Goldman family had elected not to attend the three tenors' highly-touted concert. However Donna and Daniyella were there, sitting together in the second row back from the elevated stage. When the lights went up and the three opera stars strolled forward arm in arm, Donna thought she would melt with pride over her fantastic beau. That was before Benito Geovinelli delivered his startling announcement.

"Friends, we're so thrilled to see all of you here on this wonderful evening as we celebrate our Millennial Kingdom's first Jubilee year. We are so tremendously honored to have been asked to perform here in Jerusalem on such an auspicious occasion. I would also like to be the first to congratulate our talented friend Yourgos Kirintelos, who has just informed us today that he got engaged this week to a wonderful Canadian woman named Francette Esteu. We wish them both the very best."

Sitting in the front row just four seats down from Donna's second tier chair, the shapely brunette stood up and turned around to acknowledge the thunderous applause. She did not notice the jilted American-Israeli, who sunk low in her seat as hot anger sizzled from her sweaty pores. She would get her revenge one day.

SEVENTEEN

DARKNESS AND LIGHT

Micah Kupinski was elated when asked by Athens provincial governor Moshe Salaam to stand at the head of the local reception line which would officially greet the visiting King Yeshua. The Greek Isle Construction Minister eagerly welcomed the Fountain of Life after He ceremonially entered the new regional Temple located near the old-era port of Piraeus. Next to Micah stood the two other Construction Ministers who had jointly overseen the magnificent building project with him.

The splendid sanctuary had space for nearly 10,000 humans in its long Nave and two side Transepts. Many of those in attendance were Greek construction workers who'd built the towering edifice from scratch. Apart from Micah, all of the Greek Isle ministers were positioned with Governor Eli Ben David behind the central elevated platform which faced toward Jerusalem. Sarah Goldman was hovering just above them along with several other glorified saints, including her friends Yitzhak and Shoshel, and Jonathan's twin brother David and aborted son Jesse—making a rare appearance away from the Holy Temple in Jerusalem.

The human beings were wearing special protective eyeglasses issued to each one of them as they entered the new regional Temple. They were warned they would suffer serious eye damage if they looked at the Risen Messiah without such protection, designed to block out most of the radiant light emanating from the Savior's glorious head, sandal-shod feet, and through His ceremonial robes.

Among those present in the excited crowd were Nikos and Dalya Cozantine, who had recently purchased a home half a mile north of the Summerset gated community on Naxos. Although she'd been invited to attend, Dalya's still-single twin sister Daniyella was not present. Donna Svenson had also declined an invitation from Eli, to the governor's great relief. He'd only issued it as a courtesy to his Goldman colleagues, who were all equally relieved that she stayed home in Jerusalem.

The day after the world-famous American tenor delivered his tremendous concert performance in the millennial capital city, the stunned American-Israeli woman confronted her lover over his shocking marriage announcement. Yourgos Kirintelos was still on cloud nine in the wake of the enthusiastic accolades poured upon him by many of the thousands of devoted fans in attendance. Donna had stayed away from the grandiose reception following the concert, heading straight home where she drenched her pillow in angry tears. Daniyella Bernstein attended in her place, but only to monitor the movements of the Canadian fiancée who looked absolutely gorgeous in a crepe satin gown with matching gloves. Francette Esteu's diamond engagement ring sparkled in the light as she eagerly showed it off to her future husband's exhilarated fans, lined up to greet and congratu-late the couple. Daniyella stayed well clear of that performance.

Donna didn't bother to greet Yourgos when he finally answered his mobile phone. Instead, she cut right to her chase. "What in the world's going on, Yourgos? I want straight answers right away! You and I were together in Summerset just two fricken months ago! Who is this Francette, and why didn't you tell me you were getting engaged?"

"Um, hello Donna. Why don't we…meet up at that public park near your home or something, where we can talk in person? I have lots to tell you."

"Indeed you do! Okay, let's say we rendezvous in one hour near the fountain in my neighborhood park, where we met when you were here in Jerusalem last spring."

"Sounds like a plan, Donna. I'll wear a hat and sunglasses to help disguise myself."

Donna grunted into the mouthpiece before spitting out, "Of course you will, darling. We don't want to spoil your royal wedding plans, now do we?" *Why don't you come with a sack over your puffed-up fat head,* she thought, but fortunately did not vocalize.

One hour later, the jilted American woman spotted her famous boyfriend wearing oversized dark glasses, a fake black mustache and a red baseball cap. It was one of several disguises Yourgos kept in his wardrobe for times when he wished to avoid being publicly identified.

"So what's this all about?" demanded Donna, again omitting a formal greeting to her longtime lover.

"Hi Donna, you're looking fantastic as usual." The rejected woman did not acknowledge the compliment, which anyway seemed totally tacky to her at that particular moment. "Let's sit down over there near the trees." As was his wont, Yourgos made a beeline to the park bench with Donna reluctantly in tow, feeling like a captured fish yanked out of very chilly water.

"I met Francette two years ago in Montreal, her hometown. She's a psychologist who mainly works with children, but she's also an accomplished violinist who has performed in concerts all over Canada. I met her at a dinner party after my performance in downtown Toronto."

"So this dame shrinks little brains for a living, and now I suppose you want her to shrink my mind as well? I'll warn you now, Yourgos, I won't go down without a fight!"

"Honey, *please* calm down. I'm not expecting you to just shrivel up and die. I want to remain in regular contact with you, Donna. I really do love you. It's just...."

"It's just that you need a fancier woman to show off at your side. Isn't that it Yourgos?"

"Donna, don't belittle yourself. You're a wonderful woman whom any man would be proud to have by his side, as I am. Still, you'll have to admit I'm not just another regular guy looking for a wife. However I *am* very satisfied with my beautiful lover, as you well know. We'll manage to see each other quite often, Donna, I'm sure of that. Francette doesn't want to give up her career in Montreal, so she'll only occasionally travel with me on my concert tours."

"Sure, you're no ordinary stud, Yourgos. You're an international superstar who thinks he needs a more elegant bride than me, and I suspect a younger one too. Well, this broad may be blonde on the outside, but I'm very bright on the inside, and I'm insulted you'd assume I'd be happy to act as your concubine. You can't have your French sugar-cake and eat it too. It's over Yourgos; good luck and good riddance!"

With that parting shot, Donna Svenson sprang to her feet and skedaddled away as her shaken beau wiped a tear from his eye.

The exalted Millennial Monarch had decided to privately visit each of the regional provincial capitals during His worldwide Temple dedication tour. Miri Doron and her mostly human staff worked day and night for months to prepare for King Yeshua's visit to Naxos. Fresh coats of paint were applied to all government buildings, including Eli's mansion. An elegant feast would be held there with around 200 invited guests, half human and half Kadoshim. Among them was Sarah Goldman, but not her sister Donna. Only a few of the human guests had been informed that the Anointed Messiah would attend the banquet. Otherwise the general public on Naxos would be unaware that the King of Kings was literally in their midst. He would simply appear inside the government mansion with His entourage, which included Yochanan, Foreign Minister Shaul, Prince David and other senior kingdom officials.

Governor Ben David was wearing his finest robe as he warmly greeted the Beautiful One and His traveling companions in the large foyer of his Naxos mansion. Behind him were all his cabinet ministers who bowed low as the Son of God and His esteemed entourage materialized out of thin air. After the banquet that evening, the Sovereign Lord would grace His hosts by spending the night in the largest guest room as the others went to stay at a new luxury hotel complex overlooking the increasingly busy Naxos harbor.

The city of Naxos itself now had over 20,000 year-round residents, with another 55,000 living in other parts of the green island, many of them in the new city of Gloria built on the eastern shoreline facing Patmos. Farming and tourism remained the two largest moneymakers on Naxos. Under the guidance of Finance Minister Sampson Baker and Tourism Minister Abraham Goldman, the local economy was booming. Potatoes and wine were the main agricultural exports, reaching markets as far away as Macedonia, Albania and Egypt. Visitors flocked to the Aegean island from all over the planet, especially during the somewhat warmer summer months.

The banquet featured an appetizer choice of either faux tuna on a bed of spinach leaves or tofu calamari, both garnished with sliced local lemons. The main course included faux duck in a sweet raspberry sauce, creamed Naxos potatoes, a Greek salad loaded with fresh tomatoes, onions, bell peppers and locally-produced feta cheese, and oven-baked dinner rolls. For dessert, the guests had a choice of either vanilla ice cream covered with fresh blueberries and cherries or Black Forest cake.

The Great High Priest was seated on an unadorned throne placed at the center of the head table. It faced the tall picture windows which nicely framed the aqua sea just outside of them, glistening with pink light as the waning sun slowly set in the west. Eli and his cabinet ministers sat to the right of their Eternal Ruler, with the Lord's Jerusalem entourage flanking His left. The conversation was animated as the invited dinner guests savored their food following a prayer of thanksgiving led by Rabbi Goldman.

After the main course was served by Greek waiters wearing black tuxedos, Eli rose to his feet to make a toast in honor of his distinguished guests, especially His beloved King. The governor picked up a golden goblet and uttered his toast: "Ladies and gentlemen, saints of all the ages. On this momentous occasion I lift up this cup in deepest regard for all of you and for our most gracious Sovereign Lord, Yeshua our Redeemer, who will reign forever and ever." Eli turned his gaze toward the Bright Morning Star before continuing his solemn toast. "We're so incredibly honored You've chosen to visit Naxos, our small Greek Isle provincial capital. Thank you so much for coming here and bringing our other illustrious guests with You. All are welcome to stop by anytime!"

With that, the local banquet guests rose out of their seats and elevated their crystal goblets as they toasted their visitors with shouts of "*la chaim*," to life! Standing between his earthly father Jonathan and best friend Micah, Benny Goldman felt like leaping into the air followed by some fierce dancing, but he somehow managed to restrain himself as he sipped his locally-produced Merlot.

After the festive supper was over, the Justice Minister was delightfully surprised when the Rose of Sharon requested a private word with him. The two retreated alone into a small sitting room which in a previous era might have been filled with male dinner guests puffing on Cuban cigars and drinking brandy.

"Benny, I am so pleased to hear of the tremendous judicial work you are conducting here in your island province. The official reports I am receiving are very gratifying indeed."

The young saint bowed his humble head low as he savored the Lord's gracious words. "Thank you so much, my highly-esteemed King. It's an enormous honor to serve You and Your Kingdom in this place, and I know I speak for all my cabinet colleagues as well."

The Lamb of God tenderly enfolded Benny's warm hands in His own. "Son, I want to inform you that you will soon encounter the evil tentacles our spiritual adversary still sends out like snakes into our Millennial Kingdom, despite being sealed up in bonds for a thousand years. Satan retains some significant power in our peaceful era due to the failure of some of My subjects to follow and obey the Good Shepherd. You have been carefully chosen to help uncover and confront these harmful tentacles. Never forget that the Great I Am is walking with you, and always will be."

Benny choked back tears as he gazed deeply into his beloved Savior's piercing eyes, wondering whether or not to ask for additional details. Deciding to let the Lord initiate any further dialogue, he thanked his Wonderful Counselor and once again bowed his head, finally adding he would strive, with King Yeshua's help, "to walk in Your footprints as closely as possible."

Donna Svenson was not invited to the Kirintelos/Esteu wedding. It was held in the summer of 52 DL on the western Mediterranean island of Corsica. Eli Ben David and most of his Greek Isle cabinet ministers were in attendance, along with Yoseph Steinberg's entire New York provincial cabinet. The groom was escorted up the central church aisle by his grandfather, Giuseppe Marino. His grandmother Catrina waited on the front row with her daughter Teresa Scarcelli and her earthly husband Leo. Angelica Scarcelli sat next to them along with Maria Alvarez, who wept copious tears of joy that she'd lived to see this day. Had she not gone 'by chance' to the Marino's crumbling home in New Jersey over 50 years before, the helpless baby boy now marching up the aisle looking like a prince in his gold-rimmed tuxedo would probably not be alive at all. A beaming Carmella Bernstein— who never dreamed her musical protégé would reach such a high level of international stardom—sat next to Maria under a stylish beige feathered hat, looking like a proud peacock.

Only three years old when the Conquering King descended to Jerusalem, the beautiful bride was elegantly dressed in a cream-colored wedding gown studded with red rubies. Her long brown hair, pulled to one side, nestled neatly over her bare left shoulder. She was escorted up the central aisle by her earthly father Stephane, who had been beheaded for his Christian faith by the Emperor Andre's forces along with his wife Regina. Yourgos Kirintelos' best man was his fellow tenor, Benito Geovinelli, who watched the bride's slow approach up the aisle with rapt delight. In the crowd of over 500 invited guests were many of the world's most famous celebrities, including leading film and opera stars. Alerted to the exact wedding location by a local journalist, the international paparazzi were gathering under police guard at a nearby park for their hoped-for photo opportunities when the renowned newlyweds exited the gothic church.

The married couple honeymooned on a luxury yacht that Yourgos had purchased in London during the year 47. They set sail for the western Greek islands on the other side of Italy before heading toward Crete and Rhodes. The bride was slightly annoyed by the fact that her new husband spent multiple hours talking on the phone during their pleasant voyage, attempting to negotiate the final details of a major business deal he'd been working on for some time. Along with his close friend Benito, Yourgos was trying to buy a controlling interest in Pan World Airways (PWA), which was among the most successful transport companies on earth. As the yacht entered Egyptian coastal waters, the deal was finally struck, giving Yourgos and Benito a 53% controlling interest in the thriving, New York-based airline.

Along with Sarah and Talel Goldman and Daniyella Bernstein, Donna Svenson continued to vacation annually at the shared summer home on Naxos. However unlike before her former boyfriend's wedding, she tried to avoid being there when the singing star was in residence. Despite this, she was surprised in the year 57 when Yourgos showed up without his wife during the last week of the old-world month of June. She discovered his presence one warm afternoon as she lay on her large beach towel soaking in the now virtually harmless rays (the upper atmosphere ozone layer had been both restored and reinforced when the Lord returned to earth, meaning human beings could now absorb far more UV rays without damaging their skin).

"Excuse me young woman, would you care for an ice cold brew?"

"Yourgos!" Donna blurted out as she sprang up from her mustard-colored towel. Still somewhat angry at the superstar over his assumption she'd be happy to serve as his secret sex-slave, Donna nevertheless flung her arms around his shirtless back.

Yourgos pressed her bikini-clad body closer to his chest. Finally easing his grip, he gave her a swift kiss on her left cheek. "You look wonderful my dear. It's been too long since I last saw you in Jerusalem. How've you been doing?"

Donna took a step backwards. "Not very well, Yourgos. The way you let me know about your wedding plans, the way you assumed I'd go along with being your concubine; all of that still steams me up, although not as much as before."

"I'm so sorry sweetheart. I really did handle that situation very badly. I should've told you in advance what I was intending to do with Francette. In fact, I was planning to inform you, but every time I went to phone you she'd either appear or call me! She's very protective of me, so maybe she sensed something was going on."

"Does she know anything at all about us Yourgos, and how is the marriage going?"

"I *did* tell her I'd had several girlfriends over the years, without naming names of course. Honey, you must admit that many people knew about our relationship; certainly most of your family and some of mine. So I suspect she has at least heard your name, but if so, she's never brought it up directly with me. Still, every so often she says she hopes her lovemaking is 'up to par' with my previous partners, so I'm not exactly sure what she's thinking."

"So *how* does she compare with me?"

"We have a good time together, Donna, but it's not quite like being with you. I've never known a deeper level of satisfaction than when I've been with you. I also miss your companionship."

With that, the mega-celebrity smiled as he tilted his head and passionately kissed his jilted lover on her moist lips. Donna did not resist. In fact, two minutes later she began to gently push him down onto her towel. However when they heard voices approaching the empty beach ten minutes later, they broke up their outdoor frolic and Yourgos ran to the clear water and dove in. After swimming vigorously for several minutes, he got out and slowly walked to his pile of things which he'd wisely left near the entrance of the beach. Waving to the vacationing guest couple busy setting up camp nearby, he did not acknowledge Donna, who was once again lying face up on her towel.

The unplanned encounter by the sea turned out to be the opening act in a torrid new affair between Donna Svenson and Yourgos Kirintelos. This time, it was even more illicit in that the married celebrity was cheating on his wife, who would only discover the sordid relationship many years later. Most of the time, Donna would schedule herself to be in her shared Summerset home for prearranged assignations with the superstar. The trysts usually took place in Donna's bedroom since Yourgos had a live-in Greek maid and two fulltime maintenance men who also resided on his premises. Every other year or so, the couple would meet at some remote location in Europe or North America, and once they even risked exposure by vacationing together at the same hotel in Tahiti, although they did reserve separate bungalows on opposite sites of the plush resort.

In the year 83 DL, Donna and Sarah lost their earthly mother. Esther Hazan had a massive heart attack after showering one morning at her apartment in Jerusalem. Her husband Ari was fixing breakfast in the kitchen when his wife uttered a short cry for help. After discovering her lifeless body on the bedroom floor, he phoned Sarah with the sad news. Working at her office in Prince David's palace, Sarah in turn informed the rest of the family, starting with her children, followed by Donna. While Esther's grandchildren each noted that she had surrendered her life to the Lord and would therefore rise again to eternal life at the end of the millennium, Donna did not acknowledge this comforting fact.

Sarah was annoyed when she spotted Yourgos Kirintelos and his wife Francette in the funeral crowd. She'd learned only one year before that her wayward sister was spotted at a small seaside restaurant in Naxos with the famous tenor. Sarah had confronted Donna about the revelation, but her sibling insisted it was an unplanned, one-off meal together with nothing else happening between them. Sarah was not convinced by this lie, yet didn't press the issue at that time.

Donna wiped her greasy palms against her long black dress as the famous married couple approached her at the post-funeral reception. It was the first time the cheating woman would meet her lover's elegant spouse. "Donna, this is my wife Francette. We are both so sorry about your loss."

Donna politely acknowledged her secret lover's condolences before lightly shaking hands with Francette, who smiled but said nothing. "Thank you Yourgos and Francette. It's so good of you to come to mom's funeral." Although Donna had been informed by Yourgos that he would fly to Israel with his wife from New York aboard his private jet, she did a good job of concealing that fact. Yourgos had feigned that he thought the couple should attend the funeral in order to honor Sarah Goldman and her family, who were present when his grandparents and aunt discovered him alive as a baby in the New Jersey orphanage. Francette apparently bought this contention, not suspecting he actually wanted to be there mainly for Donna's sake.

Two and a half years after Esther passed away, Yourgos confirmed mushrooming media reports that his wife was pregnant. He'd already shared the information with Donna via telephone. Although she didn't say so, she was very upset with the news, fearing her clandestine lover would pay less attention to her (it was already scant) if he had a child to attend to.

Six months later, a baby boy was born. Speaking at a press conference in Los Angeles, Yourgos revealed the child had been named Leonard in honor of two individuals: The famous composer Leonard Bernstein; related by marriage to his musical mentor, and his uncle Leo who'd been with his aunt and family when he was discovered alive in New Jersey. The boy would actually be known by the nickname Lenny. Over two decades later, he would be named a senior vice president of the ever-expanding PWA airline company.

Donna and Yourgos carried on with their secret affair despite the fact that the singer was now a proud father. However their opportunities to be alone together were much rarer than before. This naturally bothered Donna, but not enough for her to verbalize her feelings to Yourgos. The cheating woman frequently reminded herself that she had broken off the illicit relationship after learning of his engagement to Francette, not the other way around.

As she neared age 247, Donna Svenson decided to have her own baby. Before each romantic encounter with Yourgos, she'd been consuming anti-conception rice supplied to her regularly by him, since his wife had a legal prescription for the birth suppressant. Due to the vastly reduced aging process, Donna's internal organs were only just approaching the time when she would find it impossible to conceive.

Ever the conniving plotter, the American-born Israeli cooked up a plan she thought might cover the fact that Yourgos would father the hoped-for child. She phoned Brock Schmidt late one evening when she knew he'd be somewhat tipsy since he ended each and every day with several beers after having wine with his supper.

Brock's eyes lit up when he spotted his former lover's number on his cellphone face. "Hello Donna, how are you?"

"I'm fine Brock. I just wanted to call and see how you've been doing. It's been a few years since we last spoke."

"It's fantastic to hear from you, Donna. I'm doing well. I actually became a great grandfather last year, a little girl named Tammy. Hey, would you like to see her? I can invite my grandson Uri over with his wife and baby, and you could join us for a meal."

Donna smiled slyly. Her plan was unfolding better than she'd envisaged. "Oh, that would be *super*, Brock. I really do miss you honey. How about later this week? I'm free both Thursday and Friday."

"Let's do it on Thursday then. I'll confirm that with my grandson and get back to you with an exact time. I think I'll ask Uri's wife to prepare most of the meal though. I'm afraid I'm still not a very good chef."

Donna lingered longer than the other dinner guests so she could move on to Stage Two of her devious plan. As Brock placed the last dinner plate in his dishwasher, Donna approached from behind and gingerly placed her arms around his still fairly trim waist. Her ex had filled out a bit since she last saw him, but it actually made him look healthier and more attractive, she thought.

Moist lips were soon moving across the back of Brock's neck. Appearing to be around 48 years old although he was of course actually much older than that, the truck driver swiveled around and started kissing his sensual ex-lover on her ample red lips. It was only five minutes before they were nestled together in his bed. Donna had been careful to ingest a large portion of contraceptive rice before heading over to Brock's west Jerusalem apartment. She would not become pregnant with his child.

Two weeks later, she met up with Yourgos for a pre-planned tryst on the island of Cyprus. A rural home had been rented for the week by the extremely wealthy American singer. This time, Donna was careful to refrain from eating the special rice, whose effect lasted for around one week. The following month, she did not have her usual period.

Donna was elated when her gynecologist informed her that she was carrying a baby boy. She would pretend to one and all that he was Brock's son while knowing in fact that he could only be Yourgos' offspring. The deception worked, at least for awhile.

Sarah and her family were dismayed when they learned Donna was pregnant. The expectant mother, who'd moved out of Sarah's home several decades earlier, had already told her older sister that she had reconnected with Brock and was seeing him on a regular basis.

Sarah suggested at the time that she marry him, but Donna replied she was not ready to take that big step.

Brock was delighted to learn he would become a father once again, despite the fact that he was already a great grandfather. He still cared for Donna very much, although he disliked her occasional machinations. The tall Californian had no idea she was seeing Yourgos Kirintelos once again, although he did know about their earlier relationship.

The celebrated tenor was less sanguine when his lover told him she was with child. Worried he might throw her to the dogs if he knew the truth, Donna insisted the baby in her womb belonged to Brock. She might tell him the truth later on, depending on his reaction to her news. When Yourgos protested her new affair with Brock, she reminded him that he was married and therefore presumably having regular relations with his wife. "Why can you be with two women, and I can't have another man? That's totally unfair, Yourgos; and sexist I might add."

"Well, you do have a point Donna. I suppose once the baby is born, you won't want to meet up anymore. I sure hope that's not the case."

"It might be the reality for a year or two, Yourgos, but once he's a little older I can leave him with Daniyella in Jerusalem for a week or two. She's already volunteered to baby sit him."

"Great! I feel better already. So have you and Brock selected a name for the child?"

"No, but we're considering a few. We thought we'd wait until just before he's born."

"So when is he due?"

Donna had been anticipating this question. "In six months. Yourgos, I was not expecting to connect with Brock the night I conceived. We hadn't seen each other for many years, and it was a dinner at his home with his grandson and wife and baby, a sweet girl named Tammy. So I hadn't eaten any of the contraceptive rice you provide for me beforehand, and this is the unfortunate result. At least I now know for certain that I can become pregnant. You know, I've always wanted a child, so I think it will turn out alright, but I'm not sure I'll move in with Brock as he wants me to."

Yourgos was happy to hear this. "How have your relatives reacted to the news?"

"Oh, you know those 'saints.' They can be rather sanctimonious. Sarah insists I must marry Brock, but that's not going to happen."

"I'm glad to hear you're planning to stay single, Donna. Hey, here comes Francette. I've got to cut this short."

"Okay Yourgos. I'll let you know when the baby's born. Take care."

Donna put down her mobile phone and sat back on her satin bedspread. To her satisfaction, she'd managed to fool everyone, except of course the Lord.

Brock and Donna mulled over several male names, including Seth, Evan, and Brad. Then Donna put forth another name she suspected might please her famous lover. She did not tell Brock that 'Chad' had been the name of Yourgos' first cousin in the previous era, or that he'd been a little devil during his short lifetime. "You have a strong first name, Brock, and a straightforward last name. I think 'Chad' sounds like a solid name for your son. What do you think?"

"Hmm…, it does have a nice ring to it. By the way, I'm really glad you agreed to give him my family name even though we aren't married yet. As I told you, I don't want him to have the last name of your deceased Swedish husband."

"Then it's settled, Chad he will be. Oh, there goes another kick! I think he'll grow up to be a quarterback or something!" Brock enfolded his giggling lover in his arms, unaware he was being kicked in the pants by the duplicitous woman.

EIGHTEEN

GATHERING STORM

"I just can't figure it out. They must be ghosts or something!"

Benny Goldman was extremely puzzled. How were they transporting their contraband goods into his island province, and who was behind the nefarious operation? The Justice Minister was sitting in his Naxos office with Housing and Construction Minister Micah Kupinski, Foreign Minister Jonathan Goldman and Transport and Tourism Minister Abe Goldman. The four government officials were studying the latest report put together by Greek Isle Police Chief, Dimitri Simantos, and the head of the Ports Authority, Philipe Hirapolis. The two officials had detailed the growing evidence that a steady flow of illegal drugs, hard liquor and banned pornography was somehow making its way into Eli Ben David's sprawling province, as was also the case in many other parts of the world.

The Greek Isle contraband stream was first detected in the year 117 DL. However it initially appeared to be just a trickle of smuggled goods, not the flood now occurring. Benny and his colleagues at the Justice Ministry spent countless hours trying to locate the sources of the outlawed activity. It appeared the main point of entry for the apparently imported contraband was the island of Crete, which had the largest international airport in the province. However it also featured the biggest provincial seaport jutting out into the Mediterranean waters next to the rebuilt city of Iraklion, which now had a year-round population of 220,000. The possibility that the forbidden goods were coming in via private boats docking at the many small marinas located on the large island was also being investigated.

The classified report stated that an estimated five tons of banned drugs like LSD, heroin and cocaine was somehow reaching the province each year. The only consolation was that the numbers were much larger in the nearby province of Athens, but then again its resident population was also six times greater. The police chief reported around 10,000 bottles of bootleg alcohol was circulating on the black market every month, along with hundreds of thousands of banned porn magazines and films (contained on two-inch laser discs), including some featuring child molestation. Excessively violent movies, some showing actual killings and human victims being brutally tortured, were also flooding the province.

In the year 143, Benny met with his great grandfather, Rabbi Benjamin Goldman, to discuss the spiritual dimensions of the festering problem. He wanted to ascertain from the wise Religious Affairs Minister why, in his informed opinion, many human citizens in the Millennial Kingdom would risk judicial punishment by purchasing outlawed goods, most of which were clearly harmful to their physical health, not to mention detrimental to their spiritual wellbeing.

"I don't get it, Great Grandpa. How could so many people turn away from the Lord in this way? I mean, they see us Kadoshim in our glorified eternal bodies all the time. They hear King Yeshua on television and radio delivering His thoughtful talks every week on Day One. They live in a world that was virtually destroyed nearly one and a half centuries ago, and yet everyone is enjoying full peace and prosperity today. Still, many people are apparently turning to illicit sex, drugs and strong drink to get their kicks. It just doesn't make sense to me."

"Well, Benny, the Lord has reminded us many times that free will is still in operation among the people living on earth. Don't forget the world's human population is now beginning to exceed the number of Kadoshim, and that trend will only escalate in the coming decades. Almost all of them are youthful and vigorous, and like young people in the previous era, they're more susceptible than older folk to illegal drugs and alcohol, and also prone to mix sex in with that dangerous cocktail. Sadly, the fact that the Lord is visibly present on earth doesn't seem to be enough to persuade some of them to follow and obey Him."

"That's just it. How can *anyone* possibly see the glorious Lord and experience His beneficent rule every day, and still turn away from Him? Every time I see my Aunt Donna I ask myself the same question, and I don't have any satisfying answers."

Rabbi Goldman leaned forward in his mahogany chair and gently grasped his namesake's right arm. "Benny, it's no different from when the Messiah made His first appearance on earth. It wasn't just the 'uneducated masses' that rejected the incarnated Lord; in fact many common people were quite open to His message. It was precisely the leading Jewish clerics and officials who most forcefully rejected Yeshua as their Savior and Lord, as most of the ruling Roman officials did as well. You'll recall the Sanhedrin actually questioned the man who was born blind and then healed by the Redeemer. That testimony should have been enough to open their spiritual eyes, but most of them seemed to remain blind. It's the sinful nature of fallen humanity that is the real root problem here, Benny. Rebellion seems to be an extremely strong force in human hearts; and spiritual blindness too, even in the face of glorious light."

"Great Grandpa, I've been considering asking Governor Eli to approach Prince David with a request, and I'd value your opinion about my proposal. I'd like him to ask King Yeshua if He would pinpoint for us *exactly* where the contraband is coming from. What do you think of that idea?"

"Oh course, the Lord knows everything about everything, Benny, as you are obviously alluding to. However, I suspect He will not reveal that information to you. Our wonderful Sovereign often reminds us that while the iron rod has, and will be used to maintain public order when needed, He will simultaneously allow free will to run its natural course. Don't forget the book of Revelation tells us a final worldwide rebellion will take place at the conclusion of this wonderful millennial era. That prophesied fact implies that human sin, and therefore sinners, will still be quite manifest until the very end. On top of that, Satan's demons still operate on earth. While he's been bound in chains for a thousand years, they've not been sealed up yet. They work all the time to cause people to stumble and fall, and those who haven't grasped the Savior's loving hands are susceptible to their evil machinations, even during the Lord's current visible reign."

"Well, I guess I'll have a lot of work to do in the coming years running the Justice Ministry and heading up the provincial security forces! Thanks for your insights, sir. I am so blessed to be working in the same government cabinet with you, not to mention to be named after you."

"The feeling is mutual, dear one. May the Lord grant you tremendous courage and strength as you battle the enemy operating in our midst every day."

In the year 187, security forces stationed in Crete finally discovered the main source of the illegal alcohol, drugs, and pornography flow. The vital information came in a most unexpected way. A blaze broke out in the Pan World Airways warehouse at the Iraklion international airport. When firemen entered the large metal building, they heard dozens of bottles exploding in the intense heat. The bottles were packed inside several containers marked "PWA CARGO" in flames near the back wall. After the fire was successfully doused, police officers inspected the largely-destroyed crates. One was found to contain hundreds of bottles of bootleg whiskey, with banned vodka in another crate. Nearby containers were full of outlawed porn discs and prohibited drugs.

Benny Goldman was quickly summoned to the scene by the Iraklion police chief. The Justice Minister was astonished at the sheer size of the contraband haul. The drugs and other outlawed goods were hidden under legitimate cargo items such as clothing and electronic equipment due to be delivered to various business addresses all over the Greek Isle province. Police investigators discovered that false bottoms had been built into each container, with the contraband items hidden in the lower third of the crates. Some of the banned items were shipped on to their local business addresses, while others were emptied out at the warehouse. How the latter were distributed to human buyers, and by whom, was already partially known. The larger question of who was ultimately behind the smuggling operation remained unanswered.

Three years before, police officers on the island of Rhodes arrested two young men soon after they sold bootleg booze and cocaine to several students at a high school football game. However the perpetrators—just two years out of school themselves—testified under oath they didn't know the identities of their suppliers. They maintained that they simply picked up the illegal items in a stone shed located near the side of a wheat field on the island. They added they'd been recruited via a phone call to sell the contraband items after someone apparently recommended them for the lucrative job. One of the apprehended men had previously been convicted of shoplifting beer from a local grocery store, which they guessed might have been why they were contacted by their anonymous supplier.

Benny marched straight into the PWA office building next door to the lightly-damaged warehouse. He was not happy to discover that the chief administrator, an American named Ted Belington, had fled his desk and the PWA complex soon after news of the fire reached him. It was undoubtedly clear to Belington that the contraband cargo would be discovered and he would be the chief suspect in the subsequent police investigation. The Justice Minister ordered Police Chief Simantos to put out an all points bulletin for Belington's immediate arrest.

The PWA official was apprehended two days after the warehouse fire as he tried to escape the island of Crete via a small private yacht a friend had chartered for him. Confessing the obvious, Belington acknowledged he both knew about the illicit smuggling operation and had hired several thugs to unload the imported cargo and network it out to Naxos, Rhodes, and other provincial islands via private fishing boats (after appeals were made to Governor Ben David by hundreds of island residents, small-scale ocean fishing for personal consumption had been legalized in the watery province, but not for commercial sale). Belington told police investigators he didn't know who these Greek criminals were. However over time, plain clothed PIs working under Benny Goldman's supervision were able to uncover most of the smuggling network that had been clandestinely operating for many years in the island province.

Within hours of the Iraklion discovery, security raids were carried out in many PWA warehouses around the world. However, only one site, located near the Phoenix International Airport, yielded any contraband items. Evidence on the ground, especially fragments of cargo containers that had apparently been quickly ripped apart, suggested banned goods had been present in many of the warehouses, but if so, the items were rapidly disposed of.

On the one month anniversary of the PWA warehouse fire at the Iraklion airport, Governor Eli Ben David convened his entire cabinet for a special celebration of the momentous contraband discovery in his province. Jonathan Goldman was smiling broadly—thrilled it was in his son's provincial jurisdiction that the long-sought-after international breakthrough occurred. Benny's beaming grandparents and Rabbi Goldman were all equally elated.

As a surprise to the glowing Justice Minister, Sarah and Talel Goldman entered the cabinet room after all the ministers were seated. Although they'd already privately congratulated Benny during one of their weekly family Sabbath meals in Jerusalem, they soon joined the round of official accolades aimed at him. "We've been praying for you all along, son, and our Father has answered us in such a tremendous way!" proclaimed Sarah as she hugged the neck of her earthly offspring. Talel nodded in agreement as she kissed him on his left cheek. "Nice job, brother," she stated as she gave him a hi-five.

"Thanks everyone, but all the glory goes to Israel's God," Benny stated as he recalled King Yeshua's precious personal words of encouragement to him. "There's a lot more work to be done, so don't stop praying!"

Soon after returning to Jerusalem, Sarah phoned her sister Donna and asked her to come to her home for a private meeting. She'd already told her housemates Talel, Daniyella and Bet-el that she needed to speak to her sister alone, so all three had evacuated the premises by the time Donna arrived that evening from her Jerusalem apartment.

After greetings were exchanged, Sarah told her wayward sibling about the mid-day Greek Isle cabinet meeting in honor of Benny.

"That's marvelous, Sarah, I'm so glad you and Talel could be there."

"Donna, you must realize that the evidence is pointing in the direction of PWA airlines, controlled by Yourgos Kirintelos and Benito Geovinelli. This thing could become very nasty, with implications for all of us. Donna, please be completely honest with me: Are you seeing Yourgos again?"

"How many times do I have to tell you that we are not having an affair!"

Sarah frowned as she brushed some stray hair from her glistening forehead. "But reports keep coming in that you've been spotted together on Naxos. I heard just last month from Miri Doron that some of your Summerset neighbors saw you at the beach with him earlier this year."

"Oh come on, Sis! Our place is just two fricken lots down from his house, and all us humans share a common beach. Of course I'm going to occasionally run into Yourgos in Summerset, as you've done yourself. That doesn't mean we're swimming in the sheets together, and you know it. He's a married man, and I respect that fact. Indeed, Francette is actually often with him, as you well know, along with their son Lenny and their daughters Gina and Maria."

"So you don't know anything about his possible involvement with the scandal uncovered in Crete?"

"I know nothing about his business at all, Sarah, nor do I want to. Still, I'm pretty sure he wouldn't be involved in anything like that. He's a decent man, not some mafia-type criminal."

"What about Lenny? I read he's now the CEO of Pan World Airways. It seems to me he must've known something fishy was going on."

"It could be Sarah, but again, I just don't know. I've met Lenny a few times, and even had dinner with him and his wife Claudia a few years ago when they were visiting the island. To me, he also doesn't seem to be the criminal type, but he is a powerful business executive and power tends to corrupt, as they say."

As she'd done many times before, Sarah ended the conversation by urging her sister to surrender her life to the Lord. The entreaty once again fell on Donna's pierced, deaf ears.

The discovery in Crete of the Pan World Airways connection proved to be a key element in tracking down the ultimate perpetrators of the clandestine smuggling operation polluting many parts of the planet. Benny Goldman would play an instrumental role in this critical security endeavor which would unfold over several decades. Six weeks after news of the Iraklion discovery reached Jerusalem, the Greek Isle Justice Minister was summoned to the world capital to discuss the situation with Yochanan, Shaul and other senior government officials.

Yochanan warmly embraced Benny after his longtime friend entered his spacious office in King Yeshua's royal palace. "Greetings, Mr. Justice Minister! It's so good to see you; and please accept my personal congratulations on your criminal interception on the island of Crete."

"Shalom Yochanan, it's always nice to see you as well. However, I can't take any credit for the Iraklion discovery. It happened purely by chance."

"Nothing happens by chance in the Lord's Kingdom, Benny. We know you've been doggedly pursuing the criminals behind the contraband network, and we feel it was no coincidence that the breakthrough came in your province. At any rate, King Yeshua has authorized me to appoint you to head a team that will hopefully uncover the ultimate source or sources of these banned goods. You'll be joined by the London provincial Justice Minister, Clive Burrows, along with the head of our federal government security service, Avi Cohen. You may also recruit a larger team to assist you as you see fit."

"I'm so very honored by this appointment, Yochanan. I really don't know where I'll begin, but it's apparent some people connected to the PWA airline are involved in this smuggling ring. As you've undoubtedly heard, we already got a confession to that effect from the head of the airline's office in Iraklion, Ted Belington."

"Yes, and thank you for rapidly, and successfully, pursuing him— another job well done!"

"You know, Yochanan, one of the owners of the airline is the famous tenor, Yourgos Kirintelos, who I personally know. He has a summer home on Naxos and may even be secretly having an affair with my Aunt Donna. Rumors about that continue to swirl all over the place, even though there's only been circumstantial evidence to back them up so far, and she firmly denies it. All that to say; I may not be the best candidate to head up such an important investigation."

Kingdom Foreign Minister Shaul had entered Yochanan's office just as Benny brought up the PWA angle. He strode over to the Justice Minister and patted him on his broad back. "We disagree, Benny. We suspect your personal connections might actually aid your investigation. You'll enjoy our full support as you carry it out; and the blessings of our Messiah King as well. Godspeed on your efforts, my friend!"

"Godspeed indeed," added Yochanan as he stretched out his arms to give Benny a warm hug.

After holding a series of consultations at Clive Burrow's office in London, the three commissioned investigators and a team of twelve security assistants headed for PWA world headquarters in New York City, where they would be joined by five American police inspectors. Among the foreign team were Greek Isle Police Chief Dimitri Simantos and investigators from Britain, Italy and France. By prior invitation, the Kadoshim party made their initial appearance at provincial governor Yoseph Steinberg's official mansion in Brooklyn, where Yourgos Kirintelos had grown up. After greeting his overseas guests and wishing them success, Yoseph introduced them all to the US team who mainly came from his province. Then the governor took his longtime friend aside to speak privately with him.

"Benny, I know this must be a difficult assignment for you, given your personal connections to Yourgos. Let's hope he's not involved in any way. Still, he does control PWA, along with Benito Geovinelli, so he certainly needs to be questioned. Be assured my cabinet and I stand squarely behind you, whatever you discover, despite the fact that several are close relatives of Yourgos."

"Thanks so much, Yoseph; your support means a great deal to me. It's an awkward position to be in for sure, but of course I couldn't turn down the commission from our Sovereign King. Still, it's a relief to know we have your full backing. I've been told that Yourgos has little to do with the daily operations of his airline, so maybe he doesn't have any connection to the smuggling network. Like you, I certainly hope that's the case."

"I've already spoken to Maria Alvarez about it, Benny, and she's convinced Yourgos is not involved. I pray she is correct, although I know she's not exactly impartial in her estimations. She cares for Yourgos very much, as we all do."

"We'll attempt to see that justice is done, Yoseph, wherever that leads us."

Yourgos Kirintelos was the first person the three team leaders questioned after arriving at the magnificent PWA skyscraper in lower Manhattan; one of the tallest in New York rising 84 floors high. Although the talented tenor did not often work in the tower, he maintained an office there. Strategically seated next to the famous singer were two PWA attorneys prepared to take notes of the exchange and advise their client as needed.

After introductions were made, Yourgos expressed his profound shock over the discovery that his commercial aircraft were apparently being used to smuggle banned items to many compass points around the globe. "I was as surprised as anyone by this unbelievable news, gentlemen, and I immediately instructed my PWA board and son Lenny to launch a full investigation. I don't want to see illegal drugs and pornography swamp our world anymore than you do, not to mention hard liquor. Why, I even heard cigarettes loaded with nicotine were found in the Phoenix stash; as if we needed to have lung cancer plague our planet once again!"

Benny leaned forward in his chair. "It's really good to hear you've begun an internal investigation, Yourgos, but you must realize this cannot be enough to satisfy government officials in Jerusalem and in our provinces. We need to question all your senior executives and probably many of your lower-end workers in the coming weeks, as I trust you'll appreciate. We hope to have your full cooperation as we carry out this important investigation."

"You have it Benny, unconditionally. I want to get to the bottom of this at least as much as you do."

The security team next questioned Benito Geovinelli, who had flown to New York from Naples to take part in the conversation. This time, the enquiries were led by Avi Cohen, who'd served as the Israeli army's intelligence chief in the previous era before becoming a believer on his deathbed. "Thanks for agreeing to meet us today, Mr. Geovinelli. Like the others in this room, I'm a big fan of your wonderful music, as I am of Yourgos Kirintelos. However I must inform you our preliminary investigations have suggested there is a link between you and the contraband smugglers. As we speak, kingdom security forces are raiding a warehouse complex near Chicago and another one outside of Rome that we suspect are loaded with banned goods. We're aware that another company owned exclusively by you, Benito Geovinelli Incorporated, operates these complexes. So we are hereby giving you legal notice today that you're a prime suspect in this investigation."

The Italian tenor bolted out of his chair, prepared to make a fiery defense, when one of his attorneys grabbed his arm and spoke for him. "We had already learned of your security raids on several BGI premises, Mr. Cohen. Our client will make no statement about that situation at the present time. However we're prepared to cooperate fully in your ongoing investigation, but only after more facts are established."

When it became clear that nothing more would be forthcoming at the tense meeting, the lead investigators moved on to question the CEO of Pan World Airways, Lenny Kirintelos. As with the company's European co-owner, the young American man with dark wavy hair and piercing green eyes was warned he was a major suspect in the case. The short session proved to be no more revealing than the previous encounter, with the CEO's attorneys forbidding him to make any substantial statements.

The raids near Chicago and Naples yielded large volumes of banned alcoholic products, illegal drugs and stockpiles of hard-core pornography discs and magazines. Seized equipment and machinery suggested that most of the bootleg booze and some of the drugs were produced in the warehouses, along with at least some of the porn films and magazines. The contraband items were then packed into false-bottomed containers and hidden under legitimate products before being shipped to PWA warehouses in several United States provinces and others in Italy, Spain, Germany, South America and Asia. Still, it became evident after months of heavy legwork that it would be nearly impossible to prove company owner Benito Geovinelli knew about, and approved of, the criminal activity which took place on his premises. Police investigators were able to pin charges on warehouse bosses and some employees, but not on senior management based in separate offices in Rome and Chicago. Benny concluded that whoever was ultimately in charge of the smuggling operation had carefully covered their dirty tracks.

As more evidence was gathered and processed, the Greek Isle Justice Minister and his cohorts became convinced that Lenny Kirintelos was the main man who facilitated delivery of the smuggled goods to several PWA warehouses. Yet here again they were not able to prove their suspicions beyond a reasonable doubt. Several Kingdom prosecutors advised them the circumstantial evidence uncovered so far was not sufficient to secure a conviction. This situation frustrated Benny. He did not remotely like the arrogant young Kirintelos whom he thought strutted about as if he owned the world.

Three years later, a breakthrough came in a most unexpected location—the island of Naxos. Lenny Kirintelos had flown there on a short working vacation without his wife Claudia and their five children. After seeing off his father's fulltime Greek maid for a weekend visit to her parent's home on the nearby island of Paros, Lenny notified the two Greek maintenance men who lived in a nearby bungalow he was heading off in his electric Mercedes to meet some business contacts in the bustling city of Gloria.

Half an hour after the Pan World CEO exited his father's Summerset driveway, one of the fulltime workers, Alexander

Kostantos, entered the small mansion to repair a leaking drain in the master bathroom. When he pulled out three drawers adjacent to the sink to spare them any potential water damage, he discovered to his delight several laser discs with names such as *Girls in Love* stashed in the back of the bottom drawer. After finishing his job forty minutes later, the laborer gathered up his implements and placed them in his metal toolbox. Next he carefully returned the drawers to their places, but not before choosing one of the discs for immediate viewing. The single young man went into the bedroom and placed the disc in a laser machine opposite the king-sized bed. He then sprawled back on the bed and let fallen human nature take its course.

Twelve minutes into the screening, a car drove into the mansion driveway. Kostantos leapt to his feet and spurted to the window, only to discover that Lenny Kirintelos had returned home early. He ejected the disc before rushing to the master bathroom, thrusting the banned porn flick into the bottom drawer. As he was about to exit the bathroom, he heard voices approaching the adjacent bedroom. Reacting with irrational panic, the thin maintenance worker hid himself inside the curtained shower like a teenager caught smoking marijuana underneath bleachers in a school gym. At least Kostantos had his toolbox with him, which might afford a plausible excuse to be there if subsequently detected.

What happened next would change the course of Millennial Kingdom history. The airline CEO went straight to a hidden safe located behind a cedar bookcase near the large bed. Accompanying him was Francis 'Frank' Delano, an Italian-American who clandestinely worked for Benito Geovinelli, mainly carrying out hit jobs for his powerful boss.

"You'll find everything you need in here" said Kirintelos as he carefully took out a brown folder and handed it to Delano, who placed it inside his black briefcase. "Just do your job well and make sure he ends up six-feet-under, and be careful to leave no traces pointing in my direction,"

"Sure thing, Mr. Kirintelos, I'll get on it right after I return to New York. Sorry again about interrupting your day, but I felt I shouldn't contact you via my phone under the circumstances."

"You did the right thing, Frank. I didn't mind changing my plans and picking you up at the airport. This is a very important assignment as you know, and extra caution is certainly called for."

The stilted conversation intrigued the Greek maintenance man who could clearly make out every word. What he would hear from this point on would alter his personal history.

Lenny closed the safe and slid the bookcase back into its normal position. "Now that our business is done Frank, would you care to join me for a little fun this evening?"

"Definitely, sir, what do you have in mind?"

"I think you know about the place up in the hills near here my father had constructed a few years ago."

"Sure, I've heard lots of good things about it. Are we heading up that way?"

"That's exactly where I was driving when I got your phone call from the airport. So why don't you get into more comfortable clothes and we'll go up there. I'll show you a guest room where you can freshen up. If you have any condoms, bring those with you."

"Sounds like a sweet game plan, Mr. Kirintelos. I'll be ready in half an hour."

The allusions to a sex party further intrigued Alexander Kostantos. He decided to get in his truck and head for the hills after giving the Americans a decent head start. The dexterous manual worker had done some repairs at the small hilltop retreat, so he knew its exact location not far from the summit of Mount Zas. His boss Yourgos would often drive up there for a few days of what he termed "undisturbed relaxation." The stone house had no permanent staff as far as Alexander knew, and Yourgos rarely took his family or maid along with him. However Donna Svenson had been up there with him on more than one occasion.

Stationing himself in his truck down the road a mile or so, Kostantos spotted four vehicles carrying local Greek men apparently heading for the small Kirintelos retreat perched on a ridge just below the granite summit. There was no other destination beyond that after dark, although the road was routinely used during the day by hikers scaling Mount Zas.

The smell of fireplace smoke was the first thing the wiry Greek worker noticed as he slowly crept through some bushes just after sunset. As he'd done before, Kostantos noted that the view from the ridge was spectacular, facing the western Aegean dotted with Paros and several other islands. From the top of Mount Zas itself, hikers could also clearly see Mykonos, Ios, Santorini and even Patmos to the east, although only faintly.

However the view the maintenance man was seeking this warm evening was inside the Kirintelos retreat. He shimmied up a drainpipe and peered into a glass window near the kitchen sink. What he saw next would never leave him. He could easily make out the scene in the nearby living room. On the floor were about a dozen naked men and women wantonly engaged in a raucous orgy. Standing near the fire-place mantle was what appeared to be a tall muscular man whose nakedness left nothing to the imagination. It was actually a demonized hologram portraying Zeus, the Greek mythological god said to have spent his childhood in a nearby cave on the west side of the summit named after him. Periodically each of the revelers would turn their gaze toward the demonic idol whose wide eyes were ablaze with passionate lust. Kostantos could tell that among those positioned on the carpeted floor was Lenny Kirintelos.

Alexander Kostantos did not share anything with his Greek co-worker after he got back to the Summerset estate late that evening. When Lenny finally retuned home with his American guest the following noontime, the hard-working maintenance man was careful to get a good look at the visitor, offering to haul Frank's bag out to his rented car. With his conscience bothering him night and day, Kostantos finally decided after two weeks of anguished mental wrestling to go see Benny Goldman.

The Justice Minister had no idea why a common laborer would want to meet with him, only knowing he'd told his secretary it was an urgent matter. After shaking hands, the Greek worker got right to his terrible topic. "Sir, I have some news I feel I *must* share with you, even though I really don't want to. I think you already know I work for Yourgos Kirintelos and his family?"

"Yes, Mr. Kostantos, I read a memo about you prepared by my secretary after she spoke with you earlier on the phone. I think I've spotted you working in the yard a couple times when visiting the Kirintelos estate. What's on your mind today?"

"Mr. Minister, I fear that I accidentally overheard some sort of assignment for someone to be killed. I was in the master bathroom fixing a leaking pipe about two weeks ago when Lenny Kirintelos walked into the adjacent bedroom and opened his father's hidden safe. He took something out and handed it to another American man with him. I got a chance to speak briefly with the visitor the next day and so got a good look at his face. Lenny apparently handed him something and then told him to 'do your job well and make sure he ends up six-feet-under' and that it not be traceable back to him. Well, I was very upset to hear that sort of talk coming from Yourgos' son, so I followed him and his guest up to the family's hilltop retreat near Mount Zas. I looked through the window and saw that the two guys were part of a group of naked young men and women frolicking on the floor. I could see lots of banned drugs and booze near them, and some weird hologram image of a big male wearing absolutely no clothes, with a golden crown perched on his curly head like some Greek god. To be honest sir, I hate to rat on my boss' son, but whatever 'assignment' he was sending the visiting American on cannot be good, in my estimation."

"No, murder is always very bad indeed. Do you recall anything else that might help us locate the American? I presume he headed back to the States fairly quickly?"

"It sounded like he was returning to New York that same day. Oh, I did hear Lenny call him 'Frank' one time, so I guess that's his first name. Lenny himself took off for New York later that same week."

"That's all very helpful information, Mr. Kostantos. Thank you so much for your diligence in sharing it with me. I'll let you know if we need anything else, maybe a photo ID for instance."

"Okay, sir, thanks for hearing me out. I'll remain vigilant."

Two days later, Benny Goldman called Kostantos back into his office. Lined up on his desk were several pictures he wanted the worker to inspect. Two were of Francis Delano, a notorious mafia hit man well-known to the New York area police. He'd been in and out of jail four times after being convicted of felony racketeering, theft, gun smuggling and money laundering. So far, no murder charges had proved strong enough to stick to him.

"That's the man!" Kostantos proclaimed when he spotted the photos. He pointed to one mug shot taken from a police lineup and another photo of a heavyset man sitting on a motorcycle without a helmet. Both were pictures of Francis Delano. Benny immediately had his police chief contact his New York City counterpart to issue an urgent APB for the hit-man's detention.

The arrest warrant order went out slightly too late. As it was reaching provincial officials in America, Yourgos Kirintelos was just getting out of a taxi in front of the Manhattan headquarters of World News Network, where he was to appear as a musical guest on the early morning talk show. The lone bullet tore though his chest—leaving him face down in a swelling pool of blood on the sidewalk.

NINETEEN

FATHERS AND SONS

Maria Alvarez sat in the corner crying her eyes out. She had rushed to the hospital right after news reached the governor's mansion where she still lived and worked. Yourgos Kirintelos was in the emergency operating room where doctors were battling hard to save his life. Sitting next to Maria were Leo and Teresa Scarcelli and Catrina and Giuseppe Marino. Governor Yoseph and Zinel Steinberg were there as well, along with provincial Finance Minister Amos Pearlman. Missing was Yourgos' musical mentor Carmella Bernstein, who was away in Hong Kong on official business.

When he learned of the heinous drive-by shooting, Benny Goldman zipped right over to the Manhattan hospital. His earthly father Jonathan accompanied him, along with Micah Kupinski. Sarah Goldman soon appeared in the waiting room as well, along with Talel.

Just before leaving her Jerusalem office, Sarah phoned her sister to tell her the jarring news. "Honey, are you sitting down? I have something very disturbing to share with you."

Donna Svenson was gazing out her apartment kitchen window, chewing a bite of store-bought apple pie. "What's up Sis? Did dad die or something?"

"No, not that, thank the Lord. Donna, Yourgos has been shot and seriously wounded in New York. He was scheduled to perform on the WNN morning program and was just getting out of a taxi when someone fired at him from a passing car. It happened about half an hour ago. The police say the bullet tore through his chest, probably grazing his heart. He lost a lot of blood very quickly, Donna. I'm afraid to say he's not expected to survive."

"Oh Sarah, what horrible news! I can't believe it! Who would want to kill Yourgos? Are you heading to New York?"

"Talel and I are leaving very soon. Do you want me to pass along any message?"

Donna blew her nose as tears descended from the corners of her eyes. "Yes, tell his family I'm thinking of them. I'll try to book a flight out tonight. Can you help me do that?"

"Sure, I'll phone PWA at King Yeshua International Airport and let them know it's urgent you get a seat. They have two flights to New York each evening so there should be room for you. Donna, I know I've been a bit hard on you at times, but I do appreciate you care very much for Yourgos and I'm really sorry I had to share such sad news with you. I'll be keeping him and you in prayer."

The severely wounded tenor tenaciously clung to life throughout the night. By the time Donna arrived at the hospital late the next morning, his doctors announced that his chances of survival had risen to fifty-fifty. At least this was a more positive medical assessment than the initial dire forecast delivered the day before.

Donna had to bite her own bullet soon after entering the intensive care unit's waiting room. Sitting there among other relatives was Francette Esteu-Kirintelos, who had already been told that Donna was on her way to New York. Although it seemed odd to the Canadian psychologist that the woman would cross the big pond just to see her severely wounded husband, it appeared less strange when she ran into several other members of the Goldman family waiting at the hospital, including Sarah.

Francette greeted Donna politely but coolly. The fact that the American-Israeli would rush to New York so quickly only furthered her suspicions that her famous husband was having an affair with the still-beautiful Jewish woman, although Francette lacked concrete proof. Several telltale indications had come to her attention in recent years, especially reports from Yourgos' maid that the two usually seemed to be on the island of Naxos at roughly the same time, although the Greek worker had never actually seen them in bed together, nor even kissing or holding hands. However from her nearby cottage window, she'd spotted Donna enter and leave the Kirintelos home several times when Francette was not there; on one occasion just before midnight.

With doctors expressing increasing confidence every day that the world-renowned tenor would survive the drive-by shooting attack, Francette invited Donna to accompany her to his police-guarded ICU room. The suspicious psychologist wanted to measure her husband's reaction to suddenly seeing his possible tryst partner while in the presence of his wary wife. She had been careful not to mention that Donna Svenson was among his well-wishers camping out at the hospital.

"Yourgos, someone's waiting out in the hall who came a long distance to see you. I'll invite her in now. Come on in, Donna."

The wounded singer grunted audibly when his secret lover— wearing an oversized sweater and designer jeans—waltzed into the room, pulling out her well-rehearsed story as she did so. "Oh Yourgos, I'm so sorry you were viciously attacked, but very glad you survived and are starting to recover! It was so good of you and Francette to come to my mother's funeral before your son Lenny was born over a century ago. I wanted to reciprocate and come here to see you both. I have to say that despite the shooting last week, you look much better than I thought you would. Of course, I haven't seen you in several years, so you do look a little older." Donna chuckled at her tiny lie of a joke and winked at Francette, who was not sure what to make of this charade.

Yourgos Kirintelos continued to slowly recover from his close encounter with homicidal death. Fast professional work by his physicians had done the initial trick, aided by the healing leaves from the Trees of Life and considerable prayer from his family and friends. A passerby with a mobile phone had been taping the musical artist's exit from his taxi when the attack took place, so police had a video copy of the entire crime (which quickly went viral on the internet).

It took investigators just under three months to track down and incarcerate Frank Delano. He had been spirited up to the Catskill

Mountains soon after the drive-by shooting assault, hidden in the back of a van. While initially protesting his innocence, the assailant decided to come clean when police showed him a photo taken by another pedestrian that clearly pinned him to the crime scene. The blown-up picture revealed a smiling Delano sitting in the back seat of a car holding a gun just seconds after a bullet struck the American tenor. The main entrance to the WNN headquarters building was clearly identifiable in the background.

Delano's subsequent conviction for attempted murder was greatly aided by the damning testimony given earlier by Alexander Kostantos. Someone had tried to dissuade the maintenance worker from appearing at the trial, pinning a note in broken Greek on his hotel room door which threatened death if he carried on with his "crusade" against the Italian-American. The note did not have its desired effect, and the experienced hit-man was found guilty as charged and sentenced to life in prison.

With the link between Delano and Lenny Kirintelos now solidly established, criminal investigators turned their full attention to the airline chief executive. Charges were brought against him of contracting an attempted murder of his very own father. Benny Goldman was in the courtroom when the accused CEO was questioned under oath. So was Maria Alvarez, who wanted to rush up and choke the younger Kirintelos for daring to attempt to have his father's precious life snuffed out like a cockroach.

At first, the PWA executive protested his innocence, despite the fact that Delano had ended up admitting under oath that he received his commission to murder Yourgos directly from his son. However as the trial drew on, the perpetrator lost his nerve and broke down in tears, admitting he had indeed initiated the criminal hit and was also behind the international contraband operation. Lenny testified that his father Yourgos had uncovered irrefutable evidence his son was the main man fueling the smuggling operation carried out via PWA-owned jets. "I had no choice but to deal with this since my father was threatening to go to the authorities with his information. I love him, and didn't want to hurt him, but he was treading way too close for comfort. I warned him, but he said he was determined to pursue me whatever the cost. So I concluded I had to do what I did. I'm deeply sorry, mom. I really don't... know what came over me."

Despite his reference to her, Lenny tried to avoid his mother's stone cold glare. Francette was seated in the second row with Benny, Maria and other family members and friends. Her wounded husband was recuperating at home, still too weak to attend such a session. When the jury foreman announced a guilty verdict ten days later, Mrs. Kirintelos shed elephant tears as she hugged Maria, whom she had long understood was considered by Yourgos as his surrogate mother. It was at that very moment when Donna Svenson, closely following the emotional trial on WNN from her west Jerusalem apartment, decided to launch her plot to become pregnant in an attempt to give her clandestine lover another son. After all, his current son would probably now be spending the rest of his life behind bars. She began to devise the details of her plan that same evening, carrying it out with fervor a few years later.

The worldwide distribution of illegal drugs, alcohol and pornography slowed to a trickle in the wake of the two New York convictions. Benny Goldman was feted once again for his significant role in uncovering the smuggling network and pinning it on Lenny Kirintelos. Still, the Justice Minister was unhappy he'd not been able to prove that Benito Geovinelli was the ultimate force behind the illegal operation. Less than one month after Lenny was sentenced to 300 years in prison, Yourgos announced he was severing his business partnership with his longtime friend and concert partner after buying out his portion of PWA stock. Whether the authorities could prove it or not, the celebrated tenor was now convinced that his 'best man' was actually an evil brute out to harm humanity for his own personal aggrandizement. Such a person could obviously no longer be his business associate. Still, the initial realization that his friend was pulling thick wool over his eyes left Yourgos physically noxious for several days.

It would take years before Yourgos Kirintelos could even begin to deal emotionally with the startling fact that his own flesh and blood had commissioned a hit-man to murder him. Although Lenny had been somewhat rebellious as a teenager, he was basically a decent kid. He excelled at football and wrestling, and dated several lovely young women before settling on Claudia Coleman, whom he met at a college basketball game. However during his university level studies, he became addicted to pain killers prescribed to him after his knee ligaments were torn during a hotly-contested wrestling match (he could have just upped his intake of the healing Leaves of Life, but preferred to use the more traditional drugs developed in the previous era). Later he moved on to illegal amphetamines before being introduced by one of his close buddies to cocaine and heroin. He would remain hooked on these banned drugs until his arrest many years later.

After Benito Geovinelli learned of Lenny's drug habit from his in-house spies, he approached the senior PWA vice president with a proposal he could not refuse. Thus began the international contraband smuggling operation which would ultimately leave thousands of humans dead or ill from such maladies as head-on car crashes involving drunk drivers, and various illnesses including lung cancer, strokes and hepatitis. The graphic pornography contributed much fuel to sharply increased divorce rates, wife battering and pedophile assaults.

Three months after Lenny Kirintelos was convicted in a Manhattan courtroom of being an accessory to attempted first-degree murder, King Yeshua summoned Benny Goldman to His royal office in Jerusalem. He did so by using the secret name He had given Benny on millennial judgment day over 220 years before.

"Son, you have gladdened My heart by your prolific efforts to curb the sinful crime festering in Our peaceful kingdom. I am extremely proud of you."

Benny bowed his head in acknowledgment of his Sovereign Lord's precious accolades. "Thank you, Your Majesty. It was with great joy that I was able to fulfill Your commission by helping to uncover the main perpetrators behind this worldwide criminal operation."

"My child, I must tell you that the evil one is not finished with his attempts to disrupt Millennial Kingdom tranquility by stirring up harmful activities among his human followers. You will find yourself battling these dark forces in the future as well. However for now, I wish to present you with a token of Our gratitude for your tireless and faithful service."

The Reigning Lord of Lords rose up from His desk chair as several Kadoshim walked into the spacious office. Among them were Yochanan, Natan-el and Shaul. Benjamin, Abe and Rebecca Goldman were accompanied by Benny's earthly father, mother and sister. Filing in behind them was Eli Ben David, Micah Kupinski, Giuseppe and Catrina Marino, Carmella Bernstein and Yoseph and Zinel Steinberg. All bowed low before their King before greeting Benny.

After the saints had gathered around the Greek Isle Justice Minister, in walked two other Goldmans—Jonathan's twin brother David and Benny's aborted brother Jesse, who was carrying a medal resting on a small bed of velvet tucked inside a wooden box. Jesse gingerly picked up the medal and handed the box to David. Grinning from ear to ear, he then pinned the medal on Benny's robe. Made of solid gold, the shining award depicted an eagle flying high over a snow-capped mountain peak. All of the assembled onlookers, including the King of Kings, clapped and cheered as a blushing Benny wiped a tear of gratitude from his eye.

"I guess the eagle has landed his prey," the humbled government official said after the applause died down.

"Indeed it has, and it will do so again," King Yeshua replied before joyously embracing His faithful friend.

It was nearly four years after Yourgos Kirintelos survived the Manhattan murder attempt when Donna Svenson finally put her devious plan to become pregnant into action. The renowned American tenor had stopped seeing her for a second time in the months immediately after the drive-by shooting, but the couple resumed their illicit trysts one year before Donna's plan was activated. Alternating between his mansions located near Los Angeles and New York, Yourgos had meantime sincerely repented of his sins and begun to regularly attend Temple services in each of the provincial capital cities. However a visit to his summer home in Naxos had proved once again to be his undoing. He headed there for a break in the middle of a concert tour in Europe and Russia—his first since the failed homicide attempt. Figuring he would probably stop there, Donna was also on the Aegean island and the physical temptation to copulate with her had sadly proved powerful enough to overcome his new spiritual scruples.

Yourgos had absolutely no idea that Donna's subsequent baby was his offspring. However he began to suspect the child might be his son when he learned via a phone conversation with the buoyant new mother that she and Brock Schmidt had named him Chad.

"Donna, don't you know that 'Chad' was the name of my first cousin who arranged for my Aunt Teresa and Uncle Leo to be brutally beheaded by Emperor Andre's goons, along with his sister Angelica? Did you actually intentionally name your boy after that scum ball, and if so, why for goodness sake?"

"Actually, I'm only now recalling you had a cousin with that same name, Yourgos," Donna lied as she gripped her phone more tightly, not expecting his harsh reaction. She had long harbored a quiet admiration for Yourgos' first cousin, thinking it was great that he had resisted all the preaching Christians around him, even if he'd gone too far in arranging for his family to be apprehended by Andre's men. "The name was actually picked out by Brock, who thought it went well with his last name, which I agreed was the case. I think I already told you that even though we're not married—and I don't plan for that to actually ever happen—I concurred that we'd give our baby boy Brock's family name instead of mine, which of course comes from my deceased Swedish husband. It's just a coincidence that 'Chad' was also your cousin's name, Yourgos."

Despite her intentions to the contrary, Donna was eventually forced to wed Brock Schmidt in order to keep her baby. Under the law, a single mother could not raise her child with a live-in male partner if she was not legally married to him. The modest wedding ceremony took place in a Jerusalem hotel with only Sarah, Talel, the Bernstein twins and Bet-el present on the bride's side, and Brock's daughter Tina and her family on the groom's short guest list. Yourgos was not exactly thrilled with the news, but he accepted it was the only way forward if his illicit affair with Donna was to remain undiscovered.

Donna Schmidt was not happy to admit she might have to stay with Brock on a permanent basis, but at least she now had the same last name as her beautiful baby boy, whom she loved enormously. At any rate, she could dump Brock if she wanted to as soon as the child reached adulthood.

Donna carried on with her annual vacations in Summerset, usually bringing Chad with her but sometimes leaving him with Brock or Daniyella when she had a carnal rendezvous scheduled with her famed lover. Brock was happy enough to stay behind since he now had more bills to cover than ever before, and so could not afford to take too much time off. Some summers he would join Donna for part of her yearly vacation, but she always managed to find free time for herself as well.

Yourgos didn't meet Donna Schmidt's son until he was six years old. Running into his curvaceous flame and her boy at the beach, the toned tenor immediately noticed that the lad had identical eye and hair coloring to his own, which was the opposite of Brock's light Scandinavian hues. This prompted the singer to pop the question long been on his mind. "Donna, are you *certain* Chad is Brock's biological son? You and I had sex together some nine months before he was born, even though you say you also did it with Brock a couple weeks before we met up here."

"I'm pretty sure it's Brock's son, Yourgos, but if you want, I can take a swab from Chad's mouth and have it analyzed, and you can do the same; anonymously of course. Then we'll compare the DNA results."

The tests confirmed what Yourgos presumed was probably the case: The fast-growing child, who was always humming songs as he played with his friends outdoors, was indeed a product of his own loins. The megastar had decidedly mixed reactions to this confirmation. On the one hand, he was grateful to have another male child as a sort of emotional replacement for his incarcerated son Lenny. Still, he would not be able to publicly acknowledge that the boy was his own kith and kin lest he ruin his marriage and harm his career. Despite this, Yourgos was warmed by the realization that he and his scrumptious lover had parented a male child together, knowing he could occasionally see the boy on Naxos without raising any suspicion.

Donna and Yourgos jointly decided they would not tell Chad who his biological father was, at least not before he reached adulthood. This would save Brock embarrassment, even though the truck driver was privately questioning if the olive-skinned boy was not actually fathered by Yourgos. More importantly, keeping Chad in the dark would help ensure that the lad did not accidentally spill the news to Francette Kirintelos and other people, or later use the information to blackmail his real father. Although the latter prospect seemed remote, it was certainly the case that his first son had turned into a vicious betrayer, so Yourgos feared it might be something in his genes that Chad might also prove susceptible to.

The only other person who knew the truth about Chad's paternal parentage was Daniyella Bernstein. She was also the only human being who knew for sure that Donna was secretly bedding the recovered crooner once again. Donna Schmidt had confided in her adopted great niece about Chad's actual biological father one afternoon when the boy was about to turn ten. The challenged mother felt she needed to discuss some behavioral problems her son was experiencing, and thought it best if his authentic genetics was part of the conversation. On top of that, Donna knew that the younger sinner looked up to her as a role model. She wanted to boast of the full details of how she had cleverly deceived Brock into thinking he was Chad's father after luring him into the sack.

.....One day when Donna was visiting Daniyella at Sarah's southeast Jerusalem home, the two promiscuous women decided to head out to the backyard to soak up some rays while imbibing the sweet smells of the garden's perfumed flowers. Sarah had gone to the neighborhood market to pick up some fresh vegetables for the evening meal. However, she returned home much earlier than expected since the market was closed due to the sudden death of its Jewish owner that morning. He was electrocuted while rinsing off red potatoes in an industrial sink in his shop. A passing employee accidentally tripped on a power cord, knocking a nearby electric peeler into the standing water.

Sarah's kitchen window was open, letting in warm afternoon air. It also carried in the words being raucously spoken by Donna and Daniyella, seated comfortably on the back porch. Standing quietly near the window, Sarah was not happy when she detected cigarette smoke drifting in as well, but she was too intrigued by the conversation to interrupt the two participants.

"Yourgos told me he is never happier than when he's playing with our son, Daniyella. You should see the two of them together—they are real buddies! Yourgos gets to let Brock do most of the male disciplining while he just enjoys the fun of being a secret dad, even if Chad mainly regards Yourgos as an adult friend who likes to build things with him in the sand. Chad is starting to realize how well-known and wealthy Yourgos is, but I guess he'll refrain from asking for a huge allowance since he doesn't know Yourgos is his real father!"

The two females laughed jovially at Donna's joke as Sarah grimaced next to her granite kitchen counter.

When the chuckles died down, Donna turned serious. "Daniyella, I wanted to discuss something disturbing with you concerning Chad. He's still stealing things. He was recently caught shoplifting small items from a local supermarket. His pocket was full of stolen candy and gum, and even a couple of expensive pens and a lighter. Why in the world would he cop a lighter?"

"Maybe he found your hidden cigarette stash, Donna. I wouldn't worry about his thieving, at least not yet. Lots of young boys do things like that. I mean, despite all the saints floating around everywhere, boys will still be boys. Most don't carry on with things like that after they grow older, Donna, so I'm sure Chad will phase out of it. If I were you, I'd be more worried about girls."

"What do you mean?"

"Well, he's a very *cute* young guy, Donna, and I can tell the girls are already noticing him. Children may not hit puberty until age 18 or so now, but they still have curious imaginations before that. I'd say Chad is a prime candidate for future female affections."

"Oh my! If he gets in trouble, I suppose I'd only be reaping what I sowed, as Sarah would probably put it."

"Indeed I *would* say that," Sarah interjected as she marched out the back door, shocking the two human women who'd been lost in their outdoor discourse."

"How long have you been listening, Sis?"

"Long enough to hear the truth about Chad's father, plus your continuing affair with Yourgos. I'm terribly disappointed in you, Donna. Have you known all along that Chad was not Brock's son?"

In typical fashion, Donna decided to stiffen her upper lip and stand tall in her sin. "Yes, Sarah. I ate some contraceptive rice before sleeping with Brock, but not before I had sex with Yourgos in Cyprus two weeks later. You better not tell Brock anything. It could ruin Yourgos' marriage and harm our boy."

"Donna, you're digging your spiritual grave by carrying on like this. I can't just stand by and watch you literally go to hell."

"Sarah, you know I don't believe in all that stuff. Sure, there is significant supernatural power at work in this era, but that doesn't necessarily emanate from the gang now formally running the show. In fact, I read a pamphlet I found at Yourgos' home, which he said probably belonged to Lenny. It made the case that no such place as hell actually exists, and stated the current regime is suppressing native religions freely practiced in pre-Christian times. It denounced the return to puritan values under Yeshua's administration, saying the ancient wisdom religions promoted natural sex and upheld much saner moral values. I think that pamphlet made some excellent points."

"I'm not going to get into a spiritual discussion with you right now, Donna. I'm too upset with your news about Chad; not to mention the fact that you've been lying bald-faced to me all these years when you insisted you were not having intercourse with Yourgos. Don't worry Donna, I'm not planning to run off and spill the beans to Brock. That would unnecessarily upset him and risk harming your son. Still, I'll have to pray about all of this and decide if any action should be taken. You're aware that your nephew and my earthly husband are government officials in King Yeshua's benevolent millennial administration. I'm not sure that your illegal moral failings should remain hidden from the authorities."

"You'd better not betray me, Sarah, or I'll never forgive you! I want you to mind your own business!"

"It is my business Donna. You're my sister and I'm the Lord's daughter, and these trysts have been taking place in a home partly owned by me in Naxos."

"That's not true, Sarah. We mostly meet in Yourgos' home, even though that became more difficult after he got married. And I got pregnant during our visit to Cyprus. You don't know what you're talking about."

As the verbal jousting intensified, Daniyella became nauseated in her tightening stomach. The tense conversation between the two sisters ended abruptly when she vomited on the nearby lawn.

After several weeks of contemplation and prayer, Sarah decided she must inform Jonathan and Benny about her sister's illicit affair. She would then leave it up to them whether or not to do anything further with the troubling information. Both provincial officials carefully mulled over the situation, concluding any legal action would mainly serve to ruin the lives of several innocent people, especially Donna's son Chad, Francette Esteu-Kirintelos, and Brock Schmidt and his daughter Tina and family.

However, the Greek Isle cabinet ministers decided to directly confront Yourgos Kirintelos with Donna's confirmation that he was carrying on an affair with her. After phoning his private secretary to set up an appointment, they appeared together just outside the Kirintelos mansion near Hollywood California. Yourgos hoped they were coming to share good news concerning Benito Geovinelli, but he worried it might be something negative connected to his longtime lover.

Dressed in a turquoise pants-suite, Francette was standing with her husband in the mansion foyer, waiting to greet the two Goldmans who had just appeared outside the front door. "Shalom Yourgos and Francette, it's really good to see you," said Jonathan as he and Benny filed into the well-appointed foyer. After handshakes and other pleasantries were exchanged, Francette excused herself as Yourgos took his guests to his home office overlooking the backyard swimming pool.

After all three were comfortably seated, Yourgos asked, "So gentlemen, what do you have to share with me today?"

Jonathan spoke up first. "Yourgos, we need to discuss an important personal issue with you. My former sister-in-law and Benny's aunt, Donna Schmidt, has confessed to Sarah that she has been engaged in an on and off sexual affair with you for some time. As you know, this is a very serious violation of Millennial Kingdom law, particularly since you are a public figure and a married man with children. She also revealed that you fathered her son; not her husband Brock."

Yourgos coughed into his hand before responding to the unsettling news. "Well, I suppose it would be useless for me to deny the truth, Jonathan, so I won't attempt to do that. I sincerely tried to end our affair after I recovered from the shooting attack. I really did try, and actually succeeded for awhile. It's just that Donna is so…beautiful, and always very kind to me. My feelings for her only deepened when I found out that Chad was my son. I didn't know that information myself until she told me some years after the boy was born. I know it's an immoral relationship against international law, Jonathan, and I feel genuinely bad for my spouse and for Brock Schmidt."

"We don't plan to inform either your wife or Donna's husband about your affair, Yourgos," stated Benny as he opened up his briefcase and handed some pictures to the singing superstar. "However as you can see, we already possess surveillance photographs that show you kissing and fondling her. If our agents can capture these images, so can the paparazzi, given enough time. You're not only playing with spiritual fire, Yourgos; you're also threatening your marriage and your tremendous career. We may well see this grimy news reach Francette and the entire world. " Benny had already decided not to reveal that the pictures were taken by Alexander Kostantos, who was now quietly working part-time as a security agent with Benny's Justice Ministry.

"Jonathan, Benny, I can only promise that I'll seriously work to break off this affair once and for all. I do care very much for Donna, but I also love the Lord and want to serve Him and His kingdom." Yourgos began weeping before adding, "Please pray for me."

Benny stood up and put his arm around the crying crooner's broad shoulders, recalling with emotion when he and his family first saw him as a helpless baby in Maria Alvarez's arms. "We'll do that right now, Yourgos." The fêted Justice Minister uttered a prayer requesting moral strength for the famous tenor, followed by a similar prayer from Jonathan.

Yourgos Kirintelos did end his torrid affair with Donna Schmidt. Soon after meeting with the Greek Isle officials, he cancelled his annual summer vacation on Naxos to avoid running into his covert lover. However the trysts resumed again sixteen months later when Donna showed up at an outdoor concert the singer was headlining in Cape Town, South Africa. After bribing a hotel front-desk employee to reveal his room number, Donna—decked out in her most revealing dress—gently knocked on his door. It took just one warm embrace to rekindle the passionate fire in Yourgos' soul which had long burned like a blazing torch for the alluring woman.

Like his brother Lenny, Chad morphed into a highly-praised athlete during his teen years. Becoming soundly muscular like his father, he possessed keen eye and hand coordination and a great throwing arm which made him an award winner in several sports. He was also a star member of his Jerusalem high school's swimming team, which won the Israeli championship during his senior year. However like his rebellious mother, Chad was hooked on illegal nicotine cigarettes. Similar to both of his biological parents, he also had trouble keeping his zipper closed after he began to develop adult male capabilities during his senior year.

Chad found out that his real last name should be Kirintelos soon after he began studying business administration at Hebrew University in the year 239 DL. His mother's personal computer was running slowly, prompting her to request he take a look at it. While doing so, he inadvertently noticed an incoming email message from Yourgos. It began with the salutation, "Hello Sweetheart." Chad only needed to quickly scan the rest of the note to confirm it was a love letter. He confronted his mother with the revelation, and she admitted she was involved with Yourgos and that Chad was their biological son. Donna quickly added she was planning to reveal the full story after Chad graduated from university, letting him do whatever he liked with the previously-veiled information.

Although Chad enjoyed hanging out with Brock Schmidt, the news that the wildly wealthy superstar was his biological father sent goose bumps up his young spine. Now he understood more clearly why he eagerly looked forward every summer to spending as much time as possible with the talented tenor. He would surely inherit a fortune from his actual father, and maybe in the meantime land lucrative employment with his airline company, just like his much older half-brother Lenny had done.

Two months after perusing the email love note, Chad traveled alone to Naxos without his mother's awareness. He'd learned from his cousin Benny that Yourgos was expected to visit the Greek island with his wife Francette and their two grown daughters.

As he'd done many times before, the young Israeli eagerly rang the Kirintelos doorbell and was quickly let in. After greeting the entire surprised family, he asked Yourgos if he wanted to toss around a football with him on the beach. As they descended by foot to the sea, Chad indirectly revealed that he'd recently learned who his real father was.

"Yourgos, I've always liked you a lot. You were really kind to me as a boy; taking time to play with me even when I was being a bit obnoxious. I...love you...dad." Chad choked up as he embraced his biological father.

"How did you find out, son?"

"I saw a mushy email to mom from you. I'm not unhappy to learn the truth though—in fact, just the opposite. I've always really enjoyed spending time with you, Yourgos, frankly even more than with Brock. I don't plan to say anything to him by the way, at least not for the time being. He really loves mom and takes good care of her, so it just wouldn't be fair."

This time, Yourgos initiated a bear hug before revealing his thoughts. "I think that's a wise approach, Chad. My wife would go ballistic if she knew the whole story. I do care for her very much, but I love your mother quite deeply as well. And I'm, well, very pleased that I have another son; and one who is so smart and such a good athlete. You are a real hustler, you are!"

Chad beamed with pride over his newfound father's affirming comments. "I guess the fact that I can sing like a robin is no coincidence, huh Yourgos?"

"I guess not, Chad. I love you son, and you can call me dad if you want. I like the sound of that word."

Donna was delighted when Chad shared details of his conversation with her longtime lover. However she cautioned him not to let the cat out of the bag, lest such action smother his natural father's marriage and career.

The handsome young Israeli tried hard to keep the sizzling news of his venerable ancestry to himself, but he simply could not resist blabbing out loud when his famous father appeared on the common dorm television set one winter evening during his junior year at Hebrew University.

"Hey, that's my dad!" he blurted out when the tenor strode out on a London stage to perform some of his latest songs. Chad's free-flowing words were lubricated by the bottle of wine he was sharing with two male student friends.

"So that's your old man, Chadders? Did I tell you the Pope is my papa?" Dan sat back and squealed at his own witty comment.

"There's *no longer* a pope, you moron," Yuval interjected.

"Hey guys, I'm quite serious. Yourgos Kirintelos is my actual big daddy. I discovered a steamy email from him to my mom a couple years ago, and then she confessed he'd actually fathered me, not my supposed dad Brock. I'm gonna inherit a mint some day boys, so you can begin sucking up to me right away."

The tantalizing news spread like wildfire all over campus. Although not exactly a member of their generation, the American crooner was still very popular with youthful audiences, especially those of the female persuasion. Whenever Yourgos did his signature dance while coming on stage, the women went wild, both young and old. He had also acquired lots of new young fans eight years before when he released a collection of heavily-orchestrated pop songs featuring his sonorous voice. For all those reasons and more, the contention that the superstar had a son attending Hebrew University was just too juicy for containment. It was not long before the tabloid press—much tamer than in the previous era, but still quite popular with many human readers—picked up on the scandalous story. The cat was well and truly thrust out of its bag.

Francette Esteu-Kirintelos filed for divorce five weeks after the news circulated around the world. She had immediately cornered her wayward husband in their Manhattan townhouse, where Yourgos reluctantly confirmed the mushrooming media reports. Although Brock Schmidt felt humiliated by the unwanted attention, he decided to stay married to Donna. After all, they were not yet hitched when the indiscretion with the popular American singer and businessman took place. Brock didn't realize that Donna still bedded down with Yourgos whenever possible, and she did not volunteer that pertinent information to him.

Now that the truth was out in the open, Yourgos informed Chad that he'd be quite elated if the young man would agree to join his Pan World Airways corporate staff after he graduated from university. The athletic young man had no problem agreeing to this delicious proposal, expecting the position to come with a substantial annual salary and many perks. Two years later, he received another offer from a former PWA big wig that would alter millennial history.

TWENTY

FAMILY TIES

As the centuries rolled on, the world continued to enjoy the rich blessings of tranquil millennial life. No longer were wars, political revolts or coups occurring anywhere on earth. With very few physical and mental illnesses plaguing humanity, health concerns were hardly a factor in hampering world population growth. After the contraband smuggling operations were finally halted, crime rates dropped dramatically everywhere. There were no famines, droughts, floods, earthquakes or hurricanes anywhere on earth. Killer lightning bolts and tornados were likewise unheard of. Abundant food and full employment helped improve the stability of marriages around the globe, with pocketbook issues no longer a major factor contributing to family breakdowns.

Vast improvements in traffic safety made vehicular travel safer than ever. A new light-weight plastic material produced by Kadoshim scientists brought dramatic benefits to humanity. Called Trantium, the tough but pliable material was used mainly to build cars, trucks, trains and aircraft. With a cellular structure that was fluid in nature, the revolutionary material was nevertheless as durable as steel, yet far more pliant. It vastly reduced the jarring impacts of crashes, which helped cut the death rates to nearly zero on all roads, rail lines and in the air. Home and office fires still occasionally took some lives, but new building materials containing natural fire retardants derived from the bark of the Trees of Life greatly reduced the frequency and severity of such conflagrations. Forest fires were unheard of since the nightly global rains kept all of earth's vegetation well watered and healthy.

Despite the idyllic conditions prevailing everywhere on earth, illegal drug use gradually began to increase once again, beginning in the fourth century. The same was the case with bootleg alcohol consumption. Banned pornographic discs and magazines were also circulating around the world once more, especially in the big cities which had surpassed the residential numbers reached in the final decades of the previous era. Unlike the days when Lenny Kirintelos was swamping the world with illegal items via his father's large fleet of aircraft, most of the prohibited goods were coming from local sources all over the planet, and therefore more difficult to detect and put a halt to.

As was the case with his half-brother before him, Chad—who had legally adopted his biological father's famous last name, Kirintelos—played a pivotal, if totally disguised, role in the escalating crime rate. Learning from Lenny's mistakes, Chad made sure his illegal activities were extremely hard to uncover. Instead of producing drugs, nicotine cigarettes, hard liquor and pornography in central warehouses as was done by his much older sibling and Benito Geovinelli, the banned goods were made in small 'cottage industry' settings mostly located on rural farms and other remote locations. The contraband items were then trucked a little bit at a time into urban areas, hidden in false floors built into the vehicles. Most of the truck drivers had no idea they were carrying forbidden cargo, which was secretly unloaded in the middle of the night by highly-paid workers who knew the goods they were handling were questionable items, but nothing more than that. By keeping almost everyone involved in the dark, the international leaders of the new smuggling operation were able to conceal much of their criminal activity. This produced a constant stream of proscribed items entering the black market, but the volume was about half what it had been under Lenny's control.

As earth's human population rose to nearly four billion souls, kingdom officials in Jerusalem called together all 1,000 provincial Justice Ministers for a special meeting in the capital city. The year was 468 DL. King Yeshua had requested that the slow, but steadily climbing worldwide crime rate be reduced if possible before the year 500, when grand, mid-millennial celebrations were scheduled to take place in Jerusalem and many other locations all over the teeming world.

Benny Goldman was standing in a long line of officials picking up name tags at the entrance to the large public auditorium in the basement of Prince David's Jerusalem palace. He had lost his maternal grandfather, Ariel Hazan, nearly 200 years before. Although the Greek Isle Justice Minister was an ever-living saint, his remaining small human family was still very important to him. While he'd long avoided interacting very much with his errant Aunt Donna, he always looked forward to seeing his cousin Susan Feingold and her husband Aaron and their four children, plus Dalya Bernstein who had married Benny's Greek surrogate son, Nikos with whom she produced seven children.

Benny had especially enjoyed getting to know Donna's son Chad, particularly after the young man reached a human age that mirrored the unchanging youth Benny and all the Kadoshim always displayed. Nearly equal in height to Benny and with a similar muscular physique, Chad would periodically join his cousin and Micah Kupinski for vigorous swims and underwater explorations (although unlike the saints, Chad needed to come up often for air) at the private beach near the government mansion on Naxos. The two cousins also enjoyed shooting hoops together every summer on a small basketball court situated next to the mansion. Chad would frequently invite Benny to sail with him on his father's expensive yacht, along with Micah and other members of the Goldman family living on or visiting Naxos.

The prospect that his earthly mother's nephew was clandestinely behind the new wave of worldwide corruption obviously occurred to the Justice Minister, but he quickly dismissed it. Lighting rarely strikes twice in the same place, he assured himself. Having occasionally visited his half-brother Lenny in a New York provincial security prison, Benny assumed Chad knew firsthand the substantial cost he would be forced to pay if he too got involved with the mafia underworld which sadly still thrived in many major cities.

Despite his conviction that Chad Kirintelos was probably not involved in the new crime wave sweeping the earth, Benny recruited

Alexander Kostantos to keep his eyes open for any suspicious activity going on in the Kirintelos mansion in Summerset. Still working part-time for Yourgos, the Greek maintenance man cum security agent didn't detect anything out of the ordinary at the plush vacation home. Kostantos did report that the American tenor was still arranging occasional trysts on his estate with his covert lover, Donna Schmidt. However he also noted their son Chad, who married a wonderful woman named Joanna in 326 DL, seemed to be completely faithful to his wife despite his pre-marital indiscretions. Although not religiously observant, Chad had at least agreed to Benny's suggestion to send his three children to a Bible camp run by a Greek Christian ministry on the nearby island of Mykonos. The lone male and two female siblings had learned much about the Lord and the sacred scriptures at the month-long camps, which they attended every summer during their childhood years.

The international gathering of Justice Ministers opened in Jerusalem with a passionate time of praise and worship led by two saints possessing stellar singing voices. Like all of the sanctified Kadoshim enjoying eternal life in the Master's sovereign kingdom, the government officials could all carry a tune. Still, some saints were granted singing voices that outshone the rest of the redeemed. Such was the case with the two priestly worship leaders, Jesse and David Goldman.

After the stirring praise and worship came to an end, Prince David addressed the assembled provincial government officials, welcoming them to his palatial home in Jerusalem. He congratulated them for their excellent performances around the world, noting that most human beings were law-abiding people who loved their Sovereign King and gladly obeyed His commands. However the Israeli governor added it was fairly inevitable crime would continue to increase since earth's expanding population was projected to at least double before the Rock of Ages' millennial reign gave way to the prophesied new heaven and earth in just over 500 years time.

Following the eloquent speech delivered by Israel's ancient revered monarch, several cabinet ministers gave updates on the growing crime waves in their regions. Among them was Benny

Goldman, who reviewed the situation in southeast Europe. He noted that regional Justice Ministers met together every few months to keep abreast of ongoing developments in neighboring provinces. Benny then spoke of a recent discovery that was very disturbing to him and his provincial government colleagues.

"Over the past year, we were informed by several human sources that small gatherings of young people were taking place in secret locations throughout our sprawling island province. The participants are mostly males in their teens and twenties, but some young women are involved as well. We learned these humans are assembling for the purpose of reestablishing the Android youth gangs that were prevalent in the final years of the previous age. Some of you've told me the exact same thing is happening in your provinces. I for one don't believe that this disturbing development in many locations can be considered merely a coincidence. As most of you already know, we've uncovered substantial evidence that someone in America is spurring this movement on, but we're not yet certain exactly who is behind it."

In fact, the new rebellious Android youth movement was largely sponsored by none other than Chad Kirintelos. He had become fascinated over the years by the short life of his family namesake, Chad Scarcelli, who was an active Android member and local gang leader in western Connecticut. He quizzed his great aunt Teresa and her earthly husband Leo for many hours about the boy's intriguing short life, maintaining he merely wanted to know more about his pre-millennial family history. He also attempted to speak at length to Chad's sister Angelica, but she refused to talk about her long-deceased brother. However her parents were quite willing to discuss their earthly son's wicked teenage life with the prominent business executive, who had been appointed CEO of Pan World Airlines in the year 412.

Donna Schmidt's successful son was actually possessed by several powerful demons who'd also once camped in Chad Scarcelli's body. They entered their new human residence one evening in 423 DL. Chad had gone up to his father's mountain retreat on the island of Naxos for a special party organized long distance by his imprisoned half-brother Lenny. It was a similar orgy to the one discovered many years before by Alexander Kostantos. This time, instead of a demonic apparition portraying the Greek god Zeus, the demon took the naked form of Emperor Andre. Lust oozed out of its fiery eyes as the humans on the carpeted floor engaged in their reprehensible activity.

Although Chad Kirintelos had been completely faithful to his lovely wife—who came from a wealthy family living in a splendid seaside mansion on Long Island—the strong demonic influence he encountered at his father's retreat was sufficient to cause him to tear off his clothes and join the illicit action. From that moment on, Donna's son became a surreptitious devotee of the divinely imprisoned Antichrist, wanting to spread his nefarious cult whenever and wherever he could. He set up secret printing presses that began mass production of an autobiographical book called *My Journey to Glory* which Andre had authored a few years before he was crowned emperor of the world toward the end of the previous era. Banned videos of the Man of Sin were also reproduced at one of Chad's contraband factories located in a thick jungle in northern Brazil. One of the videos clearly showed Andre copulating with three beautiful women and a handsome young Asian man.

The illegal videos and books were loaded onto cruise ships at several ports around the globe. The large ocean-going vessels were owned by Chad. He'd purchased the Florida-based *Coconut Cruise Lines* in order to provide an inconspicuous cover for his international smuggling operation. Young men loyal to Andre's memory packed the illegal products at subterranean plants surreptitiously located in several provinces around the world. International Android gang leaders then distributed the books and videos in their local provinces, making sure very young people in particular were provided the banned materials free of charge. Although many refused to read Andre's hyped-up autobiography or watch the videos featuring his immoral antics, others latched onto them like they were chocolate Mars bars.

As soon as any human being fell prostrate before an object or video featuring Andre's idolatrous image—either literally or spiritually—they were instantly possessed by powerful demons who rapidly took control of their lives, as had occurred with Chad. Although the numbers in relative terms were initially rather small, this demonic activity had an immediate impact upon human society. Violence and drug abuse escalated precipitously, especially in private homes and places where illicit drinking parties and orgies were held. In some of the larger cities, the demons daringly propelled their possessed slaves to go out in public with their despicable activities in a defiant attempt to provoke millennial security forces into some sort of counteraction. They realized that media coverage of their antics would in turn bring additional recruits into Andre's growing fan base, stimulating banned emperor worship around the world.

Benny Goldman departed the Jerusalem Justice Minister's conference with renewed determination to fight the growing devilish activity with all the appropriate tools in his provincial government arsenal. The same was true with the other officials who attended the special parley. However Benny had one connection none of the other ministers possessed—a personal relationship with Lenny Kirintelos, the former worldwide crime boss, plus a close-family tie to his younger half-brother Chad.

Despite his initial conviction that Chad was probably not behind the illegal activity, the respected Greek Isle Justice Minister and other Kingdom officials worldwide were increasingly detecting circumstantial, yet substantial evidence that Benny's cousin was at least marginally linked to the growing crime spree, if not helping to spread the satanic worship of the world's fallen emperor. The damning evidence included intercepted phone calls between the PWA executive officer and known mafia bosses in several locations, including Hong Kong (which had once again become the economic capital of Southeast Asia), Buenos Aires, Los Angeles and Berlin. Although the conversations were apparently conducted in some sort of pre-arranged code, the fact that they'd taken place at all was very revealing to kingdom investigators.

So far, there was only one piece of tangible evidence that Donna's only son might be helping to promote banned emperor worship all over the planet. It was accidentally discovered by Alexander Kostantos one warm summer afternoon in the year 482 as he was fixing a malfunctioning electrical socket in the Kirintelos storage room in Summerset. Perched on a small table in a dimly lit corner of the large basement room was an object covered in blue felt cloth. Standing about three feet high, it instantly sparked the maintenance man's curiosity. The object turned out to be a forbidden golden statue of the deposed world ruler. As with most of Andre's many likenesses, the statue displayed him totally nude.

When the part-time security agent uncovered the statue, a searing hissing sound rushed forth from its elongated mouth, prompting Kostantos to cover his ears. After a report of the discovery was made to Benny, the Justice Minister reluctantly decided he had no choice but to order miniscule surveillance cameras surreptitiously installed in several rooms in the Kirintelos home. The videos later revealed that Chad was indeed a devotee of Andre's who periodically moved the statue to his bed chamber and fell to his knees in demented worship before it. On other occasions, the cameras also confirmed that Donna was still engaging in occasional trysts with Chad's famous musical father, despite the fact that the aging woman's internal biological clock revealed she was now close to 70 years old in previous-era terms.

With just 18 years remaining until special celebrations were to be held worldwide to mark the mid-way anniversary of King Yeshua's magnificent millennial rule, Benny decided he'd acquired enough evidence to confront his wayward first cousin. He only informed three other saints what he was about to do: his beloved spiritual mentor Yochanan, plus Sarah and Jonathan Goldman. With Benny's approval, Jonathan then informed Eli Ben David, who promised to keep the information under high wraps.

While Jonathan and Eli monitored the conversation via a hidden microphone implanted in Benny's Naxos office, the Justice Minister began his gentle interrogation.

"Thanks for taking time out from your summer vacation to meet with me, Chad."

"No problem, cousin. I'm always glad to chat with you, as you know. What's on your mind today, Benny?"

"I'm afraid it's not going to be the most pleasant conversation we've ever had, Chad. I've got some very serious issues to discuss with you."

The youthful American CEO stiffened his spine as he absorbed his saintly relative's ominous remark. However he still wore his usual poker face, acquired over many years of skillful lying to most of his family and friends about the darker side of his human nature. "Well, let's get to it then so I can head off for a sunset cruise on dad's yacht. Are you free to come along?"

"No, I have important work to complete before this evening, Chad, but thanks for the offer. You know I always enjoy sailing with you on the crystal blue Aegean Sea."

Although his eternal body no longer secreted mucus, Benny slowly made a sound like he was clearing his throat as he prepared to deliver his strategic blow. "Chad, you're the only son of my mother's only sister; and I've kept that fact very much in mind as I've investigated the matter I need to discuss with you today. My Justice Ministry has detected you engaging in outlawed emperor worship in your father's home here on Naxos. On top of that, reports coming in to us from other areas of the Millennial Kingdom reveal that you've been linked to various crime bosses who are both promoting the distribution of banned items like bootleg alcohol and illegal drugs, as your incarcerated half-brother before you was doing, along with facilitating forbidden emperor worship. What do you have to say for yourself?"

The still athletic airline executive scratched the two day growth on his chin as he quickly organized his defense game plan. "Well Benny, my attorneys and I would need to examine the specifics about these serious charges before I could officially comment on them, but I can tell you outright that they're false. As you know, I've made many enemies over the years due to my prominent position in the international business community, and I suspect some of them are concocting these allegations in a deliberate attempt to harm me and my reputation. Frankly, as your first cousin, I'm shocked and saddened you'd even begin to entertain them."

Benny felt a tinge of pain pierce his heavenly heart as he reluctantly carried on with his extremely difficult task. "I'm really sorry to say this to my own relative, Chad, but these are not just vague allegations. In relation to the banned emperor worship charges, my office possesses solid photographic evidence that you've privately engaged in such banned activity in your father's Summerset home; and that on a regular basis. We also have surveillance tape clearly showing the same thing occurring in other locations around the world, especially in your homes in the Bahamas, Guadalajara and in the South Pacific. In every place, other people have occasionally joined in with you, including a few well-known shady characters. Among them are several leading crime syndicate figures, who we also know you've been in regular phone contact with over the past few decades. And even though you seem to speak to them in some sort of code, just the fact you're communicating with them at all is quite damning, as you'll surely acknowledge. At any rate, we recently cracked that code, giving us much more evidence that you're engaged in the same unlawful contraband smuggling activity that Lenny pioneered."

Chad Kirintelos stiffened his back and leaned forward toward his lifelong cousin and friend. "I acknowledge *nothing*, Benny, and I'm shocked and insulted you'd bring me in here today to bring up such false allegations to my face. Again, I have many enemies who are out to destroy me, due to no fault of my own. I strongly suspect you've been duped by some of them, and I'm extremely disappointed you'd allow yourself to be taken in by my envious opponents."

"I only wish that were so, Cousin Chad. It's very painful for me to bring up such grave accusations before you today. However on the orders of King Yeshua's millennial government, I need to serve you with this inquest paper. It's a formal notification that you're under investigation into the serious legal allegations I've just spelled out to you."

Benny noticed that his relative's expression turned malevolent when he heard the Name above all names. "I'm not expecting you to fully answer the charges at this moment, Chad, realizing you have a slew of lawyers who can keep this thing tied up for some time. Still, we're certain of the veracity of these allegations, and therefore you are officially served notice of them today." With a speck of a tear forming in his left eye, Benny leaned over his desk and handed a sealed envelope to his wayward aunt's only offspring, who accepted it with a grimace. In an office down the hall, Jonathan Goldman began to openly weep as his longtime buddy Eli reached out his arm to comfort him.

Donna Hazan-Svenson-Schmidt exploded in anger when she learned that her own nephew had served legal notice of serious criminal charges on her adorable son. She immediately phoned Sarah and demanded the action be halted forthwith, as if the Jerusalem-based medical official could possibly arrange this even if she wanted to.

"Sarah, I assume by now you've heard what went down between Benny and Chad on Naxos earlier this week? My son is supposed to be on a relaxing vacation with his wife and some of his grandkids there, but instead Benny is acting just like the other moral Gestapo thought police so prominent in your worldwide 'saintly millennial reign.' Well, I for one will *not* just sit back and take this in silence! I *demand* an apology from Benny, and the immediate withdrawal of these ridiculous charges leveled against my baby boy."

"Calm down, Donna. First of all, Chad is hardly a child anymore…he's a corporate executive with one of the world's largest and most important airline carriers. And as you'll clearly recall, very similar charges were brought up in the past against the former Pan World CEO, Chad's half-brother Lenny, and these later proved in a court of law to be undeniably valid. Of course, I've not seen the latest evidence myself, but I understand from both Benny and Jonathan that the charges are absolutely airtight; to everyone's chagrin I might add. No one's been any more saddened by this than I am, Donna, at least not until you and Chad learned about the matter. I feel very bad for Yourgos as well; and naturally for Chad's fine wife Joanna and family. I assume they all know about this serious situation by now?"

"How would I know what Yourgos knows or doesn't know?" replied Donna tersely, carrying on with her silly charade that she was not in regular contact with her centuries-old lover despite the fact that the entire Goldman family and the singer's tabloid-reading international fans knew of this sordid reality. Indeed, legal charges were even then being prepared against the still-married mother herself, based upon recently uncovered concrete evidence of her ongoing illicit affair with the divorced superstar tenor, collected via the surveillance cameras installed in the Kirintelos vacation home.

"Whatever the case, Donna, I truly am sorry you have to go through this, and even more so that Yourgos has to endure it for a second time in his human life. You know, I was present when he was reunited as a baby with his remaining family at the orphanage in New Jersey, and I've had a special affection for him ever since, despite his terrible entanglement with you. Plus you're my sister, and Chad is my only nephew, and I'm just very…very…" Sarah's voice trailed off as her tender heart became overwhelmed by emotion. Her subsequent weeping was quite audible over the phone.

Donna said nothing as she also descended into the deep valley of tears. The two siblings—vastly different in so many ways yet still life-long friends—wept together miles apart for several minutes before Sarah spoke up again. "Donna, there is *no other way* forward but to surrender your lives to the Lord. Chad knows the truth about our Jewish Messiah as much as anyone does; and that is certainly the case with you too. Yeshua is Lord of Lord and King of Kings, and His benevolent reign will endure forever. He is the way, the truth and the life, and no one comes to the Heavenly Father and receives eternal life in any other manner apart from Him. As I've done for many moons now, I only hope and pray that you and Chad will act upon this fact…before it's too late."

For once, Donna did not sarcastically counter Sarah's heartfelt pleadings. Her mind was too filled with grief to respond at all. Still, she was at least listening to her redeemed sister, and even this was a minor breakthrough.

Yourgos Kirintelos was upset beyond words to learn yet another son of his had fallen into the devil's despicable trap in such a gross and harmful manner. Nearing the equivalent of the biological age of 60 in the previous era, he was finally ready to fully surrender his soiled soul to the Lord of Life, and to break off once and for all his covert affair with Donna Schmidt. He immediately phoned his beloved childhood caregiver in New York, Maria Alvarez, now an elderly woman, and confessed his many sins to her as she quietly wept tears of profound joy. The humble bondservant of her Lord was celebrating in her spirit that the daily intercessory prayers she'd faithfully uttered for her surrogate son over so many centuries were finally being answered.

Next Yourgos called his wayward son Chad—whose human existence sprang forth from his immoral love affair with an alluring woman not his lawful wife.

"Chad, I couldn't believe the news I heard about you from your mother today. Is it true? Did you actually follow so closely in your brother's wretched footsteps? And are you spreading Andre's nefarious cult? I'm frankly appalled if that's the case, even though I do love you very much, son."

The smug CEO remained defiant, insisting he was not guilty of any of the infractions Benny served him on behalf of the royal government. "I did attend a party in Paris a few years ago where some of the guests were engaged in Andre worship, dad, but I've never done that myself."

"If so Chad, why did you keep a statue of that disgusting world ruler in my basement storage compartment...I came upon it myself a few years back, so I know for a fact it was there before you apparently removed it."

"Oh come on dad! I did acquire one of those antique relics from the past era, but only as a piece of art, which you know I love...I was not planning to prostrate myself before some lifeless statue, man. I mean, give me a break...I'm the CEO of your ever- expanding world-wide airline company; not some out of work idiot with nothing better to do than fall down before some dumb idol."

"What about the other charges, which I consider far more serious: That you've been regularly communicating in code with known drug smugglers and the like, and possibly even financing their underworld operations. That is of course what sent your brother Lenny to prison, as you well know."

"It may have been Lenny's gig dad, but it's definitely not mine. I want to see their supposed 'airtight charges' before I say too much more, but if I've spoken with anyone on their blacklist it was not for the purpose of contraband smuggling or the like. We handle all sorts of cargo, as you know, and I talk to hundreds of people each week." Chad loosened his turquoise tie and undid the top button on his silk shirt. "Dad, I'm an important business leader with many contacts all over the world. This charge of some hidden illegal activity is just pure fantasy on the government's part. Let them prove it in a court of law before you get so worked up."

"Of course I love and respect you Chad, but these allegations were passed on to you by your own first cousin, who's also known and loved you since you were born. Do you really think an official as well-regarded as Benny is would participate in such action if he was not completely convinced the prosecutors have an ironclad case against you?"

"I was as shocked as anyone that my own flesh and blood, so to speak, would have a hand in this madness, dad, but that's the sad reality. I'm not sure who got to Benny, but I reminded him that I have many enemies out to get me due to my senior business position and wealth, which I of course have you to thank for, and I do thank you dad. Please just give me the benefit of the doubt."

"For sure I'm willing and able to do that, Chad. Still, that doesn't reduce my concern for you, nor lessen my conviction that the government would *not* have issued such charges against you unless there was something pretty solid to base them on. Anyway, I want to talk to you about something else, son. I've recently totally repented of my many sins against the Lord and against my own body, against your mother, and my children and extended family as well. I need to ask *your* forgiveness for giving you such a poor example of a father, even if you didn't know I was your biological father until you were a young adult." Yourgos wiped a tear from his left cheek as he continued to acknowledge his serious transgressions. "Despite warnings from many people, including Benny, I sinned grievously with your mother over many centuries, and I'm so very ashamed of that fact now. I've asked the Lord to forgive me and restore me, and to accept me into His eternal kingdom. I hope you'll do the same one day soon, Chad. In fact, today is an acceptable time to change direction."

Despite wanting to please his doting father, Chad nearly ended the call when Yourgos began speaking about the Lord. The potent demons possessing his body were loath to hear such talk, speaking into his mind that he should slam his cellphone shut at once. However Chad successfully resisted this furious 'command' because he knew his renowned father had the very down to earth power to help make or break his legal resistance to the criminal charges filed against him.

"I, um, don't really want to talk about these things now, dad. I have lots on my mind, but we can delve into this...topic some other time. I've really got to run. Joanna's coming back with our chef from the grocery store any minute and your grandson Matthew and his kids are coming over for dinner in a little while. I have to get busy and finish some business items on my computer before they arrive, dad. Talk to you later."

With that, the sincere, almost desperate attempt by Yourgos Kirintelos to reach his son with the saving gospel of salvation had come to an end, at least for the moment. "Like mother, like son," the aging singer muttered under his breath as he put his phone down while adding a little more loudly, "I guess there's really nothing else I can do but pray."

Chad Kirintelos was subsequently convicted of engaging in illegal emperor worship and cavorting with known criminal elements, several of them already imprisoned due to illegal smuggling operations and other crimes. However Kingdom prosecutors were not able to adequately prove that the airline CEO—who took a leave of absence from work before his trial began in a courtroom in Geneva—was directly involved in an international contraband network dispersing banned items. Chad had learned from his much older half-brother's many mistakes, covering his tracks like a cat pawing dirt over its smelly excrement. He was sentenced to 30 years in jail and fined 300,000 shekels.

The business executive naturally lost his position with Pan World Airways, but since he'd already amassed a huge fortune, this penalty hardly fazed him. He would be released from incarceration in a relatively short time in millennial terms, and meantime he could still run his underground operations with the aid of the many Android devotees shut up with him in his high security prison in the province of

New York City. Lenny Kirintelos was also still behind bars there, but in a separate wing. The two were granted visiting privileges every other month, which only served to increase Chad's determination to carry on with his role model's plan to flood humanity with banned materials, drugs and hard liquor that would eventually lead to a worldwide rebellion designed by Lucifer to extinguish King Yeshua's benevolent millennial rule.

TWENTY-ONE

SATAN UNLEASHED

Donna Hazan-Svenson-Schmidt drew her last breath in the spring of 749 DL. On her deathbed in Sarah Goldman's Jerusalem home, the now frail woman finally surrendered her sordid life to the beautiful Rose of Sharon. With her wrinkled human sister now looking like her grandmother, Sarah led Donna in a prayer of repentance that contained several specific references to her atrocious sins. Bending down to embrace her ailing sibling, who had developed pneumonia one week before, Sarah cried copious tears of joy over Donna's much-belated salvation. With Sarah, Talel and Bet-el surrounding her bed, the new saint departed this earth for the halls of glory just eighteen days later.

The fact that the Good Shepherd could pardon such a stubborn, heinous sinner—in like manner to the Apostle Shaul—had an immediate positive impact on Donna's longtime friend and admirer, Daniyella Bernstein. The aging twin subsequently accepted Yeshua as her Lord and Savior, immediately giving up her cigarette smoking habit as she had previously done with her occasional romps with men. After securing her eternal salvation, Daniyella moved back into Sarah's home, nesting in Donna's redecorated room.

The departed mother was able to see her wayward son just ten days before she passed away. Realizing that Donna was ill and becoming quite feeble, Chad Kirintelos had flown to Israel to visit her, utilizing one of the free tickets he was entitled to as a former PWA chief executive officer. Out of prison for over a century, the man appeared to be around 65 years old in pre-millennial human terms. Chad still carried on with his evil activities, but with such guarded subtleness that no one was able to detect a thing.

Donna, who had resisted the Lord for so long, tried desperately to convince her wayward son to accept the unmerited gift of eternal life offered to him by the merciful Lamb of God. However as soon as she brought up the sensitive topic, the demons that possessed Chad's slowly decaying body and mind ordered him to strangle her, but this time he did not obey them. Instead, he sternly informed his dying mother that he was not at all interested in worshipping Israel's Risen Messiah and did not wish to discuss the matter any further.

Chad's biological father perished at sea 35 years after his longtime lover's departure. Too old to adequately handle his small sailboat, Yourgos Kirintelos had nevertheless taken it out late one morning from the small Summerset marina with no one accompanying him. When the light afternoon breeze picked up speed, the veteran sailor had trouble keeping on course, eventually heading in the opposite direction of Naxos. Two days later the wreckage of his sailboat was located around several protrusive rocks at the entrance to a small bay on the northern shore of the island of Ios, south of Naxos. Hungry and tired, the world-renowned tenor had suffered a massive heart attack as he attempted to swim to the beach. As he was flailing in the warm water, the talented singer's last thoughts had suddenly turned tranquil as he pictured Maria Alvarez holding in her arms a young lad who was feeling extra exuberant about being alive—this time forevermore.

With just eight decades remaining before the Lord's preordained thousand year reign on earth would officially come to an end, Yourgos' younger son received his final marching orders from the wicked demons that infested him. Chad Kirintelos was to come out publicly in support of Emperor André worship, making his international pitch via laser disc. Before doing so, he would take shelter in an underground bunker located in the African province of Chad—an almost comical choice that delighted his personal demons. Although King Yeshua knew exactly where the depraved sinner was hiding in the landlocked province located due south of Libya, He did not reveal this information to anyone lest it foil the foreordained final rebellion against His benevolent rule.

Now becoming quite elderly himself, Chad sported a scraggly gray beard as he carefully laid out the supposed "logical reasons" for believing that Andre was truly divine, and therefore worthy of human worship. In his well-honed sales pitch, the former airline CEO predicted that the European demigod would soon "rise from the dead" and "lead the world in a triumphant final battle" against the Rock of Ages and his cohorts. He called upon everyone on earth, especially young people, to rally to his side. The former inmate also advocated acts of civil disobedience all over the planet, along with the legalization of banned drugs and the removal of what he termed "outdated laws" that, he averred, unnecessarily restricted human freedoms. The final scene on the vile disc showed Donna's son leading a group of young women and men in subservient prostration before Andre's glowing image. All were completely naked except for Chad, who was wearing a loose-fitting black robe over his slightly plump hairy body.

The deleterious disc rounded the world like a hurricane speeding over balmy ocean water. Android youth gangs nearly doubled in size within the space of just a few months as bootleg copies of his lying discourse multiplied everywhere. In his office on the island of Naxos, Benny Goldman watched a copy of his cousin's egregious presentation in the presence of the other Greek Isles cabinet ministers, who were all appalled by what they heard. His close friend Micah Kupinski jumped up from his seat and switched off the television set just as the disgusting emperor worship scene was beginning to unfold.

Although all understood that the prophesied final revolt against the loving Lily of the Valley had to be led by someone, the entire Goldman family was devastated by their relative's blatant admission that he was a devil worshiper, and even more so the ugly realization that he was the leading public advocate of the same. Still, no one was more upset than the hard-working Justice Minister, who had devoted untold hours trying to suppress the burgeoning tide of evil being openly embraced by millions of deceived human beings, especially younger people. Benny simply could not fathom the fact that the man leading the ultimate worldwide rebellion against the Master of the

Universe was none other than his mother's only nephew. His own flesh
and blood, so to speak, was the new False Prophet leading many on
earth straight over the cliff to eternal damnation. This reality was just
too much for the tender saint to bear.

In an attempt to help alleviate some of the intense pain and
sorrow he felt concerning his fallen cousin, Benny decided to ask for a
special audience with King Yeshua. He made the request via his
trusted spiritual mentor, Yochanan the Apostle, whom he also invited
to the session. The meeting took place in the Messiah's private office
on the top floor of His exquisite Jerusalem palace. The large French
doors behind the Lord's desk had been flung wide open, letting in the
sweet afternoon scent of miniature apple, almond and orange tree
flowers blossoming outside on the spacious balcony.

The Wonderful Counselor greeted the humble saint with a holy
kiss, as He did Yochanan. The two welcome visitors sat down on a
velvet sofa opposite a maple wood rocking chair that the Giver of Life
loved to lounge in when He had company in His private chambers.
The Son of God spoke tenderly to the Greek Isle Justice Minister after
commending him once again for the fine work he was engaged in to
fight crime in his province.

"Dear One, I know full well what is on your mind today, and I
share your anguish that sinful flesh is once again rearing its hideous
head on the world stage in the form of your cousin Chad Kirintelos
and his many cohorts. You are wondering where your rebellious relative is hiding. As you're assuming, I do in fact know his exact location,
but won't reveal that to anyone as it is predestined that someone must
lead the prophesied ultimate revolt against My peaceful millennial
rule. Exercising his own free will, he has chosen to take on that role.
To your understandable sorrow, that lot has fallen to your own kith
and kin, due to the hardness of his heart which made way for powerful
demonic possession of his body and mind. Of course, the main force
behind all of this madness is none other than Lucifer himself, as has
always been the case in humanity's long and sullied history."

The Alpha and Omega paused for a few seconds as His thoughts
drifted back to the time before time when Eden's translucent guardian

angel uttered his first word of rebellion against his Creator God. Then King Yeshua returned to His discourse. "We have offered Chad salvation via several people, including his long-rebellious mother and father who thankfully accepted My free gift of eternal life before their souls departed this earth. Still, Chad has defiantly refused to receive that generous gift."

Benny looked down before replying to his mighty, beloved Lord. "I know that I should not be so troubled, King Yeshua. I'm actually full of joy concerning the coming destruction of all of Your spiritual opponents and the final removal of sin from the earth. Yet Chad is still my late aunt's son, and I cannot help but grieve over the fact that he's morphed into a worldwide mouthpiece for Satan. I just wish...." The Justice Minister paused as tears welled up in his tender eyes. "I just wish there was more that I could do to stop him, if not to wake him up."

"He is a tool of the devil, Benny," affirmed Yochanan as he reached out his hand to pat his sweet companion on his back. "You cannot change that dear one...only Chad can make that happen."

"That is indeed the case, fine servant of the Most High God," added Israel's Sovereign as He gently rocked back and forth in His favorite chair. "However, you will have *one last chance* to help your cousin see the light, but of course it will not be an easy encounter. I will pray that you put on the full armor of the Father and will not faint, but instead fully accomplish the final mission We have in store for you."

"Thank you Your Majesty, that means so much to me." The words of a popular old hymn rushed like a swollen river into Benny's heart. While bowing his head in reverence before his Holy Lord, he shared some of them out loud: "Because *You* live, King Yeshua, I can face tomorrow. Because You live, all fear is gone. And I know for sure who holds the future. Bless you my Savior and Lord!"

Sarah Goldman was busy slicing up several russet potatoes to add to her faux chicken soup broth that was steaming on the stove. The date was the Ninth of Av in the Year of our Lord 999. Looking as trim and youthful as ever, Talel suddenly rushed into the kitchen. "Mom, quick! Cousin Chad is on television again, and he's saying something about Andre's imminent appearance!"

Sixteen months before, a virtual army of Andre's deluded followers had successfully taken control of a large portion of central Africa, using it as a staging ground for further attacks in the area directed at millennial security personnel, offices and government officials. Yeshua's administrators and police forces stationed in the province of Egypt had come under sustained assault, as had other outposts and bases in the provinces of Sudan and Libya. In the process, the rebels—several million strong—had also captured a number of satellite uplink stations that Chad was now using to spread his heinous messages all over the globe. Naturally, just one word from the Captain of the Hosts of Heaven could have instantly cut off this insurrection, but as King Yeshua had shared with Benny, it was part of the preordained outworking of God's final plan for humanity. Those people who still harbored hateful rebellion against the Prince of Peace in their soiled hearts (all the more galling since they had been living under His majestic rule) would be rooted out and judged during the coming world revolt. It was simply meant to be.

Looking close to death's door, Chad was rumbling on through his long beard about the supposed impending resurrection of the Antichrist, Emperor Andre. He said all eyes should focus on Rome where the world's supposed *real* savior would soon make his dramatic reappearance. After doing so, Andre would lead an international attack upon the "false god" inhabiting Jerusalem, stated the deranged lying prophet.

"Doesn't the book of Revelation tell us the Antichrist would be out of commission until the end of King Yeshua's rule, mom? If so, why is Chad claiming he'll soon appear in Italy?"

"Actually Yochanan wrote that the devil himself, not the Antichrist, will be released from imprisonment for a short time at the very end of the millennium, apparently in order to lead the prophesied final rebellion against the Lord's merciful reign. Revelation 19 also revealed that Andre, the Man of Sin, and the False Prophet, Urbane Basillo, would be thrown into what is called 'the Lake of Fire' at the end of the battle of Armageddon, which took place nearly a thousand years ago. The lake is said to burn with fiery brimstone for all eternity, so an extremely hellish place indeed! In light of that, Talel, I can't see how Andre would actually reappear on earth. I think Chad's 'prophecy' must be yet another ruse emanating from the father of lies."

Indeed, it was the ancient adversary himself who materialized in a well-crafted likeness of Andre's human form. The apparition, at a mansion in Rome near the site of the ancient Colosseum, came just ten days before a beautiful evening sunset would bathe Jerusalem in gold on the last day of Hanukkah. The twilight that day would mark the actual end of the Lord's exquisite millennial reign.

Invited dinner guests in Rome included hundreds of international business and political leaders who were mostly members of a pro-Andre secret society called *Andar* that had substantially grown in power and influence over the previous few decades. When the party host, a distant relative of the deceased Benito Geovinelli, rose to propose a toast to his Swiss wife who was turning 283 that birthday, the apparition suddenly appeared in the southwest corner of the mansion's elegant dining room. It resembled an apparently lifeless Emperor Andre, lying face up on top of a wrought-iron casket. Many of the assembled guests gasped in fear when they spotted the unexpected phenomenon, with a couple of them fainting from fright.

The seemingly lifeless apparition suddenly sat up as the color of blood rushed to its face, causing a number of male and female guests to scream. Grinning like a bad dog discovered chewing on its master's slipper, the devil incarnate then rose to his feet before proclaiming in a booming voice: *"The creator of all is with you! I will lead you to the gates of everlasting life and joy! Follow me and live!"*

Those guests who were already Andre's disciples fell to their knees before the beast's satanic image. Others looked on in utter astonishment. Several cameras had already been photographing the party host rising up to offer his wife a birthday toast when the apparition materialized, so the supposed 'resurrection' was recorded and rapidly distributed worldwide via demented Android gang members who made sure the deceitful disc got onto the internet and into the hands of as many human beings as possible.

Soon after taking control of northeast Africa four months before 'Andre's' appearance in Rome, the devil's mushrooming forces captured the province of North Turkey, followed weeks later by the provinces of Baghdad and Eastern Iraq. They also continued to make major inroads in fierce fighting that was spreading to many parts of North, South and Central America, Asia, Australia and Russia. In Europe the contest was less violent, with well-prepared Andre worshipers simply taking over many cities and towns with little government opposition. It was as if King Yeshua had quietly ordered his subordinates operating there to stand down for some reason.

The escalating outbreaks of armed revolt in most cities and towns around the world had become entirely unsettling to the vast majority of human beings who were faithful followers of King Yeshua, and sincerely grateful for His benevolent rule. After hundreds of years of uninterrupted peace and tranquility, billions of these innocent civilians were adversely affected by the spreading violent insurrection, inspired by an unsavory American businessman who claimed undying devotion to a worldwide emperor from the previous era. Thankfully, most people were not taken in by this satanic lie, understanding from the Lord's weekly teachings that the turbulent trouble would soon end with the complete eradication of sin and sinners from the earth, followed by the introduction of a new heaven and earth in which righteousness would dwell for all eternity.

Still, this was only partial comfort for Yeshua's suffering servants. For the first time since the nascent days of the millennial kingdom, food and electricity supplies had become scarce and expensive. People hid inside their homes for fear of burgeoning Android youth gangs that had taken control of most city streets around the globe. Communication towers were down in many places, rendering mobile phone and internet use nearly impossible. Economic activity plummeted as workers stayed away from their jobs in droves. Although nowhere as bad as the intensely dark days just before Immanuel's Second Coming to earth, the world's external condition nevertheless closely mirrored that traumatic time. Fortunately all humans who had somehow managed to live through the original tribulation period, like

Maria Alvarez, Aaron and Susan Feingold, Ari and Esther Hazan and the Bernstein twins, were already with their Maker.

Millennial security forces did their best to quell the spreading insurrection, but found in most cases they were significantly outnumbered and outgunned. In fact in a number of places, small squads of human security forces actually switched sides to join the devil and his revolting minions. Thousands of Kingdom technocrats with their own selfish interests on display crossed the aisle as well, apparently gambling that the Lord's evident restraint in the face of metastasizing evil was a sign that the prince of darkness would ultimately prevail.

With the clock approaching midnight in King Yeshua's thousand-year earthly reign, millions of well funded and trained anarchist fighters were poised to swoop into the large province of Israel from three separate directions: Turkey, Syria and Lebanon to the north; Iraq and Arabia to the east and southeast; and Egypt and North Africa to the southwest. Android leaders of the rebel forces had also managed to build a significant fleet of warships designed to strike at Israel's Mediterranean coast, effectively rendering them a fourth warfront. The Commander of the Hosts of Heaven had ordered his security officers to allow the rebels to gather all along Israel's borders, saying He wanted to offer each of them one last opportunity to repent of their rebellious ways and surrender their hearts to the Father of Lights before they perished in battle. The Merciful Savior added reassuringly that when the planned massive attack was finally launched, He Himself would take care of His rebellious opponents.

Chad Kirintelos, whose ancient parental heritage was a mixture of Jewish Israeli, Roman Italian and Greek, appeared one last time on international television, beamed out via his satellite network that had been earlier hijacked by Satan's forces. Yourgos Kirintelos and Donna Schmidt's son was in the middle of a live broadcast, pounding his hairy fist on a table while urging everyone on earth to prepare for the final attack upon the "evil rulers" who had supposedly "suppressed all truth" while governing from Jerusalem. Someone strode slowly into his dimly lit underground broadcast studio, walking right past two armed guards at the door who somehow did not seem to notice. It was Benny Goldman.

TWENTY-TWO

KISSING THE DEVIL

Chad Kirintelos stopped speaking mid-sentence when he spotted his deceased mother's nephew entering the recording studio. How in the world did the Greek Isle government official get through the intense security which surrounded the underground complex in northeast Chad, not far from the city of Fada? More importantly, what was the Justice Minister up to? Was he here to slay an old man? Chad decided he would not take time to find out. He stretched out his long index finger, switched off his microphone and jumped to his feet.

"Get out of here Goldman, and I mean *right now!*" Chad turned in the direction of the nearby master control room and shouted out "Technicians, terminate this live transmission!"

"Relax, Cousin Chad, I intend you no harm. I just wanted to talk to you face to face about…your life choices. The Lord can help you get back on the right track, my friend, and He is more than able to do it this very moment."

"I said get your butt out of here NOW Benny! I don't want to talk to you about anything! You're nothing but a wound-up robot for your 'precious Yeshua.' I don't even want to hear you utter that name!"

"Chad, our Father God loves you so very much, despite your hardcore rebellion against Him. If you'll only let the Righteous One into your life, He can and will pardon and restore you, and He can complete that action right now."

"Get out of my sight, Goldman! Guards!! Take this man out of here."

364

The two armed African men, who had somehow missed seeing the unannounced visitor enter the recording studio, rushed into the spacious room just in time to witness Chad toss his microphone in the direction of Benny's head. The metal object bounced off of an invisible protective shield that surrounded the saint's glorified body. The shield also acted as a veil which kept the guards from seeing or hearing the Justice Minister.

"What's the problem, sir?" asked the burly, pistol-toting taller guard as he rushed to Chad's side.

"What do you mean, what's the problem? *He* is the problem! Why did you allow him in here?"

"Who, sir, we don't see anyone with you in the studio, just the TV engineers on the other side of that glass. We *did* hear you speaking rather loudly just now, but thought it was probably just a dramatic moment in your televised message."

"You mean you *don't* see someone standing right there next to that brown folding chair? It's my cousin Benny Goldman; a real pain in the neck I might add. I want him out of here, pronto!"

The puzzled guards glanced at each other with discomfited expressions before the portly shorter man spoke up. "Mr. Chad, we're really sorry, but we don't see any trespassers here in the studio. Nor did we spot anyone entering it, and we've been on full alert the whole time you've been in here."

Starting to wonder if he was going crazy, Chad pushed the guards aside and spat out *"I'll take care of this myself, you idiots!"* After picking up a heavy microphone stand from his desk, the elderly man rushed as quickly as possible in Benny's direction, shouting shrilly all the while that he would kill the intruder if he did not quickly turn tail and leave. When Benny stood his ground, Chad attempted to strike his lifelong cousin on the head with his metal weapon. However the saint's protective shield prevented the intended blow from landing on his immortal body, which anyway would not have been actually wounded by the blow.

The stunned Android security guards watched in total bemusement, not sure what to make of the apparently silly scene being played out in front of them like a bizarre late night psycho flick. Ignoring them, Benny spoke again to his errant relative, but his voice was still cloaked from reaching the ears of the guards or technicians. "Chad, *please* calm down. I love you very much, my friend, and I just want to help secure the very best for you in every way. After all, you're part of my family, and we've had lots of good times together over the years. You're nearing the end of your life Chad, and you'll soon be separated from your Creator God for all eternity if you don't repent and submit your fleeting life to Him. Like I said, I would be thrilled to help you do that right now."

"I said get the hell out of here! I'm not the slightest bit interested in your stupid religious dribble! Get out, and don't come back!!" Chad picked up the aluminum-framed folding chair and began to swing it at Benny's body, but as was the case with the hurled microphone, it landed with a thud against the invisible shield. The guards were perplexed when the chair struck hard against the unseen barrier, sending Chad reeling backwards as angry curses shot like canons out of his crinkled mouth. The taller guard rushed to the infamous man's side and firmly gripped his left arm, arriving just in time to prevent Chad from hitting his nearly hairless head on the corner of his untidy studio desk.

"Cousin Chad, please stop that! You can't harm me in any way. I've been sent from the gracious Lord to afford you one last chance to change direction and receive His pardon for your grievous sins and free gift of everlasting life. Turn to Him now, my dear friend, and you'll share immortal life with your mother and father and all of us forever!"

The devil's dedicated devotee escaped the guard's grasp and fled behind his desk, pulling out a loaded revolver from the top drawer. He then began shooting wildly in Benny's direction, to the horror of the stunned guards who were standing just outside of his unsteady line of fire. The squat security man then threw himself at Chad's elderly body, knocking the gun out of his hand as one last shot rang out, striking the taller guard in his spleen. Benny rushed over and thrust his invisible right hand over the wound, praying out loud that King Yeshua would bring instant healing to it. Wondering what had just taken place, the injured guard's crimson blood stopped flowing seconds after the pain instantly disappeared. This caused the brawny 28-year-old African militiaman to render open praise to God, which only added fuel to Chad's raging fury.

Like a raving lunatic, the bearded, bald old man lunged again at his deceased mother's nephew, falling down on the tiled floor in the process and cracking the left side of his jaw. Benny then fell to his knee and prayed for instant healing, which immediately took place, to Chad's astonishment. Still, even this was not enough to melt his ungrateful frozen heart. With resumed curses flooding the television studio like stinking sewage from a drainpipe, the demonized former airline CEO vowed again to slaughter his lifelong relative, who was also once his closest friend.

Wiping tears from his tender eyes, Benny stepped closer to his lost cousin. "Look Chad, I'll leave you alone now. However before I go, I want to give you one final opportunity to surrender your rebellious life to King Yeshua, our eternal Messiah and Lord. Despite your relentless sins, He loves you very much, my friend. *Please* turn to Him and be saved!"

"Shut up Benny!" screamed Chad as he placed his weathered hands over his drooping, hair-filled ears. The two security guards gazed at each other in bewilderment before quickly exiting the room. They would leave this loaded nut-job alone with his imaginary enemy.

Two days later, Chad Kirintelos got his first opportunity to meet the 'Risen Andre' in person. The rendezvous took place in Barcelona, which had been one of the European Emperor's favorite coastal cities on earth, as Lucifer realized. The meeting took place in a private mansion near the Casa Mila in the Spanish city. Disguised as the worldwide monarch who was in fact slain once and for all by the returning Conquering King in Jerusalem just over 1,000 years before, the devil was seated on a solid gold throne. A five-tier silver crown rested on his unworthy head. A bowl full of freshly harvested purple grapes sat next to a gilded goblet on a nearby ivory table.

Chad was escorted into the elegant dining hall/throne room by two Swiss security guards dressed in traditional garb. Wearing an aqua silk robe and satin sandals, the elderly man slowly approached the deceitful devil before bowing low near his feet. The false seer then took hold of Satan's right hand and kissed the large emerald ring protruding from his middle finger.

"Your unrivaled majesty, I finally get to meet you! I am so honored, my wonderful emperor!" With his sycophantic greeting, Chad was expecting to immediately ingratiate himself with his devious master. Instead, the ersatz 'emperor' yawned as he virtually ignored his number one disciple, barking at him to rise to his feet in a voice that sounded like he was entirely annoyed by Chad's flattering verbal devotion.

"I really have very little time today, Schmidt. Let's get on with your report. How is your latest communiqué being received around the world, and what is the current status of our planned assault on the enemy millennial forces guarding my promised land?"

The once internationally successful American businessman was devastated by the cold reception from the 'exalted one,' who seemed to have deliberately used his childhood last name as an insult to him. After all, he'd been tirelessly working for 'Andre' non-stop ever since he became devoted to worshipping the emperor several centuries before. Donna Schmidt's elderly son had been expecting grateful accolades from the one he truly believed was the resurrected Emperor Andre, not this dismissive treatment. Still, like a slapped puppy, he began to dutifully deliver his report, but with only tepid enthusiasm displayed in his quivering voice.

"From all of our sources, we estimate we have at least half a billion dedicated followers around the world who are enthusiastically backing our insurrections and firmly believe in our goals. We guess another half billion people are willing to come quickly to our side if the tide of battle goes our way, as we naturally expect it will. This gives us a strong enough base to proceed with our conquest program, allowing us an ultimate and enduring victory."

"Enough about the future, Schmidt! How many men and women do we have in place today in our volunteer military force, ready for the upcoming invasion? I'd like to see around five million qualified humans involved in the final assault, or at least helping to defend our fallback positions."

"Well, as you know Emperor Andre, we have more than adequate frontline forces already stationed along Israel's northern, eastern and southern borders, and powerful naval vessels and submarines patrolling out in the Mediterranean and Red Seas. We have around four million frontline forces and another million backing them. Of course, we also succeeded in building nuclear warheads despite the many roadblocks erected by the millennial government, and this definitely tips the military balance our way."

Satan's fiendish eyes lit up at the mention of his secret nuclear arsenal. "Yes, we have the very fires of hell in our hands, as they will soon discover in Jerusalem—the city they stole from me!" Lucifer came back down to earth as he dismissed his boorish subordinate. "If that's all, Schmidt, I need to get back to other pressing matters."

Chad fingered his belly as he sheepishly affirmed that no other important items remained on his agenda. His day with the devious devil was done.

Finally getting to meet the seemingly reborn 'emperor' had been Chad Kirintelos' fanatical goal ever since Satan faked his 'miraculous resurrection' in Rome. Still, the actual encounter had been so dismal that the old man began drinking copious amounts of illegal fortified Ouzo an hour after arriving via a rebel naval boat at the small marina near his deceased father's summer home on Naxos. Two days later, his Greek maid found his naked, cold body slumped on the bathroom floor after he apparently fell down while entering or leaving the shower. The local coroner's report said he had been dead for at least thirteen hours.

Benny Goldman grasped his earthly mother's hand as he entered the Kirintelos mansion in Summerset. The two were accompanied by Governor Eli Ben David and his entire provincial cabinet, along with Talel Goldman and Shoshel Pearlman. Jonathan squeezed Sarah's other hand. He knew it would be especially difficult for his former wife to take in her nephew's lifeless body lying on his late father's bed, grieving that her only sibling's only son had rejected the Good Shepherd, not to mention the everlasting life that He so freely offers to all who acknowledge, love and follow Him.

It was an equally trying moment for the Greek Isle Justice Minister. Benny had labored so diligently to help straighten out his severely errant first cousin. He had memory reels full of vivid images featuring the myriad happy times that the two relatives had spent together over the centuries, especially during Chad's younger days. He had prayed without ceasing for his cousin, but the ultimate answer had not been what he'd so earnestly desired to receive.

The visiting entourage greeted Chad's weeping widow and his oldest daughter—who had been named Donna in honor of his mother. Attired in flowing black dresses, the two puffy-eyed females were standing together near the front entrance of their home. The visitors were escorted by the mourners into the master bedroom, where Chad's lifeless body was clothed in a gray silk suit face up on the royal blue bedspread.

Benny slowly walked over to the corpse with Sarah leaning on his right arm and Jonathan and Talel just behind them, followed by Abe, Rebecca and Rabbi Benjamin Goldman. All seven members of the Goldman family wept quietly as they approached the prone body, followed by Shoshel, Eli, Micah, and the remaining Greek Isle officials.

The sorrowful Justice Minister shut his moist eyes after looking at his relative's colorless face. *Cousin Chad, not only did you totally mess up your own life, but you swept untold numbers of other human beings with you into eternal damnation in the unquenchable fires of hell. I still can't believe that my own relative and friend would be the catalyst for the resurgence of devil worship on earth. I just can't fathom it.* Benny wiped tears of pained grief away as he took one last look at the lifeless face of his beloved close cousin and friend—a man who had horribly mutated into his fiercest adversary. Sarah and Jonathan said nothing as they placed their arms around Benny's broad shoulders. The tears being shed by all seven Goldmans and their dear friends would forever wash away the shared pain and sorrow over Chad's hellacious life and eternally lost condition.

The missile launch went off without a hitch. It was the opening salvo in Satan's final push to banish the Beautiful One from His millennial throne. Four nuclear warheads were dispatched at the same second from two locations: A submarine stationed in the Mediterranean Sea off the coast of Tel Aviv and a ground position in northeast Syria. All of the destructive warheads were blazing through the night air toward their ultimate destination—Jerusalem.

TWENTY-THREE

ALL THINGS MADE NEW

King Yeshua's human and Kadoshim security forces were placed on full war footing seconds after four enemy nuclear missiles were fired at the world's regal capital city. Radar-linked computers rapidly calculated that all of the laser-guided missiles would land within ten miles of the Temple Mount, incinerating everything in a twenty mile radius, meaning Jerusalem and its environs would be totally wiped out.

Two days before the coordinated missile launch, the fake 'Resurrected Emperor Andre' completed his plans for a massive ground and air assault on the surrounded land of Israel. First, he would obliterate the capital city of Jerusalem and all of the humans living in it. Even though he understood the Kadoshim could not be killed, their international seat of government would be annihilated, making the follow-up ground invasion that much more effective.

Two massive formations of nearly one million rebel militiamen apiece were stationed north of Israel's borders in the provinces of Beirut and Northern Syria. To clear the path for the enthusiastic volunteer Android fighters, the devil's elite fulltime military force—known as the Android Revolutionary Guards—had earlier defeated vastly outnumbered kingdom security personnel during a three-day battle sixty miles northwest of the rebuilt city of Damascus. Other Revolutionary Guards had fought hard to position themselves along the Israeli demarcation line with the province of Baghdad, which ran along the banks of the fast-flowing Euphrates River east of the Garden of Eden wildlife refuge. To the south, nearly a half-million volunteer fighters were heading in the direction of Israel from the adjacent Arabian Peninsula. Greater numbers waited for the signal to penetrate the Israeli border with the province of Egypt, located fifteen miles east of the Suez Canal. Like a pack of demented panthers sniffing blood, the well-trained and equipped volunteer fighters were ready to pounce on the detested millennial ruler and His faithful followers.

The devil incarnate made pep-rally appearances at all five border staging areas in the final run-up to the carefully-calibrated nuclear missile attack. The visits were openly broadcast live around the world via his hijacked satellite transmission system. In his first stop northeast of Beirut, 'Emperor Andre' promised the cheering throng that he would soon be ruling the world once again, largely due to their unselfish assistance: "I *am* the great I AM!! I am the first and the last, your true god and king! I will banish the dark forces from this earth forever and reestablish my magnificent rule in every spot where the sun shines down upon us from the high heavens! I am the bright morning star, the true offspring of David! Thank you all for eagerly joining our military operation to oust the prince of darkness who has deceived the world into thinking *he* is the one true God. A new era is beginning! Soon you will be feasting with me on the hills of Israel!" The fact that in natural terms, a radiation-soaked Jerusalem and its surroundings would be humanly uninhabitable for many years to come apparently did not deserve a mention from the father of lies.

At his last putrid appearance near the Suez Canal just twelve hours prior to the missile launch, Satan seated himself on a large ancient Egyptian stone that had been carved long ago into the shape of a throne. After delivering his fighting words to the assembled anarchist militiamen who had flocked to the Middle East from every province on earth, 'Andre' rose from his exalted seat as two young women approached him. They disrobed before helping the true prince of darkness do the same. Standing shamelessly naked for the entire world to see, the devil incarnate shouted out that he would "bring glorious peace, liberty and equality to everyone on earth, the most splendid place in the universe!" Then he demanded that all present fall down prostrate and worship him, which they promptly did. Lucifer's final public abomination had come to an end.

Benny Goldman had twinked to Jerusalem from Naxos first thing that morning. He had been in the Holy City most of the week as special Feast of Hanukkah celebrations were held to mark the thousand-year anniversary of King Yeshua's magnificent millennial rule. The Greek Isle Justice Minister had been personally informed by Yochanan that a nuclear assault would be launched at any time against the international capital. Benny wanted to be with his mother and other relatives and friends if Satan's nuclear-tipped warheads were indeed directed at Jerusalem. Yochanan revealed to his friend that the Lord Himself informed him of the imminent attack, foretelling it would "nearly succeed" in vaporizing the City of the Great King.

When kingdom radar centers initially detected the synchronized missile launchings at 2:46 AM that night, government emergency sirens were immediately sounded throughout Israel. It would be the last time in history that the mournful electronic wailing would be heard in the hallowed city, or in fact anywhere else on planet earth, which was about to experience a glorious metamorphosis.

Sarah Goldman was resting comfortably on her bed, praying for Chad's grieving widow Joanna and children. She had earlier visited with Benny who was back at his Jerusalem apartment. He had chosen not to reveal Yochanan's stark news to her. The Jerusalem-based health official bolted up from her soft mattress when the shrill siren pierced her room via an open window next to the bedroom closet. The distinct sound detonated vivid memories in Sarah's startled heart. She instantly recalled the jarring time just before the Antichrist began his worldwide reign when she and her children were attending a special prayer service at their congregation building in south Jerusalem. The anxious wife and mother had joined a small circle of friends who were interceding for her husband Jonathan, Eli and other believers stationed up north on the Golan Heights. They were also praying for all the other soldiers serving in the Israeli armed forces and for the political and military leaders of the land. While congregational pastor

Yoseph Steinberg was reciting Psalm 23, the siren warning began, signaling that a deadly missile attack from Syria was underway.

As she raced down the stairs in her Jerusalem home to switch on the television set in order to get details of the apparently breaking news, Sarah thought of the myriad other times she had heard security sirens wail in the previous era. Tribute sirens had been sounded throughout Israel on two recurring dates every year, one of them marking Memorial Day for the Jewish State's fallen soldiers and terrorist victims. This stirring annual event took on a whole new meaning for the grieving widow after her husband was killed in a Syrian gas attack. Another yearly sounding took place on Holocaust Remembrance Day, when a two minute memorial siren pierced the morning air in somber recollection of the millions of Jews who perished in Hitler's Nazi death camps. Sarah shuddered as she thought of the very last time she heard the sirens scream out their warning signal...as the actual Emperor Andre's United World forces were advancing on the western half of Jerusalem just before the King of the Jews returned in power and glory to the scarred sacred city.

Talel Goldman and Bet-el Preston soon joined Sarah in front of the television set, raptly listening to the millennial government's media spokesman, Shimon Nachon, announce that a hostile missile attack had just been launched against Jerusalem (the unsettling fact that Satan's forces had developed and deployed nuclear warheads was already publicly known, being first revealed three days earlier by the fake 'Emperor Andre' himself during a speech he delivered to Android loyalists in India). Human citizens of the entire province of Israel were ordered to immediately head to protective underground shelters which had been constructed in recent years all over the land as Lucifer's final worldwide rebellion—spurred on by Talel's late cousin—picked up steam.

As the severity of the situation became clearer to them, the three Kadoshim fell almost simultaneously to their knees in prayer. Sarah asked the Lord of Life to protect His loyal human followers and security forces. Talel then interrupted the prayer to ask if the other two saints thought they should all immediately will themselves over to Naxos to escape any potential nuclear blast near their home in

Jerusalem. The government spokesman appeared again on the TV screen seconds later, this time urging all of the Kadoshim residing in the land to float up into the sky over Israel in order to avoid being caught in the middle of any potential action on the ground, even if their immortal bodies could not be directly impacted by death-dealing atomic blasts.

Sarah immediately called out in her spirit for Benny and Jonathan to join her and her two companions as they ascended into the air above Jerusalem. The Greek Isle government officials appeared seconds later. All five were comforted to be together at such a time as this. "It seems Chad's despicable work is about to reach a climax," muttered Benny to no one in particular. Sarah bowed her head low at the mention of her eternally lost nephew, relieved that his horrendous legacy would soon be eliminated from the earth but still shaken that her sister's only son had helped lead so many astray. Tears soon appeared in her glowing eyes. They would be the last ones that Sarah Goldman, or any other saint, would ever shed. The First and the Last, the Beginning and the End, would soon wipe every tear from all eyes. There would be no more sorrow or mourning at all, for the former things were passing away. The Father God, the Master of the Universe, was about to make all things new.

The Kadoshim joined hands and willed themselves into the upper atmosphere above the targeted Holy City, rising some ten miles into the air. Millions of Kadoshim joined them; all anxiously watching to see what would unfold.

Less than one minute later, the fiery tails of the four incoming ballistic missiles appeared on the upper horizon. Computer models showed that within three minutes, the ultimate weapons would strike their designated targets. One warhead was meant to obliterate the Temple Mount and the nearby government palaces belonging to King Yeshua and Prince David. Another was headed toward the south of Jerusalem, where Sarah had her home. A third missile was aimed at the northern portion of the millennial capital and a fourth was set to wipe out the western suburbs of the Holy City stretching down to the coastal plain.

Suspended in the air well out of harm's way, Benny was pleased when his aborted brother Jesse and Jonathan's twin brother David and other members of the extended Goldman family materialized in the same location. The broadening band was quickly joined by Eli Ben David and the remaining Greek Isle cabinet ministers and several other close friends, including Shoshel Pearlman and her father Amos, the Steinbergs, Teresa and Leo Scarcelli, Carmella Bernstein and other New York City provincial officials who had come with all the Kadoshim to witness the final act of history. The hovering saints all sighted the advancing enemy missiles, prompting Jonathan's thoughts to flash back to the chemical rocket attack which ended his human life on the Golan Heights over ten centuries before. Although that assault and subsequent ones left tens of thousands of Israelis dead or wounded in their atrocious wakes, he was confident in his heart that this time the missile blitz would not end up the same way.

Indeed, all of the Kadoshim knew that the Ancient of Days was fully able to protect His beloved people and land, and so most were not surprised when the night sky was suddenly awash with light as if it was noontime on a cloudless day. A towering wall of fire had descended from the heavens in every direction surrounding the Holy Land, encircling it like some gigantic security belt. The four nuclear-tipped missiles would roll into the sizzling barrier in just a few seconds, rapidly ending up as final ashes in the devil's deep lock box filled with the remains of countless weapons of warfare that had killed or maimed millions of human beings over the ages. The madness was finally coming to an end, never to return again.

The blazing wall of fire—unleashed and erected at the command of the Captain of the Armies of Heaven-slowly began to edge away from Israel's borders. As it did so, the heathen Android militiamen stationed in the provinces of Lebanon, North Syria, Baghdad, Northern Arabia, Egypt and those on nearby ships at sea were quickly incinerated, losing in the process both their human lives and their final possibility to inherit eternal life (although thousands *did* quickly surrender to Him when the wall of fire first appeared). Millions of international supporters of the deluded rebels and their ruthless lying leader soon found themselves scooped up in the powerful hands of harvesting angels who would cast them into a furnace of fire to await their final judgments, as the Jewish Messiah had warned would occur at the consummation of the age. The Lord God of Israel was cleansing the entire planet of those remaining wicked, unrepentant sinners who defiantly refused to love and obey Him and to receive His merciful free gift of eternal salvation.

Within ten minutes, all of the world's rebellious sinners were removed from the earth. However the devil who deceived them was hiding out in a deep underground bunker beneath an armory near the city of Tyre. A violent earthquake began to shake the area; the first seismic activity to rattle anywhere on earth in over a thousand years. Two strong angels appeared on either side of Lucifer, who had just fallen off his chair as the quake continued to rock the region. As the tremors subsided, the heavenly warriors swooped up the vile deceiver into their steely hands, ferrying him up an airshaft to a field located directly above the bunker. Then they placed the one who had corrupted the whole earth upright next to a twisted old olive tree.

Without warning, the luminous Lord of Glory suddenly appeared twelve feet away from the tree, accompanied by a small squadron of shimmering angels. Two of the angels held small television cameras that were broadcasting the scene live around the world.

King Yeshua spoke directly to His ancient adversary, quoting His own words delivered long ago via the Hebrew prophet Ezekiel: "You were the anointed cherub who covers, and I placed you there in the Garden of Eden. Your heart was lifted up because of your beauty. You corrupted your wisdom by reason of your splendor. I cast you to the ground. I put you before kings that they may see you. By the multitude of your iniquities, in the unrighteousness of your trade, you profaned your sanctuaries. Therefore I have brought fire from the midst of you and it has consumed you. I have turned you to ashes on the earth in the eyes of all who see you. All who know you among the peoples are appalled at you." King Yeshua strode several steps closer to the quivering beast before completing His quote: "You have become terrified, and you will cease to be forever!"

The Conquering King stretched out his powerful right arm and pointed His thick index finger at Satan before proclaiming in a thunderous voice: *"You are banished to the lake of fire and brimstone, where the beast and the false prophet are already being tortured day and night forever!"* Four angles rushed over to the evil one and seized his arms and legs, lifting him high into the air as he shouted out biting insults at them. One minute later, Lucifer was eyeball to eyeball with the real Emperor Andre and his false prophet Urbane Basillo who were writhing in pain in the deepest part of the Lake of Fire-the same horrible condition they had justly endured for a thousand years.

No longer would the prince of darkness wreak havoc on earth. No more would the vile deceiver unleash his wretched machinations on humanity. The wicked inventor of lies was banished forever, imprisoned in the fiery hell that he himself had gleefully enslaved so many fallen souls in over the long ages. The Righteous Judge of All the Earth had spoken and acted, and it was done.

Israel's Mighty Messiah King soon reappeared in His Jerusalem palace as television footage of the triumphant banishment was rebroadcast around the world. Yochanan, Natan-el, Prince David and Moses accompanied the Great High Priest as He marched victoriously out onto His private balcony. Still hovering in the air but now located just above the Holy City, millions of Kadoshim began to clap and cheer, hailing the Giver of Life who had completely delivered the world from Satan's iniquitous spell once and for all.

Five minutes later, all of the buildings in Jerusalem, including the two royal palaces, were dissolved at the Lord's command. The hallowed Shekinah fire that had swirled up and down inside the holy Jerusalem Temple for a thousand years was the only thing still visible, apart from the hovering Kadoshim who were rejoicing in the ultimate victory that their Mighty Savior and King, the lover of their souls, had just won.

As the fantastic transformations were taking place in the Millennial Kingdom's international capital city, they were also occurring all over the globe. It was the prophesied culmination of the Day of the Lord. The elements comprising the earth were destroyed by intense heat as the world and its works were burnt up. The heavens above disappeared with a roar, changed into raw atomic energy. A new heaven and earth in which righteousness would dwell forever was about to be created by the magnificent Master Builder.

Just seconds before the earth melted like wax, the remaining humans living on it were supernaturally transferred to a holding area near the assembled Kadoshim—awaiting their final judgments from the King of Kings. It was time for the prophesied Great White Throne Judgment to begin. The King of Glory took His exalted seat on a towering throne which suddenly materialized, made out of glistening white marble dotted with gargantuan pearls. The disappearing continents gave up their dead, as did the dissolving seas. All who had perished from the beginning of time, starting with Adam and Eve, came to life and joined the other humans in the holding area, waiting to appear individually before the hallowed throne.

As each person, both great and small, stood before the Righteous One, final judgment was pronounced upon them. The Kadoshim—who had already experienced their own individual judgments soon after Israel's Messiah-King returned to earth—watched silently from above. Each individual from Adam on received an equitable sentence that reflected his or her deeds, heart condition, and especially their responses to the free gift of eternal life offered to them by Israel's Merciful Messiah. A few especially vile rulers who had committed mass murder were consigned to the very depths of hell where the devil and his two notorious comrades were already bound up forevermore. The relatively few babies and very young children who perished during the millennium were granted eternal life, along with the billions of older people who had gladly worshipped the King of Kings.

Among those entering everlasting life despite their earlier grave sins—due to their subsequent confessions of faith in the Lord and true, if belated repentance—were Donna Schmidt and Yourgos Kirintelos. Their gracious pardons, like the ones earlier granted to the Apostle Shaul, King David, Batsheva and many others who lived in the previous era, aptly illustrated the fact that the Precious Savior, the just Lamb of God, desires that no one should perish, as the sacred scriptures confirm.

Watching the proceedings from above, Sarah and her earthly Kadoshim relatives were elated when a positive sentence was issued to

Chad's widow, Joanna, who had been a quiet disciple of the Lord despite her demonized husband's open rebellion against Him. The same was happily the case with their daughter Donna Kirintelos and her sister Francette, but not their brother Leonard who had supported his father's rebellion against the Great I AM. The Goldmans' joy was shared by Chad's great grandparents, Giuseppe Marino and his earthly wife Catrina, and other relatives watching from above. Sarah clapped with delight as her resurrected earthly parents, Ariel and Esther Hazan, were among the billions who rejoiced over the glorious gift of eternal life, receiving their individual heavenly bodies immediately after they gratefully heard the Lord say, *"Well done, good and faithful servant. Enter into your eternal reward."*

In earthly terms, it took several days for the Great White Throne Judgment to be completed; with every single person who had ever lived on earth, apart from the Kadoshim, appearing individually before the royal judgment seat. Each saw their earthly life flash before them, followed by the Lord's righteous pronouncement of their final sealed judgment. The entire process took less than one minute per person in human time, but seemed significantly longer than that to the participants.

The thunderous voice of the Son of God rang out soon after the last humans had either been accepted into King Yeshua's heavenly kingdom or exiled into the Lake of Fire, which was also known as the Second Death. "Shalom to each one of you, My beloved children! You successfully completed your personal human journey of life in the sin-soaked fallen world, being united forever with the Heavenly Father and His Firstborn Son. The Holy Spirit of God dwells in each and every one of you, making you forever one with the Father and His beloved Son. Come now and enter into your everlasting inheritance in the New Jerusalem above. She is free, she is our real mother, and you are her precious children."

From the dissolved heavens directly above the eradicated earth, the radiant New Jerusalem began to descend like a beautifully-adorned bride being tenderly carried by her beloved bridegroom down a set of marble stairs outside a wedding chapel. The glorious Holy City had no need for a sun or a moon to shine on it since the luminous Lord God of Israel reigning in the midst of it would serve as its spectacular enduring light.

The New Jerusalem was headed for the same region in the dissolved universe where the dissipated planet had circled the sun-star for many eons. It was laid out like a mammoth cube, with the height of its shimmering jasper walls—fifteen-hundred miles tall—equal to its length and width. Everything inside the square walls was comprised of pure gold that was translucent like crystal glass, illuminating the city with a brilliance that outshone the disbanded sun. The heavenly city featured twelve gates made of choice pearls. Each was named after one of the twelve tribes of Israel, expressly linking the magnificent New Jerusalem with the earthly Jewish people who had sprung from Jacob's loins in ancient days. Twelve foundation stones became visible to the greatly expanded band of Kadoshim as the Sacred City continued its descent, displaying the names in Hebrew of the Lion of Judah's faithful Apostles. The saints of all the ages would soon discover that there was no need for a Holy Temple there since the Lord God Almighty and His resurrected Sacrificial Lamb were resident in it.

Seconds after the New Jerusalem arrived at its preordained eternal destination at the center of a newly created earth, the Lord of Lords shouted out a proclamation first recorded in the final chapter of Yochanan's Book of Revelation: *"I am the Root and Offspring of David, the Bright Morning Star!"* Then He added, *"Come now and follow Me into your eternal rest and reward!"* The jubilant Kadoshim gathered outside the gate named after the tribe of Judah, the main entrance into the new sacred city that was akin to the far less illustrious Jaffa Gate of old. The distinct sound of thousands of trumpets filled their ears as the Matchless One began to parade through the gate into the marvelous new city, followed by His closest associates including Yochanan and Prince David.

Not far back from the front of the procession, Benny Goldman began to hum an old hymn of praise to his well-loved Faithful Friend. Soon he was actually singing the song's chorus out loud, which was quickly noticed by Sarah and Jonathan Goldman and other surrounding family and friends including Eli Ben David and Micah

Kupinski, who were all gleefully entering their New Jerusalem home hand in hand.

"Your kingdom will reign forever and ever! Your Kingdom will reign forever and ever! Amen!!"

The chorus spread like wildfire through the ranks of the marching Kadoshim, with all skillfully joining in the harmonious celebratory song. Sarah grabbed hold of the arms of her earthly husband, son and daughter as a series of worshipful anthems arose in honor of the Father God of Israel and Immanuel, the beautiful Light of the World, who would never again be called the Son of Man. However as all began melodiously singing one of the most beloved hymns of all time, the words were coming out a bit differently from the original version. Saturated in never ending glory, the completed Body of Messiah was joyfully proclaiming the fact that they would *never* cease thanking and praising the magnificent Holy One of Israel.

"When we've been here ten trillion years, bright shining like the sun! There's no less days to sing God's praise than when we first begun!"